AFTER THE FIRE

Fredrik Welin is a seventy-year-old retired doctor. Years ago, he retreated to the Swedish archipelago, where he lives alone on an island. He swims in the sea every day, cutting a hole in the ice if necessary. He lives a quiet life. Until he wakes up one night to find his house on fire. Fredrik escapes just in time, wearing two left-footed wellies, as neighbouring islanders arrive to help douse the flames. All that remains in the morning is a stinking ruin and evidence of arson. The house that has been in his family for generations, and all his worldly belongings, are gone. He cannot think who would do such a thing, or why — and without a suspect, the police begin to believe he started the fire himself . . .

SPECIAL MESSAGE TO READERS

THE ULVERSCROFT FOUNDATION
(registered UK charity number 264873)
was established in 1972 to provide funds for
research, diagnosis and treatment of eye diseases.
Examples of major projects funded by
the Ulverscroft Foundation are:-

- The Children's Eye Unit at Moorfields Eye Hospital, London
- The Ulverscroft Children's Eye Unit at Great Ormond Street Hospital for Sick Children
- Funding research into eye diseases and treatment at the Department of Ophthalmology, University of Leicester
- The Ulverscroft Vision Research Group, Institute of Child Health
- Twin operating theatres at the Western Ophthalmic Hospital, London
- The Chair of Ophthalmology at the Royal Australian College of Ophthalmologists

You can help further the work of the Foundation
by making a donation or leaving a legacy.
Every contribution is gratefully received. If you
would like to help support the Foundation or
require further information, please contact:

THE ULVERSCROFT FOUNDATION
The Green, Bradgate Road, Anstey
Leicester LE7 7FU, England
Tel: (0116) 236 4325

website: www.foundation.ulverscroft.com

AFTER THE FIRE

HENNING MANKELL

TRANSLATED FROM THE SWEDISH BY MARLAINE DELARGY

LARGE
PRINT

First published in Great Britain 2017
by
Harvill Secker

First Isis Edition
published 2019
by arrangement with
Vintage
Penguin Random House

A catalogue record for this book is available
from the British Library.

ISBN 978–1–78541–766–5 (hb)
ISBN 978–1–78541–772–6 (pb)

Published by
F. A. Thorpe (Publishing)
Anstey, Leicestershire

Set by Words & Graphics Ltd.
Anstey, Leicestershire
Printed and bound in Great Britain by
T. J. International Ltd., Padstow, Cornwall

This book is printed on acid-free paper

To Elise

This is a freestanding continuation of *Italian Shoes,* which was first published in 2006. This narrative takes place eight years later.

Much has he learned who knows sorrow.

From *The Song of Roland*

Contents

PART ONE

The Ocean of Emptiness

CHAPTER
ONE

My house burned down on an autumn night almost a year ago. It was a Sunday. The wind had got up during the afternoon and by the evening the anemometer indicated that the gusts measured over twenty metres per second.

The wind was coming from the north and was very chilly in spite of the fact that it was still early autumn. When I went to bed at around half past ten I thought that this would be the first storm of the season, moving in across the island I had inherited from my maternal grandparents.

Soon it would be winter. One night the sea would slowly begin to ice over.

That was the first night I wore socks to bed. The cold was tightening its grip.

The previous month, with some difficulty, I had managed to fix the roof. It was a big job for a small workman. Many of the slates were old and cracked. My hands, which had once held a scalpel during complex surgical procedures, were not made for manipulating broken tiles.

Ture Jansson, who had spent his entire working life as the postman out here in the islands before he retired,

3

agreed to fetch the new slates from the harbour although he refused to accept any payment. As I have set up an improvised surgery in my boathouse in order to deal with all his imaginary medical complaints, perhaps he thought he ought to return the favour.

For years now I have stood there on the jetty by the boathouse examining his allegedly painful arms and back. I have brought out the stethoscope which hangs beside a decoy duck and established that his heart and lungs sound absolutely fine. In every single examination I have found Jansson to be in the best of health. His fear of these imaginary ailments has been so extreme that I have never seen anything like it in all my years as a doctor. He was simultaneously the postman and a full-time hypochondriac.

On one occasion he insisted he had toothache, at which point I refused to have anything to do with his problem. I don't know whether he went to see a dentist on the mainland or not. I wonder if he's ever had a single cavity. Perhaps he was in the habit of grinding his teeth while he was asleep, and that's what caused the pain?

On the night of the fire I had taken a sleeping tablet as usual and dropped off almost immediately.

I was woken by a light being switched on. When I opened my eyes, I was surrounded by a dazzling brightness. Beneath the ceiling of my bedroom I could see a band of grey smoke. I must have pushed off my socks in my sleep when the room got hot. I leaped out of bed, ran down the stairs and into the kitchen through that harsh, searing light. The clock on the wall

4

was showing nineteen minutes past midnight. I grabbed my black raincoat from the hook by the back door, pulled on my wellington boots, one of which was almost impossible to get my foot into, and rushed outside.

The house was already in flames, the fire roaring. I had to go down to the jetty and the boathouse before the heat became unbearable. During those first few minutes I didn't even think about what had caused this disastrous conflagration; I just watched as the impossible unfolded before my eyes. My heart was pounding so hard I thought it would be smashed to pieces inside my chest. The fire was ravaging me in equal measure.

Time melted away in the heat. Boats began to arrive from the other islands and skerries, the residents rudely woken from their sleep, but afterwards I was unable to say how long it took or who was there. My gaze was fixed on the flames, the sparks whirling up into the night sky. For one terrifying moment I thought I saw the elderly figures of my grandmother and my grandfather standing on the far side of the fire.

There are not many of us out here on the islands in the autumn, when the summer visitors disappear and the last of the yachts return to their home harbours, wherever those might be. But someone had seen the glow of the fire in the darkness, the message had been passed along, and everyone wanted to help. The coastguard's firefighting equipment was used to pump up seawater and spray it on the burning building, but it was too late. All it changed was the smell. Charred oak timbers and wall panels, burned wallpaper and linoleum flooring combined with salt water to give off an unforgettable stench. When dawn broke all that remained was a smoking, stinking ruin. The wind had dropped — the storm had already moved on, heading towards the Gulf of Finland — but it had fulfilled its spiteful task, working together with the blaze, and now there was nothing left of my grandparents' pretty house.

That was when I first thought to ask myself: how had the fire broken out? I hadn't lit any candles or left any of the old paraffin lamps burning. I hadn't had a cigarette or used the wood-burning stove. The electrical wiring throughout the house had been renewed just a few years ago.

It was as if the house had set fire to itself.

As if a house could commit suicide as a result of weariness, old age and sorrow.

I realised I had been mistaken about a key aspect of my life. After performing an operation that went disastrously wrong and led to a young woman losing her arm, I moved out here many years ago. Back then I often thought that the house in which I was living had been here on the day when I was born, and that it would still be here on the day when I no longer existed.

But I was mistaken. The oak trees, the birches, the alders and the single ash tree would remain here after I was gone, but of my beautiful home in the archipelago only the foundations, hauled to the island across the ice from the long-defunct quarry at Håkansborg, would remain.

My train of thought was interrupted as Jansson appeared beside me. He was bare-headed, wearing very old dark blue overalls and a pair of motorcycle gloves that I recognised from the winters when the ice had not been thick enough to drive across, and he had used his hydrocopter to deliver the post.

He was staring at my old green wellingtons. When I looked down I realised I had pulled on two left boots in my haste. Now I understood why it had been so difficult to put one of them on.

"I'll bring you a boot," Jansson said. "I've got a few pairs back at home."

"There might be a spare pair down in the boathouse," I suggested.

"No. I've been to look. There are some leather shoes and some old crampons people used to fix onto their boots when they went out on the ice clubbing seals."

The fact that Jansson had already been rooting around in my boathouse shouldn't have surprised me, even if on this occasion he had done it out of consideration. I already knew that he was in the habit of going in there. Jansson was a snooper. From an early stage I had been convinced that he read every postcard that passed through his hands when the summer visitors bought their stamps down by the jetties.

He looked at me with tired eyes. It had been a long night.

"Where will you live? What are you going to do now?"

I didn't reply because I didn't have an answer.

I shuffled closer to the smoking ruin. The boot on my right foot was chafing. This is what I own now, I thought. Two wellingtons that aren't even a pair. Everything else is gone. I don't even have any clothes.

At that moment, as I grasped the full extent of the disaster that had befallen me, it was as if a howl swept through my body. But I heard nothing. Everything that happened within me was soundless.

Jansson appeared beside me once more. He has a curious way of moving, as if he has paws instead of feet. He comes from nowhere and suddenly materialises. He seems to know how to stay out of another person's field of vision all the time.

Why hadn't his wretched house on Stångskär burned down instead?

Jansson gave a start as if he had picked up on my embittered thought, but then I realised I had pulled a face, and he thought it was because he had come too close.

"You can come and stay with me, of course," he offered when he had recovered his equilibrium.

"Thank you."

Then I noticed my daughter Louise's caravan, which was behind Jansson in a grove of alders alongside a tall oak tree that had not yet lost all its leaves. The caravan was still partly concealed by its low branches.

"I've got the caravan," I said. "I can live there for the time being."

Jansson looked surprised but didn't say anything.

All the people who had turned up during the night were starting to head back to their boats, but before they left they came over to say they were happy to help with whatever I needed.

During the course of a few hours my life had changed so completely that I actually needed everything.

I didn't even have a matching pair of wellingtons.

CHAPTER
TWO

I watched as one boat after another disappeared, the sounds of the different engines gradually dying away.

I knew who each person was out here in the archipelago. There are two dominant families: the Hanssons and the Westerlunds. Many of them are sworn enemies who meet up only at funerals or when there is a fire or a tragedy at sea. At such times all animosity is set aside, only to be resurrected as soon as normal circumstances resume.

I will never be a part of the community in which they live despite all those long-running feuds. My grandfather came from one of the smaller families out here, the Lundbergs, and they always managed to steer clear of any conflict. In addition, he married a woman who came from the distant shores of Åland.

My origins lie here in the islands, and yet I do not belong. I am a runaway doctor who hid in the home I inherited. My medical expertise is an undoubted advantage, but I will never be a true islander.

Besides, everyone knows that I am a winter bather. Every morning I open up the hole I have made in the ice and take a dip. This is regarded with deep suspicion by the permanent residents. Most of them think I'm crazy.

Thanks to Jansson I knew that people were puzzled by the life I led. What did I do, out here all alone on my island? I didn't fish, I wasn't a part of the local history association or any other organisation. I didn't hunt, nor did I appear to have any interest in repairing my dilapidated boathouse or the jetty, which had been badly affected by the ice over the past few winters.

So, as I said, the few remaining permanent residents out here regarded me with a certain measure of distrust. The summer visitors, however, who heard about the retired doctor, thought how fortunate I was to be able to retire to the tranquillity of the archipelago and escape the noise and chaos of the city.

The previous year an impressive motor launch had moored at my jetty. I went down to chase the unwanted visitors away, but a man and a woman carried ashore a crying child who had erupted in a rash. They had heard about the doctor living on the island and were obviously very worried, so I opened up my boathouse clinic. The child was placed on the bench next to the area where my grandfather's fishing nets still hung, and I was soon able to establish that it was nothing more than a harmless nettle rash. I asked a few questions and concluded that the child had had an allergic reaction after eating freshly picked strawberries.

I went up to my kitchen and fetched a non-prescription antihistamine. They wanted to pay me of course, but I refused. I stood on the jetty and watched as their ostentatious pleasure craft disappeared behind Höga Tryholmen.

I always keep a good store of medication for my own private use, and several oxygen cylinders. I am no hypochondriac, but I do want access to drugs when necessary. I don't want to risk waking up one night to find that I am having a heart attack without being able to administer at least the same treatment as I would receive in an ambulance.

I believe that other doctors are just as afraid of dying as I am. Today I look back and regret the decision I made when I was fifteen years old to enter the medical profession. Today I find it easier to understand my father, a permanently exhausted waiter; he looked at me with displeasure and asked if I seriously thought that hacking away at other people's bodies was a satisfactory choice in life.

At the time I told him I was convinced that I was doing the right thing, but I never revealed that I didn't think I had any chance whatsoever of gaining the qualifications to train as a doctor. When I succeeded, much to my own astonishment, I couldn't go back on my word.

That's the truth: I became a doctor because I had told my father that was what I was going to do. If he had died before I completed my training, I would have given up immediately.

I can't imagine what I would have done with my life instead; I would probably have moved out here at an earlier stage, but I have no idea how I would have earned a living.

The last boats disappeared into the morning mist. The sea, the islands, greyer than ever. Only Jansson and I were left. The stinking ruin was still smoking, the odd flame flaring up from the collapsed oak beams. I pulled my raincoat more tightly over my pyjamas and walked around the remains of my house. One of the apple trees my grandfather had planted was a charred skeleton; it looked like something from a theatre set. The intense heat had melted a metal water butt, and the grass was burned to a crisp.

I felt an almost irresistible desire to scream, but as long as Jansson stubbornly hung around, I couldn't do it. Nor did I have the strength to get rid of him. Whatever happened, I realised that I was going to need his help.

I rejoined him.

"Can you do something for me?" I said. "I need a mobile phone. I left mine in the house, so it's gone."

"I've got a spare one at home that you can borrow," Jansson replied.

"Just until I manage to get a new one."

Obviously I needed the phone as soon as possible, so Jansson went down to his boat. It's one of the last in the archipelago that has a so-called hot bulb engine, which has to be started with a blowtorch. He had a faster boat when he used to deliver the post, but the day after he retired he sold it and started using the old wooden boat he had inherited from his father. I have heard everything about that boat, including how it was built in a little boatyard in Västervik in 1923 and still has its original engine.

I stayed where I was, beside the smoking ruin. I heard Jansson spin the flywheel. He stuck his head out of the wheelhouse hatch as he waved goodbye.

Everything was quiet in the aftermath of the storm. There was a crow sitting in a tree contemplating the ruin. I picked up a stone and threw it at the bird, which flapped away on weary wings.

Then I went over to the caravan. I sat down on the bed and was overwhelmed by sorrow and pain, by a despair that I could feel all the way down to my toes. It made me hot, like a fever. I let out a yell so loud that the walls of the caravan seemed to bulge outwards. I began to weep. I hadn't cried like that since I was a child.

I lay down and stared at the damp patch on the ceiling, which to my eyes now resembled a foetus. The whole of my childhood had been shot through with an ever-present fear of being abandoned. At night I would sometimes wake and tiptoe into my parents' room just to check that they hadn't gone off and left me behind. If I couldn't hear them breathing I was terrified that they had died. I would put my face as close to theirs as possible until I was sure I could feel their breath.

There was no reason for my fear of being left alone. My mother regarded it as her life's work to make sure I was always clean and nicely dressed, while my father believed that a good upbringing was the key to success in life. He was rarely at home because he was always working as a waiter in various restaurants. However, whenever he did have time off or was unemployed because he had been sacked for some perceived insolence towards the maître d', he would open up his very own training academy for me. I would have to open the door between our kitchen and the cramped living room and pretend to show a lady in ahead of me. He would set the table for a fine dinner — perhaps even the Nobel dinner — with countless glasses and knives and forks so that I could learn the etiquette of eating and drinking while at the same time conversing with the elegant ladies sitting on either side of me. Now and again I would be faced with the winner of the Nobel Prize in physics, or the Swedish foreign minister, or the even more distinguished prime minister.

It was a terrifying game. I was pleased when he praised me but constantly worried about doing something wrong in the world into which he led me. There was always an invisible venomous snake lurking among the glasses and cutlery.

My father had actually worked as a waiter at the Nobel dinner on one occasion. His station had been down at the end of the furthest table, which meant he had never been anywhere near the prize-winners or royal guests. But he wanted me to learn how to behave in situations that might arise in life, however unlikely.

I don't remember him playing with me when I was a child. What I do remember, however, is that he taught me how to do up my own tie and how to knot a cravat before I was ten years old. I also learned how to fold serviettes into a whole array of artistic shapes.

I must have fallen asleep eventually. It's not unusual for me to seek refuge in sleep when I have suffered some kind of trauma. I can drop off at any time of the day, wherever I happen to be. It's as if I force myself to sleep, in the same way I used to search for hiding places when I was a child. I set up secret dens among the bins and heaps of coal in the yards behind the apartment blocks where we lived. I would seek out thickets of undergrowth among the trees. Throughout my life I have left a series of undiscovered hiding places behind me. But none of these hiding places has ever been as perfect as sleep.

I woke up shivering. I had left my watch on the bedside table in the house, so that was gone. I went outside and looked at the ruin, which was still smoking. The odd ragged cloud was scudding across the sky; judging by the position of the sun, I guessed it was somewhere between ten and eleven o'clock.

I went down to the boathouse and carefully opened the black-painted door, because the hinges are in poor shape. If I pull too hard, the door comes off completely. There was a pair of dungarees and an old sweater hanging on a hook inside; among the tins of paint I also found a pair of thick socks that my grandmother had knitted for me many years ago. They had been far too big at the time, but now they were a perfect fit. I searched among the spent batteries and rusty tools until I found a woolly hat advertising a television set that had been sold in the 1960s. ALWAYS THE VERY BEST PICTURE it said in barely legible letters.

The mice had been at work — it looked as if it had been peppered with pellets from a shotgun. I pulled it on and went back outside.

I had just closed the door when I spotted a paper bag on the jetty. It contained a mobile phone, some underwear and a packet of sandwiches. Jansson must have come back while I was asleep. He had also left a note on a torn-off piece of a brown envelope.

Phone charged. Keep it. Underpants clean.

Next to the bag stood a wellington boot for the right foot. Mine were green, but this one was black. It was also larger because Jansson has big feet.

There was another note inside the boot.

Sorry, haven't got green.

I wondered briefly why he hadn't brought the other half of the black pair, but Jansson operates according to a logic I have never understood.

I took the bag and the boot back to the caravan. Jansson's flimsy underpants were far too big, but there was something deeply touching about the fact that he had brought them.

I kept my pyjama jacket on as a shirt and pulled on the dungarees and the sweater. I found some paper bags in a drawer, screwed them up and used them to pad out the black wellington boot then sat on the bed and ate a couple of Jansson's sandwiches; I needed the strength to decide what I was going to do.

A person who has lost everything doesn't have much time. Or perhaps the reverse is true. I didn't know.

I heard the sound of an approaching boat. I could tell it wasn't Jansson; after all the years I have spent living out here, I have learned to identify different types of engine and individual boats.

I listened as the vessel came closer and closer, and identified it as one of the coastguard's smaller boats, a fast thirty-foot aluminium launch equipped with two Volvo diesel engines.

I put down the sandwiches, put on my holey hat and went outside. The blue-painted boat swung around the headland before I had reached the jetty.

There were three people on board. To my surprise, a young woman was at the helm. She was wearing the coastguard uniform, her blonde hair spilling out from beneath her cap. It was the first time I had seen a woman working on a patrol boat.

She looked alarmingly young, little more than a teenager in fact.

The man standing legs wide apart in the prow, holding the mooring rope, was called Alexandersson. He was about ten years younger than me and the direct opposite of me in physical terms: short and overweight. He was also short-sighted and his hair was thinning.

He was a police officer. A few years ago, after a spate of break-ins at closed-up summer cottages early in the spring, he had called on all the permanent residents to see if we might have noticed anything suspicious. They never found out who was responsible, but Alexandersson and I got on very well. I had no idea whether he knew anything about my past, but after his first visit I thought he could have been the brother I never had.

He owned a little summer cottage on one of the small skerries, which were known as Bräkorna. Whenever he came to see me, we would have a cup of coffee, talk about our health, then discuss the wind and the weather. Neither of us had any reason to get into more serious issues. We would quite happily sit in silence for long periods of time, listening to the birds or the wind soughing in the treetops.

Alexandersson had been married for many years, and his children were grown up. Then all of a sudden his wife left him. I have no idea why; I never asked. I sensed a deep sorrow within him. Perhaps I recognised myself in his grief? Yet another of those questions I am incapable of answering.

Alexandersson landed clumsily on the jetty. He looped the rope around one of the bollards before shaking my hand. A man I had never seen before came out on deck and also jumped ashore. He had seemed unsure of how to behave on a boat that was never completely still. He shook my hand and informed me that his name was Robert Lundin and that he was a fire investigation officer. I couldn't place his accent right away, but I suspected that he came from somewhere up in Norrland, away from the coast.

The young woman had switched off the engine and made fast the stern mooring rope. She came over and nodded to me. She really was very young.

"Alma Hamrén," she said. "I'm very sorry about your house."

I nodded in return, suddenly on the verge of tears. Alexandersson realised what was happening.

"Shall we go and take a look?" he said.

Alma Hamrén stayed with the boat; she was composing a text message, her nimble fingers flying.

No one commented on my odd wellington boots. I couldn't even tell whether they had noticed; surely they must have done?

Smoke was still rising from various spots in the ruins of my house.

"Do you have any idea how the fire might have started?" Alexandersson asked.

I explained that there had been no candles burning, and the stove had gone out by the time I went to bed. I had been asleep for less than two hours when I woke to find the whole house ablaze. I also told him that the wiring had been renewed, and that I couldn't see any logical explanation as to why the fire had broken out.

Lundin remained in the background, listening. He didn't ask any questions. I realised it was his job to establish the cause of the fire; I hoped he would succeed. I wanted to know what lay behind this disaster.

Alexandersson and Lundin began to walk around among the debris. I kept my distance, observing their slow progress. Occasionally one of them bent down; they reminded me of watchful animals.

I suddenly felt dizzy and had to lean on the old water pump for support. Alexandersson noticed that I wasn't feeling well and gave me a searching look. I shook my head and went over to the caravan. I sat down on the steps and made an effort to breathe deeply. After a few minutes I stood up; the dizziness had passed. I set off back to the site of the fire, but stopped as I rounded the corner of the caravan and saw the two men standing among the sooty remains of the roof timbers. They were talking; I couldn't make out what they were saying, but I immediately had the feeling that they were deliberately speaking quietly, as if they didn't want anyone else to hear.

From time to time Alexandersson glanced in my direction, but I was still hidden by the greenery surrounding the caravan.

I knew, even though I didn't know. They were discussing the cause of the fire. Saying there were no external factors. Wondering whether I could have started it myself.

I held my breath, trying to make sense of it. Could they really believe that I was capable of such a thing? Or was it just that they had to consider every possibility, no matter how bizarre?

I stayed where I was until they resumed their slow, meticulous examination of the site. From time to time Lundin took photographs.

I pushed aside the low branches and went to rejoin the men.

"How's it going?" I asked.

"It takes time," Alexandersson replied. "It's difficult."

"Very difficult," Lundin agreed. "There's nothing obvious."

The young woman called Alma Hamrén was sitting on the bench where I usually examined Jansson when he turned up with his imaginary aches and pains; she was still busy with her phone.

They carried on working for a couple of hours, then said they would probably be back later in the day. I told them I might not be here; I had to go over to the mainland to do some shopping.

I stood on the jetty until the boat had disappeared beyond the headland, then I went back to the remains of the house. They had placed some of the items they had found on a small sheet of plastic.

There were fragments of electrical cables, some half-melted fuses from the fuse box, and at the edge of the sheet I saw something I vaguely recognised. When I bent down to take a closer look, I realised what it was.

It was one of the buckles from the shoes that Giaconelli, the Italian shoemaker, had made for me some years ago.

At that moment I understood that I really had lost everything.

Nothing remained of my seventy-year life.

CHAPTER
THREE

I stood there gazing at my burned-down house. If I stared at the ruins for long enough, it was as if the building rose again from the sooty ashes.

The site reminded me of a war zone: it could have been the result of exploding grenades, tossed from passing tanks.

I was feeling more and more shaken. The sight of the blackened apple tree filled me with both sorrow and disgust. It was like an attack on the memory of my grandparents. I imagined that it would produce black, putrid apples. No one would be able to eat them. The tree was alive, yet at the same time it was dead.

I moved closer. The ruins were also a burial ground. The whole of my former life had been cremated. During those few violent hours last night the house had been transformed into an oven.

I experienced a vague but growing sense of loss for everything that had gone. I think I was most upset about my logbooks, which is what I called my diaries. The black-covered books hadn't even crossed my mind as I rushed out of the house, and now they were nothing more than ashes. I could have carried my life in my arms; instead I had fled empty-handed out of the dragon's mouth. I thought about Giaconelli's shoes. The only thing left of them was the charred buckle on Alexandersson's plastic sheet.

It looked like an insect, perhaps one of the stag beetles I used to see in the summer when I was a child. They had disappeared, although no one seemed to know why. I had once asked Jansson whether there were any among the clumps of oak trees on the islands of the archipelago, and he had asked all the permanent residents when he delivered their post. No one except old widow Sjöberg, who lived in her isolated house on Nässelholmen, had seen a stag beetle since the 1960s. There were plenty around her place, she claimed, but she was notorious for lying about virtually everything, including her own age.

In death Giaconelli's handmade leather shoes, which he had given me as a present, had been reduced to a charred black stag beetle. I wondered what the buckle was made of. The silver candlestick I had given my grandparents on the occasion of their golden wedding anniversary was gone, the silver now simply part of the remains of the fire.

But the buckle had survived. I wouldn't be able to ask Giaconelli what material he had used; after many years up in the forests of Hälsingland, where he had set up his shoemaking business surrounded by opera music pouring out of an old transistor radio, he had abruptly returned to Italy.

It seemed he had abandoned his workshop in haste. He didn't have many friends, and none of them had any idea what had happened. He hadn't even closed the

24

front door. It had been standing open, banging in the wind, when a neighbour came over to see if the shoe-maker could fix the loose sole of one of his work boots.

Giaconelli had completed all his orders before simply getting up from his chair and disappearing.

Later I found out from my daughter Louise that he had gone back to Italy by train, to his home village of Santo Ferrera north of Milan, where he had taken to his bed in a simple boarding house in order to die.

I had no idea what had happened to the workshop, or to his tools and all those lasts in the shape of people's feet. Louise hadn't told me, so presumably she didn't know either.

I picked up the buckle. The last time I had spoken to Louise was two weeks ago. She had called late one night from a noisy cafe on the outskirts of Amsterdam, when I had just fallen asleep. She wouldn't tell me what she was doing there, even though I asked her twice. The conversation was very brief. She was calling to check that I was still alive, and I in turn asked her if she was all right. Perhaps we regard each other as two patients, carrying out our doctors' rounds together through a series of telephone calls?

The buckle was a charred memory of a pair of handmade shoes, and of a time when there had been stag beetles on the island. I wondered how Louise would react when she found out that the house that would one day have been hers had burned down.

I didn't know my daughter well enough to gauge her reaction. Louise might simply shrug her shoulders and never mention the matter again, but she might also fly into a rage, blaming me for failing to prevent the fire. She might decide that I was a pyromaniac, even though there was nothing whatsoever to suggest that I had started the blaze.

I put down the buckle, went back to the caravan and finished off Jansson's sandwiches, then went down to the boathouse, where I had a small open plastic boat with an outboard engine. It's eighteen horsepower, and if the weather is good and the sea is calm, I can get up to twelve knots. I started the engine, sat down on a mouldy cushion and reversed out of the boathouse. I rounded the headland and increased my speed.

When I looked back I was horrified. I had always been able to see the roof and the upstairs windows of my house above the trees, but now there was only a gaping hole. I was so shaken by the discovery that I almost ran aground on Kogrundet, which lies just beyond the headland, managing to veer away only at the last minute.

I switched off the engine when I reached open water. The sea was empty, not a sound, no boats, hardly even any birds. A lone sea duck was skimming along just above the surface of the water, heading for the outer skerries.

I shivered. It came from deep inside. The boat drifted with the invisible wind. I lay down and stared up at the sky, where the clouds had begun to gather. There would be rain tonight.

The water lapped gently against the thin plastic skin that formed the outer shell of my boat. I tried to decide what to do.

The mobile Jansson had given me rang; it could only be him.

"Is there something wrong with your engine?" he asked.

He can see me, I thought, turning my head. But the sea was still empty. There was no sign of Jansson's boat.

"Why would there be something wrong with my engine?"

I shouldn't have snapped at him; Jansson always means well. I sometimes thought that the enormous amount of mail he had read before delivering it over all those years was a kind of declaration of love to the dwindling population of the islands. I think he felt it was part of his duty as a seafaring postman to read every postcard sent or received by the summer visitors. He had to keep himself informed about what these people who turned up for the summer thought about life and death and the permanent residents of the archipelago.

"Where are you?" I said.

"At home."

He was lying. If he was at home on Stångskär, there was no way he could see me slowly drifting along. That disappointed me. When I came to live on the island I decided never to let other people's behaviour get me down. The fact that Jansson wasn't always completely truthful didn't usually bother me — but when I had just lost my home in a devastating fire?

I suspected he was perched on a rock somewhere, clutching his binoculars.

I told him I had switched off the engine because I needed to think through my situation, and now I was going to head for the mainland to do my shopping.

"I'm starting her up now," I said. "If you listen you'll hear that she's running perfectly."

I ended the call before he could say anything else. The engine started and I sped away, heading for land.

My car is old but reliable. It's parked down by the harbour on the mainland, outside a house that belongs to a strange woman whose name is Rut Oslovski. No one calls her Rut, as far as I know. Everyone says Oslovski. She allows me to park there, and in return I check her blood pressure from time to time. I keep a stethoscope and a blood-pressure monitor in the glove box. Oslovski's blood pressure is too high, in spite of the fact that she has been taking metoprolol for the past few years. She's not even forty, so I think it's important to keep her blood pressure under control.

Oslovski's left eye is made of glass. No one seems to know how she lost her eye. No one knows very much about Oslovski, to be honest. According to Jansson, she suddenly turned up here twenty years ago after being granted asylum. At the time her Swedish pronunciation was terrible. She later claimed to have come from Poland and become a Swedish citizen, but Jansson, who can be very suspicious, pointed out that no one had ever seen her passport or any proof that she really was a Swedish citizen.

Unexpectedly, Oslovski turned out to be a skilled mechanic. Nor was she afraid of taking on hard physical work in the late autumn or early spring, repairing jetties when the melting ice had damaged the structure, leaving them crooked and unsafe.

She was strong, broad-shouldered, not beautiful but friendly. She kept herself to herself for the most part.

The handymen in the area kept a close eye on her, but no one could say that she took work away from them by charging too little.

When she first arrived, Oslovski lived in a small cottage in the pine forest, a few kilometres from the sea. After a while she bought the little house down by the harbour, which used to belong to a retired pilot.

Jansson had spoken to his colleague who delivered the post in the harbour area; Oslovski never received any letters, nor did she subscribe to any newspapers or magazines. Did she even have a mailbox out on the street?

Sometimes she disappeared for several months and then one day she would be back. As if nothing had happened. She moved around like a cat in the night.

I moored the boat and went up to my car. There was no sign of Oslovski. The car started right away; I dread the day when it gives up and decides it's time for the scrapyard.

It usually takes me twenty minutes to drive into town, but on this particular day the trip was much faster. I slowed down only when I realised I was putting myself in danger. I was beginning to suspect that the fire had destroyed something inside me. People can have load-bearing beams that give way too.

I parked on the main street, which is in fact the only street in town. It lies right at the end of an inlet poisoned by heavy metals from the industries that were here in the past. I can still recall the stench of a tannery from my childhood.

The bank is a white building right next to the toxic inlet.

I went up to the counter and explained that I had no bank cards and no ID; everything had been lost in the fire. The clerk recognised me but didn't seem to be quite sure what to do. A person without any form of ID always constitutes some kind of threat nowadays.

"I know my account number," I said, reeling off the numbers as he entered them into his computer.

"There should be about a hundred thousand kronor in there," I said. "Give or take a hundred."

The clerk peered at the screen, as if he couldn't believe the information that had appeared.

"Ninety-nine thousand and nine kronor," he said.

"I need to withdraw ten thousand. As you can see, I'm wearing my pyjama jacket instead of a shirt. I've lost everything."

I deliberately raised my voice when I explained what had happened. The whole place fell silent. Behind the counter there were two women in addition to the clerk who was helping me, and three customers were waiting their turn. Everyone was staring at me. I made a ridiculous bow, as if I were acknowledging silent applause.

The clerk counted out my money, then helped me to order a new card.

I went over to a cafe on the other side of the street. I had picked up a free pen and a couple of withdrawal forms in the bank, and I sat down and made a list of what I needed to buy.

It was a very long list. When I had filled both the slips and my serviette, I gave up.

I wondered how I was going to bear the pain and sorrow. I was too old to start again. The future had nothing to say. I could neither hear nor see any way out.

I screwed up the slips and the serviette, finished my tea and left. Then I went to the only clothes shop in town and bought shirts and underwear, sweaters and socks, trousers and a jacket, paying no heed to either quality or price. I put my bags in the car, then headed for the shoe shop to buy wellington boots. The only pair I could find had been made in Italy. That annoyed me. The assistant was a young girl in a headscarf whose Swedish was very poor. I tried to be pleasant, even though I was cross because they didn't have ordinary Tretorn wellingtons.

"Don't you have any Swedish wellingtons? Tretorn?" I asked.

"We have these," she replied. "No others."

"It's ridiculous not to sell classic Swedish wellingtons in a Swedish shoe shop!"

I was still doing my best to be civil, but she must have seen through my tone of voice. I could see that she was scared, which annoyed me even more. I had asked a perfectly simple question that wasn't supposed to be rude or threatening.

"Have you any idea what I'm talking about?" I asked.

"We have no other boots," she said.

"In that case I'll leave it. Unfortunately."

I walked out. I couldn't help slamming the door behind me.

There were no wellingtons in the ironmonger's either, just work boots with steel toecaps. I bought a cheap watch, then made my way to a shop down by the harbour to stock up on food. There was an LPG stove in the caravan, plus a few pans. I didn't buy anything I wanted, but I didn't buy anything I didn't want either. I filled my black plastic basket with indifference.

As I was passing the chemist's I remembered that my medical supplies had been destroyed in the fire, so I went inside. As a doctor I am still entitled to purchase prescription-only drugs.

Before I went back to the car I also bought a pay-as-you-go mobile phone.

I suddenly realised I had no electricity on the island.

I drove back towards the harbour. I still had about half of the money I had taken out. I parked the car in the usual place; the door to Oslovski's house was shut, and a rotting crow lay on the gravel path. Perhaps Oslovski was off on one of her mysterious trips?

I put my bags in the boat, then went to the chandlery. They had wellington boots, and they were made in Sweden. Or at least they were Tretorn anyway, but they didn't have my size. I ordered a pair and was informed that it would be at least two weeks before they arrived.

The owner of the shop is called Nordin. He's always been there. He spoke as if he had mourning crêpe in his voice when we talked about the fire. Nordin has a lot of children. He has been married three or four times. His present wife is called Margareta, but they have no children.

Jansson claims that Nordin does magic tricks for his children, but I have no idea whether that is true or not.

I felt chilled to the bone when I emerged onto the quayside. I went over to the boat, took a shirt out of one of the plastic bags, then went into the cafe above the chandlery. I ordered coffee and a Mazarin. When I picked the pastry up it disintegrated into a pile of dry crumbs.

I sat down at a table with a view over the harbour, unpacked my mobile phone and used the charging point on the cafe wall.

A man who will soon be seventy years old has nowhere to live because his house has burned down. He has no worldly possessions left apart from a boathouse, a caravan, a thirteen-foot open boat and an old car. The question is: what does he do now? Does this man have a future? Does he have any real reason to go on living?

I stopped dead right there. My daughter Louise — why hadn't I thought of her first of all? I was ashamed of myself.

Whether it was my crumbling Mazarin or what I had just been thinking I couldn't say, but the tears began to flow. I wiped my eyes with my napkin. The scene was the very epitome of loneliness and isolation. An old man sitting in a deserted cafe on an autumn day, the only customer in a harbour establishment to which the yachts and cruisers will not return until next summer.

I realised I had to call Louise. I would have preferred to wait, but she would never forgive me if I didn't tell her what had happened right away. My daughter is a volatile individual who lacks the tolerance and patience I believe I possess. She reminds me of her mother Harriet, who made her way across the ice using her wheeled walker some years ago, then died in my house the following summer.

My train of thought was interrupted as the door of the cafe opened and an unfamiliar woman of about forty came in. She was wearing exactly the kind of green wellingtons I had been searching for, plus a warm jacket and a scarf wound around her neck and head. When she took it off I saw that she had short hair and was very attractive. She went over to the counter and contemplated the unfortunate Mazarins.

Suddenly she turned and smiled at me. I nodded, wondering if I had met her before and forgotten. Veronika, who ran the cafe, emerged from the kitchen, and the woman ordered coffee and a Danish pastry. She came over to my table. I didn't know who she was.

"May I join you?"

She pulled out the chair without waiting for a response. A ray of pale autumn sunshine lit up her face as she sat down. She reached for the yellow curtain and pulled it across, shutting out the sun.

She smiled again. She had nice teeth. I smiled back but was careful to show only a little of my upper teeth;

they still look reasonably good. My daughter Louise inherited her mother's genes as far as her teeth are concerned, and unfortunately they are not as good as mine. Sometimes when Louise has been visiting and has got really drunk, she has quite unexpectedly attacked me because her teeth are not as white as mine.

"My name is Lisa Modin," the woman said. "And you must be the man who watched his house burn down last night. My sympathies, of course. It must have been a terrible experience. After all, a house and a home is like an outer skin for a human being."

She spoke with a slight accent that could have been from Sörmland, but I wasn't sure. And I was even less sure about why she had come to sit at my table. She took off her warm jacket and hung it over the back of the chair next to her.

I still didn't know what she wanted, but it didn't matter. In a moment of madness the very fact that she had sat down at my table made me start to love her.

An old man doesn't have much time at his disposal, I thought. This sudden love is all we can hope for.

"I'm a journalist. I write for the local paper. The editor asked me to go over and talk to you, take a look at the site of the fire. But when I went into the chandlery to ask how I could get to your island, they said you were probably in the grocery shop. Which you weren't — but you were here."

"How did you know it was me?"

"The man in the chandlery described you as best he could. It wasn't difficult to work out, particularly as there was no one in the grocery shop, and there's no one else in here."

She took a notepad out of her bag. The music from the radio in the kitchen suddenly seemed to irritate her; she got up, went over to the counter and asked Veronika to turn it down. After a moment the radio fell silent.

Lisa Modin was smiling as she came back to the table.

"I'll take you over," I said. "If you can cope with a small open boat."

"And you'll bring me back?"

"Of course."

"Are you still living on the island? I mean, your house burned down."

"I have a caravan."

"On an island? I thought it was really small. Is there a road?"

"It's a long story."

She was holding a pen but hadn't yet opened her notepad.

"The news about the fire is one thing," she said. "My editor is dealing with that; he'll speak to the police and the fire service. He wants me to write a more in-depth article about what losing your home like that means to a family."

"I'm on my own."

"Don't you even have pets?"

"They're dead."

"Did they burn to death?"

She seemed horrified at the thought.

"Dead and buried."

"And you don't have a wife?"

"She's dead too. Cremated. But I do have a daughter."

"What does she have to say about all this?"

"Nothing so far. She doesn't know yet."

She gave me a searching look, then she put down her pen and drank her coffee. I noticed that she was wearing a ring with an amber stone on her right hand. No ring on her left hand.

"It's too late today," she said. "But how about tomorrow? If you have time?"

"I've got all the time in the world."

"Surely not, if everything you owned has gone up in smoke?"

I didn't reply because of course she was right.

"I'll pick you up tomorrow," I said instead. "What time?"

"Ten o'clock? Is that too early?"

"It's fine."

She pointed to the window. "Down there?"

"I'll be by the petrol pumps. Wear something warm. And we might have rain tomorrow."

She finished her coffee and stood up.

"I'll be there at ten," she said and left the cafe.

I heard the sound of a car starting. I wondered if she knew my name.

I travelled home across the dark sea. The boat was full of plastic bags. I thought about Lisa Modin and the movements of her hands as she wound her scarf around her head and neck. I felt a sense of excitement and anticipation as I contemplated the following day.

I rounded Höga Tryholmen expecting to see the coastguard's boat moored at my jetty, but it wasn't there. I pushed my boat into the boathouse and carried all my bags to the caravan. I had switched on the small fridge and the heater before I left and the place felt nice and warm. I checked the LPG gauge; there was plenty of fuel in the cylinder.

I unpacked my new clothes and glanced at where they had been made. The three shirts were all manufactured in China. I moved on to the underclothes and socks: also China. The jacket was made in Hong Kong, so from now on I would be going around entirely dressed in clothes from China. Until my new wellingtons arrived, nothing that I was wearing to keep out the cold would be from anywhere other than faraway China.

I hung up the shirts, wondering why it seemed important. Was I just looking for something to complain about? As if the last thing that remains for a man who is growing old is the ability to complain?

I put on a shirt, a sweater and the jacket. The remains of the fire had now stopped smoking; however, the acrid stench of the seawater-sodden oak timbers was still unpleasant. It made me feel sick if I got too close. I walked slowly around the ruins of my house to see if there might be something salvageable after all, apart from the buckle from one of Giaconelli's shoes. I didn't find anything. The feeling that I was contemplating a war zone returned.

I stopped when I reached the plastic sheet. I frowned. Something had changed. I stood there for several minutes before I gave up. I had noticed something, but I couldn't say what it was.

I glanced at my new watch. I feel helpless if I don't know what time of the day or night it is. Perhaps it's because my father was such a poor timekeeper; on at least one occasion he was sacked from the restaurant where he was working for turning up late three days in a row.

I went up to the highest point on the island, from which I could see in all directions. My grandfather built a bench so that he and my grandmother could sit up there on warm summer evenings. I don't know whether they talked to each other or sat in silence, but once when I was a child, a few years before they died, I picked up my grandfather's binoculars and trained them on my grandparents. Much to my surprise I discovered that they were holding hands. It was a clear expression of tenderness and gratitude. They had been married for sixty-one years.

The bench is falling apart. I haven't looked after it. I have neglected it, like so many other things on the island.

I stood there staring out across the archipelago. My gaze settled on a little skerry to the east of my island. The skerry belongs to me too, but it doesn't have a name. It consists of no more than a couple of rocks and a small hollow in which a few trees grow. The hollow is deep enough to be protected from the wind. When I was a child I often built a den there. From the age of ten, when I was a strong swimmer, my grandparents allowed me to sleep over there when the weather was good.

When I was a teenager I had a tent on the skerry during the summer. Now I was looking at the place with different ideas. A thought had struck me, but I hadn't quite processed it yet.

I continued my walk around the island. On the western side I caught a glimpse of two mink disappearing among the rocks. Otherwise everything was quiet. It was as if I was all alone in a deserted world.

I stopped when I reached the plastic sheet again. Now I realised what I had noticed earlier. Lundin and Alexandersson had been back while I was away, then they had left without any indication as to whether they would return.

I couldn't prove it, but I was absolutely certain.

They suspected me of having started the fire. There was no obvious cause, so they had to investigate the possibility that I was an arsonist.

I knew I had done nothing, but how would I cope with being suspected of a crime?

My life had been turned upside down once before, when my career as a doctor came to an end following a botched operation. Had I now been afflicted by another disaster? How much could I bear?

I went to the boathouse and took down the blood-pressure monitor I use when Jansson turns up with his imaginary pains. I unbuttoned my Chinese-made shirt, rolled up my sleeve and took my blood pressure: 160 over 98. That's unusually high for me, so I checked the other arm too: 159 over 99. I wasn't happy with the result, even though I understood that it was probably because my house had burned down. I had had a shock. I had bought the medication at the chemist's earlier; I didn't normally take metoprolol, but it would bring down my blood pressure. If necessary I could also take an Oxascand tablet, a tranquilliser I use occasionally.

I took my pulse: 78. A little high but nothing serious. As I put the monitor back in the boathouse, I heard the sound of an engine in the distance. It was so far off that I couldn't work out which boat it was, and after a little while it died away.

I remembered that there was an old wind-up alarm clock in the boathouse. I had no idea whether it still worked; I searched among the tools and took it outside. The spring held when I wound it up, it started ticking and the hands began to move. I set it to the right time and put it down beside me on the bench. Right now that clock, my mobile phone and the Chinese shirts were my most valuable possessions.

The wind had got up. The weathervane on top of the boathouse was hovering between south and west. I picked up the clock and got to my feet.

I couldn't wait any longer. I had to try and get hold of my daughter.

CHAPTER
FOUR

Louise is forty years old. As I said, the last time we spoke she was in Amsterdam. I presumed she had friends there but saw no reason to tell me anything about them. Of course she could also have been driven to the Dutch city by one of the political projects to which she devoted her time.

She doesn't only write to presidents and dictators. More than once she has caused a scandal by throwing bags of rubbish at reactionary politicians. Sometimes it seems to me that she is an anarchist who has got lost along the way, at other times she appears to be a right-thinking radical woman who resorts to hopeless methods. Whenever I have tried to engage in a political discussion with her, I have always lost. Even if she hasn't managed to convince me with her arguments, she has crushed me with her constant interruptions.

I have no idea how she supports herself, but she doesn't seem to be short of money, and she has a stubborn streak which I envy.

When Harriet surprised me with the news that I had a daughter, Louise was already an adult. At the time she was living inland in a melancholy area of southern Norrland. It was her mother who took me to see her.

Harriet had told me only that we were going to visit someone on the way to the forest pool that was our official destination. It wasn't until after the door of the caravan opened and I was faced with a complete stranger that I found out she was my daughter. Needless to say it was one of the most overwhelming and important moments of my life. I had a child, a daughter, who was born when she was already over thirty years old.

She was living in the caravan, which was later transported to the island on an old cattle ferry. She stayed here until Harriet had died and we had burned her body in my old wooden boat, which had been lying there rotting on the shore. Shortly afterwards Louise disappeared. I eventually found out what she had been doing through a picture in the newspaper in which she was shown dancing naked in front of several international politicians whose actions she despised.

I hardly know her at all, but I wish I did. She has become increasingly fond of this island, and I have promised her that she will of course inherit everything when I am gone. The alternative would be for me to sell my home or to donate it to the local history society, but I don't need the money, and the society seems to consist mostly of people bickering among themselves about what it should really be doing. I don't want my grandparents' house — if it is rebuilt — to be turned into a badly run summer cafe.

A few years ago several young women lived here for a period of about six months. They had been evicted from a home for vulnerable girls run by the woman whose arm I had so unfortunately amputated by mistake. She had forgiven me, and I had been so pleased to be able to help the girls when they were homeless. However, they were restless souls, and living on this isolated island soon began to increase their anxiety levels. They left when a place on the mainland became available, and I never saw them again.

I was glad they weren't here now that the house had burned down. I shuddered at the thought that one of them could have died in the fire.

I sat on the bed in the caravan for a long time before I managed to pluck up the courage to call Louise. I hoped she wouldn't answer, then I could wait until the following day with a clean conscience. She picked up after four rings. Her voice was as clear as if she were standing just outside the caravan.

As usual I started by asking if I was disturbing her. I wasn't. Then I asked where she was. In the past we always began a phone call by enquiring how the other person was; now we want to know where they are.

She didn't answer, which meant that she had no intention of revealing her whereabouts. I didn't push it. If I am too inquisitive she often takes her revenge by not responding for several weeks when I call her.

I told her what had happened.

"The house burned down. Last night."

"What house?"

"My house. The one you were supposed to inherit."

"The house has burned down?"

"Yes."

"Oh my God!"

"Indeed."

"What happened?"

"No one knows. The whole place was ablaze when I woke up. I didn't manage to save anything except myself."

"Not even your diaries?"

"Nothing."

She fell silent, trying to process what I had said.

"Are you hurt?"

"No."

"But surely there must be an explanation?"

"The police and a fire investigation officer have been here poking around in the ruins. They couldn't find a cause."

"Houses don't just burn down for no reason. Are you sure you're not hurt?"

"I'm fine."

"What are you going to do now?"

"I don't know."

"Where are you living?"

"In your caravan, for the time being."

Another silence. At least her surprise hadn't turned to anger at me.

"I'm coming home."

"There's no need."

"I know, but I want to see it with my own eyes, see that everything is gone."

"You can believe what I say."

"I do."

I could tell from her voice that she didn't want to talk any more. She said she would be in touch very soon, and we ended the call. I lay down and noticed that I was sweating. In spite of everything, right now Louise was the only person I could talk to about what had happened.

After a while I got up and went outside. I put Jansson's phone in a small metal box under the bench on the jetty, then I sent him a text to let him know that he could come and pick it up. I also placed a fifty-kronor note in the box to cover the few calls I had made. At the end of my message I said that I would prefer not to have any visitors.

I sat down on the bench and leaned back against the wall of the boathouse; the red paint was flaking.

When I woke up it was twilight. I shivered and walked back up to the caravan. All at once I found the gathering darkness frightening. There was no glow from the windows that were no longer there. The light outside the boathouse wasn't working either. I was surrounded by darkness. I switched on the LPG light inside the caravan and dug out an old paraffin lamp that Harriet had once given to Louise. I opened a tin of soup and heated it up. When it was ready I switched off the LPG light, leaving the softer glow of the paraffin lamp.

I went to bed early that night. As I lay there I realised how tired I was. I didn't even have the energy to worry about the following day. It was as if the fire had consumed all my strength, along with my house.

I woke from a dream about a storm. With the help of the old alarm clock I worked out that I had slept for nine hours. I don't think I've slept for that long since I was a child. As usual I got up immediately. If I stay in bed, anxiety spreads through my body. I put on my raincoat and realised that I had forgotten to buy a towel the previous day. I decided to sacrifice the yellow Chinese shirt. I headed for the boathouse, where at the very end of the jetty there is a ladder leading into the water. I climbed down and floated away on my back.

It was cold. I guessed that the temperature of the sea was seven or eight degrees. The wind had strengthened during the night, and the weathervane on top of the boathouse was veering between west and south-west. I hadn't remembered to buy a radio either, I thought as I clambered out of the water. I rubbed my skin dry with the yellow shirt in order to get my circulation going. I avoided looking too closely at myself; as I get older, I find my body increasingly repulsive. This morning I thought I looked more decrepit than ever.

I hurried back to the caravan and got dressed. After a cup of coffee and a couple of sandwiches, I called Directory Enquiries and eventually managed to get hold of Kolbjörn Eriksson. He is the same age as me, and returned to the archipelago after spending many years as an electrician aboard a cargo ship sailing between Europe and South America. These days he lives in a house he inherited from his uncle, who was a member of one of the better-known seal-hunting families out here on the islands, Kolbjörn repaired my electric cooker a while ago, and he is also the man who renewed all the wiring in the house.

He answered immediately. When I told him who I was, I thought I heard him let out a groan.

"My house has burned down, but you probably know that already."

"I was there," he replied. "I don't suppose you remember."

I had absolutely no recollection of seeing him among those working in vain to extinguish the blaze. How could I not recall his characteristic face, his bald head, his height and his slightly reedy voice?

"I don't remember anyone who was there," I replied. "But thank you for trying to help."

"What happened?"

"It was definitely nothing to do with the wiring you renewed," I reassured him.

"You didn't leave a candle burning?"

"No. We'll have to wait and see what conclusion the investigators reach."

I almost told him that I was probably suspected of arson, but I managed to stop the words before they flew out of my mouth.

"I need electricity," I said. "I'm living in the caravan at the moment; I need light and heat."

"I've already thought about that. I can come over today."

I was due to pick up Lisa Modin in three hours.

"Tomorrow," I said. "And could you bring some outside lights and some lamps that I can use inside the caravan, if you have any?"

Kolbjörn promised he would be there the following day; we agreed on seven thirty. I put the phone in my

48

pocket and went down to my boat, which started first time. I headed for the skerry with no name. I switched off the engine, flipped it up and made my way in using an oar. The bottom of the boat scraped against the rock. There was no need to make it fast because I would be able to see it from wherever I was on the skerry. The wind was a south-westerly, and the waves were lapping against the stern.

I found a few bones from a herring gull on the rocks. I had been finding such things, including entire skeletons, ever since I was a child. But I didn't want to think of the skerry as a graveyard. I went down to the hollow between the two rocks; beyond lay the open sea, with the odd reef barely visible on the horizon.

When I was little I used to think of the reefs as the backs of whales, emerging from the sea.

I still do.

I paced out the hollow; the caravan would fit. With ropes and a block and tackle it wouldn't be impossible to transport it from a ferry to the spot between two dense clumps of alders. I decided to carry out the plan that had come into my mind the previous day. I was sure that my daughter would approve. I was going to relocate the caravan.

I walked around the skerry. The wind felt fresh out here, with no islands to get in its way.

I got back in the boat and headed for the harbour. There was still an hour to go before I was due to meet Lisa Modin. I went to see Nordin and asked if he had ordered my wellingtons. He had. He looked almost insulted at the question.

I also bought a life jacket for Lisa. I have an old one that I never use. After mooring the boat I had taken it out from the little storage area in the stern, and had tried in vain to wipe off the oil and fish scales.

I was astonished when I paid for Lisa Modin's life jacket. Nordin agreed that it was expensive, but of course he didn't set the price.

Some construction workers were sitting in the cafe drinking coffee. They were in the middle of resurfacing the jetty where the coastguard patrol boats are moored. Apparently one of them had spotted a perch a few days earlier, and there was a loud discussion about whether he might have been mistaken. Everyone knows that perch has practically died out in the archipelago. I haven't seen any in the water by my boathouse for almost three years. The odd shoal of dace has drifted by, but nothing else.

I listened distractedly to their conversation. The Baltic Sea was dying. Its decline was insidious. Parts of the seabed invisible to the naked eye were already dead, leaving nothing but a sterile underwater desert. The increasingly intense algae blooms were like an outbreak of psoriasis every summer. The sea was shedding its skin while being suffocated at the same time.

The construction workers left without reaching any agreement on the existence or otherwise of the perch. I was alone in the cafe. Veronika was in the kitchen, listening to the radio. I had noticed that she turned down the volume when I came in.

50

Veronika is the granddaughter of one of the last pilots out here. She has a brother who was born with hydrocephalus and lives at home with his parents. Veronika has a small apartment squeezed in between the grocery store and the cafe.

She is friendly and attentive, but permanently anxious, afraid of doing something wrong or saying something inappropriate. Sometimes I think she will always be here in the cafe, serving customers until old age takes its inevitable toll. I wonder what she really longs for. There must be something.

I went to the toilet and contemplated my reflection in the mirror. It was what it was. My hair was thinning but neatly combed. My expression was grim. I attempted a smile. I tried to picture Lisa Modin without any clothes on. I immediately felt embarrassed.

I discovered a mark on the blue Chinese shirt I had put on this morning, a small flaw on the collar. This made me so angry that I was on the point of ripping off the shirt and throwing it in the bin in the toilet, but I managed to calm myself down. If I pulled up my jumper by a few centimetres, the flaw wouldn't show.

I still had twenty minutes before Lisa Modin was due to arrive. I went to the grocery shop and bought a brioche loaf. The place was just as empty as the cafe had been. There were hardly any people left on the islands, just as there were hardly any fish left in the sea.

I went down to the boat and waited. There was a light breeze blowing across the water. A rain front was building over to the east, but it was unlikely to reach us before the evening.

The construction workers were banging away on the jetty, the smell of asphalt filling the air.

I looked down into the water. No fish. Not even a little shoal of whitefish.

Ten o'clock. No sign of a car. Had she decided not to come after all?

At that moment a pale blue car came racing down the hill; the driver slammed on the brakes when it reached the parking area. Lisa Modin got out. She was wearing the same jacket as the previous day. I stood up and waved. In my eagerness I exaggerated the gesture; the boat rocked and I almost fell in the water. I banged my knee on one of the oars and sat down in the bottom with a thud. I don't know if she noticed; I was back on my feet by the time she reached the boat.

"Sorry I'm late," she said.

"No problem."

I took her handbag and helped her into the boat. She was wearing gloves. I gave her the life jacket and cast off. She settled down on the seat in the middle with her back to me. I headed out of the harbour and increased my speed. Nordin was standing outside the chandlery smoking his pipe. He's one of the few people I know these days who stubbornly refuses to give up smoking.

Lisa Modin didn't say a word throughout the whole journey, she just sat gazing out across the islands, the rocks and the open sea. A sea eagle drifted high above us on the thermals. That was the only time she turned to me. I nodded towards the bird, which appeared to be suspended on invisible strings.

"A golden eagle?" she called out.

"Sea eagle."

Those were the only words we exchanged. I slowed down as we approached my jetty. The site of the fire was clearly visible. I manoeuvred carefully into the boathouse.

She didn't need any help getting ashore. We went straight up to my burned-out house. She walked around the blackened remains once, twice, the second time in the opposite direction. I stood by the charred apple tree, watching her. For a brief moment she reminded me of Harriet when she was young, although Harriet had never had such short hair. Suddenly I didn't know if my desire was focused on a memory or on the woman walking around the ruins.

Lisa rejoined me, shaking her head.

"What happened?"

"I was asleep, and I woke up because the room was full of a searing light. I ran straight outside."

"I spoke to Bengt Alexandersson on the phone. He said the cause of the fire is still unclear."

"Did he say anything else?"

"No. Just that the cause of the fire is unclear."

I immediately felt that she wasn't telling the truth. Alexandersson must have said something else. Did she know that I was suspected of having set fire to my own house?

I turned away and slowly walked back to the boathouse and the bench. I no longer had the desire to invite her into the caravan for a cup of coffee. She followed me and sat down beside me with her notepad and pen in her hand.

"How do you survive?" she asked.

"You get out of the house as fast as you can."

"That's not what I meant. How do you survive when you've lost everything you own?"

"We really need very little in order to live."

"But what about all the memories? The family heirlooms? The photograph albums? The floors you have always walked on, the wallpaper you have seen every day, the doors you have opened and closed?"

"The most important memories are preserved in my mind. I can't weep over the fact that everything is gone. I have to decide what to do. I have no intention of allowing the fire to steal my life."

"Are you going to rebuild the house?"

"I don't know yet."

"But you were fully insured, of course?"

"Yes."

"Including the contents?"

"I don't know."

She jotted a few things down. I noticed that she used shorthand. She was still wearing her gloves. I ought to ask her what Alexandersson had really said.

She suddenly pulled a face and bent her head. I could see that she was in pain.

"I'm wondering if I've slipped a disc," she said. "But maybe it's just a stiff neck?"

I got to my feet.

"I run a kind of doctor's surgery from this bench," I said. "Would you like me to check?"

She looked as if she thought I was joking.

"I could examine you," I said quietly. "It will only take a couple of minutes."

She hesitated, but then she took off her scarf and unbuttoned her jacket. I felt her neck, gently pressing the vertebrae. Then I asked her to move her head and neck according to my instructions. I suspected it could well be a slipped disc, but she would need an X-ray to confirm my diagnosis.

Her body was warm. I wanted to rest my face against her skin. I asked her to carry out a few unnecessary movements just so that I could leave my hands where they were.

She put her scarf back on and promised to go for an X-ray. I suggested that we go into the caravan for a cup of coffee while we continued our conversation. First of all she took a couple of photographs of me sitting on the bench with the sea in the background, then she wanted me to go and stand right at the end of the jetty looking out to sea. I did as she said.

The caravan was very cramped with two people inside it at the same time. I sliced the brioche and set it out on a plate and served coffee in mismatched cups, which were all I had. I sat at the table on a stool, while Lisa sat on the bed with a cushion behind her back. She asked me about the history of the house and the island, how long I had lived there and how I saw my future.

The last question was the most difficult to answer. I simply said that I hadn't yet made any decisions. The fire was still burning inside me.

"That's a beautiful way of putting it," she said. "Beautiful and terrifying."

When she didn't appear to have any further questions, I asked her how she had ended up working for the local newspaper. She told me she had split up with her husband and left Strängnäs, where she had been working for another local paper. She had moved here a year ago for the job, and I had a feeling that she wasn't particularly happy.

She had no children. I didn't ask, she just told me.

"What will you be doing in ten years?" I wondered.

"Hopefully something I can't even imagine today. What about you?"

"I'll give the same answer as you."

"But you'll still be here? In a new house?"

I didn't reply. We sat in silence as the alder branches tapped against the roof of the caravan.

"I've never been out in the archipelago before," she said. "Strangely enough. Now I can see how beautiful it is."

"It has a particular beauty just before the winter. There's nothing lovelier, although some people see it as desolate and frightening."

"I heard about one of the outer skerries where poor fishermen and their families used to live long ago. Apparently you can still see something of the foundations of their houses, and no one can understand how anyone could survive out there. I'd like to see that. But if I've understood correctly, no one is allowed to go ashore?"

"That's only during the birds' breeding season. You can go there at this time of year."

"Have you been there?"

56

"Many times. I can show you if you like."

She immediately accepted my invitation.

"Next Wednesday?" she suggested. "If you have time? I realise you have a lot to think about at the moment."

"I've got all the time in the world."

We carried on talking about the fire. She asked me to describe my former house, room by room. I told her about the rough oak timbers in the walls, how the trees had been felled in the northern reaches of the archipelago and dragged across the ice by horses. My grandfather had told me that one of the wagonloads had gone down near a small insignificant shallow that was known as Kejsaren, for some reason. Even if the ice was thick, treacherous cracks could appear in the vicinity of shallows or close to long shorelines. The horse, which according to my grandfather was called Rommel, had gone straight through the ice along with the driver, who was only twenty years old. No one had been around, no one had heard the screams. It wasn't until late at night that the search had begun, by flickering torchlight. The following day the crack had sealed itself, and neither horse nor driver were found until the spring came and the ice loosened its grip.

I felt as if I was walking through my house once more. The cumulative impressions left by several generations had been obliterated in just a few short hours. Invisible traces of movements, words, silences, sorrows, suffering and laughter had disappeared. Even things that are invisible can be reduced to soot and ashes.

As we walked down to the boathouse I was already looking forward to Lisa's return. Right now that was more important to me than the blackened ruins of my house.

I dropped her off in the harbour by the petrol pumps. We shook hands. I waited until she got into her car and drove off.

Back on the island I discovered that Jansson had been to collect his phone. He had placed a bag of freshly baked crisprolls in the metal box.

Jansson is a man of many talents. On one occasion he revealed that he was interested in how people had executed one another over the centuries. It turned out that he knew everything about strange, barbaric methods of execution. I listened in astonishment and with growing revulsion to the catalogue of human brutality until he abruptly stopped, as if he had realised that he had said too much.

But the most remarkable thing about Jansson is his clear, sonorous tenor voice. On Harriet's last birthday he surprised us all by suddenly getting up from the table in the midsummer twilight and singing Schubert's "Ave Maria", the sound echoing across the water. We were all deeply moved and equally taken aback. No one knew he had such a powerful voice. However, when he was subsequently asked to join the church choir, he said no. No one has heard him sing since that birthday party, when Harriet sat with a garland of flowers in her hair just a few weeks before she died.

I took the crisprolls up to the caravan, where I sat down and made a list of all the things I had to sort out.

I also looked at my financial situation and discovered that, thanks to my thriftiness over the years, it wasn't nearly as bad as I had feared. I had around two hundred thousand kronor in various bank accounts, plus a quantity of stocks and shares.

I opened a couple of tins and made myself something to eat, then went for a walk around the island. When I got back I fetched an old transistor radio from the boathouse. I didn't expect it to work, but when I put in the new batteries I had remembered to buy the previous day, it actually made a noise. I listened to a lecture by a professor at the University of Lund who was talking about the healing properties of magnetism. As a doctor I obviously don't believe in the miraculous power of magnets, but the professor had a pleasant voice. I didn't really care what he was saying.

Then came the news and the shipping forecast. The outside world becomes more incomprehensible with each passing day. I am losing track of which terrorist groups are killing each other. A Palestinian boy had been burned alive outside Jerusalem. This terrible bulletin ended with a report about a group of rebels in Iraq who had been crucified by their opponents. Their hatred was based on different opinions on what constituted the true religion. Both parties believed that they were serving the same god.

There was no god in my caravan. Perhaps he wandered around the island at night? Perhaps he slept in the boathouse? I had no intention of ever letting him in here, not even if he was frozen stiff. When it came to contact with gods, I was capable of inhumane behaviour.

I woke early the following day. During the night I had dreamed of an armada of ancient motorboats surrounding the island. The beams of their headlights shone at my caravan with such intensity that it reminded me of the fire. I woke up thinking the caravan must be burning. I ran out into the darkness stark naked. My heart carried on pounding for a long time, even after I had realised it was only a dream.

I lay awake for ages. The wind rocked the caravan slightly, like a vessel bobbing around on its moorings.

Eventually I dozed off and slept until six o'clock. I went down to the boathouse and took my morning dip. The thermometer was showing seven degrees. The yellow Chinese shirt served as a towel once more. I made coffee and sardine sandwiches. Just to be on the safe side, I checked the tin to make sure it didn't say "Produce of China", but in fact the fish had made the long journey from Lagos in Portugal.

At seven thirty Kolbjörn arrived in his big aluminium ferry. Apart from his electrical expertise, he also has an in-depth knowledge of different forms of marine propulsion. This particular vessel was driven by a jet stream, which meant it didn't need a propeller.

We chatted for a while down by the jetty. He had brought some outdoor lights as well as a couple of table lamps for the caravan.

The electric cable to my island comes ashore on the south side. There is a sign to say that dropping anchor there is forbidden. I asked Kolbjörn if he would like a cup of coffee, but he declined; he wanted to get straight down to work. He had only glanced in passing at the site of the fire; it was as if he would prefer not to see it.

I asked if he needed an unqualified labourer. Once again he declined; he would rather work alone. When I wondered whether we should discuss his fee for the job, he muttered something unintelligible in response.

I knew he would charge me next to nothing. As far as he was concerned, I was a person in dire straits who needed support.

My mobile rang. I didn't recognise the number and when I answered I heard an eager voice wanting to sell me outdoor furniture made of durable plastic. Before I ended the call in an outburst of rage I gathered that the price had been slashed now the summer was over. The salesman didn't call back.

As I slipped the phone in my pocket I heard the throb of an engine; it was the coastguard. This time Captain Pålsson was at the helm, with Alexandersson and a man I had never seen before on board. They hove to next to Kolbjörn's ferry and came ashore. Alexandersson was in uniform, while the other man wore an overcoat with blue overalls underneath.

Alexandersson introduced him.

"Detective Inspector Sture Hämäläinen. The police are investigating the cause of the fire too."

Hämäläinen was short and chubby, and his face was so pale I thought he was wearing white make-up. He shook my hand.

"It's just routine," he said. "Apart from anything else, you'll have problems with the insurance if the cause of the fire can't be established."

He spoke Swedish with a Finnish accent. At least he wasn't made in China, I thought grimly.

We went up to the house. Kolbjörn and Alexandersson nodded to one another.

"I'm not a pyromaniac," I said. "Why would I set fire to my own house?"

I was speaking to Hämäläinen, but he didn't reply. He was staring at the ruins. I wasn't even sure if he had heard what I said. Then he began to walk slowly around the plot.

"Why are the police involved?" I asked Alexandersson. "Do you really think I'm responsible for this?"

"Of course not."

"What does he think he's going to find?"

"The cause. He's very good."

"Let's hope you're right."

I noticed that I was getting annoyed. Alexandersson understood. We didn't say anything else.

Kolbjörn was busy fixing up an external light down by the boathouse,

"Who's the stranger?" he wanted to know.

"A detective inspector who's going to try and find out if I set fire to my own house."

Kolbjörn dropped his screwdriver. I bent down and gave it back to him.

"I'm not an arsonist," I said. "I'm going shopping. There's a flask of coffee in the caravan."

I didn't go shopping. I chugged aimlessly around the islands instead, then I decided to go out to Vrångskär, the skerry I would be visiting with Lisa Modin in a few days.

I went ashore, pulled the boat up behind me, then found a place to sit under a distorted pine tree where the ground was dry.

I could see storm clouds gathering on the distant horizon. I gazed out to sea, thinking that soon I would have to decide what I was going to do.

Had my life gone up in flames? Did I still have the desire to imagine anything beyond the humiliation of old age? Could I find a new will to live?

Basically it came down to just one question: did I want to rebuild the house or should I let Louise inherit the site of a fire?

I carried on staring out to sea, hoping that an answer would drift ashore. But nothing turned up.

However, I did make up my mind that I wouldn't wait any longer; I was going to move the caravan to the skerry and the hollow between the two rocks. No doubt Kolbjörn would be able to run a cable from the island to the skerry; he wouldn't hesitate to break the law if that was what it took to solve an emergency energy issue.

The decision gave me the strength to get to my feet. I went down to the boat, breaking off one of the last roses of the summer on the way, and set off for home.

The two boats were still there. Kolbjörn was in the process of fixing up the wiring in the caravan, while Alexandersson and Hämäläinen were still at the site of the fire.

"Have you found anything?" I asked.

I couldn't help noticing the fleeting glance they exchanged. It worried me, but it also irritated me. A mixture of worry and anger leads to fear.

"What have you found?" I persisted.

"Indications that the fire started simultaneously in several places," Hämäläinen said.

"What kind of indications?"

"There are signs that an accelerant was used."

"So the fire was started deliberately?"

Hämäläinen grimaced and shook his head. Alexandersson looked troubled, scraping his foot at the ash around the foundations.

"So I'm suspected of starting the fire," I said.

Hämäläinen shrugged, then looked me straight in the eye.

"Did you?"

"Did I what?"

"Start the fire."

I turned to Alexandersson. "Who is this fucking Finn you've brought with you?"

I didn't wait for a response, but stormed off down to the caravan. Kolbjörn, who was outside balancing on a ladder, could see that I was upset. But he didn't say anything.

A little while later I heard the coastguard's boat start up. I waited until the throb of the engine had died away, then I went outside. I explained to Kolbjörn that I was thinking of moving the caravan to the skerry without a name. Could he help me? I knew he had an old cattle ferry. He would also be able to solve the problem of finding a block and tackle to get it into the right place in the hollow.

He promised to see what he could do. Sorting out a supply of electricity would be no trouble either.

He finished work just before dusk fell. A lantern shone outside the boathouse.

I switched on the lamp he had placed on the small table in the caravan. It would be easier to make decisions now, I thought. The light would help me.

That evening I ate unmemorable fish soup. I was fast asleep before midnight.

CHAPTER
FIVE

The following day I spent a long time searching the boathouse for something to write on. The only thing I could find, in a box of worn-out paintbrushes, was a tattered notebook in which my grandfather had kept a record of the oil changes he had carried out on his car, a PV444 that he owned in the 1950s. The book was stiff with dried oil, but there were several blank pages that would serve my purpose.

I was about to push away the box of brushes when I discovered another object right at the bottom, under a few sheets of well-used sandpaper. It was a black yo-yo, made of wood and with the string still intact.

I hadn't held a yo-yo in my hand for sixty years. Had my grandfather or grandmother secretly performed tricks with it? Or could this be my own childhood toy?

I went out onto the jetty, slipped the middle finger of my right hand through the loop and tried to make the yo-yo dance. I could just about get it to travel up and down the string once.

I'm not quite sure what happened next. I felt dizzy and collapsed onto the bench; the dizziness was followed by nausea. There was no pain in my chest or my left arm. I sat completely still, trying to breathe calmly. The yo-yo dangled lifeless from my right hand. Slowly I began to feel better. I tried to think of it as nothing more than a funny turn, but then I realised I was having a panic attack that was spreading through my body. I thought that each breath, each moment would be my last.

I staggered up to the caravan and lay down on the bed, convinced that I was going to die right there and then. I swallowed two tranquillisers with a mouthful of cold coffee, but the panic continued to grow. I felt as if I had a herd of horses inside my head, bolting in all directions. I slammed my hand against the wall to chase them away, but to no avail.

By the time the attack had passed and I tried to sit up, the sun was no longer shining in through the skylight. I switched on the transistor radio. After a few minutes a classical music programme was interrupted by the news. It was two o'clock. I had been battling the panic and terror for at least five hours.

I switched off the radio and went outside. The sun was still strong. I carried on down to the boathouse. The notebook containing my grandfather's record of his oil changes was lying on the jetty. I picked it up and put it in my pocket.

Now the attack was over, I thought that perhaps it had been caused by old age. Until now I had believed that the passing years didn't mean much. I was ageing, but slowly, almost imperceptibly. Growing older was like a mist silently drifting across the sea.

But perhaps that was no longer the case. Now suddenly I was an old man, afraid of dying. Taking that step across the invisible border was the final element. It was a step I feared much more than I had realised.

All at once I knew I needed to talk to someone. I don't know when I last felt that urge. I keyed in Jansson's number, but as the phone started to ring I cancelled the call. I didn't want to talk to him; instead I called my daughter, but once again I changed my mind before she could answer.

I heard the throb of an engine in the distance. After a little while I realised it was the coastguard's boat, and that the sound was getting closer. I wondered if I had time to cast off and slip away on my boat in order to avoid seeing Alexandersson and whoever he had brought with him, but it was too late.

Pålsson was at the helm. I had no idea what had become of the blonde girl, Alma Hamrén. However, both Alexandersson and Hämäläinen were on board. We shook hands and went up to the site of the fire.

"Have you got anywhere?" I asked.

Alexandersson glanced at Hämäläinen.

"We have no explanation for the fire," Hämäläinen said. "But we do have a number of clues."

"Like what?"

"As I told you last time, the fire seems to have started in several places simultaneously."

"And how would you interpret that?"

"It's too early to say."

I didn't ask any more questions because I knew I wouldn't get any straight answers. I left them up by the ruins and went back to the caravan. I put the notebook on the table and found a pen. But I didn't write anything. I had nothing to say. There was a little mirror hanging on the wall, and I could see my unshaven face. I looked like a highwayman. Or perhaps I looked the way an arsonist is supposed to look. I made a note to buy razors and shaving foam. That was the first thing I wrote in my grandfather's old notebook.

I lay down on the bed and must have fallen asleep. I was woken by someone knocking on the door; it was Alexandersson.

"Did I wake you?"

"Of course not. Who the hell sleeps in the middle of the afternoon?"

He shook his head apologetically.

"We'd like to ask you a few questions. Well, not me — Hämäläinen."

We went back up to the ruins, where Hämäläinen was waiting. The sun was low in the sky now. The rain I had been expecting had gone away.

This is when it happens, I thought. This is when they accuse me.

The yo-yo was in my pocket. I wondered whether to whip it out and try to make it dance while Hämäläinen was asking his questions.

I left it where it was and looked him in the eye.

"There's still this feeling that the fire started in several places at the same time."

"Is it a feeling or a fact?"

He didn't answer my question.

"It's impossible to pick up a specific odour," he said instead. "But in all four corners of the house there are signs that a highly flammable liquid has been poured out and ignited. It leaves particular marks on burning wood."

"That's ridiculous!"

"Ridiculous or not, it's something we have to investigate further."

"What did you want to ask me?"

"Do you have access to petrol or diesel?"

"I have a boat engine that runs on petrol. Apart from the tank on board, I have a can with a reserve supply of twenty litres."

"Could we go down and take a look at it?"

"The tank on board or the reserve supply?"

"I was thinking of the reserve supply."

Alexandersson remained a few steps behind. I unscrewed the cap, and once the petrol fumes had dispersed, it was obvious that the can was empty. "I realise you will interpret this as further evidence against me. A reserve is no use unless it's full."

I was so agitated that my voice was hoarse. I could hardly speak.

"We need to carry out a chemical analysis of the remains of the fire," Hämäläinen said.

"I didn't burn down my house!" I shouted. "If that's what you're accusing me of, then I suggest you arrest me right now!"

I held out my hands in a pathetic gesture, inviting him to slap on the handcuffs. Which he didn't do, of course.

"I'd like you both to go to hell now," I said. "Carry out your investigation, but let me know when you're coming so that I can make sure I'm not around."

I took out my mobile and read out the number. Alexandersson put it into his own phone. Hämäläinen just stood there staring down at the bare boards of the jetty.

Silence fell, and I could feel my anger turning to despair. The road from failed doctor to suspected arsonist was not long.

"Is there anyone you can think of who might have set fire to your house?" Hämäläinen suddenly asked.

"Someone who knew I was asleep in there, and was prepared to risk my being burned alive? Or maybe that was the aim — is that what you mean?"

"There can be many reasons for starting a fire."

"Don't a lot of arsonists simply enjoy seeing the fire spread, consuming everything in its path?"

"That's pyromaniacs. Arsonists have a motive, even if it is obscure."

"I have no enemies out here in the archipelago."

"What about elsewhere?"

I thought about it. Harriet had hated me for many years, but she was dead and I didn't believe in ghosts. I couldn't come up with anyone else.

"Not that I know of," I said. "But of course there could be people after me that I'm totally unaware of."

The conversation foundered. Hämäläinen returned to the site of the fire, while Alexandersson and I remained on the jetty and talked about the autumn weather. If it had been spring, we would have talked about the spring weather. I sometimes wonder how many hours of my life I have spent conversing with various people about the wind and the weather.

Hämäläinen came back carrying several plastic bags containing samples of burned material.

Alexandersson was keen to make a move. Pålsson, who never said a word, started the engine.

"What happened to Alma?" I asked. "Your blonde companion?"

"She's got flu," Alexandersson said. "She'll be back when she's better."

"Well, if she needs a doctor you know where I am."

I immediately regretted my comment. Alexandersson stared at me in surprise. I could understand why. What use would I be to a young woman suffering from flu?

I stood on the jetty and raised my hand in farewell. It felt as heavy as a stone. My brief outburst had worn me out.

I went back to the caravan, lay down on the bed and tried to think. But my head was spinning. That herd of bolting horses was back.

How long I lay there I don't know. Eventually I left the caravan with a vague idea of cleaning out the boathouse. Many years ago, when I first moved to the island, I had a good clear-out, but haven't touched it since. Even if you live as simply as I do, life seems to consist mainly of amassing a huge amount of rubbish that has no importance or value whatsoever.

There is an inner room in the boathouse where my grandfather kept his nets. It also contains the stool he used to sit on while mending torn nets. Some of them are still on the walls, but they are so fragile that they would fall apart if I so much as touched them. None of them would be any use for fishing. My grandfather made many of his own nets, and they constitute a memory of him that I have no wish to get rid of.

I began by clearing a shelf behind the old flounder nets. Under a pile of tools I found a little brown book that I'd never noticed before. The room was dark and the light wasn't working, so I took the book outside and sat down on the bench. To my surprise I saw that it was very old. It had been printed in Stockholm in 1833, and was based on an original text in German. It didn't say who was responsible for the translation, but the author's name was D. J. Tscheiner. The Swedish title was *Anwisning till Sångfåglars Fångst och Skötsel — A Guide to the Capture and Care of Songbirds*. I flicked through the pages, wondering how such a thing had ended up with my grandfather. It was very difficult to read.

My curiosity was aroused, and I went back inside. After a while I found what I first assumed was part of a discarded eel trap, but then I realised it was the remnants of a plaited birdcage. It was as if I had discovered some totally unknown aspect of my grandparents' lives. A birdcage and a 181-year-old book?

I carried on searching until I had gone through the entire room and there was only a box of old glass jars left. I found a mummified mouse in there, but the jars were empty. I sniffed them but couldn't determine what they might have contained. They weren't labelled.

Apart from one — virtually the last one I picked up. I took it outside. It contained something grey, a congealed jelly-like substance. It gave off a faint smell that I thought I recognised, but I couldn't put a name to it, and it was hard to make out what was written in ink on the white sticky label. After much pondering I decided it said *Fågellim* — Birdlime. I wasn't sure whether it was my grandfather's or grandmother's handwriting. To be honest, I don't think I'd ever seen anything they'd actually written.

Birdlime?

I tried to put together the old book, the jar and the birdcage to form a whole. The key clue was of course the title of the book: *A Guide to the Capture and Care of Songbirds*. The remnants of the cage fitted in with this. But the jar and its contents? Had I read the label correctly? Was birdlime something that was used to trap larks and finches?

I had no recollection of a birdcage in the house when I was a child. Nor could I remember any talk of birds apart from the eider ducks and velvet scoters my grandfather shot when he was out hunting.

I decided to wait until my daughter arrived before trying to find the answers to my questions. She has a computer that helps her solve most problems that arise.

Songbirds and birdlime.

I carried on rummaging around in the boathouse. I found plenty of dead swallows that had got caught up in various discarded tools and been unable to free themselves. The place was like a swallows' graveyard. Some were adults, others little more than fledglings. They must have barely flown the nest before becoming trapped, never to escape.

74

Then I found my old tent from my childhood, with an equally ancient sleeping bag lying next to it. I took both items out onto the jetty, assuming they were rotten and would have to be thrown away. However, the tent and the sleeping bag were intact and the pegs were still there. I couldn't resist the temptation of pitching the tent on the grass. The process came back to me straight away. When the tent was up, I was surprised at how small it was.

I threw the sleeping bag over the washing line to air, then I crawled inside the tent. The pale autumn light produced a greyish-green glow.

As I sat there on the green groundsheet I experienced a great sense of calm, a feeling that I had distanced myself from the disastrous fire for just a little while. The horses in my head had stopped galloping around. I made up my mind to erect the tent out on the skerry that very afternoon. I needed to get away from the remains of my house and the charred apple tree.

I set off at about six o'clock. I had tried out the sleeping bag; the musty smell still lingered, but it was usable. I had eaten dinner early, then packed some sandwiches, a flask of coffee and a bottle of water.

I dragged the boat ashore on the skerry and moored it by the same rock I had favoured when I was a boy. I put up the tent in what had been my usual spot. I spread out the sleeping bag and lay down. The uneven ground beneath me was instantly familiar.

I got up, gathered twigs and branches in the semi-darkness and piled them up in a crevice in the rock. However, as I knelt there with a box of matches in my hand, I decided not to light my fire. I had had enough of flames. I left the branches where they were and went back to the tent. I hadn't brought any source of light with me, so I lay on top of the sleeping bag, had a cup of coffee and ate a couple of sandwiches. The wind came and went in sudden gusts. I was filled with a sense of liberation. For the first time since I rushed out of my burning house, I was able to think clearly once more.

I had made up my mind to move the caravan, but I didn't want to make a decision about the house until my daughter came home. It was more about her future than mine.

I thought about Lisa Modin and her impending visit. I pleaded with her in my thoughts. I didn't hurt her, didn't cross the line with my hopes of perhaps experiencing love again in my old age.

These pleasant reveries carried me slowly into the diffuse landscape where reality slips into sleep and dreams.

I woke up shivering. Before I crawled into the sleeping bag I went outside. The sky was full of stars, and there was hardly a breath of wind. There are flight paths directly above this part of the archipelago, but after eleven o'clock at night it's usually quiet.

I couldn't see the moon. There had always been autumn nights, and there would always be autumn nights even when I was no longer around. I was a temporary guest in the darkness, and I would never be anything else.

I slept badly. If a stray gust of wind shook the tent flap, I was immediately awake. I would lie there for a long time before nodding off, only to be woken again a little while later.

I thought about Louise, wondered what she was doing. I wondered when she would come home. I thought back to the time when I had been a doctor and to the years after the disaster when I had lost all sense of direction in my life. I passed one crossroads after another.

It was a night of broken sleep and shattered contemplation. At dawn, when the first ray of light appeared over the sea, I got up and left the tent. I jumped up and down to shake some life into my body, frightening a lone swan on the shore. It flew away on heavy wings. I looked at my watch. Fourteen minutes to seven. It was a cold morning. Far away on the horizon, a cargo ship was ploughing northwards through the waves.

I left the tent where it was and simply folded up my sleeping bag. I took the flask, the bottle of water and the greaseproof paper my sandwiches had been wrapped in down to the boat. I pushed it off the rock and jumped in.

The engine didn't start. That had never happened before. I had no tools with me, nothing I could use to adjust the spark plugs. I doubted that any water had got into the fuel tank.

I made several more attempts to start the engine, then I flipped it up and took to the oars. I decided to call Jansson. I don't know anyone who can deal with a recalcitrant engine better than him, apart from the professional mechanics on the mainland, of course. I didn't like having to contact him, but I couldn't see any other option. There was no way I could ask him to pick up Lisa Modin, take us out to Vrångskär, then pick us up a few hours later.

I rowed home, moored the boat and made a dozen or so further attempts to start the engine. Still nothing. I sat down on the bench and called Jansson. He promised to be there within the hour. He asked a few questions about what the engine sounded like when I pulled the cord, in much the same way as I asked questions when he came to me with his imaginary aches and pains.

"It won't start," I said. "It sounds perfectly normal. There's just one problem. It won't start."

"I'm sure we can get it going," Jansson said.

He arrived an hour later, to the minute. I went into the boathouse with him. He pulled the cord several times; the engine didn't start.

"I'm sure we can get it going," he said again.

"Come up to the caravan if you want a cup of coffee," I said.

Jansson probably wanted me to stay and keep him company. While I was grateful for his help, I couldn't cope with the endless, unrelenting stream of his words, particularly if he started talking about macabre execution methods or something else that lay buried in his bizarre store of knowledge.

I went through the drawers in the caravan and found a pack of cards. The only form of patience I know is

Idiot's Delight. I played a few games, and of course it didn't come out. After an hour or so I went to see how Jansson was getting on. He had removed the protective housing, unscrewed the spark plugs, and was shining his torch on the internal workings of the engine.

"Have you found out what's wrong?" I asked.

"Not yet. But I'm sure it's nothing serious."

I didn't ask any more questions. He carried on working, and I watched him in silence for a little while. I was just about to go back to the caravan when I thought about my phone.

"Can you set the clock on my mobile? I don't trust these cheap watches."

Jansson switched off the torch, put down the tool he was using and took my phone. In less than a minute he had set the time, calibrating it with his own watch.

"I'm not very good at the technical stuff," I said.

"It's very simple. If you like I can show you what else it can do."

"Thanks, but the time is really all I need."

"You can use it as an alarm clock, but maybe you know that already."

"I don't need anything to wake me up."

I stayed a little while longer, watching as Jansson continued his meticulous examination of my recalcitrant engine. Then I went back to my cards.

Even though Jansson insisted it was nothing serious, it took him another three hours to identify and fix whatever was wrong. I was having a cup of coffee when he knocked on the door.

"All done," he said.

"What was it?"

"Nothing, really. But those are the trickiest problems to solve."

"Coffee?"

"Thanks, but I'll get off home. It took a bit longer than I expected."

We went down to the boat. The housing was back on, the tools all put away.

"Start her up," Jansson said.

I clambered down into the boat. The engine started straight away. I switched it off and tried again. Same result.

I climbed out and walked along the jetty with Jansson. I asked how much I owed him. He looked offended and said I didn't owe him anything.

"There was nothing wrong," he insisted.

"There must have been something — it took you hours!"

He mumbled something unintelligible, got into his boat and started her up. I cast off his mooring ropes and he reversed away from the jetty, one hand raised in farewell.

I wondered if he sang in his beautiful voice when he was alone in his boat, speeding across the waves.

A bank of cloud was approaching from the south. I went over to the mainland to shop for food and also put an A4 pad of lined paper in my basket. The rain arrived when I was about halfway home, hammering against the boat. I was soaked to the skin by the time I reached the boathouse.

Back in the caravan I changed into the remaining unused Chinese shirt. I had no dry trousers so I hung the sodden pair over the edge of the table and wrapped a blanket around my legs.

I fell asleep early that night.

The following day the rain had gone. I went over to the mainland again and bought more clothes from the same shop.

There was no sign of Oslovski when I picked up my car, nor when I came back. I called in at the chandlery to ask if my wellingtons had arrived. They hadn't.

Alexandersson and Hämäläinen didn't turn up. I cleaned the caravan, thinking of very little apart from Lisa Modin. I avoided going anywhere near the site of the fire. However, I did dream about my grandparents for the next two nights. They were talking to me, and they looked exactly as I remembered them from my childhood. But in my dreams their voices were inaudible. They were talking to me, but I couldn't hear a word they said.

In the evenings I read the book from 1833, the one about the capture and care of songbirds. I still couldn't work out the connection between my grandfather and the birdcage. I had put the jar of birdlime on the shelf above the kitchen sink.

I woke earlier than usual on the morning I was due to pick up Lisa Modin. The sun still hadn't shown itself when I went down for my dip.

After breakfast I got into my boat and tried the engine. It started right away. I was nervous about seeing

Lisa. I tried to set aside any expectations. She was still a young woman, in contrast to the old man I had become. The omens were hardly favourable when it came to love.

I moored by the petrol pumps an hour before she was due. I wandered around and saw that the repairs to the coastguards' jetty had been completed. The big vessel was out; I knew that they had an extensive area to patrol.

There is a noticeboard on the quayside by the bus stop. One of the things that brings home the passage of time most powerfully to me is the sight of old, peeling posters about summer festivals or outdoor dance parties. There were also handwritten adverts for smoked whitefish or live rabbits. The bus timetable was shredded, but I couldn't tell whether the wind or an angry traveller was responsible.

I walked up to my car. Oslovski's door was closed, but the dead crow had been removed. I didn't hang around; I didn't want to risk Oslovski appearing and demanding that I take her blood pressure.

A cat that I think belonged to the grocery shop was padding across the quayside. Its presence reinforced the sense of desolation. A graveyard of summer memories. I stared at the window display in the chandlery: rucksacks, tins of paint, a selection of anchors.

I still had half an hour left before Lisa Modin arrived. I walked right to the end of the jetty, balancing on the rubble that made up the outer defences of the harbour, then came back again.

It was ten past ten when her car appeared, by which time I had begun to think she wasn't coming. She parked outside the chandlery's storage depot, which isn't actually allowed.

She was wearing a bright yellow raincoat, with an old-fashioned sou'wester in her hand. A small rucksack hung over one shoulder.

"I'm always late," she said apologetically.

"No problem. It's many years since I was in a hurry."

I took her rucksack and held out my hand to help her into the boat, but she put one foot on the step cut into the quayside and grabbed hold of the iron ring. I cast off and started the engine. The sound sliced through the silence. I caught a glimpse of Veronika at the window of the apartment next to the grocery store and waved at her.

The weather was calm. We puttered slowly out of the harbour. Lisa Modin was sitting in the prow; she flung her arms wide.

"Which way are we going?" she shouted.

"North-east," I replied, pointing. I increased my speed.

Lisa seemed to be enjoying the fresh autumn air. She closed her eyes.

I set my course towards the island of the poor people.

CHAPTER
SIX

The sea opened out, the skerries grew sparser, smaller, barer, the low-growing plants cowering in the crevices in the rock. Bracken, crowberry, cotton grass, sometimes even dwarf cornel. Further out there was salt grass and sea spurrey, silver cinquefoil and violas. We couldn't see them from the boat, but I knew they were there.

Cool spray from the choppy waves blew in our faces. Vrångskär itself was quite isolated, at the far reaches of the archipelago. It was mainly composed of gneiss rock, its steep sides plunging into the sea. I slowed down as we approached the southern headland. Lisa Modin looked at me and smiled.

We rounded the skerry, with its small deep-cut inlets and heather-covered areas of flat land. The bedrock itself was grey, mixed with serpentine streaks of dark red sediment. Towards the north there was a tumbledown cairn which had once acted as a navigation mark for one of the navy's secret shipping lanes.

"Where did the people live?" Lisa asked.

"There are dips and hollows that can't be seen from the sea," I explained. "They built their houses where there was some protection from the wind."

On the western side there is a natural harbour where the skerry divides in two, with a steep rock face on either side of the inlet. I switched off the engine and allowed the boat to drift towards the shore.

In order to get to the large low-lying area we had to take the long way round, scrambling over slippery moss-covered rocks. I offered to carry Lisa's rucksack, but she shook her head and looped it over her shoulder.

We passed a dense thicket of wild roses. I broke off a late autumn bloom and gave it to her.

"This was planted by people," I said. "According to someone who knows, it's been growing here for almost two hundred years."

She tucked the rose into the breast pocket of her raincoat, and soon the hollow that had once housed a settlement was spread before us.

Many years ago my grandfather and I had accompanied a group of archaeologists on a summer expedition to Vrångskär. I could still remember in detail what the team leader had said about the fishing community that had disappeared so long ago.

I showed Lisa the remains of the foundations; at most six houses and the same number of outhouses had stood here. The possibilities for animal husbandry were limited because there was only enough fodder for one or two cows. People had moved out here in the eighteenth century, and the level of poverty they suffered is unimaginable today. The total population of Vrångskär was in the region of forty individuals, and their livelihood depended on fishing. Nets and rowing boats were the essential elements of their lives. If the nets were out when a storm suddenly blew up, they had to go and bring them in. There are many tales of men and women who failed to save their nets. I have never forgotten one story which took place in the 1790s. A storm swept in from the north-east with no warning. Nils Eriksson, a young fisherman, and his wife Emma immediately went out to rescue their nets, but their boat capsized. Neither of them could swim, and they both perished. Emma was later found entangled in one of their own nets. Nils' body was never recovered.

Five young children were orphaned that day. There is no record of what happened to them.

I led Lisa over to the best-preserved foundation. According to the archaeologists, this had been one of the largest houses on Vrångskär. It consisted of a single room that may have housed as many as ten people.

We sat down on a flat rock beside the place where the poorest of the poor must have constantly wondered if they were going to survive. God knows how they coped during winters when the ice was neither thick enough to travel over, nor thin enough to break through so that boats could be used.

"But someone must have lain down in the grass on a summer's day, looked up at the sun and thought: this is my home," Lisa said.

I don't know why I did it, but I got up from the rock and lay down in the sparse yellow autumn grass.

"The people who lived here had neither the strength nor the time," I said. "Women gave birth out here; I expect they lay down then. Most babies died during the first few months."

Lisa looked at me.

"Tell me more," she said. "Show me what else there is to see."

I rejoined her and pointed to a couple of stones in the grass that might also have been part of the foundations of a house once upon a time.

"I come out here sometimes and sit and look at those stones. Occasionally I get the feeling that they are moving with immense slowness. I think perhaps they are on their way back to the place from which they originally came. This skerry is in the process of reverting to what it used to be, before the people arrived."

Lisa nodded, her expression pensive. I carried on talking although I didn't have much more to add.

"The last inhabitant of Vrångskär was an old woman; I think her name was Sofia Karlsson. She had come out here as a young serving girl, and had married one of the last resident fishermen. When he died, she stayed here on her own. That was in the 1830s. Many of the people who lived here had moved closer to the copper mine that had opened further out into the archipelago. I don't suppose life was any easier there, but perhaps it was less lonely. Some emigrated to America, and others simply disappeared. Apart from Sofia. No one knows how she coped all by herself during those last years; her final winter must have been one long episode of protracted suffering. She was almost ninety years old. One day she slipped on an icy rock and broke her leg. She managed to drag herself back to her house, but of course there was no way she could contact anyone.

Some time later a seal hunter turned up and found her dead in her bed in the bitterly cold house. She was buried in the churchyard on the mainland. No one has lived on Vrångskär since then."

"And the stones began to move back? That's a lovely thought."

Lisa rose to her feet and wandered around the site of the former settlement. From time to time she vanished behind a projecting rock, before reappearing. I stayed where I was, watching her. Perhaps I was like the people who used to live here, while she belonged to the new age?

We unpacked our picnic and ate without saying very much. Occasionally our hands accidentally touched as we reached for the same slice of bread or a hard-boiled egg.

After lunch we climbed to the highest point on the island. The wind blowing off the sea was stronger up there, but I didn't think there was any reason for us to set off home right away.

"An archaeologist once found a bear's tooth up here," I said. "No one has ever come up with a sensible explanation as to how it got here. The odd wolf might have been spotted on the islands further in, but there are no tales of bears."

"Where's the tooth now?"

"I don't know; in the vicarage, perhaps? There were a number of priests serving the archipelago who were interested in nature."

"Who's the priest now?"

The question took me by surprise.

"I never go to church. I have no idea who the priest is."

"I'll ring up and find out. I want to see the bear's tooth."

We started to clamber down; I warned Lisa about the slippery moss, but I was the one who stumbled, not her. When we reached the boat I took her rucksack to put it on board but I wasn't looking where I was going; I lost my footing on a rock at the water's edge and fell in head first. I was soaked to the skin. I'm used to taking a dip every morning when it's cold, but naturally I dry myself immediately afterwards. This was quite different. I started to shiver as soon as the water penetrated my clothes, and of course I didn't have anything to change into.

I was embarrassed, but Lisa was worried in case I had hurt myself.

"I'll survive," I said. "But I think we'd better get back. I'll call in at home and put on some dry clothes before I take you to the mainland."

I shook with cold the whole way. I went as fast as I could. Lisa offered me her jacket, but I didn't want it.

I moored at the jetty and hurried up to the caravan while Lisa made her way to the site of the fire. I stripped off, dropping my wet clothes on the floor, and rubbed myself dry with one of the dirty Chinese shirts. I didn't have much to change into, but I got dressed and put on the raincoat I had rescued from the burning house.

Lisa was standing by the ruins, bouncing up and down on the balls of her feet because she was cold.

"Sorry about the sooty raincoat," I said. "It's what I pulled on when I ran out of the house."

She looked at me, then gently stroked my cheek. It was so unexpected that I recoiled, as if I thought she was going to hit me. I fell over, and both of us burst out laughing. She reached out and helped me up.

"I'm not dangerous," she said.

"And I'm not in the habit of falling over."

I almost embraced her, pulled her close, but there was a hurdle within me that I just couldn't get over.

We went back down to the jetty and the boathouse.

"I'm going to write about Vrångskär," Lisa said. "I'm going to ask my dopey editor to give me the space for a series of articles."

"I'd be more than happy to take you out there again."

"I'll bring a camera next time. It will need to be soon; I don't want to get caught out by the snow."

"You've got a month before you need to worry about that. At least."

We eased away from the jetty. Every time I pulled the cord I was prepared for the engine not to start, but Jansson had done a good job.

Out in the bay I spotted Jansson and his boat in the distance. He seemed to have a passenger on board. He was heading in my direction, but no doubt his destination was one of the islands further north, Olsö or Farsholmen.

I moored by the petrol pumps and walked Lisa Modin to her car. There was an angry little note tucked under one of the windscreen wipers: "Don't fucking park here!" She looked at me in horror as she passed it to me.

"Who's written this?"

"I don't know. Maybe someone from the harbour-master's office. But it's nothing to worry about."

I screwed up the note and shoved it in my pocket. She threw her rucksack on the back seat and got behind the wheel.

"Thank you," she said. "I'll be in touch very soon."

I gave her my number and she put it in her phone. She was smiling as she closed the door and turned the key. She shot up the hill at high speed. The fact that she was in such a hurry made me jealous; who was waiting for her?

I went over to the litter bin outside the chandlery and threw away the message. When I turned to go back to my boat, I saw another person in the otherwise deserted harbour. It was Oslovski. She was hobbling along as if she had injured her foot or leg. I really, really hoped she wasn't going to ask me to check her blood pressure. Right now all I wanted to do was go home and get warm in my caravan.

Oslovski was very pale and looked tired.

We stopped and shook hands; I noticed that her hand was sweaty, which was unusual. I had a strong feeling that she had changed in some way, although I couldn't put my finger on how. There was something about her usually clear gaze that I didn't recognise.

We exchanged the standard pleasantries about the weather and our health. I asked if she had been away, but she merely smiled and didn't answer.

At that moment I realised she was afraid. I didn't know why, but I was immediately convinced that I was right. She was standing there in front of me, but at the same time she was moving away. Something in the background was frightening her.

"I'm on my way home," I said. "But if you want me to check your blood pressure, we can go up to the car."

She shook her head. "I'm fine. No aches and pains, and my blood pressure is either too high or too low."

She wanted to go, but I couldn't help trying to keep her there. As long as I was talking to her, she would have to stay.

"This harbour was built for herring fishing," I said. "There isn't a single professional fisherman left today. The trawlers have rotted away or been sold to Africa."

"To the Baltic states," Oslovski replied, unusually forcefully.

I saw no reason to contradict her.

"Anyway, they're all gone," I said. "The trawlermen and the owners. All dead and gone."

"Old age and death," Oslovski said. "I once read a quotation hanging on the wall of a carpenter's workshop. It said that we shouldn't take life seriously because we're not going to survive it in any case."

She abruptly turned and glanced at the hill up which Lisa Modin had recently disappeared, and at the little side road leading to her house and my car. She was afraid of something. It could only be people, surely?

I went down to the boat. During my many years as a doctor I often encountered those who were afraid — every single day, in fact. I spent several weeks one summer working on a temporary basis in the oncology department of one of the largest hospitals in the country. There was a spate of illness among the other doctors in the department, which meant that for ten days I was the one who had to deliver the gravest news to a series of patients. I remember one young man particularly clearly; he had woken up one morning with a stiff neck. He was examined by an orthopaedic specialist who suspected it could be something more serious, and a scan had led to the correct diagnosis.

There I sat, with the results in front of me. The stiff neck was a serious, probably incurable cancer. The primary tumours were in his left lung, and the pain in his neck was a metastasis lurking in one of the vertebrae at the top of his spine. And now I had to deliver the news. The notes informed me that Sven Roland Hansson was born in 1951, which meant he was nineteen years old. In 1970 the chances of curing cancer were still extremely limited. Today six out of ten cancer patients survive. In 1970 the figure was probably only three or four.

As I called him in from the waiting room, I knew that I would probably be giving him a death sentence. In such situations it was normal practice to have an experienced nurse present; I had asked a sister who had worked in the department for many years to sit in with me.

Sven Roland Hansson was what we might have called a bit of a misfit back then. He was wearing a green jacket and scruffy jeans. He regarded me and the nurse with distaste, making it clear that he was in a hurry and really didn't want to sit down when I offered him a chair.

I had asked the nurse how I should approach the diagnosis, and she had told me to get straight to the point. If something was serious, there was no "kind" way of saying it. The important thing was for the patient himself to understand that the doctor sitting opposite him was treating his fate with the gravitas it deserved.

There would be a whole programme of further investigations before the medical team decided on the best course of treatment. That wasn't really anything to do with me because I didn't have the specialist knowledge; I was only here because of a desperate shortage of doctors.

Eventually Sven Roland sat down. I could see that he was starting to feel afraid. It was obvious that he had only just realised the significance of the fact that he was in the oncology department.

Slowly and carefully I explained the seriousness of his illness. The colour drained from his face. He understood.

Suddenly he began to scream. It was as if someone had burned him, or stabbed him. I have never heard anyone scream like that, neither before nor since. That is why I will never forget it. I had seen those who were suffering greatly die in a silence suffused with fear; I had heard people groan with pain, but I had never seen a metamorphosis like this one. He was yelling so violently that his chewing gum flew out of his mouth and landed on my white coat. I didn't know what to do, but fortunately the nurse stepped in. She took his hand, but he pulled away and carried on screaming. Then she took a firm grip of his shoulders as if he were a small child and shouted to me, telling me to give him a sedative.

A year later I happened to notice his name in a newspaper. In those days it was uncommon for anything other than a black cross to appear in a death notice, but Sven Roland Hansson's little box was adorned with a guitar.

I had a friend who specialised in treating drug addicts. He played the guitar, and he informed me that the picture showed a Telecaster, one of the most important electric guitars ever made.

I thought I had seen something of Sven Roland Hansson's fear in Oslovski's face. Those frightened eyes told the same story.

I started the engine and slowly made my way out of the harbour. Oslovski was standing up on the road trying to hide behind a tree as she watched me leave. I pretended I couldn't see her and increased my speed as I passed the outer pier. When I glanced back over my shoulder, she had disappeared.

Perhaps it was the cold, perhaps it was Oslovski's fear, but I shivered. I tucked my chin inside my jacket and set a course for my island.

As I rounded the headland I saw someone standing on the jetty with his arms wrapped around his chest to keep warm. At first I thought it was Alexandersson and his colleague, but where was their boat?

Then I realised it wasn't a man waiting for me; it was my daughter Louise. In the midst of my astonishment I understood that it was she who must have been on board Jansson's boat when I was on my way back to the mainland with Lisa Modin.

I don't like being surprised by unexpected news or visits. Harriet had completely floored me one day by informing me that Louise was my daughter. I never doubted that it was true, nor did Louise even though we bore no resemblance to one another. I could see Harriet in her face and perhaps something of my father's features.

She did not have my build, nor Harriet's. She was strong and sturdy. If we got into a physical fight, I was pretty sure Louise would win. At the same time she was a very attractive woman. When we were in town or at a cafe, I had noticed that men turned to look at her when she walked by.

I didn't really understand what made her tick. She was a closed book, so much so that I was always ready for her to do something unforeseen. I had tried to get used to the situation, but without success.

Her sudden departures also irritated me, as did the fact that she never told me when she was planning to return. All she had said on the phone when I told her about the fire was that she would come. Not a word about where she would be coming from or when she thought she might appear.

I chugged into the boathouse. Before I had time to fasten the mooring ropes she flung open the door. The sunlight dazzled me, and I saw her only as a black shadow framed in the doorway.

She came towards me and we embraced. Her face was wet against my cheek. She was crying, or she had been.

We went outside. I had a lump in my throat and was afraid I might break down. That was one thing we had in common at least: we were both mourning the old house.

As usual Louise had very little luggage with her, just a small brown case. She always had more baggage when she left than when she came back.

We put the case in the caravan, then continued up to the site of the fire. Catching sight of Louise from behind, I had the feeling that it was Harriet walking in front of me.

That surprised me because Louise and Harriet were so fundamentally different. Was it an illusion? I stopped to look at her. Louise immediately turned around, and I caught up with her. The apple tree resembled a stage prop made of black crêpe paper.

"When you weren't here I thought you'd got in your boat and simply headed out to sea, but Nilsson said he'd seen you sailing towards the mainland as we were on our way over."

"Jansson. Not Nilsson."

"Jansson. Did I say Nilsson?"

"Yes."

"He was the one who sang so beautifully on Mum's last birthday."

"How did you get hold of him?"

"I got off the bus down by the harbour and asked the driver. He's the one who was called Nilsson. He called Jansson, who promised to pick me up right away. There was something odd about the bus, incidentally."

"Oh?"

"I was the only passenger."

"That's not unusual at this time of year."

"I've never been the only passenger on a bus before. Never. Not anywhere. I have, however, been the only passenger on a huge airliner — in Mali. There were two pilots, two air hostesses, and me."

"What were you doing in Mali?"

"A sandstorm had prevented me from landing in Dakar. Do you know where that is?"

"In Senegal. So you can speak French?"

"I can get by."

"What were you doing there?"

"I was visiting an area from which slaves used to be shipped overseas. I went to see a remarkable door opening."

"What does that mean?"

"I'll tell you later."

She carried on up to the ruins of the house, which were still covered by a layer of malodorous soot. Several small birds searching for food among the mess flew away as we approached.

"My room was just here. If I'd climbed on your shoulders I could have reached my window."

She came and stood directly in front of me. I could see that not only had she been crying, she was also extremely tired. Usually when she returned from her frequent travels to mysterious destinations, she had a healthy tan. But not this time.

There was always so much I wanted to ask her. And she so rarely gave away anything about her life.

"Tell me what happened."

"I fell asleep around ten thirty. Two hours later I was woken by a searing light that found its way into my brain. It was very hot, unpleasantly so. The house was ablaze; I rushed outside. Thinking back, I remember the roar of the fire. It was as if some kind of monster was breathing oxygen onto the flames."

"But how did it start?"

"No one knows — not the police, not the fire investigation officer, not me."

"Are there many options?"

"There's a rumour that I set fire to my own house."

"Why would you do that?"

"Perhaps because I've lost my mind?"

"Have you?"

"What do you think?"

"Don't answer a question with another question!"

"I'm not crazy. I'm no arsonist. When I woke up, the whole house was on fire. Whatever the cause might have been, it wasn't me playing with matches."

"A house doesn't just burst into flames. Could mice have chewed through the wiring?"

"Only if there was a gang of four mice working together who also had access to petrol."

I told her what Hämäläinen had said. She listened but didn't ask any questions. Instead she walked slowly around the house, pausing at each corner. I wondered if she would be the one to discover the cause of the fire. She took her time, and eventually she stood staring at the charred objects on the plastic sheet. I went over and picked up the buckle from Giaconelli's shoes. She recognised it at once when I handed it to her.

"You didn't even manage to save the shoes."

"I didn't manage to save anything except myself."

She crouched down and replaced the buckle. I had a feeling that she was preparing for some kind of funeral. I crouched down beside her, even though my knees protested.

"Giaconelli's death . . ." I said. "All I know is that he went back to Italy and died in a boarding house."

"His kidneys were failing. He didn't want to become reliant on dialysis, so he decided to make sure his life had a decent end. He left everything in Hälsingland and went home to the village north of Milan where he grew up. In two weeks he was dead. His friends let me know."

"What's happened to the workshop where he made his shoes?"

"His neighbours are keeping it as a museum, but because they're all quite old, no one knows how long they will be able to honour his memory."

Louise straightened up. I tried to do the same and almost toppled over. I grabbed her leg and she helped me up.

We went down to the caravan. She sat on the bed; I sat at the table. I poured us both a cup of coffee from my Thermos.

"There's not enough room in here for both of us," she said.

"I've already made preparations. You know the skerry to the east of the island, the one with no name? I've put up my old tent over there."

"Isn't it cold?"

"My old sleeping bag is nice and warm."

"Surely it must be rotten by now? I remember seeing it when I was here before, when Mum died. I couldn't understand why you hadn't thrown it away."

"It smells a bit musty, but things soon get aired out here, because it's always windy."

She lay down.

"I've had a long journey. I'm tired."

"Where have you come from?"

She didn't reply, she merely shook her head. That annoyed me.

"Why can't you answer? I'm not asking what you've been doing, I'm just wondering where you've come from."

She opened her eyes and gave me the same challenging look that I had sometimes seen in Harriet's eyes. However, she still didn't answer. Instead she turned her back on me and drew up her knees, making it perfectly clear that she intended to get some sleep.

All I could do was to make some sandwiches quietly and get out a tin of soup that I could warm on the camping stove I had moved from the boathouse to the skerry. The caravan belonged to my daughter.

She had arrived too soon and too precipitately. I hadn't had time to get used to the idea that my house had burned down, let alone the realisation that Louise had come home.

I walked around the island, following the shoreline heading south as I recalled virtually every rock from my childhood. I had spent so much time down there with my fishing rod, stopping at certain selected spots to try my luck.

I no longer had a fishing rod. And there were no fish left in the sea.

Louise was fast asleep when I got back. I gently placed a blanket over her legs. She didn't move.

Dusk was falling as I walked down to the boathouse, and there was a bank of cloud over the sea. It had come creeping in without my noticing. The temperature was dropping.

I thought I should take my new A4 pad over to the tent with me so that I could write down everything that had happened, but I decided to leave it. I didn't want to risk waking Louise by going back into the caravan.

I pushed the boat out of the boathouse, and instead of starting the engine I rowed across to the skerry. It didn't take long, because of the following wind.

The hollow was sheltered. I lit the camping stove and warmed my soup. I had pulled the sleeping bag up over my legs so that I wouldn't get cold. It was as if I was sitting there surrounded by myself, by the child I had been in all its manifestations.

I thought about Lisa Modin, about my daughter, about Harriet, who had died a few years ago.

After my meal I sat there in total darkness. I was very tired.

I was just about to go inside the tent when I saw a light. It was coming from the island, but I couldn't work out what it was.

I screwed up my eyes; eventually I realised that it must be Louise, standing on the jetty and flashing the torch I had left on the table in the caravan.

I shouted to her, but the wind was too strong and carried my words away. The flashes were irregular, but I knew she wouldn't do such a thing unless it was important.

It occurred to me that she didn't have my phone number. I went down to the boat and rowed into the darkness, the same darkness in which I had been lying when the fire began to burn behind my eyes. Could it be happening again? Could the sea catch fire and force me to row in a certain direction in order to save myself?

I rested my oars and turned around.

The torch on the jetty had gone out.

CHAPTER
SEVEN

I moored the boat by the jetty; Louise wasn't there. Nor had she switched on the light on the wall of the boathouse. If she had really wanted to make sure I saw her signal, she would have used the powerful exterior light rather than the feeble torch.

I was just about to call out to her when I saw a glow in the caravan window. I stopped dead. She obviously hadn't noticed the light being switched on outside.

A large, heavy bird flapped away in the darkness. From time to time over the years I had caught a glimpse of an eagle owl following a trail that no one else knew.

I went up to the caravan but paused before I reached the door. The curtain wasn't fully drawn across the oval window. I had never spied on my daughter before, but now I crept forward and cautiously peered inside.

Louise had stripped to the waist and was sitting at the table, shuffling the pack of cards. She wasn't playing patience; she seemed to be completely lost in thought. I had never seen her semi-naked. I moved back silently so that she wouldn't notice me if she suddenly glanced at the window.

104

I didn't want to be caught out, but nor did I want to stop looking into her world. She must have turned up the heating; that was why she was only half-dressed.

I contemplated my daughter. After a few minutes I knocked on the door. She didn't react. I knocked again.

"Who is it?"

"It's me. I saw you signalling with the torch."

"The torch?"

"Yes."

"Hang on."

The caravan rocked as she got to her feet. She had pulled on a sweater by the time she opened the door. She let me in, frowning at me.

"What are you talking about? What torch?"

I had just spotted the torch lying on the draining board. I pointed to it and said, "I was about to get inside the tent when I saw you standing on the jetty, flashing the torch in my direction. I tried to shout to you, but the wind was too strong and you couldn't hear me. So I got in the boat and rowed over. Why didn't you use the light outside the boathouse? You could have switched it on and off — it's like a floodlight!"

Louise didn't say anything for a moment; she looked searchingly at me, then nodded towards the stool. I sat down and unbuttoned my jacket. It was very warm inside the caravan. She remained standing by the door.

"I have no idea what you're talking about," she said eventually.

I reached over, picked up the torch, pointed it at her and switched it on and off several times.

"This is what I saw; you were down on the jetty signalling to me over on the skerry. What did you want? I was worried."

She didn't answer. I realised that something wasn't right, but I knew what I had seen.

"I haven't been down to the jetty with the torch."

"I'm not imagining things."

"You saw it flashing?"

"Yes."

"Was it Morse code?"

"I don't know. It was very erratic, like an uneven pulse."

She shook her head. I thought I could sense a vague anxiety within her; did she think I was going senile?

The idea frightened me. I can't think of anything worse than being physically healthy, and someone, perhaps my daughter, explaining to me one day that my brain and my memory are deteriorating. Even all those years ago when I was training to be a doctor, my fellow medical students and I would sit and discuss the worst fate we could imagine. Most of us felt the same: dementia was far more terrifying than physical pain.

"You have to believe me: I haven't been down to the jetty. Why would I lie about such a thing?" Louise said.

"But if it wasn't you, who was it?"

"Are there strangers creeping around on the island?"

"Not as far as I know. Perhaps the arsonist has come back?"

Once again she frowned. "The only person who's come back is you."

"I haven't been seeing things!" I insisted.

"In that case we'd better go outside and search for the intruder."

Silence fell; needless to say, we didn't go outside.

"Have you eaten?" she asked.

"Yes."

"Coffee?"

"No, thanks — it would keep me awake."

"How about a glass of rum?"

"Why would I want a glass of rum? You know I don't drink spirits."

"That's not true — sometimes you knock it back like nobody's business."

"That's a completely different matter — I'm *drinking* then!"

"Is there anything I can get you?"

"I ought to row back to my tent and go to bed."

"You'll get lost, rowing in the dark."

"It's not far."

"I want you to stay here. When darkness fell I was quite scared of being alone. I thought I could see people with charred black bodies moving around outside. You can take the bed and I'll lie on the floor; if we gather together lots of clothes, blankets and cushions it will be soft enough. I'm going to have a glass of rum, then we'll play cards for a little while before we go to bed. In spite of the fact that the house has burned down and someone seems to be wandering around signalling with a torch."

"I just don't understand who it could have been."

Louise didn't reply. She dug a half-empty bottle of dark rum out of her bag and poured herself a glass. She knocked it back, pulled a face and poured herself another. I hadn't noticed it before, but she emptied the glass exactly as her mother used to do. Harriet had never drunk much, but when she did she downed it as if it were something deeply unpleasant.

Louise put her glass down on the table.

"What are you thinking about? The torch?"

"I'm thinking that I see Harriet when I look at you."

"What do you see?"

"You both knock back your drink in exactly the same way."

"Our tolerance is different though. She used to fall asleep after a couple of glasses; I either get melancholy or furious. I never know in advance what's going to happen. But you needn't worry; I'm not trying to get drunk tonight. It makes me shudder when I think about everything that's gone, everything that can never be restored."

"I don't think I've fully grasped what's happened, but tomorrow we need to start talking about the future."

Louise pushed away her glass and picked up the cards.

Card games have always bored me. We started to play poker. She won nearly all the time, whether she had a better hand than me or not. I couldn't read her face; I had no idea when she was bluffing. Occasionally I thought she was letting me win out of sympathy. Every time my pile of matches was nearly gone, I won and had to carry on playing.

108

Neither of us said a word. Louise was totally focused on the game while I frequently made mistakes.

At eleven o'clock she decided we should take a break. She went outside for a pee, then came back in and made sandwiches. She had a cup of coffee; I drank water. Then we carried on playing. By midnight I still hadn't managed to lose all my matches. I threw down my cards and said I'd had enough. Louise wasn't happy, but she nodded. I went out to empty my bladder; I could hear her making preparations for the night. A faint crescent moon was just visible; the cloud cover had lifted. I waited until it was quiet inside the caravan, then I tapped on the door and went back in.

Louise had made her bed on the floor and had already settled down. Her eyes were closed as she wished me goodnight. I undressed, climbed into bed and switched off the lamp. The external light from the boathouse was shining in through the window; I got up to close the curtain.

"Leave it," Louise said. "It makes the night less dark."

I went back to bed. My tiredness was a very heavy burden. I was simply too old to start all over again.

Oslovski popped into my head. She had always been a woman who hid strong emotions, but that had changed. When I met her on the quayside it was obvious that she was afraid. She had even shown me where her fear came from: the outside world, a threat somewhere behind her.

Before I fell asleep I made a mental note that tomorrow I must convince Louise that the decision about what ought to happen next was hers alone. If she still saw herself living on the island in the future, then she must make up her mind what the new house should look like. I had taken out a very good insurance policy years ago in which it was stated that such an old house couldn't possibly be rebuilt as it had once been. There would be no oak beams forming the framework. Under the terms of the policy, Louise had a free choice.

But what if the charred black ruin scared her away? What would I do if she suggested selling the island, if she said that she wanted part of her inheritance right now, while I was still alive? Could I take on the huge responsibility of having a new house built? Or would I live in the caravan on a permanent basis? Perhaps I could ask a local handyman to extend the boathouse, enabling me to live behind wooden walls rather than the laminated plastic of the caravan?

I could have my car brought over from the mainland and hitched up the caravan, as if I were getting ready to be transported across the Styx by car instead of by ferry . . .

I had almost dropped off when I was roused by Louise's voice. She was talking quite loudly, as if she assumed I was still awake.

"I'm going to make a garden."

I heard the words clearly, but I didn't understand. If there was one thing I thought I knew about my daughter, it was that she and I shared the same distaste for poking around in the soil with a trowel in order to get something to grow.

"And where is this garden going to be?"

"Here."

"Nothing grows on this island. The soil is very poor, and it's full of stones. The oaks and the alders take any nutrients there might be."

"Obviously I shall make a garden that's suitable for the prevailing conditions."

"I've never known you show any interest in plants."

The caravan rocked as she leaped up, wrapped a blanket around her body and switched on the lamp. She sat down at the table as I lay there blinking in the light.

"I went to the village where Giaconelli is buried. He had told me about a beautiful garden behind a wall that was almost completely hidden by ivy. I found the wall and climbed over it. The garden was overgrown, but I'm sure it had once been lovely. As I walked around I realised that I wanted to make a garden somewhere else. Giaconelli had shown me this one, but at the same time he knew that I would go my own way. The Ocean of Emptiness is what I want to create."

"What's that?"

"I'll tell you tomorrow. I'm turning off the light now."

Before I dozed off I tried without success to work out what she had meant by the Ocean of Emptiness.

I woke just after six. Louise was fast asleep with the covers pulled over her head and one foot sticking out, as if it had detached itself from the rest of her body. Cautiously I covered it with the end of the blanket. She twitched but didn't wake up.

I picked up my clothes and one of the blue Chinese shirts to use as a towel, and went down to the jetty. The morning was dark and chilly. The wind had changed and was coming from the north. I took a deep breath and stepped down into the water. The cold struck my body hard as usual. It seemed to me that there was a certain point in the autumn when the feeling was exactly the same as it was immediately after the ice had broken up in the spring. Two contrasting seasons were somehow united.

I counted to ten as I always do before climbing out. The Chinese shirt left little blue threads all over my body as I rubbed myself dry. After I had got dressed I looked at the thermometer: three degrees. The wind was gusting slightly. The bitter chill from the north bit into my face and hands.

I sat down on the bench, huddled up in the darkness as the dawn began to break. What was it Louise had said late last night? The Heaven of Emptiness? No, the Ocean of Emptiness. It still didn't make any sense to me.

The caravan door opened, and Louise shouted that it was breakfast time. She was dressed and had put up her hair with several slides.

"I wish I could tolerate cold water like you," she said when we were sitting at the table.

The coffee she made was always far too strong for my taste, but as I knew what to expect, I didn't complain.

"You're going to have to jump in sooner or later. We don't have a bath tub, or any way of heating water."

"There's a shower for sailors in the harbour."

"I very much doubt if it's open now."

"Do you think they'd refuse to let us use it, knowing that your house has burned down?"

She was right, of course. We finished our breakfast in silence. Louise cleared the table, insisting I couldn't help as there wasn't enough room in the caravan for us both to move around at the same time. We decided to go over to the mainland later, when the shops were open.

"The Ocean of Emptiness," I said when she had finished.

"I'll show you, and I'll explain."

Outside, the wind was still gusting and the cloud cover dense and low. It was eight o'clock. Louise marched determinedly up to the patch of grass behind the ruins of the house. If you sit on a rock and look towards the grass, you also have a clear view of the sea. She pointed to a flat rock and I sat down.

She told me about a trip she had made to Japan the previous year. She is fascinating when she wants to be. I often think she has a much stronger relationship with words than I have.

Needless to say, I had no idea that she had been to Japan, just as I knew nothing about her visits to Paraguay and Tasmania. Apparently she had gone there because she was thinking of importing special paper dragons to Europe. She mentioned it in passing, and I didn't ask what had happened to that idea. She told me that she and a friend had visited Kyoto and the Zen Buddhist temple of Daisen-in, where she had stood before a garden made of stone and gravel, with not a blade of grass to be seen. The garden had been laid out in the sixteenth century, with the aim of creating a mystery in the landscape which would make it easier for visitors to concentrate when they were meditating.

"I became utterly still," Louise said. "It was as if I had found something I had been searching for, even though I didn't know it. I sat down on a bench and I was immediately drawn into that world of stone. I felt a great calmness, but I was excited at the same time. I immediately decided that one day I would make my own garden, as a nod to the Ocean of Emptiness — that was the name of the garden before me. And because nothing grows on this island, as you pointed out, I can't think of a better place to create my garden of rocks and gravel. Then they can reach out their stony hands and wave to one another from Sweden and Japan."

She suddenly broke off and ran back down to the caravan. She returned with a black and white photograph.

"The Ocean of Emptiness," she said. "This is what it looks like."

I sat there for a long time holding the picture. Louise left me and wandered around the patch of grass that she was intending to transform into something resembling the image in my hand.

I didn't understand what she had found so captivating about the garden in Kyoto. Gravel, stone, maybe sand, a few small mounds that looked like petrified bubbles on the smooth ground.

114

My life seemed to be full of rocks and stones at the moment, I thought. There was nothing left of my house apart from the foundations. The previous day I had taken Lisa Modin to Vrångskär, where remnants of rock had reminded us of the people who had tried to survive there in spite of unimaginable poverty. I had talked about the fact that I sometimes believed that the stones that had been used to build houses on the skerry all those years ago were on their way back to the places from which they had come.

And now this.

I tucked the photograph in my inside pocket. Louise came and sat down beside me.

"What was it you saw?" I asked. "A picture can't convey what you actually experienced."

"You'll understand when I've made my garden here."

"Are you serious?"

"I'm always serious."

"I know, but are you going to make this garden before we build a new house?"

"Perhaps."

"Well, it's your decision."

She nodded without saying anything, then she bent down and picked up a piece of stone that had splintered away from the rock on which we were sitting. She got up and placed it in the middle of the grass.

"My garden begins with a single stone," she said.

"You need to decide what you want to do with the house."

"Tonight. Let's go."

Louise sat in the prow, facing forward. I reflected on what she had told me about the Japanese garden. I was struck by a thought that came out of nowhere. I was so taken aback that I slowed down. She turned and looked enquiringly at me. I slowed down even more, until the engine was idling.

"Why have we stopped?"

I moved to the middle seat in order to get closer to her.

"Did you say the Japanese garden was something to do with Buddhists?"

"They believe it was created by a monk called Soami."

"And he was a Buddhist?"

"A Zen Buddhist."

"I don't know the difference."

"I can explain when we get home, if you like."

"I'm just wondering if you're intending to turn our island into a Zen Buddhist temple? Have you become a Buddhist?"

Her reaction to my questions was an outburst of rage. She picked up the plastic bailer and threw it at me. It contained rainwater, which splashed all over my face. I threw it straight back at her, and we sat there attacking one another with the bailer flying between us until she accidentally threw it overboard, and I had to fish it out with one of the oars.

"I'm not religious," she said. "You don't have to be religious to make a garden."

I didn't reply, I simply accelerated towards the harbour.

116

The shower block was locked. Louise tugged at the door several times, then we went into the chandlery. Nordin was unpacking a box of heavy-duty gloves when we walked in.

My wellingtons hadn't arrived. And of course Louise lost her temper when Nordin told her that the showers wouldn't open until May next year. He understood that our need was great, but at the same time he couldn't go against the council's decision. I wished Louise wasn't so fiery. I have rarely, if ever, found that anger helps to solve a problem. Sometimes it seemed to me that my daughter had a need to fly into a rage.

Nordin was astonished at her behaviour. He probably wasn't used to people raising their voices because of something for which he wasn't even responsible. I tried to intervene, to calm things down, but Louise pushed me away.

"Who do I talk to at the council?" she demanded.

"I don't know," Nordin replied. "Various people look after the showers."

"Who has the keys? Who makes sure there's hot water?"

"During the season it's me."

"So that means you have the keys?"

"I can't hand them over out of season."

"People need a shower even though it's autumn."

Both Louise and I saw Nordin glance towards a key cupboard on the wall. That was enough for Louise to march over, open the cupboard and grab the key attached to a large piece of wood with SHOWERS

117

written on it in luminous ink. Without a word she left the chandlery with her rolled-up towel under her arm.

Nordin was shaking. It was as if someone had robbed him, not of possessions but of an obligation that he had sworn a symbolic oath to defend and uphold. I realised that he needed a solace I was unable to provide.

"She doesn't mean any harm," I said feebly. "She just feels dirty. The sea is too cold for her. We'll sort it out with a couple of big bowls, some buckets and an electric hotplate."

I left him with his half-unpacked box of gloves and went over to the shower block. I could hear the sound of running water; Louise had brought soap and a bottle of shampoo wrapped in her towel.

As I stood there in the bitter wind, I thought that it might have been better if she hadn't come back. I would have been able to handle the disastrous fire more easily without her. However, I knew that wasn't entirely true. Without Louise I would never be able to make a decision about what to do with the remains of my life. My pipe dream about some kind of relationship with Lisa Modin was nothing but a way of escaping reality.

Louise emerged with wet hair, the towel wound around her head.

"Did he die?" she asked.

I felt a sudden urge to hit her, slap her hard across the face. Needless to say, I didn't. I simply snatched the key, which was dangling from her fingers.

"I don't like you upsetting my friends," I snapped. "If you'd left it to me, Nordin would have given us the key. Stay here while I take it back and apologise. I'll tell him you're too embarrassed to do it yourself."

She opened her mouth to protest. In a vain attempt to put an end to the impossible situation, I yanked off the towel, which was the same shade of yellow as my Chinese shirt. It landed on the wet quayside.

"I'll be back in a minute," I said. "If you're here, we'll go and do some shopping. If you're not, I'll assume you've gone off on one of those trips you never bother to tell me about."

I turned away and went into the chandlery. The box of gloves still hadn't been unpacked. Nordin was sitting on his stool by the counter where he cut fishing line and mooring rope to the lengths customers wanted. He was clutching a pencil in one hand. He didn't look at me as I put down the key in front of him, together with a fifty-kronor note, mumbling an apology on Louise's behalf.

I have to admit I wasn't entirely truthful. I said that Louise had been very badly affected by the fire.

Nordin put down the pencil, got up and replaced the key. I had a feeling that he wanted to be alone. I shut the door behind me and went up to Oslovski's house to fetch my car. The gate and the front door were closed. There was no sign of Oslovski.

As I was about to pull out onto the road, I glanced in the rear-view mirror and saw a curtain move. I caught a glimpse of Oslovski's face before the curtain fell back into place. So she was at home. And she was still afraid.

I was filled with a growing sense of unease. First of all my daughter's quarrel with Nordin, and now

Oslovski peeping through her window, frightened of being seen. Something was happening. My burned-down house was merely a part of something bigger.

I picked up Louise, who had wound the towel around her head once more. We drove in silence. I had to slam on the brakes when a fox ran across the road.

I had never seen a fox around here before; plenty of elk and deer, but no foxes. I had also heard from Jansson that the number of wild boar was increasing.

"Look out!" Louise said.

"It's the fox who needs to look out."

As usual I parked behind the bank. While I went shopping for groceries, Louise took off somewhere else. I noticed that the shoe shop was closed, in spite of the fact that it was within normal opening hours.

We met back at the car. I recognised the plastic bags Louise was carrying; she had been to the shop where I bought my Chinese shirts. We drove to a DIY store just outside the town and bought a hotplate, light bulbs, large bowls and buckets. I don't know whether Louise found the silence uncomfortable, but I was beginning to lose patience, driving around with a daughter who didn't say a word.

We loaded the last of our purchases into the car.

"I'm hungry," I said. "But if you're going to carry on like this, I don't want to eat with you."

She was holding a red woolly hat that she'd bought. She pulled it on and burst out laughing.

"Of course we're going to eat together! I think it's nice that we don't always have to talk. The world we live in is full of unnecessary chatter."

We went to a restaurant in a ten-pin bowling alley, where we ate fried fish and drank water. The construction workers I had seen down by the harbour the other day were sitting at one of the tables. To my surprise they were still discussing whether or not one of them had actually seen a perch.

We had coffee after our meal. The construction workers left. Louise placed her hand on my arm.

"I want to rebuild the house so that it's as much like the old one as possible. That's where I want to live at some point in the future."

"Of course you do," I said.

We headed back to the harbour. I wondered whether Louise felt as relieved as I did. We drove in silence once again, but it was a different silence now.

A fox ran across the road in exactly the same spot as earlier.

"A different fox," Louise said. "This one was smaller."

"Are you sure it wasn't bigger?"

"It was smaller."

I didn't argue with her. Today had been difficult enough as it was. I dropped her off at the boat and unloaded all our bags and boxes, then I took the car back to its usual place. There was no sign of movement behind Oslovski's curtains. I realised I was worried about her. Where did her fear come from? Why was she hiding?

I walked down to the quayside. To my surprise I saw that Nordin had put up the CLOSED sign at the chandlery. I had a horrible feeling that he was sitting inside weeping. Once again I felt a spurt of anger at my daughter's behaviour, but I had no intention of saying anything. Not right now, anyway.

I cast off from the quayside.

"I want to drive," Louise said.

I sat down in the prow; she yanked the cord and started the engine. She had been a boxer when I first met her, and she was fast and strong. She knew the shipping lane, although I did think she was a bit too close to the shallow known as Bygrundet, which was invisible.

As we rounded the last headland I saw Jansson's boat moored at the jetty. He was sitting on the bench. We slid inside the boathouse and I left Louise to unload the boat while I went to see what Jansson wanted.

Syrén, the new postman, had given him a letter for me. Perhaps those responsible for the mail still thought I didn't want any correspondence?

It was from the police. I opened it; I was required to attend an interview at the police station in town with regard to suspected arson. I had to be there in four days, at eleven o'clock.

Jansson looked enquiringly at me.

"There's no reply," I said. "You don't need to wait."

I stood on the jetty and watched him go. I wondered how many people in the archipelago already knew that I had been called in for questioning.

Was I the last to know?

PART TWO

The Fox Runs towards Golgotha

CHAPTER
EIGHT

The next few days felt like a long period of waiting. At night the horses charged around inside my head. I didn't say anything to Louise about the letter I had received. She had seen Jansson give me the envelope and had looked at me curiously, but she didn't ask questions.

As we ate dinner in the caravan that first night, we started chatting again. We talked about the contents of the LPG cylinder, the fact that we needed a new frying pan, and washing powder to keep our clothes clean. We avoided anything that might require a serious approach.

After we arrived home I had spent the day in the boathouse while Louise stayed in the caravan. At one point I peeped in through the window; she was sitting on the bed talking on her phone. I tried to make out what she was saying, but without success. Her expression was grave. Perhaps she was angry or sad; I couldn't tell. When she ended the call I moved away and went back to the boathouse. I had opened a tin of tar — not because I was going to use it, but because I loved the smell. Tar runs through the ages out here in the archipelago.

Behind the boathouse lay an ancient leaky skiff that I hadn't bothered putting in the water for the last few years. I pushed it in now and saw that it wasn't in as bad a state as I had feared. I fetched the oars and old tin bailer and clambered in. I would be able to use the skiff to travel back and forth between the island and the skerry where I had pitched my tent.

During my childhood there had been a large rowing boat on the island. It was black, completely soaked in tar, and my grandfather used it when he went out fishing with nets. At first my grandmother used to row, but when I was old enough to manage the oars, and to understand what to do with the nets, the responsibility passed to me.

I remembered an incident that had taken place when I was ten or eleven years old. My grandfather spotted a deer, swimming along. He dropped the net he was holding, pushed me out of the way and grabbed the oars. He caught up with the animal, stood up and hit it on the head with one of the oars.

The oar snapped in half. The deer carried on swimming, but my grandfather leaned out of the boat and managed to seize one of its horns. He took out his Mora knife and slit its throat. It happened so fast that for a few seconds I didn't realise what was going on. It was only when he dragged the dead animal on board, his hands dripping with blood, that I understood. The deer stared at me with huge, shining, unseeing eyes.

I had met death.

From that day onwards I was always a little afraid of my grandfather. I had seen something in him that I had never previously suspected. Snapping the necks of fish as he picked them out of the nets was one thing, but I had been completely unprepared for this slaughter out at sea.

When we came ashore and he hauled the dead body onto the jetty, I threw up. He looked at me with distaste but said nothing. He shouted to my grandmother, and together they butchered the deer. By then I had walked away.

It was at least fifty-five years since that day, and yet I could still see that powerful gesture as he slit the animal's throat. He exuded pure hatred as he brought the oar down on its head. I think he would have carried on rowing with the broken oar all the way to the Finnish coast in pursuit of the deer if necessary.

Even as a ten-year-old, the incident made it clear to me that people are never completely what we believe they are. Including me. There is always something unexpected within those we meet, those we think we have got to know.

I rowed back, dragged the skiff ashore and bailed out the water that had found its way in. I wondered whether to dig up one of the anthills on the island in order to seal the skiff, but I decided against it. I knew that my daughter would be furious if I killed a colony of ants just to make an old skiff watertight.

She was sitting on the bench at the top of the island. I sat down beside her. It was time to tell her.

"I've been called in for questioning by the police," I said.

"Why?"

"They think I burned down the house."

"And did you?" she asked without looking at me.

"No. Did you?"

I got up and went back down to the boathouse. A mixture of anger and fear was growing inside me. I no longer thought that I would be able to control what was going on.

There have been periods in my life when I have briefly turned to drink because of sorrow, fear or anger. Right now I wished I had a bottle of vodka, brandy or schnapps to take with me to my tent.

I was nudging the skiff towards the water when I realised that Louise had followed me.

"I'll come with you," she said.

"Where? To the tent?"

"To the police."

"I don't want you to come with me."

"I don't care. You won't be able to cope."

There was an old cork float in the skiff. I picked it up and threw it at her.

"You're not coming with me!" I yelled. "Why do I need someone with me when I know I didn't set fire to my house?"

I didn't wait for an answer; I just slotted the oars into the rowlocks. Needless to say, one of them slid straight into the water. As I reached for it, just as my grandfather had reached out when he grabbed and killed the deer, I was soaked by a wave. I don't know if Louise was still standing on the shore but I rowed out stern first so that I didn't have to look. When I had rounded the headland I turned the skiff. There she was, arms folded. She reminded me of a Native American chief, watching as the white man in a Chinese shirt rowed towards his fate and his half-rotten tent.

I lay awake most of the night, longing for something to drink. I wanted to get drunk, to liberate myself from the insanity of being called in for questioning by the police. When I eventually fell asleep, it was with the perception that I had come close to crossing a line. How would I cope with growing older, with a burned-out house and with the experience of living in a no-man's-land where no one asked after me? Or where everyone thought I had gone crazy and started running around with cans of petrol and a box of matches?

Even my daughter was starting to regard me as more and more of a burden. I was no longer the longed-for father who had finally come into her life.

When I woke at dawn, I might as well have been drunk the night before. Tiredness made me feel hungover. I crawled out of my sleeping bag and went outside. The sea was grey, the air cold, the wind still light but somehow threatening, as it can be sometimes when a storm is approaching. Two eider ducks were bobbing up and down on the water. I clapped my hands and they flew away — heading directly north, oddly enough. I watched them until it was no longer possible to make them out against the sky.

I didn't row back to the island until the afternoon. The caravan smelled fresh and clean when Louise opened the door. We ate a simple dinner but didn't talk much. Afterwards she walked down to the boathouse with me.

"Why were you signalling with the torch?" I asked her.

"I wasn't. You must have been seeing things."

There was no point in asking again. If she didn't want to tell me, then she wouldn't.

We were both people who lied, I thought. But we lied in different ways.

I slept just as badly over the next few nights. The days were all the same, all uniformly grey. I walked around my skerry trying to prepare myself for what was waiting for me at the police station.

The evening before the interview, we had food in the caravan, played a game of cards. Once again Louise accompanied me down to the jetty.

"I'm coming with you tomorrow," she said.

"No."

We didn't say any more.

That night I slept heavily; I was exhausted. My last thought was that I hadn't taken my morning dip for several days, which was depressing.

I rowed back to the island in the morning feeling well rested at last. However, when I reached the boathouse I discovered that the boat with the outboard motor was missing. I knocked on the door of the caravan, but there was no reply. When I went in I saw that the bed was made and Louise's rucksack was gone. She hadn't left a note.

I called her mobile; there was no answer, and I wasn't able to leave a message. I slammed the door behind me as hard as I could. A piece of the roof edging came away. I left it dangling and went and sat down on the bench by the boathouse. I knew my daughter well enough to realise there was no point in waiting and hoping she would be back in time to enable me to get to the police station.

I did what I had to do: I called Jansson. As usual he answered right away, as if he were sitting there with the phone in his hand. He was like a striking cobra.

"There's nothing wrong with my engine this time," I said. "But I need a lift to the mainland."

"When?"

"Now."

"I'm on my way."

"Thank you."

I ended the call before he could ask why I couldn't use my own boat.

My clothes were still in the caravan. The dangling roof edging was in the way of the door, so I ripped it off and threw it on the grass. I chose the least dirty Chinese shirt, then searched around to see if Louise might have hidden a bottle of wine or spirits, but I couldn't find anything.

I sat down on the bench and waited. Jansson arrived after precisely twenty-six minutes. Of course he noticed that my boat was gone, but he didn't say anything. Perhaps he thought he was transporting a prisoner, because he knew my interview with the police was scheduled for today.

We travelled to the mainland without exchanging a single word. He refused to accept any payment when we arrived, but I placed a one-hundred-kronor note under a fishing spoon on the seat and walked away without mentioning that I would need a lift back when the police had finished with me.

Nordin was outside the chandlery cleaning seagull shit off a window. We said hello; I had the distinct feeling he also knew where I was going.

Before I left the quayside I looked around the harbour, but there was no sign of my boat. I didn't understand where Louise had gone. Perhaps I should be worried? I pushed the thought aside; she wasn't the kind of person who would put herself at risk unnecessarily.

Oslovski's house was deserted. The curtains were closed, no sign of life. I picked up my car and set off. Once again I had to brake to avoid a fox that ran across the road. When I had recovered from the shock I thought angrily that the next time it appeared in front of my car, I would do my very best to kill it. The fox was running towards Golgotha, even though it didn't know it.

It took an hour to reach the town. About halfway there was a modest little roadside cafe where I usually stopped. It's always been there; I remember it from when I was a child. In those days it was run by a lady who wore bright red lipstick, and spoke in an almost incomprehensible dialect. I remembered fizzy drinks and a plate of meringues. Today I drank coffee and chewed on one of the dry Mazarins that seem to have infected every cafe in our country.

I was the only customer. I could see myself at the empty tables, in different manifestations and at different ages. The loneliness is palpable when you are surrounded by empty tables and chairs.

The door opened and a woman with a wheeled walker manoeuvred her way in. I remembered Harriet's slow progress across the ice a few years earlier. I couldn't picture myself with a walker. The thought was terrifying, revolting. Would I really want to live if my legs wouldn't carry me?

The woman bought a cinnamon bun and drank a glass of water. The waitress carried the tray for her as she groped her way along, feeling for the edge of the table and the chair before she sat down.

I wondered what she was thinking. In my eyes the earth was already dragging her down. She was slowly fading away, and eventually she would disappear completely.

I picked up my coffee, poured it into a paper cup and left the cafe. I had never had anything to do with the police before, apart from routine business such as renewing my passport or reporting some minor damage to my car when someone drove into it on one occasion. Now I was suspected of a serious crime. I knew I was innocent, but I had no idea what conclusions the police had reached.

I sat there and acknowledged my anxiety. The car had become a confessional.

The police station was newly built, of red brick. Behind what I assumed was bulletproof glass sat a receptionist in civilian clothing. I told her who I was and showed her the letter. She picked up the phone and said: "He's here."

After a few minutes a young police officer came through the door leading to the various departments. He wasn't in uniform either. He held out his hand.

"Månsson."

His grip was firm, but once we had shaken hands he withdrew quickly, as if he were somehow afraid of getting stuck. I followed him into the depths of the building, where at last I caught a glimpse of a uniformed officer. It was reassuring; in my world policemen wore a uniform and carried a baton.

Månsson couldn't have been more than thirty years old. I thought he was fashionably dressed, but what did I know. For some reason, perhaps a trend that had passed me by, he was wearing different-coloured socks.

We went into a small conference room. There was another plain-clothes officer over by the window, absent-mindedly feeling the compost around a potted plant. He was a little older, maybe thirty-five. He didn't shake hands, merely nodded and informed me that his name was Brenne.

We sat down. The chairs were green, the table brown. There was a tape recorder. Brenne switched it on, but it was Månsson who took charge.

I wished I had brought my yo-yo with me. Not so that I could get it out, unsettle the two officers, but to calm myself. Feeling its weight in my hand would have helped more than a solicitor.

Månsson glanced down at a file on the table, then began to speak, directing his words at the microphone. I got the feeling he was already sick and tired of what was in front of him.

134

"Interview with Fredrik Welin. The time is eleven forty-five. Detective Inspectors Brenne and Månsson are both present." He turned to me, then went on: "You have been called in for questioning about the fire which destroyed your house. You are aware that's why you're here?"

"I'm not aware of anything. But yes, my house has burned down. Everything I owned is gone. I bought the clothes I'm wearing just a few days ago. Poor quality, made in China."

Both Månsson and Brenne were looking at me curiously. Obviously my response wasn't what they had been expecting.

"Our investigation hasn't revealed a natural explanation for the fire," Månsson continued. "We have, however, established that it started simultaneously in at least four different places at the corners of the house. We therefore have reasonable grounds to suspect that the fire was deliberate."

"I know that, but I didn't do it."

"Have you any idea who might have done such a thing?"

"I have no enemies. Nor is there anyone who stands to gain financially from my house burning down."

"You were fully insured?"

"Yes."

So far the interview had followed the pattern I had been expecting. Nothing I didn't know, nothing to explain why the finger of suspicion was pointing at me apart from the fact that there was no alternative.

Brenne broke his silence by asking if I would like a coffee. I declined. He left the room and returned with mugs of coffee for himself and his colleague.

The tape recorder was switched back on. I was still missing my yo-yo. The interview seemed to be going round in circles: when exactly had I fallen asleep, when had I woken up and rushed outside, did I have any enemies who might have wanted me to burn to death. I gave them the times as best I could, and continued to deny that I had any idea who might have started the fire.

Eventually I got fed up of the constant repetition.

"I know I'm here because you suspect me," I said. "I can only reiterate that you're on the wrong track. I haven't a clue how the fire started or who might have wanted to harm or kill me. I've told you everything I know."

Månsson gazed at me in silence for a long time, then he spoke into the microphone, saying that the interview was terminated, and switched off the tape recorder.

"I'm sure we'll be in touch again," he said as he got to his feet and adjusted his pink tie.

Brenne said nothing. He had gone back to the potted plant on the windowsill.

Månsson showed me out. I felt a surge of relief as I walked away from the police station. I left the car and went into one of the big department stores nearby. There was a sale in one of the clothing concessions, and I bought several items after carefully checking that none of them were made in China. I had lunch at an Italian restaurant in the galleria; the food wasn't good.

It could have been made by Brenne or Månsson, I thought. It contained more fatigue and sorrow than nutrition.

I bought two bottles of vodka at the nearby state-run liquor store, then I went to collect my car. I saw two police officers dragging along a woman who had passed out from drink. One of the officers looked like Lisa Modin. The resemblance was so striking that I thought it was her at first, but then I realised that the officer's face was thinner and covered in freckles.

Before I headed back towards the harbour and my island, I called Louise again. This time I was able to leave a message.

"Where the hell did you go?" I said. "I had to swim to the mainland to get to the police station on time."

I didn't ask her to pick me up. Instead I called her again.

"I got beaten up," I said in my second message. "I'm probably going to lose the sight in my left eye."

I drove through a landscape filled with beautiful autumn colours, but at the same time it filled me with uncertainty. In the past the seasons had never affected me, but over the last few years the cold and the darkness evoked a growing sense of unease.

I stopped when I reached the place where I had bought my Chinese shirts. The shoe shop was closed. There weren't many customers in the grocery shop. I filled my basket with things that I didn't necessarily need to cook; everything could be eaten cold. I carried my bag to the car, then wondered briefly whether I should try to find out Lisa Modin's home address. The temptation was strong, but I resisted and set off for the harbour. It was three o'clock in the afternoon. The hilly road wound its way through dense forest, except in a few places where it was possible to glimpse the waters of a lake and eventually the sea, shining among the dark trees. If you didn't know better, the forest could seem endless.

There were few side roads. In fact there was really only one, leading north. The sign, which I don't think had ever been cleaned, bore the name of a place called Hörum. It was seven kilometres away. I had passed that sign for years, ever since I was a child, but I had never had any reason to go to Hörum. I had no reason now either, but I instinctively turned off, the decision made so quickly that I didn't even have time to brake. The gravel sprayed up around my wheels, and I only just managed to avoid skidding off the road and driving straight into the trees.

I drove towards Hörum without knowing why. When I was a child I used to dream about a road that led nowhere, that simply kept on going for ever and ever. That feeling came back to me now. Hörum was the name of a place that didn't exist. I slowed down, but I didn't turn around. I was going to make that journey into the unknown, the journey I had always imagined.

I stopped and switched off the engine. I cautiously opened the door, as if I might disturb someone. Outside the car the world was silent; there was no wind in the dense forest. I don't know how long I stood there, I just know that I closed my eyes, thinking that soon I wouldn't exist any more. I had only old age left. Soon that too would end, and then there was nothing.

I opened my eyes; I ought to turn back. But instead I got in the car and kept on going.

I drove down a steep hill, and then the trees began to thin out. I passed a few houses by the side of the road; some were empty, dilapidated, while others were perhaps still occupied. I stopped the car again and got out. No movement, not a sound. The forest had crept right up to the houses, swallowing the rusty tools, the overgrown meadows. A lost autumn bumble bee buzzed past my face. The two houses that might have been occupied, or at least still had curtains at the windows, lay in the middle of the little village. I saw a mailbox with the lid open; there was a sodden, half-rotten newspaper inside. It was the local paper that Lisa Modin worked for; three weeks old, its main story was about a horse that had died after being driven too hard in a trotting race.

But no people. No one peeping from behind their curtains, as I had seen at Oslovski's house. No one wondering who I was. Right at the end of the village lay the house that was in the worst state. The grass was overgrown, the gate hanging off its hinges into the ditch. I went into the garden. The remains of a kick sled were hidden among the bushes. The porch door stood ajar; I went inside the deserted house. The rooms were empty, the wallpaper was peeling off, a broken table had been overturned. There were few traces of the former inhabitants. A dead mouse lay on the stairs. The whole place seemed to be a sad sarcophagus, waiting for the walls to collapse and bury everything that had been there, once and for all.

I went upstairs. In one of the bedrooms the roof had fallen in, and the floor had rotted because of the rain.

But there was a bed. I stopped dead. It was made up with sheets that couldn't have been there for long; they were clean, ironed, perhaps even unused.

I went into the three other bedrooms: no beds or other furniture. Only in that one room, where the rain came in, was there a made-up bed.

Behind the peeling wallpaper I found a newspaper that had once been used to provide insulation. 12 May 1934. A landowner born in 1852 had passed away. A priest by the name of Johannes Wiman had spoken at his funeral.

There was a combine harvester for sale, and Svea Förlag were advertising a book that "seriously considered the difficult Jewish question". The price was three kronor, and speedy delivery was guaranteed.

The newspaper crumbled away between my fingers. But who slept in that bed? The question stayed with me as I left the house.

I returned to my car and drove back to the main road. When I parked at Oslovski's house, I could hear someone hammering. The garage door was ajar; she must be at home. I pushed the door open and she turned around. Again I saw her fear, but as soon as she realised it was me, she relaxed. She was holding a bumper.

The day Oslovski bought the house, a truck had arrived with a vintage car in pretty bad condition.

Nordin had seen the whole thing and had wondered what kind of strange female car enthusiast had moved in.

Now, after all these years, I knew the car was a 1958 DeSoto Fireflite four-door sedan, and that Oslovski was restoring it from something resembling a heap of scrap metal to a shining vintage car. I had shown no interest whatsoever, but she had informed me that it had 305 horsepower and that the compression was 10:1. Needless to say I had no idea what that meant, just as I didn't understand the significance of the fact that the tyres were Goodyear, size 8 x 14.

However, I had realised how much passion this strange woman put into her car. When she had been away, she often returned with spare parts gleaned from some scrapyard.

"A new find?" I asked, nodding in the direction of the bumper.

"I've been searching for this for four years," Oslovski said. "I eventually found it in Gamleby."

"Do you need many more parts?"

"The clutch. I'll probably have to go up north to find something suitable."

"Can't you advertise?"

"I want to find everything myself. I know it's stupid, but that's just the way it is."

I nodded and walked away. After only a few metres I heard her eager hammer blows once again. I wondered where I would find the old car that could fill my life with meaning. Perhaps that was why my house had burned down? So that rebuilding it would give me a purpose?

As I was carrying my bags to the quayside I noticed an ambulance in front of the chandlery. Nordin was carried out on a stretcher. I put down my bags and ran. Nordin's eyes were closed, an oxygen mask over his nose and mouth. The paramedics were very young.

"I'm a doctor and a friend," I said. "What's happened? Is it his head or his heart?"

One of the paramedics looked dubiously at me. He had freckles, and spots around his nose.

"I'm a doctor," I repeated in a louder voice.

"His head, we think," said the man, who was really no more than a boy.

"Who made the call?"

"I've no idea."

I nodded and stepped back. Perhaps I should have gone with Nordin to the hospital, but when the door closed and the ambulance drove off, I just stood there.

I was surrounded by too much death, too much misery. Had Nordin been so upset by my daughter's appalling behaviour that he'd had a stroke?

Veronika came running down from the cafe, wondering what was going on. I explained as best I could.

"Why didn't you go with him?" she said. "You're a doctor."

I didn't have a satisfactory answer to give her, and in any case she seemed to have lost interest in me.

"I'll call the family," she said. "Someone needs to lock up, and they won't know what's happened."

Suddenly we heard the ambulance's siren; it was already quite a long way off. We stood in silence, both equally upset. Veronika ran back upstairs, and I fetched my bags and put them under the projecting roof of the kiosk which sells smoked fish in the summer.

I walked out to the end of the quay as a light drizzle began to fall. I executed a few dance steps to shake off the bad feeling from the empty house and from what had befallen Nordin.

Then I called Jansson. He answered on the second ring. Of course he would come and pick me up.

I waited for him under the roof with my bags. The faint smell of the summer's smoked fish lingered in the air.

CHAPTER
NINE

Before I had even managed to stow my bags in the boat, Jansson wanted to know what was the matter with Nordin. How he could already know that something had happened was one of those mysteries I would never solve. He was like an old-fashioned telephone exchange operator, who put through calls then listened in.

"It could be some kind of stroke," I said. "I'm not sure."

"Is he going to die?"

"Let's hope not. Can we go now?"

Deep down Jansson is afraid of me. Not just of me, but everyone. His constant desire to help, to be of service, hides his anxiety that we will all turn on him. He is afraid that we will tire of him and stop contacting him when we need help.

I noticed it now. He cowered as if I had delivered a physical blow, then started the engine and began to reverse out of the harbour — much too quickly, as if he feared my impatience.

I usually feel slightly guilty when I have been too sharp with people, but to my surprise I experienced a certain satisfaction at having given Jansson a bit of a scare. I made it clear that I had had enough of his ingratiating self-importance. His friendliness irritated me until I could no longer control my impatience. Several times when he had complained about his imaginary aches and pains I had been tempted to lie, to tell him that he was suffering from a fatal illness. I had never done it, but as I sat in his boat on the way home I thought it would soon be time to give him a serious fright. I would deliver a death sentence when he was lying on the bench outside my boathouse being examined by these doctor's hands, which he respected more than anything in the world.

We met the coastguard's biggest patrol boat, on its way back to the harbour after a tour of inspection along the coastline. I thought I could see Alma Hamrén at the wheel. My bags toppled as we bounced over the swell in the wake of the large vessel.

The wind had got up. Jansson pulled his old woolly hat low down over his forehead. He looked like a frozen animal, standing there steering his boat. I tried to prepare myself for the forthcoming encounter with my daughter, if she had returned. The important thing was not to lose my temper. I couldn't bear the thought of us staring at one another with loathing.

However, I wasn't sure whether I wanted to be alone, or whether I wanted her to stay. I couldn't make up my mind.

I sat facing the direction in which we were going. The wind was against us and felt cold on my skin. I caught sight of something black, breaking the surface of the water. If it was a log we could easily have an accident. I waved my arms at Jansson, trying to tell him to veer to one side, but he misunderstood me and cut the engine.

"There's something in the water," I shouted.

Jansson swung to the side and moved the boat slowly forward. He spotted the object that I had seen, but we still couldn't make out what it was. Jansson stood up, steering towards it with one foot. During all those years as a postman in the archipelago he had come across many strange, sometimes frightening things in the sea. He once found a human body, almost completely decomposed, which was never identified. After that incident he came to my little private clinic by the boathouse and complained that he was sleeping badly. He said he had the feeling that the body had been partially eaten, and as there were unlikely to be any flesh-eating monsters in the Baltic Sea, he had started to imagine it was the remains of a cannibal's supper.

This time it was a dead seal. Not a cub, but a fully grown grey seal. It stank. The eyes had been pecked out by gulls or eagles. Jansson prodded it with the boathook while breathing through his mouth.

"It's been shot," he said. "With a shotgun."

Using the boathook as a pointer, he showed me where the pellets had hit the back of the animal's head.

"It's pure vindictiveness," Jansson said angrily. "Someone has amused themselves by shooting the seal without bothering to deal with it afterwards."

"Let's go," I said. "If it's dead, there's nothing we can do."

"I ought to tow it ashore and bury it. I don't want it lying here stinking."

"You can do that when you've dropped me off," I said firmly.

I looked away; Jansson increased his speed.

As we turned in towards the jetty, I could see that my boat wasn't there. Louise still hadn't come home. Jansson noticed the same thing.

"Your boat isn't here," he said as he hove to.

"Louise had a few errands," I said.

I quickly unloaded my bags, then gave Jansson two hundred kronor before he had time to protest. I placed the notes under the bailer so they wouldn't blow away. He reversed out, no doubt heading back to bury the stinking seal. I waved and carried my bags into the boathouse.

It had been drizzling on and off, but at the moment it was dry. It didn't look as if Louise had been back to the caravan during the day: everything was exactly the same as when I had changed my clothes in the morning.

I sat down on the bed and called Directory Enquiries to find out the number for Veronika's cafe. It was a while before she answered. In the background I could hear the sound of lively customers, even though it was still only afternoon. Veronika seemed stressed.

I asked if she had been in touch with Nordin's family. She had, and she now knew that Nordin had suffered a serious brain haemorrhage. His prospects were uncertain. She gave me the number of the hospital and I jotted it down on the back of a magazine about health food that Louise had brought with her.

"It sounds as if you're busy," I said.

"There's a very strange event going on here," she replied.

"What do you mean, strange?"

"A young woman has won twenty-five thousand kronor a year for the next twenty-five years, so she's invited all her friends to a party, in the middle of the day. It's important income, both for me and the cafe."

"Do I know her?"

"I shouldn't think so. Her name is Rebecka Karlsson; she's twenty-two years old and she's never had a job. Nor has she been to college. She lives at home with her parents, who have always supported her. He's a blacksmith, and her mother is a care assistant in an old people's home. It's disgusting, a person like that winning so much money!"

I expressed my agreement and we ended the call. I went back outside. The ruins of my house looked eerie in the dull afternoon light.

Something dangling in the sooty apple tree caught my attention. When I got closer I saw that it was a message left by Louise. She had clearly used the same pen with which I had made a note of the hospital's phone number: *Top of the hill!*

Nothing else. Just those four words. I looked around to see if there were any further notes in the alders and oaks, but their branches were empty. I suspected that the most important part of the message was the exclamation mark at the end. She wanted me to go up to the top of the little hill where my grandfather's bench was located: there were no other hills on the island.

When I got to the top I was expecting to find another note from Louise, but there was nothing on the bench or attached to the little juniper bush. I sat down, wondering if I had misunderstood her. Or did she want me to sit here wondering about some wild goose chase?

I gazed out across the sea, and then I understood. My boat was drawn up on the nameless skerry where I had pitched my tent.

I went back down to the caravan and dug out the old pair of binoculars that had been there ever since Harriet's day. Now I could see Louise. She was sitting on a rock on the eastern side of the skerry with her back towards me, looking out over the sea. I stared at her until the effort of holding the binoculars made my hands begin to shake.

It was cold, and it had started drizzling again. I didn't understand my daughter. She probably didn't understand me either. In spite of all our efforts, we were doomed to misunderstand one another.

I returned to the caravan, switched on the light, plugged my phone into the charger and wondered what Louise was actually up to. Dusk fell. I took the torch and went up the hill to check on her. She had lit a small fire outside the tent, but she was sitting in the shadows; I couldn't see her even with the binoculars. She was hiding in the darkness in a strange game of cat and mouse.

She must know I'm here, I thought. She must have heard Jansson's boat. And she probably suspects that I'm sitting on this bench looking over at the skerry.

I was suddenly overwhelmed by exhaustion. From my years as a doctor I could remember a similar tiredness after long days and nights on call. Laboriously I got to my feet. Back in the caravan I made myself something to eat; it was far too salty and had a metallic taste, but I ate every scrap, then lay down on the bed.

When I woke up I didn't know where I was at first. Something in my dream was holding onto me. I was standing on the jetty, watching Harriet swim towards the land. But she wasn't swimming in the sea, she was in the forest pool in Norrland that I had once promised to show her, the pool we had finally visited the year she died. In my dream the wind was not soughing in the tops of the trees around the pool; instead there was a whining noise that sounded like some kind of machinery. It was unbearable to listen to.

I sat up. It was ten o'clock; I had been asleep for a long time. There was no sign of Louise. I called her phone, but she didn't answer. I started to leave a message but broke off after a few words. What was the point? I made coffee. The wind had picked up, and it was pouring with rain. I lay down again; all I wanted to do was go back to sleep.

Instead I grabbed my torch and went out into the rain. The mossy rocks were even more treacherous now, and I fell over twice on my way up to the bench. When I eventually made it I could see that the fire on the skerry had gone out, or been extinguished. The place was in darkness.

So Louise had decided to stay over there. She had taken over my tent and left me the caravan.

150

My wet hair was plastered to my forehead. I flashed the torch a few times, but needless to say there was no response.

I slithered down the hill, wondering why Louise was torturing me like this. I sat down at the table and began to play patience. It didn't come out, of course. I gathered up the cards and made a decision.

Tomorrow I would ask Louise to leave my islands. I couldn't have her here.

I lay awake for hours. The pillow carried the faint scent of the soap she used, which made it impossible for me to stop brooding over why she was out there in the darkness in my tent.

Over and over again I got up, flicked through books and magazines that had been here since Harriet's time.

I might have dozed for an hour or so around daybreak, but when the autumn morning filtered through my window, I got up. I had a cup of coffee, then went up the hill with Harriet's binoculars. There was no sign of movement around the tent. The flap was closed.

I knew exactly what to do now. I bailed out all the water that had gathered in the skiff and set off for the skerry. The sun had just risen above the horizon, and the water shone like a mirror. It was the coldest autumn day so far this year. Several gulls were screaming and fighting over some invisible prey a short distance away. It might have been the rotten seal, if Jansson hadn't already towed it ashore and buried it under a pile of seaweed and sand.

I rowed around the skerry. When I had only a few strokes left before the depths turned into a steeply shelving shallow leading onto the rocks, my gaze fastened on something that appeared to be floating just metres below the surface. I slowed down and leaned over the side. At first I couldn't make out what it was, then I realised it was part of a drift net that had broken free, and was now at the mercy of the winds and the currents. It was festooned with dead fish, a diving duck and ribbons of seaweed. I had never seen an escaped fishing net before. As I gazed down into the silent water, the net reminded me of a prisoner who has scaled a high wall and is now fleeing for his life. Or perhaps it was more like a stray dog, and no one knew where it was going.

The sun disappeared behind a bank of cloud, and I could no longer see the net. I clambered ashore on the far side of the skerry, then hauled the boat up onto the rocks, taking care not to make any noise. I secured the mooring rope with a heavy chunk of stone that had fallen away, then made my way towards the tent. I couldn't be sure that Louise wasn't lying awake in there. If she heard footsteps outside, she might be scared. I didn't want that. Even if we regularly launched symbolic attacks on one another, I didn't want to frighten her.

I crouched down, put my ear to the fabric of the tent and listened. Could I hear her breathing or not? The sun slipped in and out behind the scudding clouds. I straightened up and went over to the sheltered spot where I usually build a fire. The surface of the rock was blackened from my earlier efforts. Louise had chosen a different place that was less suitable. I gathered up branches, twigs, a plank from an old fish box that had drifted ashore, and covered the whole lot with moss. Then I lit a fire. There wasn't a breath of wind; the smoke rose straight up into the sky.

I settled down to wait. I had yet to decide how I was going to explain my presence outside the tent.

I fed the fire with more branches and twigs. From time to time I scrambled around the skerry in order to keep the cold and the tiredness at bay.

One hour passed, almost two.

I heard something from inside the tent, but at first I couldn't work out what it was. I moved closer, put my ear against the side.

My daughter was weeping. I hadn't seen her cry since Harriet died. She was sometimes unhappy, downhearted, but never enough for the tears to fall. At least not as far as I was aware.

It was upsetting, hearing her cry. I had no idea what to do. I went back to the fire, thinking that it was probably best if I left and returned to the island. But I couldn't put out the fire without her hearing the hiss of the water as I doused the flames.

I sat there listening to my daughter. I looked at my watch so that I would know how long she cried for. She stopped after fifteen minutes. She must be in terrible pain, I thought.

Silence. I carried on waiting.

I heard her yawn, then she opened the tent flap. The zip stuck, as it always did for me. Her hair was standing on end. It was a few seconds before she noticed me; she froze in the opening as if she couldn't decide if I really was there. Then she got to her feet and went behind one of the rocks that provides shelter from the east. When she came back she had combed her hair. She fetched the pillow from inside the tent and sat down by the fire.

"You could have made some coffee, seeing as you're here," she said.

I didn't reply. I had no intention of asking any questions until she explained why she had taken the boat when she knew I had to get to the police station. Just like her mother Harriet, she has the ability to confuse people when she doesn't have the upper hand, and then she steers the conversation in a completely different direction.

I always thought I was considerably more intelligent than Harriet, but I have come to realise that my daughter is a dangerous opponent.

"How did it go?" she asked.

"How did what go?"

"The interview with the police. Did they beat you up like you said in your message?"

"With batons."

She suddenly seemed tired. She became someone else, pale and shrunken. I thought vaguely that she must have looked exactly like that when she was a child, when she lived with Harriet and didn't even know I was her father.

"Can't we have a conversation like adults for once?" she said.

"They didn't beat me up. They suspect me of having started the fire, but they have no evidence. And I didn't do it, either deliberately or by accident."

"So how did it happen?"

"I want answers just as much as you do."

Louise got up, went into the tent and came back with a bottle of water. She constructed a stand so that she could hang the coffee pot above the fire, then she fetched the Thermos flask and my cup, which I had left in the tent. She gave me the mug and kept the cup for herself. There were a couple of spoonfuls of instant coffee in the bottom of the mug.

A gust of wind came from nowhere and blew smoke in her face. The smell of the fire reminded me of the night my house burned down.

"I might as well say it here as anywhere else," Louise suddenly blurted out. "And I might as well tell you now as later."

I don't really like the taste of instant coffee. It brings back those long years as a medical student when I never drank anything else.

I put down the mug. Her words made me feel anxious. I thought about Harriet and her incurable illness. Was there something wrong with Louise too? My heart was pounding, just as it had when I rushed out of the burning house a few weeks ago.

"What's the matter?" I said. "It sounds serious."

"It is."

I kicked over my mug, and coffee splashed over the side of the tent.

"Tell me, please."

"I'm pregnant."

She hurled the words at me as if I were a crowd to whom she was delivering an important message.

Curiously enough, they instantly evoked a memory, something I thought I had long since forgotten. Before my relationship with Harriet, when I had just started medical school, a young woman had stood in front of me, radiant with happiness, and told me she was pregnant. She was studying to be some kind of chemical researcher. We had met at a student party. Untroubled by whether what I was saying was true or not, I had showered her with declarations of eternal love, painting a picture of our future together, our family. She had believed me. Now she was pregnant. I faced her happiness with dumbstruck horror. I didn't want children, not with her or anyone else. I remember her heart-rending despair when I more or less forced her to have an abortion. If she didn't go through with it, I told her, I would leave her. Which I did anyway, as soon as she had got rid of the foetus.

Now Louise was hurling those words at me. She wasn't radiant with joy, however; there was a kind of caution about her, as if she were simply stating something that had to be said.

I couldn't take it in. I had never imagined her as a mother. I don't think Harriet had either. I had once asked her about Louise's boyfriends, and she had simply replied that she knew nothing about her daughter's sexuality. I never asked again. From time to time, when Louise disappeared or returned from her mysterious trips, I had naturally wondered if there was a man in the background. I had never found any evidence of a secret lover. I must admit that I do poke around in her bags and pockets now and again, but I'd never come across the slightest hint about that part of her life.

"Did you hear what I said?"

She impatiently interrupted my train of thought.

"Of course. But it might take me a while to understand it."

"I'm pregnant. It's fairly straightforward, wouldn't you say?"

"You don't get pregnant on your own."

"That's the only question I won't answer," she said. "The identity of the baby's father is my business."

"Why?"

"Because that's how I want it."

"Do you know for sure who it is?"

I didn't have time to think that question was a mistake before she leaned across the fire and punched me in the face; I didn't realise my nose was bleeding until the blood trickled down onto my top lip. Louise didn't say anything, even though she must have seen it. I had a dirty handkerchief in my pocket; I scrubbed at my face and the flow of blood stopped.

"I won't ask," I said. "And of course I have no doubt that you know who the father is. How far gone are you?"

"Three months."

"And everything is as it should be?"

"I think so."

"You think so?"

"I haven't been to see a doctor, if that's what you're wondering."

"You have to make an appointment!"

We weren't conversing; as usual we were sparring with one another. My phone rang; a welcome interruption.

It was Veronika.

"Did I wake you?"

"No."

"I wanted to let you know that Axel died."

At first I didn't understand who she meant. Axel? I didn't know anyone called Axel. Then I realised that was Nordin's name. Axel Nordin.

"Are you still there?" she asked.

I could tell from her voice that she was upset. Or maybe she was afraid? Young people often react to sudden death with fear.

"I'm still here."

"He passed away just after four o'clock this morning. Margareta called me; she was devastated."

I knew that Nordin's wife was called Margareta. I also knew that they didn't have any children, which was a great source of sorrow to them. The whole thing felt very strange and unpleasant, bearing in mind that I was sitting here talking to my daughter about the fact that she was expecting a baby and that her dreadful behaviour might have contributed to Nordin's death.

I stood up and walked out onto the rocks.

"I don't think I'm going to open the cafe today," Veronika said.

"I understand. I assume the shop will be closed too," I said. "Who will take over?"

"It's owned by the fishermen's association. You'd have to ask them."

"I've ordered some wellington boots," I said. "I hope I'll be able to get hold of them."

Veronika wasn't impressed, and to be fair I wished I hadn't mentioned my wellingtons.

"Who cares about something like that right now?" she said.

I didn't respond to her question; I simply said I would get in touch with Margareta, and we ended the call.

When I went back to the fire, Louise was inside the tent. Her expression was grim when she eventually emerged.

"Nordin is dead," I informed her. "He had a brain haemorrhage and passed away in the early hours of this morning."

"Who?"

"The man in the shop where the keys to the shower block are kept."

I thought I saw a fleeting look of worry pass across her face, but it was gone in a second.

"It can't have anything to do with me," she said. "I didn't give him that much of a hard time."

"Nobody is suggesting it's anything to do with you. All I know is that he's dead."

Louise got to her feet.

"Let's go. It's cold."

"Where are we going?"

"Around the island."

"This isn't an island. It's a skerry."

"What's the difference?"

"The size, maybe."

We clambered over the rocks, slithering and sliding across the stones at the water's edge. Louise moved with confidence, while I was always afraid of losing my balance. At one stage she was ahead of me, up on a high rock from which she could look down on me. She stopped and turned. She didn't say a word, she just gazed at me. Then she carried on, still without a word.

I felt a surge of rage that immediately ebbed away. I'm afraid I am hopelessly, furiously envious of all those who will continue to live when I am dead. I am equally embarrassed and terrified by the thought. I try to deny it, but it recurs with increasing frequency the older I get.

I wonder if other people feel the same way? I don't know, and I am never going to ask, but this envy is my deepest darkness.

Can I really be alone in feeling like this?

We returned to the fire, which had almost gone out.

"You must realise . . ." I began.

"Realise what?"

"That I often wonder what you live on. You never ask me for money. I have no idea what you do."

She smiled at me, then she quickly headed for a clump of alders, bumping into me as she pushed past.

"I need a pee."

"Watch out for the ticks."

After a moment she came back and sat down.

160

"Go home," she said. "Take the motorboat. I'll be over in a few hours, but right now I want to be left in peace."

"We still have a lot to talk about. Not least what we're going to do about the house — particularly now there's a new generation on the way."

"I know. We've got all the time in the world to talk to one another, haven't we? About houses and children."

I pushed the boat out, flipped down the engine and started her up. I decided to take a little trip before returning to the island. Much to my surprise, beyond the outer skerries, the nameless hogsbacks that barely broke the surface, where great shoals of herring used to gather, I spotted a lone sailboat heading into the wind, out towards the open sea. It was strange to see pleasure sailors so late in the year. I followed the boat with my gaze and could see only one person on board, but I couldn't make out if it was a man or a woman at the helm. Then I turned and went home. I moored the boat and sat down on the bench. I tried to come to terms emotionally with what Louise had said: she was pregnant. I couldn't feel the unreserved joy I should be experiencing, which worried me. Why did I carry my emotions as if they were a burden?

At least we had started a conversation; I hoped it wasn't already over.

I went up to the caravan, glancing at my watch on the way.

It wasn't there. I checked my pockets, then went back to see if it was in the boat. Nothing.

I tried to come up with an explanation; the bracelet was made of steel and was hardly likely to have broken.

My mobile rang, interrupting my thoughts. It was Jansson.

"Nordin is dead," he said.

"I know."

"I'm going to be one of the bearers at his funeral. Are you?"

"Surely he must have closer relatives than me?"

"It's terrible, the number of people dying these days."

"That's what people usually do," I replied.

Then I said he was breaking up and I pretended I couldn't hear what he was saying. I ended the call.

Jansson could wait. I might be in a hurry, but right now everything would have to wait.

I had to think of Louise's child as the best thing that could happen to me.

CHAPTER
TEN

I went up the hill and looked over at the skerry. When I saw Louise climb into the skiff, I went down to the boathouse and waited for her. The boat wobbled as she stepped onto the jetty; I thought she was going to fall, but she managed to grab hold of one of the bollards.

"That was a close thing," I said.

"No, it wasn't. There's nothing wrong with my balance. Besides, you probably don't know that I used to practise walking on a tightrope when I was a child."

I wondered if she was making it up; Harriet had never said that our daughter had tried the art of funambulism.

"Can you tell me what time it is?" I asked. "I've lost my watch."

"Quarter past twelve."

"I don't know where my watch is."

"You just said that."

"It's strange that it's disappeared; I was wearing it when I rowed across to the skerry."

"I haven't seen it."

"I mean, a watch can't just disappear, can it?"

"It's probably still over there."

I was surprised that she sounded so indifferent, but I didn't pursue the matter. I would find it if I carried out a proper search. I dismissed the idea that I could have dropped it in the water.

Louise headed for the caravan; my telephone rang as she slammed the door, the whole structure shuddering. I didn't recognise the number, so I didn't answer. When it stopped ringing I put it back in my pocket.

It immediately rang again; this time I did answer, but hesitantly, afraid of being surprised by someone delivering bad news.

It was Lisa Modin.

"Am I disturbing you?"

"Not at all. Was it you who just rang me?"

"Yes. Are you on your island?"

"Where else would I be?"

She laughed.

"I'm calling as a journalist," she said.

I was immediately on my guard. It was as if her voice suddenly changed. She wasn't ringing to talk to me, but on behalf of the newspaper.

I said nothing.

"I believe the prosecutor is preparing to charge you because there are reasonable grounds to suspect you of arson."

From nowhere a knot formed in my stomach. I almost groaned in pain.

"Are you still there?" Lisa said.

"I'm still here."

"Is it true, what I just said about the prosecutor?"

"I don't know."

"You don't know?"

"I haven't heard anything since I left the police station. No one has called; I haven't had a letter. Perhaps you could explain how you know something that no one has told me?"

"It's my job as a journalist to find out what's going on."

"But nothing's going on, is it?"

"So you haven't been charged?"

"No."

The conversation broke up. Her voice came and went, but neither of us could hear what the other was saying. I waited for her to call me back. I tried to call her but without success. The phone masts don't always cover the archipelago. Nordin once asked me to sign a petition protesting about the poor service; I signed, but of course it led nowhere.

I went over to the caravan. The temperature was dropping; I wouldn't be able to sleep in the tent for much longer.

I was just about to knock on the door when I changed my mind. I wasn't ready to talk to my daughter yet. Instead I sat down among the old fishing nets in the boathouse. I tried to gather my thoughts, to go back to the night when that bright light suddenly woke me. I had a great deal to process, otherwise I would end up in the midst of insoluble chaos.

But I couldn't gather my thoughts. All I could hear was Lisa Modin's voice in my head, asking if I'd been charged. How could she possibly know? Was it a rumour, or was it true?

As I sat there in the darkness, I began to feel afraid. I began to doubt my recollections of that night. Could I have set fire to the house after all, without realising it? Could I really be charged without any solid evidence?

The fear turned to nausea. I put my head between my knees, as I had been taught when I was studying to be a doctor.

How long I sat like that I don't know. The nausea had metamorphosed into a headache when I felt a hand on my shoulder. I heard myself cry out as I straightened up with a jolt.

"What's the matter with you? Why are you sitting here?"

I hadn't heard Louise come into the boathouse.

"I don't have many other places to sit."

"It's cold here. I thought we were going to talk. I've been waiting for you."

We went up to the caravan. I followed a few steps behind her, feeling like a stray dog that nobody really wants to take care of.

She made some coffee.

"Do you want something to eat?"

"No."

"You mean, no, thank you."

"No, thank you."

"You have to eat."

I didn't protest when she made me a couple of sandwiches. I really was very hungry. She looked at me searchingly, as if she expected me to start the conversation, but I had nothing to say. The truncated

166

phone call from Lisa Modin had chased away all rational thought.

It was Louise who first heard the boat approaching. She raised her head and then I heard it too. I opened the door. I had no doubt that it was Jansson's boat.

"It's the postman," I said. "Go down to the jetty and tell him I'm not here."

"But the boats are both there — he'll be able to see them!"

"Well, tell him I've drowned!"

"I have no intention of lying. If you don't want to see him, you can sort it out yourself."

I realised she wasn't going to change her mind. Jansson was my problem. I pulled on my jacket and went down to the jetty. When Jansson rounded the headland, I could see that he wasn't alone. Lisa Modin was sitting in the prow, her face turned to avoid the icy wind.

It made no sense. Only a little while ago she had been on the other end of the phone, and now she was here.

Jansson hove to, and Lisa jumped ashore. Jansson stayed in the boat and gave me a sloppy salute, raising a hand to his black woolly hat.

Lisa was wearing a raincoat and carrying a sou'wester.

"I expect this is a bit of a surprise," she said.

"Yes."

"I was standing on the quayside when I called you."

"With Jansson?"

"That was pure coincidence — he just happened to be there."

I looked at Jansson; he had heard what Lisa said, and he nodded.

"I won't stay long," Lisa assured me, "but our phone call was cut off."

Jansson picked up the local paper Lisa Modin wrote for, and began to read. We walked up to the caravan. The door was closed, and I couldn't see any sign of Louise through the window. I could, however, hear the radio.

"My daughter is here."

"That's good — it means you don't have to be alone."

We went up to the ruins; the smell of the fire still lingered, although it wasn't quite as strong now.

I felt an overwhelming urge to put my arms around her, to let my frozen hands find their way inside her clothes. But of course I did no such thing.

We stood looking at the ruins.

"What are you thinking now?" she asked. "Now a little time has passed?"

"Nothing," I said. "I still don't understand what's happened."

"I have to be honest," she said. "Apparently the prosecutor's office has decided to embark on a preliminary investigation which will probably lead to charges against you. As the house was fully insured, the assumption is that the motive was insurance fraud. But you still claim you know nothing?"

"About the fire or the charges?"

"Both."

"Absolutely. If I hadn't woken up, I would have burned to death. In which case it would have been a successful suicide attempt, not insurance fraud."

She pushed the sou'wester into her raincoat pocket. I noticed that her hair was even shorter now.

"I have to write about this," she said. "But I'm only allowed a short piece, not a more detailed report."

"It would be better if you wrote that I didn't set fire to my house and that all those who are spreading rumours should be chased down into hell."

"That's not where prosecutors and police officers usually end up."

I went up the hill; Lisa followed at a distance. Why was she here? Did she think I was going to confess to starting the fire?

I sat down on the bench while she stood a little way off, gazing out to sea. Suddenly she pointed.

"Look!"

I followed her finger but couldn't see anything. However, when I got to my feet I understood. Beyond the skerry where I had pitched my tent, the wind was stronger; a windsurfer dressed all in black was heading straight out to sea at high speed. They were often around in the summer, but never this late in the autumn. In contrast to normal practice, the little sail and the board were also black. From this distance it looked as if the man or woman was skimming across the surface of the water on bare feet.

"He must be freezing cold," Lisa said. "What if he loses his grip?"

We watched the windsurfer until he disappeared behind Låga Höholmen. After a while he popped up on the other side, still heading straight out to sea. Something about the sight of him, the black sail, the speed, made me feel ill at ease. What kind of person does that on a bitter October day?

I seized Lisa's hand. It was cold. She let me hold it for a little while before she gently withdrew it.

A dry twig snapped behind us. I turned to see Louise on her way up the hill. Lisa saw her at the same time. Louise's hair was all over the place, and she seemed upset. Her expression was hostile to say the least.

"This is Lisa Modin," I said. "She's a friend."

Lisa held out her hand, but Louise didn't take it.

"Louise is my daughter."

Lisa had immediately picked up on Louise's animosity. They stood there staring at one another.

Louise turned to me. "Why haven't you told me about her?"

"We haven't known each other very long."

"Are you sleeping together?"

Lisa Modin gasped. Then she started to laugh.

"No," I said. "No, we're not."

Louise was about to speak, but Lisa got there first.

"I don't know why you're being so unpleasant. Just to clarify things: I wanted to ask your father some questions. I'm a journalist. I've got my answers, and now I'm going to leave."

"What was it you wanted to know?"

Lisa glanced at me, but I had nothing to say. This was about me, but I wasn't a part of what was going on.

"The police believe the fire was the result of arson. That means your father is a suspect."

Both Lisa and I were completely taken aback when Louise stepped forward and yelled, "Get the fuck out of here! It's hard enough without journalists running around all over the place!"

Lisa was dumbstruck. I could see the anger in her eyes, but she walked away, down the hill. She got into Jansson's waiting boat, and Louise and I stood watching as he started the engine and disappeared around the headland.

The wind was even stronger now. My daughter had robbed me of one of the few hopes I had for the future: that Lisa Modin might become more than a passing acquaintance, more than someone I showed around the archipelago from time to time.

"I want you to leave," I said. "If you're going to chase away the few people I like, I don't want you here."

"Do you really think she's interested in you? She's at least thirty years younger than you!"

"She hasn't let me down so far. Even if we're not sleeping together."

We didn't say anything else. By the time we got down to the caravan, the wind speed had increased further. I looked at the dark clouds piling up in the west; if it had been a little later in the year, I would have expected snow overnight.

We ate dinner together, then drank a cup of tea. I don't like the blend Louise favours. It tastes of unidentifiable herbs, which doesn't appeal to me at all. But of course I didn't say anything.

We were both tired. We reached a tacit decision that I would sleep in the caravan. We played cards until it was late enough to go to bed. Louise lay awake for a long time, but eventually her breathing became deeper and heavier. Then I fell asleep too.

The following day I rowed across to the skerry to look for my watch. Louise didn't want to come with me because she wasn't feeling well.

Perhaps that was when I really grasped the fact that she was pregnant. Now I got it. My daughter was going to have a child, and I hadn't a clue who the father was.

I rowed slowly, trying to picture this unknown man, but there was only a crowd of men milling around, as if the gates had just opened before a football match.

I spent a long time searching for my watch, but without success. I even pulled out a few tent pegs to see if it might somehow have ended up under the groundsheet, but it was nowhere to be seen. My watch had disappeared, and that was that.

For two days nothing much happened. The wind rose and fell, at times almost reaching gale force. Louise and I spent most of our time in the caravan. I resumed my habit of taking a dip in the cold water in the mornings. I tried to persuade Louise to come with me, but she refused. When I had finished, she washed herself at the water pump. I could hear her puffing and blowing, cursing the icy water.

I wondered why we were behaving so oddly: two adults who couldn't bring themselves to discuss the new generation that was on its way. What was it that made both of us so ill equipped for something that would be a normal conversation for normal people?

We did, however, talk about the matter of rebuilding the house. As long as the police investigation was ongoing and the prosecutor was considering his options, I wouldn't receive a payout from the insurance company, but we couldn't stay in the caravan when the winter came.

At around lunchtime on the second day I called my insurance company. It took a while to get through to someone who was able to access my details. He introduced himself as Jonas Andersson. I searched my memory, but I had no recollection of ever having met him. He spoke much too quickly and seemed keen to end the conversation as soon as possible. He hadn't heard about the fire because I hadn't yet submitted a claim. Nor had he read anything about the suspicion that the fire had been started deliberately. Perhaps I was speaking to a young man who belonged to the generation that had given up reading altogether — not just newspapers, but books as well?

The brief conversation with Jonas Andersson was an ordeal. I didn't mention that the police investigation might well result in charges against me. He could find that out for himself. Most importantly, he was able to confirm that my premium had been paid on time.

My insurance was valid. The company would pay the full amount necessary to rebuild the house, although of course it would never be as solid a piece of workmanship as the house that had been built in the nineteenth century. There would be no oak beams in the walls, nor would the porch boast the same ornate carpentry as my old house.

I wondered if the insurance also covered charred apple trees, but I didn't ask. Jonas Andersson probably wasn't interested in that kind of thing.

I was sitting in the caravan while I made the call; Louise stood by the door, listening. Andersson's voice was quite loud, so she probably heard everything he had to say. At the end of the conversation he said that he or someone else would come out to inspect the site of the fire. He used a strange expression: the site of the fire would be visually assessed. This would happen within a few days.

He didn't ask where I was living at the moment, nor did he comment on the fact that all my possessions had gone up in flames. I assumed his main responsibility was to ensure that the company didn't pay out unnecessarily.

"The insurance is valid," I said when we had ended the call. "Unless of course I'm charged and convicted of arson."

"What happens then?"

"I'll end up in prison. And the insurance company won't pay for a new house."

The weather had gradually improved. After the blustery winds came clear skies and unexpected warmth. Once a day I went up the hill to look for the windsurfer, but the sea was empty. No boats, no black sails.

When the migration of the birds is over, the archipelago is quiet. The sound of the waves and the sighing of the wind, nothing more.

One evening I came across Louise looking very disheartened. She was sitting on the bench by the boathouse with her head in her hands. I had just come down the hill when I saw her. I watched her for a few moments but didn't make my presence known. More and more we seemed to spend our time secretly watching one another. We were afraid. My fear stemmed from the fact that I felt as if I knew less and less about my pregnant daughter. And perhaps in me she saw what old age does to a person.

It was ten o'clock in the morning on the first Tuesday in November when I heard the sound of an engine. The wind was coming from the south and the archipelago was quiet, so I heard the boat from a long way off. It wasn't Jansson. I didn't recognise the engine at all. I had never seen the boat that rounded the headland; it was a white plastic vessel with a powerful inboard motor, and it had the unusual name *Drabant II*. I wondered what kind of an idiot had given the boat a horse's name.

For once both Louise and I went down to the jetty to meet our visitor.

It was a representative from the insurance company, but not Jonas Andersson. The man introduced himself as Torsten Myllgren. He couldn't have been more than twenty-five years old. I had always imagined that assessors would be experienced individuals who had checked out and dealt with many different types of insurance claim. Torsten Myllgren appeared to be an overgrown teenager.

The person driving the boat was considerably older; with a limp and sweaty handshake. He introduced himself in a high-pitched voice as Hasse, if I heard him correctly. When I asked Louise, it transpired that she wasn't too sure of his name either.

We went up to the site of the fire. I was expecting Myllgren to inform me that he knew the police were investigating the possibility of arson, but he said nothing. He was wearing orange overalls, and I was pleased to see sturdy green Swedish wellingtons on his feet. I almost asked him where he had bought them. He was carrying a large notepad, and started jotting things down as soon as we reached the blackened ruins.

Hasse lit a large cigar, standing in a spot that was sheltered from the wind by the caravan. I wondered if he was employed by the insurance company to ferry their representatives around the archipelago. The cigar smoke drifted up to Louise and me as we watched Myllgren stomping around. From time to time he stopped and took pictures with his phone. He also used a small Dictaphone to make verbal notes.

"What's he looking for?" Louise said. "I mean, he can't tell what the house used to be like."

"I don't know. You'll have to ask him."

"I'm glad I don't wake up next to a man like that every morning."

I was taken aback by her comment, but at the same time I realised she had given me an opportunity to ask the most important question of all.

"Which man do you want to wake up next to?"

"You'll find out when you meet him."

176

Asking any more questions would be pointless.

We carried on watching Myllgren.

"What's he searching for?" Louise said.

"The truth. If it exists."

Louise took my arm. She nodded in the direction of the hill and my grandfather's bench. We had only just sat down when she started talking.

"You remember I was in Amsterdam when we spoke on the phone a few weeks before the house burned down?"

"Yes, I remember. It sounded as if you were in a cafe."

"What do you think I was doing in Amsterdam?"

"I don't even want to hazard a guess."

"I'll tell you. I go there several times a year. As you know, the Rijksmuseum — the national gallery of the Netherlands, where a number of Rembrandt's paintings are preserved — is there. I never tire of looking at his work. No one could fail to be moved by these masterpieces. If such people do exist, then they must be completely immune to art. However, I wasn't actually there to see the pictures; I was there to help other people visit the gallery. There is a small group, mostly from Holland but also from other countries, who have set up an agreement with the Rijksmuseum. We collect money, we organise cars and ambulances. Our aim is very simple: we offer terminally ill individuals whose life expectancy is very short and who long to see Rembrandt's paintings just once more the opportunity to make a final visit. Once every four months the gallery opens just for these people, who arrive on stretchers or in wheelchairs. They are lying down or half-sitting, often in severe pain because they have all temporarily eschewed any form of analgesic in order to have a clear head when they face Rembrandt. Most of them want to see his self-portraits, mainly the ones in which he is an old man. This meeting, face to face, makes the transition between life and death less painful. Perhaps you thought I was in Amsterdam because drugs are regarded differently in Holland, that I went there to smoke weed? That wasn't the case. Now you know something about me that you didn't know before."

The sound of a radio blared out from the boat; it was very loud but didn't seem to disturb Myllgren.

"What kind of music is that?" I asked.

"It's called techno," Louise said. "But that probably doesn't help you."

It was a beautiful autumn day with glorious colours, a clear sky and almost no wind. I thought about what Louise had told me.

An hour passed, and now Louise had disappeared into the caravan. I paced back and forth by the site of the fire, as if I didn't want to leave Myllgren alone to do his job. A herring gull with a limp was keeping watch on a rock nearby. I had seen it there before; I had thrown it scraps of food a few times.

Myllgren closed his notepad, almost as if he were bringing down the clapperboard on a film set to mark the beginning of a new take. He tucked a plug of snuff under his top lip, tugged at his overall, which seemed to be chafing at his crotch, then headed in my direction.

He stumbled over one of the foundation stones that was partially buried under the remains of the fire. As he went down I heard a bone in his leg crack. He yelled out in pain and dropped his notepad.

He lay there like a wounded animal, clutching his left leg. You didn't have to be a doctor to see that the leg was broken between the ankle and the knee.

Louise had heard his scream and came running up from the caravan. Hasse, who was sitting in the boat, also realised that something had happened. We gathered around Myllgren, who was struggling to cope. If my house hadn't burned down I would immediately have given him a pain-killing injection, but as it was I could offer him only tablets. He was very pale, and made me think of a soldier in a trench who has been shot and can feel the life seeping out of him.

"You've broken your leg," I said. "You need to go to hospital."

"We'll carry him down to the boat," Hasse said, who clearly didn't grasp the severity of the situation.

"The coastguard will have to come and pick him up," I said. "If we carry him without a stretcher, we could make things even worse."

I asked Louise to fetch a blanket.

"You'll have to move your boat," I said to Hasse. "Otherwise the coastguard won't be able to get in."

He opened his mouth to protest, but I raised my hand and pointed to the jetty. He decided to cooperate. I called the coastguard, then crouched down next to Myllgren. He was so young, and I was impressed by his determination not to give in to the agonising pain.

The coastguards arrived in less than half an hour. They put Myllgren on a stretcher and carried him down to their boat. Alexandersson was in charge; he was an experienced man who had carried many stretchers in his life.

Hasse had moved his boat, which was drifting just off the jetty. When Myllgren was safely on board, Alexandersson turned to me.

"I was buying paint yesterday," he said. "Maggan asked about you. She said your boots had arrived. She's going to run the chandlery now that Nordin is gone — for a while anyway, until his brother takes over."

I knew that Nordin's brother was a plumber. Perhaps he would make a good job of running the shop?

Alexandersson stepped aboard, and the boat reversed out. Hasse followed in his white *Drabant II* once the coastguard had rounded the headland.

"My wellington boots have arrived," I said to Louise, who was sitting on the bench.

"In that case we can pick them up tomorrow. We need to do some food shopping anyway."

I heard Alexandersson turn the engine up to full throttle, the dull roar bouncing off the rocks of the islands and skerries.

I felt sorry for Myllgren, but at the same time I was glad my wellington boots had arrived.

CHAPTER
ELEVEN

The wellington boots didn't fit.

Nordin's wife Margareta was considerably bigger than I remembered. She must be suffering from some kind of disease. No one can get that fat just through overeating. She could hardly make her way between the shelves and counters in the shop. When I walked in she was contemplating a display of landing nets. The bell above the door pinged; she turned around and knocked over a stand full of thick socks. The thought that I was looking at a large, clumsy animal that had somehow got into a very small shop made me want to laugh, but I managed to maintain my composure.

I said hello, offered my condolences and said that I was pleased my wellingtons had arrived. I sat down on a stool while Margareta went to fetch them. I took off the odd wellingtons I had been wearing ever since the fire. She brought the new ones in an open box: green, shiny Tretorn wellington boots with pale yellow ridged soles. As usual I started with the left one. I couldn't get it on. I tried the right one, but that was no use either. I checked the number stamped on the side; it was the wrong size.

"They're the wrong size," I informed Margareta, who was busy picking up socks. I wondered how she managed to bend down without falling head over heels.

"I don't know anything about that. It wasn't me who sent the order."

"Did only one pair arrive? Didn't he order more?"

"Only this pair."

I put the wellingtons back in the box.

"In that case we need to reorder," I said. "I'm a size forty-three, not forty-one. My feet aren't that small."

She wrote down the numbers on the back of an envelope lying next to the till.

"Perhaps you could ask them to process the order quickly," I said, getting up from the stool. "It took an awful long time for this pair to arrive, and they don't fit me."

"I don't know much about all this," Margareta complained.

She seemed to think I was holding her personally responsible for what had happened.

Through the window I saw Louise arrive on the quayside in my car. Margareta bent over the socks once more, and I found it very difficult to resist the urge to push her over. If I just poked her bottom with one finger, I was sure she would go. I pulled on my mismatched wellingtons and left the shop. I have found it easier to control my wicked impulses as the years have gone by.

Louise drives erratically and much too fast. Even though I didn't teach her to drive, she seems to be just as bad a driver as me. It's not just the speed; we both fail to pay enough attention and get far too close to the middle of the road.

I suddenly wondered if she actually had a licence. I'd never seen it.

We travelled through the autumn forest. I asked her to be careful where the trees were at their thickest, because there were a lot of elk moving around. Just a few years ago a wealthy company owner who had a large summer home in the archipelago had died in a head-on collision with a bull elk. Louise showed no sign of slowing down or paying more attention; she didn't even answer me.

I rarely if ever know what my daughter is really thinking. Her inner world is hidden behind ramparts and barricades, all invisible but still impossible to breach. I am probably equally incomprehensible to her. What do my defences look like? Are they easier to get past?

On the brow of a hill we met a truck that was far too big and wide for the road. Even though Louise swerved as far over to the verge as possible, we passed each other with just centimetres to spare. She seemed unmoved, while I was stamping hard on the non-existent brake pedal in front of me.

"You drive too fast," I said angrily when I had regained my composure.

"The truck was driving too fast."

I had expected her to snap at me, but her response was totally indifferent, as if nothing had happened.

"Did you find your watch?" she suddenly asked.

183

I looked down at my left arm, as if my watch might have magically reappeared.

"No. No watch."

"You must have dropped it when you were rowing."

"No, I know that for sure."

"How do you know?"

"I just do."

"You don't really need a watch. Life can't be measured anyway."

"It's time we measure. Not life."

She glanced at me but said nothing.

As a doctor I had been forced to contemplate the fleeting nature of life every single day. Unlike priests, who droned on about the brevity of life as a reminder of the eternal life awaiting us beyond the here and now, a doctor saw what this brevity really meant. A stream of images always scrolled through my mind when I thought about how death came without warning. Not even seriously ill patients, usually very old, with no way out and where the end could reasonably be expected to come at any moment, were ready to die. They might claim they were ready when speaking to visiting relatives, but it was rarely true. When the relatives had left and the dying patient had cheerfully waved them off, they would be overcome by tears, terror and bottomless despair as soon as the door closed.

Those who understood death best were the children. That wasn't only my experience; it was something we doctors often discussed. How could it be that often very young children, who ought to have their whole lives before them, behaved with such calm composure when they were dying? They would lie quietly in their beds, knowing what was to come. Instead of the life they would never have, there was another unknown world waiting for them.

Children almost always died in silence.

I don't often think about my own death, but as I sat there in the car with Louise driving so badly, thoughts of the end came into my head. I used to believe that doctors died a different death from those people we can characterise as patients. A doctor is familiar with all the processes that lead to the heart, the brain and other organs ceasing to function; therefore a doctor ought to be able to prepare himself or herself in a different way from people with a different life and a different profession. Now I realised that was far from the truth. Even though I am a doctor, death is just as mercilessly unwanted, just as difficult to prepare for as it would be for anyone else. I do not know if I will die calmly or desperately resisting. I know absolutely nothing about what is to come.

I looked over at Louise, who still seemed distracted. What was she thinking? Did death even form a part of her view of the world? What had Harriet's death meant to her? What did the child she was expecting mean to her? And what did the child mean to me?

There was a heavy downpour as we parked behind the bank; people ran to get out of the rain. We stayed in the car and divided up the errands between us. I was surprised when she asked me to do the food shopping; I thought she would want to take care of that herself.

However, she said she had other things to do, although she didn't explain what they were.

We decided to meet for lunch at the restaurant in the bowling alley in an hour, then we sat in silence waiting for the rain to stop. I wondered whether I should drive into town to buy a pair of wellingtons instead of waiting for the new order to arrive at the chandlery. I didn't reach a decision.

When the rain stopped we went our separate ways. I was heading for the grocery shop when I heard Louise calling to me. She waved, ran back and gave me the car keys.

"You might be finished before me," I said.

"No, I won't."

She turned and hurried away. I wondered why she was in such a rush and what she was going to do. I watched her until she went into the bank.

It took me half an hour to buy the food I thought we would need for the next week. The shop was almost empty. The assistant, who was approximately the same size as fru Nordin, had nodded off at the till. I bought a couple of crossword books, then I put my bags in the car and wondered whether to go to the chemist's but decided not to bother; I didn't really need anything at the moment.

It was too early to go to the restaurant, so I walked up to the old railway station, which was no longer in use. The tracks had been ripped up long before I moved to my grandfather's island. I peered into various shops to see if Louise was in there, but there was no sign of her. The window display had changed in the shoe shop where I had failed to find any wellingtons, and now featured autumn and winter shoes. I tried to peer inside, but without success. When I reached the station I remembered all the times I had arrived here as a child and been met by my grandfather. I always made the trip with a sense of freedom when the school term ended in the spring. A sense of freedom that now, all these years later, seems totally incomprehensible. Are we really the same person, the child I used to be and the adult I am today? The thought of my distant childhood made me desperately sad. I left the station as quickly as I could.

I stopped outside a modest antique shop and contemplated the items crammed in the window. I tried to imagine the people whose former possessions now lay there with price tags like little white tails. Who had owned the fob watch with an inscription on the case? Whose was that elegant cut-throat razor?

For many years my father had a special pen when he worked as a waiter. It was with that pen and only that pen that he took orders on his notepad and wrote out the bills. It had been given to him as an extra tip by an elderly gentleman who frequented the restaurant where my father happened to be working; the gentleman finished his meal that day and stated that he wouldn't be coming back. He didn't say why, or where he was going, but a few days later my father read in the newspaper that he had committed suicide. He had shot himself in the head. From then on, my father never used any other pen. When he died I searched for it for a long time, but I never found it. What he did with it remains a mystery.

Another downpour was on the way. I hurried to the restaurant and got through the door just before the rain came down. Louise wasn't there, but it was still only fifty minutes since we had parted company. It was lunchtime, so many of the tables were occupied; I sat down in a corner to wait for her. When she hadn't appeared after half an hour, I ordered some food at the counter, paid and began to eat. If she didn't turn up at the agreed time, that was her problem.

There was still no sign of her when I had finished my meal. I waited a few more minutes, then went and got a cup of coffee. It had stopped raining. I put down the coffee cup on my table and went out into the street. I couldn't see Louise anywhere.

I began to wonder why she had come running back to give me the car keys. Something wasn't right. Something was going on, but I couldn't work out what.

The coffee tasted bitter. I drank half of it, then pushed the cup away. The restaurant was beginning to empty. Over by the counter the girl on the checkout dropped a glass on the floor. A heated exchange broke out between her and a man who I assumed was the owner of the restaurant. I couldn't say what language they were speaking. The argument stopped as quickly as it had started. Still no sign of Louise. I decided to wait another ten minutes, then she would have to fend for herself. She had a phone, she could call me, but my phone hadn't rung, and I hadn't received any text messages.

I tried to tell myself that something had happened. An accident. But I couldn't summon up any anxiety. She had simply ignored our agreement to have lunch together before we drove back to the harbour.

Eventually I decided I couldn't wait any longer. The sun was shining when I left the restaurant. Louise wasn't waiting by the car. I had already got in when I spotted a note tucked underneath one of the windscreen wipers. Had I been given a parking ticket? Angrily I flung open the door and grabbed the note.

It wasn't a parking ticket. Louise had left me a message. The paper wasn't wet, so she must have put it there after the rain had stopped — ten, fifteen minutes ago at the most.

The message was very short: *Go without me.*

I looked around to see if she was anywhere nearby, but there was no sign of her. I drove up and down the street, to no avail.

I drove down to the harbour. The heat of the sun was suddenly very noticeable; it was almost like a summer's day. I parked and looked around for Oslovski. Everything seemed to be closed up. I went over to the garage; there was no one around, but something gave me pause for thought. Oslovski was always very tidy; each of her tools had its place, either on a shelf or hanging on the wall. Now they were spread all over the dirty concrete floor.

I went back to the house and did something I had never had the courage to do in the past: I knocked on Oslovski's door. Once, twice, three times. No one came. The curtains were drawn. I put my ear to the door, but I couldn't hear any movement inside.

I took my bags down to the boat. Margareta Nordin was sitting outside the chandlery soaking up the sun. Somehow this seemed like a betrayal of the grief she should be feeling at the loss of her husband.

"This heat is a bit strange, isn't it?" I said.

"Everything is strange," she replied. "I'm sitting here trying to grasp the fact that my husband is dead."

"We can never make sense of death," I said. "It doesn't obey any laws or follow any rules. Death is an intractable anarchist."

She looked curiously at me, not surprisingly. My words sounded peculiar to me as well, even if they were true.

Alexandersson was standing smoking outside the coastguard's office as I walked towards my boat. When he spotted me, he hurried inside, thinking I hadn't seen him. Had things really gone so far that no one wanted to talk to me?

I tossed my bags into the boat, cast off and pushed away from the quay before I had even started the engine. I didn't care if I got wet when I sat down; I just wanted to get away as quickly as possible.

Of course the engine decided to play up. I had almost drifted out of the harbour before it fired. I assumed Alexandersson was standing by a window watching the whole thing. I wondered if he regarded me with contempt or sympathy. I thought he probably saw me as a shady character, someone who had turned out to be a criminal.

190

I headed for the island. The wind was warm, considering it was a November day. I was about halfway when I slowed right down and let the engine idle.

I realised that Louise had gone. She hadn't bothered to pack a suitcase, but I knew that when I got back to the caravan I would find that her passport was missing together with her money, her credit cards, everything she needed in order to move on. She had planned this; she had never intended to come to the restaurant. That was why she had given me the car keys; she knew exactly what she was going to do. She had probably caught a bus into town but I had no idea what she had done next, nor where she was going.

She had taken her unborn child with her. Its father was waiting for her somewhere.

I allowed the boat to drift. Her disappearance filled me with disappointment, but there was something else, a feeling, a rapidly growing suspicion.

I remembered when Louise and I had been out on the skerry. How she had brushed against me when she went to pee. When I got home and was on my way up to the caravan, I had discovered that my watch was missing.

The realisation hit me like a hammer blow. Louise had taken my watch. That must have been what happened. I had a daughter who was a skilled pickpocket.

At first I refused to believe it; it was too astonishing, too frightening. But in the end it was impossible to deny the truth. Louise was a pickpocket. She made her living by stealing. There was no other explanation.

She had asked me about my watch in the car simply because she wanted to know if I suspected anything.

191

My answer must have convinced her that I had no idea of the reason behind the disappearance of my watch.

I swore out loud, at Louise and at my own stupidity. I no longer wanted anything to do with her. I didn't need her, or a grandchild. She had stolen my watch and gone off to some unknown man who was the father of her child.

I moved into the prow of the boat, stretched out my legs and closed my eyes.

I fell asleep, thanks to a combination of weariness and sorrow. I had been dreaming of Harriet when I woke because the engine had cut out. She was standing by the burned-out ruins of my house, and she looked exactly the same as she had done on the day when she made her way across the ice using her wheeled walker. In spite of the fact that it was late autumn in my dream, as in reality, she was dressed for winter, complaining that she was freezing cold. When I embraced her and bade her welcome, she bit me on the arm.

Still half-asleep, I stumbled to the stern and pulled the engine cord. When I got back to the island, I went straight up to the caravan. Louise's passport, money and various credit cards were gone. At the bottom of her bag I found my watch. I was furious; I hurled it at the wall, but when I picked it up it was still going. I put it on and lay down on the bed. The door of the caravan was ajar; there wasn't a breath of wind.

"Louise," I said out loud to myself.

Just that. Nothing else. I wasn't calling to her, I wasn't pleading with her or begging her to come back. I just said her name.

I decided to row across to my skerry. Settling down with the oars always filled me with a great sense of calm. It didn't take many strokes before the unease had left me. I rowed with no sense of urgency, resting often. I pictured Louise in different situations: on a bus, on a train, walking into an airport, aboard a ferry. I wondered why she had chosen this particular day to leave. Had I driven her away by asking too many intrusive questions about how she made a living? Or was she unable to cope with the thought of her father being accused of arson?

A pickpocket. Yet at the same time she was helping terminally ill people to see Rembrandt's paintings for one last time — it didn't make sense.

I rested on my oars once more. Perhaps she really did believe I'd burned down my house?

I was sweating by the time I reached the skerry. I walked towards the tent, then stopped dead. Someone had been there and hadn't managed to hide the telltale signs. Not Louise, but someone else.

I had made a fire on a pile of stones; they had been moved, and the pile had grown. I opened the tent and crawled in; my sleeping bag was in the right place, but it was zipped up. I always leave it open during the day to air.

I went back outside. Who had used the tent and lit a fire? I searched the whole skerry for further evidence but found nothing. I returned to the tent and sat down on the rock where I usually balance a plate of food or a cup of coffee on my knees. Was it my imagination? No,

I wasn't wrong. Someone had come to the skerry, rearranged my fire stones and gone inside my tent.

If it had been summer I could have understood it more easily; some kids paddling kayaks might have spent the night there. But in late autumn? It couldn't be any of the permanent residents of the islands either.

Before I rowed back, I placed a little brown stone shaped like the point of an arrow just beneath the edge of the tent flap. If anyone undid the zip, the stone would move. It was safe from the wind, and no one would suspect that it was a trap.

I made myself something to eat. From time to time I went up the hill and looked over at the skerry through my binoculars, but there was no one there. When I had finished my meal I sat down at the table and turned my attention to one of the crossword books, but I couldn't concentrate. I tore up the paper grocery bags and tried to make a list of things that had happened over the past few weeks: the fire, the suspicion of arson and, not least, Louise's pregnancy.

I sat there scribbling until I noticed that I had started drawing grotesque, swollen faces. I screwed up the piece of paper and threw it on the draining board.

I went up the hill one last time. It was too dark to use the binoculars, but I wanted to see if someone had lit a fire by the tent. Nothing.

Once again I wondered who could have been there, and suddenly I remembered the made-up bed in the empty house in Hörum.

I took one of my sleeping tablets and went to bed. The scent of Louise hit me as soon as I put my head on

194

the pillow, bringing me to the verge of tears; I missed her.

I thought about her unborn child; I hoped she had gone to the man who was its father.

Just before the sleeping tablet began to take effect, my parents came into my mind. When I was a child, I once hid underneath the dining table. My parents thought I was asleep. I did it because I thought it would be an exciting adventure, not because I suspected something was going on that might affect me. I sat there looking at their shoes and bare feet. My father, whose legs ached after a long day and evening at the restaurant where he was working, always took off his shoes and socks when he got home — before he had even taken off his hat or coat. It was as if he couldn't bear to have anything on his feet. After a particularly hard day my mother would prepare a footbath for him, and he would sit there with his feet in a bowl of water while they ate or had a cup of coffee or a glass of wine. My mother, on the other hand, always wore shoes. I can't recall ever having seen her bare feet during my childhood.

It was on one of those footbath evenings that I hid under the table. I could hear the clink of wine glasses. Then I heard my mother say that she would really like me to have a brother or sister. I remember trembling inside. It had never occurred to me that I might have a sibling. I had always thought of myself as an only child, and I had expected the situation to remain unchanged. There was no need for any more children. When I heard my mother express her wish, I felt as if it wasn't a sibling she hoped for; she wanted to swap me for another child. I was a failure, I wasn't enough for them.

My father didn't reply, but the wine glasses clinked once more. I realised I had to protect myself against my mother's attack on me. I sank my teeth into her leg just above the shoe, and I bit her as hard as I could. She screamed and tried to pull her leg away, but I hung on. She got up, still screaming, knocking over her chair in the process, and dragged me out from under the table, where I was still clinging on. She was finally able to free herself. I remember looking at my father. He was holding his glass of red wine, his hand frozen on the way to his mouth. He was staring in surprise, or perhaps it was horror, at his son, who had blood all around his mouth like some repulsive vampire.

That was the only time my mother hit me. She did it not out of viciousness, but out of fear. I can understand how unexpected and frightening it must have been to be bitten on the leg while she was sitting quietly with her husband, enjoying a glass of wine.

I yelled out in pain and terror when she hit me, but I was most scared of being given away.

That evening I changed from being a child to something else, although I didn't know what it was until many years later. I wasn't a child, I wasn't an adult, I was someone living in a land that didn't exist. My mother felt guilty for the rest of her life because she had hit me, even though we never talked about it. Every time she looked at me, I could see that she was wondering whether I had forgiven her or not. When she died, all our questions remained unanswered. All I know today is that I never had a sister or brother. Perhaps my violent protest under the table played its part. My father spoke of it only once, when I was thirteen or fourteen years old. He had just been sacked from a restaurant where he had fallen out with the maître d' over certain routines. He had applied for a new job at one of the restaurants in the Tivoli amusement park, and took me with him to Copenhagen. My mother had merely looked at him with heavy eyes when he announced that the family might be moving to Denmark.

When we arrived at Tivoli, we had an hour before he was due to meet the maître d'. It was May, warm when the sun was shining, chilly as soon as it went behind a cloud. We drank lemonade and shivered when the sun disappeared. Without any warning, he asked me about that evening when I had been sitting under the table: why had I bitten my mother? His tone was friendly, calm, almost tentative. He didn't usually sound like that when he asked me questions; he might as well have been wondering what I would like to eat or drink.

I told him the truth: I had bitten her because I was scared that I was no longer enough for them.

He never mentioned the incident again. Years later I thought that perhaps he understood my reaction, that he felt the bite was somehow justifiable.

He didn't get the job in Copenhagen. A few weeks later he started work at the restaurant in the central station in Stockholm and stayed there for six years, the longest he ever worked in the same place. Occasionally my mother and I would go for a meal when he was on duty. As I watched him hurrying from one table to another, I vowed I would never become a waiter.

I must have dozed off while I was thinking about my parents; I was woken by the sound of my phone ringing. I sat up in the darkness, alarmed by the noise of the phone inside the caravan.

It was a man, but I didn't recognise the voice.

"Fredrik?"

"Yes?"

"Just want to warn you."

"What about?"

"You're going to be arrested, possibly tomorrow."

"Who are you?"

"A friend, perhaps. Or just someone who wants to warn you."

He ended the call. I replayed the brief exchange in my mind; the voice was completely unfamiliar. I couldn't decide whether it had been disguised or distorted in some way. Perhaps the man had put a handkerchief or his hand over the phone?

I was scared. My hands were shaking.

I didn't sleep much that night. I was already up by the time dawn broke. I still didn't know what to make of the phone call. I went out and took a dip in the ice-cold water. By the time I had dried myself and got dressed, I had made a decision. I had no intention of staying on the island, or on the skerry where my tent was. Nor was I planning to run away. I simply wanted to give myself time to understand what was happening around me.

A grey morning. Slight northerly breeze. Through the binoculars I could see that no one had moored a boat on the skerry. I tucked the money I had left in my jacket pocket and set off without bothering to lock the door of the caravan. The engine started right away. The last of the birds had migrated to warmer climes. I sailed to the harbour and moored at the far end of the inlet, where a half-submerged fishing boat had lain for many years. Fru Nordin had not yet arrived at the chandlery. The bread delivery van was parked outside the grocery shop. The cafe wasn't open either.

I picked up my car from Oslovski's. I could see that the tools were still strewn across the concrete floor but had been used. They were lying in different places, different combinations. Oslovski had been in there, working on her car.

I didn't knock on her door, nor did I see any movement behind the closed curtains.

I drove away. You might say I had a plan, but whether it could be realised was something that no one, least of all me, was able to say with any certainty.

CHAPTER
TWELVE

The three-storey building was in a residential area on the outskirts of the town. When I was a child there was nothing here but fields and meadows where cows grazed. The apartment blocks had been built in the 1960s, and looked exactly like all the others that had been erected in those days.

I parked outside the block closest to the edge of the forest. From the top floor I thought it would be possible to see the deep inlet leading out to sea.

It had been easy to find. I had called Directory Enquiries, and they had given me Lisa Modin's address.

I ate in the restaurant at the bowling alley then went for a walk along the track by the inlet. Whenever I met anyone, I looked down at the ground. I had the feeling I might be recognised.

I didn't get back to my car until about two o'clock. Someone had stuck a flyer under one of the windscreen wipers, informing me that cloudberries would be on sale in the square between twelve and two the following day. I wondered if there really were cloudberries so late in the year.

I could see the front door of Lisa's apartment block. I checked out every window through my binoculars, but the curtains, potted plants and lamps gave me no clue as to which flat was hers.

I got out of the car and went over to the main door, which wasn't locked. There was a list of residents' names on a board to the left of the staircase; the building didn't have a lift. Someone had scrawled *GRINGO* on a wall with a red marker pen; someone else had crossed it out and written *JUNGLE BUNNY* instead.

Lisa lived on the top floor. There were two apartments: Modin L. and Cieslak W. Should I go up and ring her doorbell now? No, it was too early in the day; I wanted to be sure she was in.

I sat in the car for almost four hours before Lisa turned up. I had seen children coming home from school, dropping their bicycles carelessly outside the block. A caretaker had oiled the hinges on the outside door. An elderly man with a wheeled walker, moving incredibly slowly as if he thought he might collapse with every new step, had shuffled inside. He had a bag of shopping looped over the handle of his frame; he seemed like a thousand-year-old man who had passed through the ages and had finally reached this grey concrete box with its unbarred windows and tiny built-in balconies with barely enough room for more than two people.

During all those hours of waiting I avoided thinking about what the anonymous voice on the telephone had said. Nor did I have the strength to examine my reasons for leaving the island and hoping that Lisa Modin would provide me with a place of refuge for a few days. What I wanted more than anything was not a place to sleep, but someone to talk to about everything that had happened. I didn't really know her and she didn't know me, but now that Louise had sneaked out the back way, so to speak, I had no one else to turn to.

I wanted both clarity and solace, but of course I didn't know whether Lisa would be able to give me what I needed. She might not even let me in when I rang the bell and she saw who was standing outside her door.

A woman emerged from the apartment block. She reminded me of Harriet. Harriet as a young woman, when I first met her and we had our brief, chaotic relationship.

That was forty years ago. I had just qualified as a doctor. We met, as people often do, through friends of friends. I knew right from the start that Harriet wasn't the great love of my life, but I found her attractive. I soon realised that I meant more to her than she did to me, so I pretended that my love also went much deeper than erotic need. I still feel ashamed that I deceived her, made her think that I shared her feelings. Even when she made her way across the ice using her wheeled walker, suffering from terminal cancer, I still couldn't tell her how I had felt all those years ago. The last thing I robbed her of was the truth.

The woman carried on down the hill. I was on the point of giving up, going back to the island and waiting for the police to come for me. It was pointless, this search for a hiding place that didn't exist.

I suddenly missed my mother and father, the siblings I had never had, Jansson with his imaginary aches and pains, Harriet, Louise, Oslovski, even Nordin, who had messed up the order for my new wellington boots.

And I wondered if there was anyone who missed me.

Lisa Modin came walking up the hill at ten to six with her rucksack over one shoulder, carrying a bag from the shop where I bought my groceries. She was wearing a red beret, and had a scarf wound around her neck. I slid down as far as possible in my seat. She went inside, and a few minutes later a lamp was switched on in the apartment on the top floor closest to the invisible inlet. I caught a glimpse of her as she opened a window.

I got out of the car and crossed the road. As I reached the door a group of teenage boys came out, talking about a girl called Rosalin; apparently they all wanted to undress her and go to bed with her.

I climbed the stairs slowly in order to avoid getting out of breath. I could hear accordion music coming through one door and a loud telephone conversation through another. The wheeled walker was on the first-floor landing, so I concluded that this must be where the thousand-year-old man lived. Did he only need the walker when he was outdoors? Or did he have another one, specifically for indoor use?

I reached the top floor and paused to catch my breath. Although I had taken my time, my pulse rate had still increased. On Lisa Modin's door there was a picture of a man with a camera in his hand. When I read the caption at the bottom I learned that he was a photographer called Robert Capa, and that the picture had been taken in France at the end of the Second World War. I had never heard of him, but if Lisa had put his picture on her door, then he must be important to her.

I listened for a moment; I couldn't hear anything from inside the apartment. I opened the letter box a fraction and listened again. The light was on in the hallway, but I still couldn't hear a thing.

I hesitated. How would I explain the fact that I had simply turned up without contacting her first? What was I actually expecting?

I made several attempts to ring the doorbell, but kept drawing back my hand at the last second. I realised how pointless the whole thing was, and I had lost my nerve. If I drove back to the harbour now, I would have time to row over to the island before it was completely dark.

I set off down the stairs. After a couple of steps I turned, went back up and immediately rang the bell. I wanted to run away again, but I stayed where I was. Lisa flung the door open, as if she had been disturbed. When she saw me she frowned, but she was smiling at the same time.

"You," she said. "The man whose house burned down."

"I hope I'm not disturbing you."

She didn't reply; she just stepped aside and let me in. A big black cat was sitting on a mirrored shelf, contemplating me with displeasure. When I tried to stroke it, it jumped down and ran off.

Lisa handed me a coat hanger.

"The cat's name is Sally," she said. "Even though he's a tom. He doesn't like strangers."

I hung up my jacket and kicked off my boots.

"I don't want to disturb you," I said again.

"You've already said that, but I'm curious — why are you here?"

"I've got nowhere else to go."

She was wearing a green dressing gown. She tightened the belt around her waist, waiting for me to say something else. I didn't.

She showed me into her living room. On the way we passed the half-open door of her bedroom. The duvet was thrown back; presumably she had been lying down when I rang the bell.

It was indeed possible to see the blue waters of the inlet from the living-room window. Lisa had positioned an armchair and a table with a pile of books on it in the spot which gave her the best view. There wasn't much furniture, and hardly any pictures. A door led into another bedroom, while the kitchen was an open-plan arrangement.

She gestured towards the red sofa in front of a glass coffee table; its legs suggested that it might be from an Arab country.

"What can I offer you?"

"Nothing."

"In that case I'm going to make a pot of tea, then you can have a cup if you change your mind."

She went into the kitchen and I looked around the living room. There was nothing to indicate the presence of a man. I couldn't be sure, but there was no harm in hoping. When she had poured water into the teapot she disappeared into her bedroom and came back fully dressed.

She served the tea in white cups, and placed a plate of biscuits on the table.

"So," she said. "Why have you come here?"

"I don't know where to start."

"I usually find the beginning is the easiest place."

I already knew I wasn't going to tell her the truth, but I also knew that for a lie to work, most of what you say must be true. It is only the conclusions that can contain the lie, twisting the story on its own axis. At the same time I thought the truth was impossible to deliver on this occasion, because I didn't know what it was.

"You know the beginning," I said. "The accusation that I'm an arsonist. I'm not."

"So surely it's important for you to defend yourself? No one is convicted without solid proof of their guilt."

"I've already been convicted. I had a phone call to say I was going to be arrested. I've also received several anonymous letters."

"I thought you said you didn't want any post delivered to your island?"

"They were lying on the bench by the boathouse. I don't know how they got there."

Lisa looked at me pensively. The tea was very sweet, nothing like the blend Louise had left in the caravan.

"My daughter has gone away," I said.

"Why?"

"Don't ask me. She didn't even tell me she was going."

"That sounds like very strange behaviour."

"My daughter is strange. I also think she makes her living as a prostitute."

I have no idea where that came from.

"That sounds alarming," Lisa said after a brief silence.

I noticed that she was on her guard now. I realised I might have gone a step too far.

"I don't want to talk about it," I said. "And I'd like you to forget what I just said."

"You can't just make yourself forget something, but I'll try. I still don't know why you've come to see me."

"I've got nowhere to go. No one to talk to."

"That's not quite the same thing. You could have phoned me."

"I'll leave right away, if that's what you want."

"That's not what I said."

"I couldn't stay on the island. I hardly know anyone around here. The only person I could think of was you, but now I realise I shouldn't have come."

Lisa was still looking at me with a certain wariness.

"I hope you won't write about this," I said.

"Why would the local paper be interested in this?"

"I don't know."

"As you're here, it's probably best if you tell me what's going on. I still don't understand why you've left the island."

I realised that my lies had made me unsure of what to say next, but there were moments during that long evening when I almost told her the truth: that I wanted her to take me into her bed. That was all.

Perhaps she knew what I was thinking? It was very late and we had drunk a bottle of wine when she suggested I should stay over on the sofa.

"But don't get any ideas," she added.

I felt like saying that it was always worth getting ideas, but at least she was letting me stay.

She made up a bed on the sofa, cleared away the cups and glasses and gave me a towel.

"I'm tired," she said. "I need to sleep. First thing in the morning I'm off to visit two elderly siblings who live on a remote farm with no mains water supply and no electricity."

I had hoped I would be able to give her a hug at least, but she merely nodded, switched off all the lamps apart from the one next to the sofa and disappeared into the bathroom. I decided not to get undressed until I heard the bedroom door close behind her.

I sat there in the pale light shining in from the street down below. I had draped the towel over the lampshade.

Nothing had turned out as I had hoped. The childish disappointment I felt reminded me of my clumsy teenage attempts at dating.

I walked around the silent apartment. Listened outside Lisa's room. I had the feeling that she was standing just behind the door and quickly moved away. I opened the door of the other bedroom. There was a bed, but the room was clearly used as a study. On a desk by the window stood a computer and an old typewriter. I flicked through a pile of papers which contained barely legible notes and a few incomplete manuscripts. Daily newspapers were stacked up on the floor. I was listening the whole time; I didn't want to be caught by Lisa if she emerged from her bedroom.

There were several framed photos on a shelf. I guessed they were from the 1930s or 40s, men and women posing for the photographer with smiling faces. However, there was nothing more modern, no pictures of people who might be Lisa's parents or other relatives.

The apartment was strangely empty. It seemed as if her life and mine had some similarities after all.

I sat down at her desk and carried on looking through her papers. I turned on the lamp and read some letters, holding the paper in one hand while the other hovered over the switch. I didn't want to be caught snooping. I have often expressed my contempt for those who pry into the lives of others, yet I have that same tendency myself.

One letter was from a reader complaining about the way Lisa had written about a serious matter involving the mistreatment of animals. A number of cows had been neglected, and had had to be slaughtered. The man who had sent the letter was called Herbert, and he felt he had been insulted and unfairly hung out to dry. At the bottom Lisa had put: *No reply.* Another letter was so full of hatred that I was astonished. I had received an anonymous phone call, but Lisa got letters. An anonymous man wasn't attacking her for some article she had published; he was simply telling her how arousing he found the thought of sleeping with her. The fact that he had sadistic fantasies became clear after the first few lines.

This time Lisa's note said: *Can he be traced?*

I turned off the lamp and got to my feet. There was a wardrobe on one wall, containing her clothes. I inhaled the smell of her and picked up a pair of high-heeled shoes.

As I stood there with the shoes in my hand I heard a noise behind me. I spun around so fast that I banged my head on the wardrobe door, but there was no one there. It was just my imagination. I put down the shoes exactly as I had found them. I was about to close the door when something right at the back caught my eye. At first I couldn't make out what it was: possibly a small Swedish flag? However, when I took it out I discovered that it was an embroidered cloth. Above the Swedish flag was the word "Schweden", and below it a black swastika on a red and white background.

I could see that it was old; the white fabric had acquired a yellowish tinge. I put it back in the wardrobe. Next to it, on another hanger, was a black leather bag. I took it out and opened it. It contained a number of Nazi war decorations, including a gold-coloured clasp with an inscription on the back which I interpreted as "close combat clasp". There was also an Iron Cross, although I couldn't tell which grade, and a knife in a case that had belonged to a member of the Waffen-SS. At the bottom of the bag was a photograph of an unshaven man in a German uniform. He was smoking a cigarette and smiling into the camera. On the back of the photograph was the name Karl Madsen, and in different handwriting someone had added: "Eastern Front 1942".

I put the bag back in the wardrobe and left the room. There still wasn't a sound from Lisa. It was quarter to three in the morning. I lay down on the sofa without getting undressed and fell asleep. In my dream Louise was walking along a street I didn't recognise. I didn't recognise her either; she looked completely different, and yet I still knew it was her. When I tried to call out to her, she turned and smiled. Her mouth was like a black hole; she had no teeth.

When I woke, it was ten past four. The whole situation, the fact that I was in Lisa's apartment, felt like a dream. I went over to the window and looked down on the open space illuminated by a swinging street lamp. My car was in the shadows.

I went into Lisa's study again. Once more I opened the wardrobe and took out the embroidered cloth with the Swedish flag and the swastika. Why was it hanging there among her clothes? What did the contents of the black leather bag mean?

I couldn't find any answers.

I was on my way back to the sofa, but I couldn't resist listening outside Lisa's bedroom door again. Everything was still silent. Gently I pushed down the handle and opened the door a fraction. The blind was pulled only halfway down, and the street lamp shone onto the bed where she was lying.

I don't know how long I stood there in the doorway, gazing at her. In the pale glow she looked like the women I have been with during my life. There weren't many, apart from Harriet, but they were all lying in that bed looking just like Lisa Modin.

Eventually I lay back down on the sofa and dozed off, even though I really didn't want to. When she woke up I wanted to be sitting here so that I could tell her I hadn't slept a wink. I hoped that would arouse her sympathy.

I came back to life every fifteen minutes or so, in a state somewhere between sleep and drowsiness. When I heard the alarm clock in her bedroom, immediately followed by the sound of the radio, I sat up, combed my hair and waited. She opened the door softly, so as not to wake me. It was six o'clock. She was wearing her dressing gown. She nodded when she saw me sitting there; I nodded back as she disappeared into the bathroom. I heard the sound of running water. When she came out she had a towel wrapped around her hair. She went back into the bedroom; I stayed where I was. It was still dark outside.

She was dressed when she reappeared.

"I thought you'd be asleep since you were so tired," she said. "But you're up and dressed already."

"I haven't slept," I said. "I didn't even get undressed."

"Have you been sitting on the sofa all night?"

"I lay down from time to time."

She shook her head and looked worried.

"I'm fine," I said. "At least I've had peace and quiet here. Nobody knows where I am."

"Not getting any sleep isn't going to help."

"Sleeping isn't going to help either."

She went into the kitchen and began to prepare breakfast. I waited on the sofa until she said the coffee was ready. I was hungry but only had a cup of coffee. She tried to persuade me to have a sandwich, but I refused.

She got up, taking her coffee with her.

"I've got a couple of things to do," she said. "I'll be leaving in half an hour."

When she had gone into her study I quickly made a sandwich while trying to work out how I could stay in the apartment. I didn't want to go back to the island.

Lisa came out of her study. She topped up her cup, went over to the window and looked out towards the inlet; the sky was growing lighter now.

"Why did you come here?" she asked. Her voice was different, deeper. She was still gazing out of the window.

"I tried to explain last night; perhaps I didn't do a very good job."

"You've been snooping," she said, turning to face me.

I felt my pulse rate increase, as if I had avoided a car accident by the narrowest of margins.

"I don't know what you're talking about."

She put down her coffee cup on the draining board; I could see her hand trembling.

"You've been in my study. You've been going through my papers, and you've opened my wardrobe. I can't say exactly what you've done or why, but I can tell when something has changed."

"I'm not in the habit of going through other people's things," I said huffily. "Whatever you might think, you're wrong."

Lisa looked tired. She shook her head slowly.

"I'd like you to leave now. I thought you really needed help and a place to sleep, but now I don't know who you are or why you've come here."

"I can assure you I haven't been in your study."

She shook her head again. I didn't know how she had discovered what I had been up to during the night, but I knew I wasn't going to be able to convince her that she was mistaken.

"In that case I'll go," I said, getting to my feet.

She followed me into the hallway and watched as I put on my jacket and my wellington boots. I opened the door, then asked her, "Who's the man in this picture?"

"Robert Capa. He's a photographer; I admire him more than any other journalist or photographer. He died when he was reporting from a war zone in Asia; he stepped on a landmine."

I made my mind up there and then, with one foot outside her door.

"One day you must tell me why there's an embroidered cloth in your wardrobe with the Swedish flag and a swastika on it. Who made it? You must tell me all about it, but not right now — you're obviously in a hurry."

I didn't wait for her response because I didn't want to hear it. I hurried down the stairs, and as I reached the

214

wheeled walker outside the old man's apartment, I heard Lisa's door slam.

I got in the car, lowered the back of my seat and fell asleep almost immediately.

When I woke up two hours later I was frozen through and felt sick. I took my pulse. It was much too rapid: ninety-seven. I got out of the car and walked around for a couple of minutes to shake some life into my body.

A little while later I parked by the bank and waited in the car until the liquor store opened. I bought half-bottles of vodka so that I could slip them into my jacket pocket, and ten cans of beer to ease the hangover that was bound to follow.

I went to a small cafe I had never been to before and had a couple of sandwiches. Since I was alone I added a good slug of vodka to my coffee cup. I saw no reason to wait until I got home. There were no police checks on the short stretch of road between here and the harbour. I wasn't used to drinking spirits, so I felt the effects immediately. A warming sense of calm flooded my body.

I left the cafe, got into my car and had another swig of vodka before I set off. I was drunk, but I was still capable of keeping the car on the road and avoiding a collision with the oncoming traffic. I felt extremely cheerful. I was convinced that my parting comment to Lisa had hit home.

I parked outside Oslovski's house, which still appeared to be deserted. I listened for sounds from her garage but heard nothing.

I went down to the boat with my stash of booze; I didn't bother looking over at the chandlery to see if fru Nordin was there. The two coastguard patrol vessels were moored at the quayside. I clambered into my boat and left the harbour. A gentle offshore breeze was blowing, and just as I was picking up speed the sun emerged from behind the clouds. I set a more northerly course so that I could take a longer route home, travelling between islands with summer cottages closed up for the season. At one point I thought I caught a glimpse of a wild boar among the trees, but I couldn't be certain. The water opened out into the wide expanse of Ramfjärden. In the distance I could see the outer sunken reefs and the open sea. I intended to head east when I had gone about halfway to the open sea; I would soon be home. However, instead I switched off the engine. I moved to the prow and fell over when the boat rocked. One of the oars slid into the water, but I managed to fish it out before it drifted away. I sat down and carried on drinking. The sun was lovely and warm. I took off my jacket.

I didn't think about anything — not Lisa Modin, not my daughter, not the unknown police officers I would soon be talking to. I drank. Exhaustion from the almost sleepless night caught up with me, and I fell asleep.

I was woken by the boat bumping into something. When I sat up I was staring straight into Alexandersson's face. He was leaning over the rail of the larger patrol boat, which loomed above me like an enormous whale. I looked in the other direction and realised that I had drifted all the way to the outer reefs, where the open sea was waiting. I was already caught up in the sea swell. I didn't know how long I had slept, but I was still extremely drunk.

"I think it's best if you come aboard," Alexandersson said.

"Fuck off," I replied as I stumbled to the stern and pulled the cord. The engine started immediately; I reversed away from the reef and set off towards my island. I thought Alexandersson would come after me; I was drunk, and could be arrested for being in charge of a vessel while under the influence.

However, the coastguard made no attempt to stop me. When I reached the island I ran the boat straight up onto the shore, but managed to flip up the engine before the propeller sustained any damage.

I tottered up to the caravan. Before I lay down I did something I never usually do.

I locked the door.

CHAPTER
THIRTEEN

I was woken by the sound of someone knocking.

It was the second day after the coastguard had found me drifting in my boat. I had carried on drinking when I'd got back to the island, and hadn't begun to sober up until the following day. I was constantly expecting the police to come and pick me up.

The occasions in my life when I have drunk heavily have been few and far between, and I have always been alone when they happened. They follow the same path: I drink, I remain silent apart from yelling into the emptiness now and again. I fall asleep easily but usually wake up after a short time.

When I had started to sober up and felt the remorse gradually ebbing away, I went up to the bench on the hill with my binoculars. I looked over at the tent on the skerry, but there was no sign of anyone. However, I couldn't be sure that the mysterious visitor hadn't been there.

I noticed that I was listening for the sound of an engine the whole time. There wasn't a breath of wind. I made myself something to eat when I remembered, but I hardly touched it and threw it to the gulls on the rock down by the boathouse where my grandfather used to sit mending his eel traps when I was a child. Slowly my thoughts returned to the night I had spent in Lisa Modin's apartment.

The events to which the embroidered cloth bore witness, and the contents of the black bag, belonged to the past. It was seventy-five years since the war broke out, since the Nazi threat had seemed unstoppable. I was born after the war, Lisa Modin much later than me. Obviously there was something in her past that was still alive as far as she was concerned, but she didn't have the items on display. It wasn't something she wanted on show.

The most important question in my mind was of course the identity of the smiling man blowing cigarette smoke straight into the photographer's eye. Who was Karl Madsen?

Remorse was replaced by depression and self-loathing. Every time I was overcome by those feelings I thought about my father and his many failures. I remembered him coming home after long shifts and immediately sitting down at the kitchen table, forcing my mother to listen to his complaints about all his difficult colleagues and the maître d's, not to mention the diners he had to put up with. I never heard him accept responsibility for any tricky situation that had arisen; it was always the other person who had been in the wrong. When I was a child, I thought my father was an amazing man who never made any mistakes, but as time went on I realised that of course he was simply blaming someone else. That was also why he burdened himself with what sometimes seemed like a bottomless sorrow over a life that had turned out to be a failure.

My mother was his polar opposite. She was happy to take the blame for everything that happened in our home. If I came home with bad marks from school, it was her fault; she should have made sure I had peace and quiet to do my homework. If I got a nosebleed because I'd been fighting in the playground, she was responsible; she should have warned me about the boys who had attacked me.

I began my second day after my major drinking session by going down to the jetty and taking a dip in the ice-cold water. When I had rubbed myself dry I was even able to manage a substantial breakfast. Afterwards I poured the remains of the vodka down the sink but kept the cans of beer I hadn't yet drunk.

In the afternoon I lay down for a sleep only to be woken by the sound of someone knocking. I opened the door to find Lisa Modin standing outside. She was dressed in the same way as on the day we went over to Vrångskär. She was pale and seemed nervous. I stepped aside and let her in.

"How did you get here?" I asked when she was sitting at the table. I had offered her the bed, which was more comfortable, but she chose the stool.

"My editor has a small boat; I came on my own. I was afraid of running aground because I only knew the general direction, not how far away from the islands I needed to stay, but it was fine. I hope I'm not disturbing you."

"You're not disturbing me. Can I get you anything?"

220

"Tea?"

We drank tea. I didn't like the taste; Lisa didn't seem very keen either. I could tell from her face, but she didn't say anything. I waited.

I had once been sent for by my senior consultant when I was a newly qualified doctor. I didn't know why he wanted to see me, so I sat down and said nothing. The consultant, who was both stern and rather self-important, didn't say anything either. We sat in silence for perhaps ten minutes, then he looked at me and thanked me for coming. When I mentioned this strange encounter to one of my contemporaries, he said I should have asked for a pay rise. That was why the consultant had sent for me. He knew I wasn't happy, but he would never have started the conversation about my salary.

I topped up Lisa's cup. She still didn't say anything. I looked at her, remembering the night I had seen her in her bed.

"I wasn't lying," I said.

She looked questioningly at me.

"I wasn't snooping. I made a mistake in the night when I needed the toilet. I opened the wrong door, and then the wardrobe. I might have tripped. But I don't read other people's letters. I don't poke around in other people's belongings. Nor do I allow anyone to poke around in what is mine. Or was mine. Now my house has burned down, there's nothing left."

When I stopped speaking she looked at me for a long time, presumably trying to decide whether to believe me or not. Trusting what a person says is always a risk.

The truth is always provisional, while lies are often solid.

"I came here because I want to explain," she said. "At the moment I don't care whether or not you got lost in the night. You're wrong if you think I was trying to hide something."

She got to her feet.

"Can we go outside? It's not raining or windy. I need air; it's so cramped in here."

I pulled on my wellingtons, grabbed my jacket and opened the door. The sun was shining; late autumn in the archipelago was still mild.

We walked around the island and eventually sat down on the bench at the top of the hill.

She began to talk. Her family came from Germany. Her grandmother Ulrike had married Karl Madsen, a member of the infamous Waffen-SS. He had belonged to one of the units responsible for appalling outrages in Poland while Ulrike had remained in Bremen. Lisa's mother Roswita was born when the war was over, in the autumn of 1945, following Karl's last visit home towards the end of 1944.

Ulrike, who had been born in 1917, died at the end of the 1970s. Until that day Roswita had believed that her father had died while defending Berlin, before the city fell in May 1945. However, as she went through everything her mother had left behind, she realised that Ulrike had lied to her. Karl Madsen had been lynched in Krakow a few months before the end of the war, hanged on a makeshift gallows in one of the city's squares. He had been recognised because of his involvement in indescribably brutal actions during the conflict in Poland. There was no indication in Ulrike's papers of what he had done, nor was there any explanation as to why the photograph of Karl Madsen had been taken somewhere on the Eastern Front. It seemed likely that he had fought on the front line for a short period; a soldier's life was always full of gaps.

We set off for a brisk walk around the island again because Lisa was cold. When we got back to the bench, she continued her story.

"I hardly remember my grandmother. I was only six or seven when she died. We were already living in Sweden by then; I was born in Uddevalla. My mother met a sailor called Lars Modin, who was fifteen years older than her and had moved here from Germany. Ulrike came too, with her few memories of my grandfather. My first recollections are of sunshine: warm summer days, a great stillness. My grandmother had her own apartment on the top floor of our house. She used to eat with us, but I never went up to visit her; she wanted peace and quiet. I was frightened of her — not because she was strict, but because she hardly ever spoke. I don't remember her voice. Then she died, and my mother passed away too when I was thirteen. She was only forty, but she had a massive brain haemorrhage. I stayed with my father until I was twenty; he died a few years ago. A lovely old man who kept himself smart in his room in a care home. I didn't learn much from Roswita about my German heritage; it was only when my father died that I found the items that you came across in my wardrobe. There isn't really any more to say."

I had no reason to doubt the veracity of what she said. I realised that was the most important thing I could tell her.

"That's a remarkable story, and I believe you. And of course I won't tell anyone else."

"I had to explain, but I don't want to talk about it any more. It's my story, not yours, not ours. Mine."

I offered to cook her a simple meal, and to my surprise she accepted the invitation. Louise had left a fish pie in the freezer compartment; I put it in the microwave and got out the cans of beer I had bought. We ate and drank and talked about anything apart from what she had just told me.

We said nothing about her journey home, we just carried on chatting and finished off the beer. I had a lot of questions I wanted to ask her. I was convinced that she would soon move away; I felt as if she didn't fit in at all in the small town where she lived and worked. However, I didn't mention it. I had come to realise that she liked to choose the moment when it came to sharing information about herself.

"I'll have to stay the night," she said when it was almost midnight.

I had been expecting her to say that.

"We'll manage somehow," I said. "You take the bed and I'll put a mattress on the floor. It's a bit cramped, but it's OK."

I put a pan of water on the hob and gave her a towel.

"I'll go and see to the boats; when you've had a wash and got into bed, turn out the light. I can find my way around in the dark."

"I've never slept in a caravan," she said with a laugh. "I've never even slept in a tent."

I picked up my jacket and was just about to leave when she touched my shoulder.

"I can take the mattress," she said. "The bed is yours. But don't expect anything."

I just shook my head and went outside. When I turned I saw that she had drawn the curtain.

I switched off my torch and stood motionless in the darkness. I could hear the sound of a cargo ship in the distance, ploughing through the waves, although I couldn't work out in which direction it was going. It was a moment of absolute timelessness. I have always felt that time, the passage of the year, was a growing burden, as if days and years can be measured in grams and kilograms. The timelessness I experienced as I stood there on the jetty was almost like weightlessness. I closed my eyes and listened to the night breeze. There was no past, no future, no worry about Louise, no burned-out house. Above all there was no botched operation, no young woman who had lost her arm.

I felt tears scalding my eyes.

It wasn't me, standing there on the jetty. It was the child I had once been.

I managed to pull myself together. I wiped my eyes and noticed that the light in the caravan had gone off. I went into the boathouse and fetched a bar of saltwater soap, then I stripped off and climbed down into the

225

ice-cold water. I worked up a good lather, then dipped under the surface. By the time I got dressed my fingers were blue, my legs were shaking and my teeth were chattering.

I jumped up and down on the jetty to get my circulation going; only to get cramp in one leg. I had to massage my calf muscle before I was able to walk back up to the caravan. The pain had driven home the truth: I was a man of almost seventy who was tired, slightly hungover and wanted to sleep more than anything. Softly I opened the door; the light from the small lamp in the kitchen area cast a faint glow over the room. Lisa had turned to face the wall; only her head was visible above the covers. No doubt she was awake but wanted me to think she was asleep. I rolled out the mattress, fetched a pillow and a blanket from the cupboard, undressed to my underpants, switched off the lamp and lay down.

When I was studying medicine, before I met Harriet, a group of us went to a bar. It was someone's birthday; he had plenty of money, and was treating us. At the end of the evening I joined forces with one of the female students because we were going in the same direction. It was winter, cold and icy. She was a fairly anonymous member of the group; not pretty or funny, just pale and quiet. She spent most of her time alone and seemed perfectly happy to do so; she never really sought out the company of anyone else. Just before we were about to say goodnight, she slipped on a patch of ice. I caught her before she fell, and suddenly I was holding her close. It happened in a second. We could feel each other's bodies through our thick winter coats. Without either of us saying anything, I went home with her. She had a small bedsit; I can still remember the scent of soap. As soon as we got through the door she was tearing at my clothes. I still think she was the most passionate woman I have ever met. She raked her nails down my back and bit my face. When we finally fell asleep at dawn, the sheets were spattered with blood. A glance in the bathroom mirror told me that I looked like someone who had been hit by a hail of shotgun pellets.

We didn't speak during the night. In spite of her wildness she didn't utter a single word. When I woke up in the morning, she was gone. She had left a brief note on the table.

Thanks. Close the door when you leave.

Later that day we met in a lecture on ethics. She nodded at me as if absolutely nothing had happened. I tried to speak to her during the break, but she simply shook her head. She didn't want to talk. I'm not even sure she wanted to remember.

I never went to her apartment again after that night. When we qualified, we went our separate ways; many years later I saw her name in a death notice. She had died suddenly, and was mourned by her parents, brother and sister. She was forty-two years old and working as a GP in the northern province of Västerbotten at the time.

When I saw the notice I felt a deep and unexpected wave of grief. I missed her, although I didn't understand why.

"I can tell you're not asleep," Lisa said.

She didn't turn over. Her words bounced off the wall.

"I never sleep particularly well," I replied.

She rolled over. I could just make out her face in the light shining faintly through the curtain.

"I was asleep," she said. "Then all at once I woke up and didn't know where I was. It's worse than the worst nightmare, that split second when you don't know where you are. It's as if you don't know who you are either. While I was dreaming someone has taken my face and my body and replaced them with something I don't recognise; I don't know who they belong to."

"I never have nightmares in the caravan. It's as if there isn't room in here. Nightmares need space, or a proper bedroom at least."

"It's the opposite way round for me."

The conversation stopped as abruptly as it had begun.

"I have to repeat what I said when you slept on my sofa," she said after a while. "I hope you're not expecting anything just because I've stayed over. But perhaps you've already got the message?"

"One always expects something," I replied. "But that doesn't mean you have anything to worry about."

"What is it you expect?"

"Do I have to answer that?"

"I can't force you."

"Well, of course I'm expecting you to ask me to join you in bed, and then we'll make love."

Lisa laughed. She didn't sound annoyed or surprised.

"That's not going to happen."

"I'm too old for you anyway."

"I've never slept with a man I wasn't deeply in love with." She turned to face the wall once more. "Let's go to sleep. If we carry on talking I'll be wide awake."

"You started it," I pointed out.

"I know. Go to sleep."

It was a long time before I nodded off. The temptation to get up and squeeze into the bed was ever-present. Either she would open her body to me or push me away.

I stayed on the mattress and listened to her breathing gradually grow heavier until she was asleep.

In my dream the searing light was there once more. I tried to get out of the burning house, but to no avail. The staircase was missing. There was no way down from the first floor. When I turned around, my grandmother was standing there. She shouted to my grandfather to tell him that dinner was ready; they were having boiled pike.

At that point the dream ended abruptly, with no conclusion.

I was woken by the sound of an engine. I sat up and discovered that the bed was empty, and Lisa's clothes and handbag were gone. I ran outside; her boat was just pulling away. When she saw me she waved and pointed to the jetty. I walked across the damp grass; she had left a folded piece of paper under a stone on the bench. The name of her newspaper was at the top.

You were sleeping so deeply that I didn't want to wake you. But at least you know a little bit more about who I am now.

I climbed down into the water. The cold sliced through my body. I counted to ten out loud before heaving myself onto the jetty, then I ran back to the caravan and got into bed.

I woke several hours later, finally feeling rested. I decided I needed to work out how I was going to deal with the risk of being arrested. As I yanked back the curtain the fitting came away from the plastic wall; I threw the curtain out of the door. If it didn't want to be there, I wasn't going to waste time trying to fix it.

I went outside. If I was going to be able to think clearly, I needed to move. I put my binoculars around my neck and made my way down to the skiff. It was half full of water, and I had to bail it out before I set off for the skerry where my tent was.

The wind was a north-easterly. Far away on the horizon I could see a dark bank of cloud. I rowed to the skerry as fast as I could in order to warm myself up and get my circulation going.

The tent was empty, but I could see straight away that someone had made a fire among the stones. Next to a juniper bush lay empty tins that had contained American corned beef. There were no other traces of the person who had been using my campsite. I walked around the skerry to see if I could find anything; an empty milk carton was jammed between some smaller rocks, but it could simply have drifted ashore.

230

I wondered whether to leave a message for the mysterious visitor. I crawled into the tent and stretched out on my sleeping bag.

As I lay there with the grey light seeping in through the porous fabric, I thought that Lisa Modin was closer to me than I had dared to believe possible. The age difference between us was considerable, but I was starting to believe that she needed me in some way, just as I needed her.

It was an exciting prospect. I headed home without leaving a message on the skerry. To give myself more exercise, I rowed around my island before mooring at the jetty.

I would make a plan. Not just for the next few days, but for the future. I would suggest to Lisa that we took a trip together. If there was a place she dreamed of visiting, I would pay for us to go there. If she didn't have anywhere specific in mind, I would make suggestions. Somewhere hot. The Caribbean perhaps, or even further afield — a Pacific island.

For the first time since the fire I was in a good mood. I hurried up to the caravan, eager to start formulating my thoughts. As I stepped inside, my phone rang. I recognised the number.

It was Louise. She was talking fast, and her tone was forced. The line was bad too; I asked her to slow down. She said she didn't have much time. I could tell that she was frightened and on the verge of tears. Stammering, almost shouting when I interrupted her to say that I could hardly hear her, she told me that she had been arrested. She was being held by the police in

Paris and needed my help. I tried to ask her what had happened, but she wasn't listening; she just kept repeating that she needed help.

The connection was broken. Her voice echoed inside my head. I tried her number but couldn't get through.

I had never heard her sound so scared. I went outside, taking the phone with me in case she called again. I sat on my grandfather's bench even though the wind had increased, and I immediately started to shiver.

My passport had been lost in the fire, but I knew that it was possible to obtain a provisional passport at the larger Swedish airports. I called the bank and managed to speak to the clerk who had helped me before. My new card had arrived.

I didn't need to give the matter any more thought. I called Jansson and asked him to pick me up in an hour. Naturally he wondered if the engine was giving me trouble again.

"No. I just need transport, nothing else."

I dug out an old bag left over from Harriet's time and packed my Chinese shirts, my underwear and my phone charger. I gathered up the cash I had, then wrote a note to Alexandersson. I didn't want anyone to think I'd done a runner. I told him that my daughter was in trouble and needed my help, and I hoped to be back in a few days.

I was waiting on the jetty when Jansson arrived, punctual as usual. We shook hands; he was always very particular on that point.

"I expect you're going to the harbour," Jansson said. "When do you want to come back?"

"I don't know."

The sea spray was fresh and cold as we sped across the water. Jansson dropped me off by the petrol pumps, and I gave him a hundred kronor as usual. By the time he left the harbour I was already on my way to the coastguards' office. I had folded the piece of paper and written Alexandersson's name on one side.

As I was passing the chandlery I couldn't resist popping in to ask Margareta if my wellington boots had arrived. They hadn't.

"I'm going away for a few days," I said. "Perhaps the boots will be here when I get back."

"You can never tell when orders will arrive," Margareta said. "You can't rely on anyone these days."

Oslovski wasn't at home, but when I looked in the garage, all the tools were in their proper places.

The curtains were closed.

I got in the car and drove off.

I hoped to find a flight leaving for Paris that evening. I would leave my country with a slight bow.

PART THREE

The Bedouin in the Bottle

CHAPTER
FOURTEEN

During the drive to Arlanda many thoughts about Louise passed through my mind, along with memories from my younger days: hitchhiking by the roadside, travelling from town to town, sometimes even crossing the border into a new country. I remembered drivers who had stopped, but turned out to be drunk. On one occasion I was picked up by a young woman. She was driving an expensive sports car, and there was barely room for my rucksack between my legs. In broken English she informed me that she had just murdered her husband. I recalled with particular clarity that she said she had stabbed him in the back. She tried to excuse her actions by saying that he hadn't had time to realise what was happening; I don't know what I said in response. She suddenly slammed on the brakes and told me to get out of the car in the middle of nowhere in the dark. I don't remember how I continued my journey.

Just as my hitchhiking to Paris always led me to Belgium, especially the city of Ghent, if I travelled by train I always ended up in the central station in Hamburg at three o'clock in the morning. I used to change trains there for Paris, where I would either stay or go on to Spain or Portugal, perhaps even across to North Africa. Homeless beggars used to wander around the deserted station in Hamburg; this was only about fifteen years after the end of the Second World War, so I always imagined that these elderly men in their long, dirty overcoats were soldiers who had survived the Western or Eastern Front. There was a dark imprint of horror in their eyes. However, I don't recall ever giving any of them money, either because I had no German currency or because I felt too poor. The pale light transformed the enormous space into a theatre set, where the actors had left long ago but the lighting technician had forgotten to switch everything off before he went home. The few nocturnal wanderers, the passengers and the cleaners were acting out a drama that had no beginning and no end.

When I had reached Arlanda and parked my car, I stepped straight into a world swarming with people. Long queues stretched from every check-in desk. I hadn't a clue what to do. I couldn't tell you when I was last in an airport.

It was a while before I managed to pull myself together sufficiently to start looking for a ticket office. According to one of the big electronic information boards, the 19:30 Air France flight to Paris was delayed by two hours. That was the only departure I could find, but luckily there were still spaces. I paid with the credit card I had collected from the bank earlier in the day. I was holding the ticket in my hand when I realised I had an important question for the woman behind the glass in her blue uniform.

"I've left my passport at home," I said. "As a Swedish citizen, I assume I can travel to France without it?"

"As long as you have ID, that's fine," she replied. "Otherwise the police here in the airport can issue a passport which is valid for one journey."

I went and sorted out a provisional passport, then changed some money, found the right check-in desk and went through security. In the departure hall I bought a cheap suitcase on wheels. I transferred the contents of Harriet's old bag into it and purchased some more shirts and underwear. I sat down by one of the huge windows overlooking the tarmac, where the planes were squatting at their gates like beasts in their stalls.

I called Lisa Modin; she answered just as I was about to give up hope. I briefly explained what had happened — my daughter's cry for help, my hurried departure.

"Can I ask you a favour?" I said. "I haven't even managed to sort out a hotel. Could you possibly use your computer to find something that's in the city centre but no more than three-star? From tomorrow — the plane's delayed, so I'll be arriving in the middle of the night."

"How much do you want to spend? And for how many nights?"

"I've no idea about the cost — three-star is three-star. I need the room for at least two nights."

"No problem."

She called me back after twenty minutes to say that she had found a hotel.

"It's called the Hotel Celtic, and it's in Montparnasse, Rue d'Odessa, not far from Rue de Vaugirard,"

At first I wondered if she was joking. Of all the thousands of streets in Paris, Rue de Vaugirard is the one I know best. During my longest stay in the city, in 1963, I rented a room on Rue de Cadix, just off the far end of that long street, right next to the Porte de Versailles. It was a forty-minute walk from Montparnasse. When I was out and about at night I often saw packs of huge rats by the kerb moving from one drain to another. Some of them were as big as cats. It was frightening; I felt as if they could change direction and attack me at any moment.

At night my footsteps echoed on the cobblestones. My shoes were brown and far from clean. I had been given them by someone I met by chance in a jazz club in Rue Mouffetard. He thought the shoes I was wearing, with the left-hand sole coming away, looked dreadful. Late that night I accompanied him and his girlfriend to one of the streets behind the Jardin du Luxembourg. He lived right at the top of a house in one of the tiny garrets that had once provided accommodation for servants. He didn't want to come all the way down again, so he tossed the brown shoes out of the window. They hit the cobblestones with a short, sharp smack. I put them on there and then, and they fitted perfectly.

"Are you still there?" Lisa asked. "Shall I make the booking? There are rooms available."

"Yes, please. Will they want my credit card number?"

"I'll give them mine to secure the booking, then you can pay with yours."

"Won't you come with me?"

Only when I heard myself say those words did I realise that that was what I had been planning ever since I asked her to find me a hotel. I wanted to entice her to come with me, even though I would be searching for my daughter.

"What do you mean?"

"Exactly what I say. Come to Paris. I'll pay for everything. To say thank you for the night I spent in your apartment."

"A trip to Paris is a big thank you for an uncomfortable sofa."

"You're wrong."

She laughed.

"You've got my phone number," I went on. "Call me when you arrive and I'll meet you."

"I'm not coming. We don't know one another."

"I know myself. I mean what I say."

"Where are you?"

"I'm at Arlanda, waiting for my flight. I don't think I've ever felt more lonely in my life. I can't imagine what it will be like when I'm dead."

"What do you mean?" she said again.

"That death seems to be a very lonely place, and an equally lonely state."

"I've got work to do. I can't just swan off to Paris."

"Write about Paris. Write about the arsonist who's on the run, looking for his daughter."

"Have you managed to get hold of her?"

"No. I'm getting more and more worried."

She didn't say anything for a long time; life seemed to stop. Lisa Modin was present but silent. I was waiting for her to say that she loved me. I didn't love her, I just had an overpowering need for a woman, any woman, and I was ready to say anything in order to persuade her.

When I was younger, a woman I had dumped accused me of being like a spider, catching my prey then watching it struggle. I never ate my victims, I just scuttled away to spin a new web.

"Are you coming or not?" I asked when the silence began to feel uncomfortable.

"Not."

"I'll wait for you."

"What exactly are you expecting?"

"Nothing. Company, that's all."

"This conversation is making me uneasy."

"That wasn't my intention."

"I'll text you the address of the hotel."

"Thank you."

"I can't talk any more right now."

"Why not?"

She ended the call, and neither of us rang back.

The plane was indeed two hours late by the time we took off. When Paris finally lay glittering below us, we had to wait in a holding pattern before we were allowed to land. I stayed in my seat, observing my fellow passengers as they grabbed their outdoor clothing and hand luggage. It was as if they had all lost vital time and were now pushing and shoving to get off the plane as quickly as possible. I watched the whole thing with growing astonishment. A flock of people, desperate to flee. But from what? Cramped seats, fear of flying or their own lives? Had I been like them once upon a time, a person who regarded time as a game where winning or losing was all that mattered? I knew I had, but now that time really was an issue for me, the important thing was to be careful with whatever I had left.

I was the last person to disembark. One of the stewardesses was yawning so widely that I could almost hear her jaw crack. It reminded me of an occasion when I had arrived in Paris by train, having developed severe toothache the previous night in Hamburg. It was a very cold winter and I had stayed put on the train when it stopped at the Gare du Nord until a sour-faced conductor flung open the door of my compartment and ordered me to get off. I was sixteen years old at the time, escaping from a muddled decision to leave school.

The airport, with its many escalators, reminded me of a factory I had visited with my father when he was running the canteen there for a brief period. We arrived early in the morning, just before the first shift was due to clock on. I had the same feeling now as I approached passport control and customs. I was waved through without anyone asking for my passport or ID; no one was interested in my suitcase either.

The night was chilly as I emerged through the glass doors, looking for the airport bus. However, I immediately changed my mind. Why go to my hotel and sit around in reception until late afternoon, when my room would be available? I went back inside the terminal building and found some empty plastic chairs. I lay down, using my suitcase as a pillow, and soon fell asleep. Unfortunately I woke up every time someone came near me. I had learned the art of dropping off for just a few minutes at a time during the years I spent on call at various hospitals.

It was just after seven o'clock when I sat up. My body was frozen stiff. I had a cup of coffee and a croissant in a cafe that had just opened. The black woman who served me had a noticeable scar down one cheek and part of her ear on the same side was also missing. I wondered which African civil war with its concomitant slaughterhouse she had managed to escape from. Liberia? Rwanda? I smiled at her to show that I understood, but she looked tired; perhaps she was also someone who could no longer trust people.

I sensed so many of the dead behind her. Family, friends, strangers who had not managed to get away, unlike her.

By quarter to eight the airport was beginning to fill up. I went outside and got on a bus showing the Opéra as its final destination. Half the seats were occupied by a large number of Chinese men and women who belonged to a tour group. The group leader moved up and down the aisle, chatting to them. I found a seat right at the back, wondering if I ought to mention that my shirt was made in China.

A black family with an enormous amount of luggage were the last to board before the bus set off with a jolt. The journey into the city centre was drawn out and tedious, with frequent delays. The view from the window was the same as the view in so many other countries. The densely packed traffic induced in me a feeling of despair about the world into which I had been born and in which I happened to live. What were these people, many of them alone in their cars, thinking? Were they thinking at all?

I carried on staring out of the window but decided to ignore the traffic and turn my attention instead to how I was going to track down Louise. My French was far from perfect, but I could usually make myself understood and grasp what others were saying to me.

I got off at the Opéra, which looked almost exactly the same as it had fifty years ago when I saw it for the first time. I had intended to walk to Montparnasse, but after a glance at the Metro map I realised the distance was too great. As a young man I had happily walked from the city centre to the outskirts to visit a flea market, or simply in order to get to know different areas, but now it was too far. I made my way underground and found the line which would take me to Montparnasse, with one change at Châtelet. I remembered that the line going east from Châtelet used to have the most up-to-date trains. Those new trains had rubber wheels that hissed instead of scraping and squealing. I couldn't get a seat and was squashed up against several women talking to each other in low, intense voices.

By the time I emerged it had started to drizzle, but I knew where I was going. Rue d'Odessa was quite close by, and it took me ten minutes to get to my hotel, during which time I kept having to duck to avoid open umbrellas that threatened to poke me in the eye. It was ten o'clock. I wouldn't be allowed access to my room for several hours. The brass nameplate did indeed show three stars. The building dated from the end of the nineteenth century and the stone was somewhat crumbling, as if the place was slowly but imperceptibly falling down. The main door was up a short flight of steps, and an African girl was busy cleaning the glass with the name of the hotel etched upon it. She smiled and opened the door for me.

The compact reception area, adorned with brown wallpaper and wooden panelling, smelled of lavender. A thick, worn rug covered the floor. It was dark red, with a motif of smiling mermaids woven into it. A man was standing behind the counter, looking at me with what I perceived to be an odd expression. Then I realised he had a glass eye, just like Oslovski.

I produced my credit card and my temporary passport, and told him in halting French that I had a room booked. He immediately found my name on his computer screen and said that a different card had been used to secure the booking. I explained that this was my wife's card, but that I wanted him to use the one I had just handed over.

"Will I be able to get into the room at two o'clock?" I asked.

The receptionist wore a name badge announcing that he was Monsieur Pierre. His expression was friendly as he said, "You can go up now. We had a guest who left very early, poor man — at half past four."

He nodded in the direction of the black girl who was still polishing the glass door.

"Rachel has already cleaned your room."

He took down an old, heavy key with the number 213, pointed towards the lift and bade me welcome.

My room overlooked a courtyard at the back. Just as in the reception area, everything was in shades of brown, and once again there was the scent of lavender. The place wasn't large, but Rachel had done her job well. I took off my shoes, folded back the bedspread and lay down. I gazed up at the ceiling, where a network of thin black cracks extended across a white background.

The ceiling was like a fog that was beginning to lift.

I took out my phone and tried Louise's number once again. Still no answer, still no possibility of leaving a message.

I thought about the ruins of my house. About the tent out on the skerry, used by some unknown person.

And now room 213.

I remembered what Louise had told me about the Japanese garden known as the Ocean of Emptiness.

Suddenly there was just one thought in my head. I didn't want to die of a heart attack or a stroke in this hotel room. Not before I had found my daughter. I sat up; I had to start searching for her. I went over to the window; it was raining harder now.

I caught a glimpse of a rat disappearing among the rubbish bins.

I left the room. The lift was busy and didn't arrive even though I pressed the button several times. I met

Rachel on the stairs, carrying a pile of clean sheets. She smiled at me again, and I thanked her for cleaning my room so well. I gave her a five-euro note and carried on down the stairs.

When I glanced over my shoulder, she was standing there watching me.

CHAPTER
FIFTEEN

In reception I asked Monsieur Pierre if I could borrow the Paris telephone directories. He immediately offered to look up the number I wanted on his computer, but I declined; I didn't want to tell him that I was going to make a list of all the prisons and police stations in the city.

He gave me the heavy directories; I also asked him for a pen and some paper, then settled down in the closed bar. I spent almost an hour jotting down addresses and phone numbers. I also found the name of the prison where I had spent an afternoon, a night and several hours the following morning in the spring of 1968.

I had realised that my visit coincided with the student riots only when I was looking for cheap accommodation around the Latin Quarter. I ended up right in the middle of utter chaos — burning cars, tear gas, riot police, a boiling sea of people. Of course I was aware of the student movement in Europe, but I had never been a part of it. I had just started training to be a doctor and never joined in the political discussions over lunch or at break time. I distrusted those who became doctors in order to travel to poor countries. I wanted to be a doctor so that I could earn a good salary and have the freedom to choose where I worked. The thought of going off to Africa or Asia was complete anathema to me. I regarded my colleagues who were contemplating such a course of action as naive; I had no doubt that they would change their minds or regret their decision. Today I think I was probably wrong.

I had gone to Paris for a week because my exams were over. I went alone, looking forward to strolling along the boulevards. I had no plans other than to immerse myself in the anonymity of the city.

I found a small, shabby boarding house not far from the Sorbonne, then went out for something to eat. There were no demonstrations, no burning cars, no ranks of riot police. I turned into a side street where I knew there were a number of restaurants. It was a very short street, and in seconds two police cars arrived and blocked off both ends. A large number of officers poured out and arrested everyone in sight. There was no explanation; I was simply thrown in the back of a dark blue police van with barred windows and driven away. We were an odd mixture of men and women, French workers, students and foreign tourists. Nobody knew what was going on. One of the women started to cry. I don't remember whether I was afraid or merely surprised. However, I do recall that I was very hungry.

I didn't get any food until the following day. We were delivered to the police station on the Île de la Cité and bundled into a gigantic windowless cellar. I counted over two hundred people sitting on the stone floor or on the benches lining the whitewashed walls. I could

250

see no connection between the members of this disparate group. Some of the women might have been prostitutes, judging by their clothing, but most were perfectly ordinary people. No doubt many of them were just as hungry as I was.

Our passports or ID documents were taken away, but no one would tell us why we had been arrested. During the night a rumour spread, alleging that it had nothing to do with the student protests. Apparently some hitchhikers had murdered a driver somewhere between Rouen and Paris. I looked around the enormous prison cell and couldn't see anyone that looked like a hitchhiking killer.

In the morning I was taken to an interview room, where I explained that I was a medical student, that I had a week off and was staying in a boarding house in Paris. The officer sighed, returned my passport and suggested that I should avoid open areas for the rest of my visit. As I was hungry and tired after a sleepless night on the concrete floor, I immediately replied, "I'm on the side of the students, of course."

I went straight to a cafe and ordered coffee and sandwiches. I spent the rest of the week sticking close to the walls of buildings whenever I ventured out, and I felt a surge of anxiety every time I saw a police car.

I gave the directories back to Monsieur Pierre and left the hotel, taking care not to leave any fingerprints on the newly polished glass doors.

The sun was shining through a thin mist. I was struck by the fact that the people I saw, with very few exceptions, were younger than me. It had never been more noticeable. I was part of a marginal group on my way out of this life. Every person who passed me drove the point home as they hurried towards destinations of which I knew nothing.

When I was young I was one of those people who used to run up the escalator. I was always in a rush, even if I wasn't actually going anywhere in particular. One desolate Midsummer's Eve in Stockholm I went to visit the Museum of Modern Art in Skeppsholmen. Afterwards I followed an attractive woman, who must have been ten years older than me, taking care to keep my distance. My only aim was to watch her walking in front of me. We had reached Norrmalmstorg when she suddenly stopped, turned and smiled. I caught up with her and she asked what I wanted.

"Nothing," I said. "I guess we're just going in the same direction."

"No," she replied. "We're not. And you are going to stay here and stop following me, otherwise I won't be smiling."

I watched her turn into Biblioteksgatan. At that moment I wasn't the oldest person on the street.

The memory of that long night in the prison cell had made me hungry. I strolled down the street and couldn't help calling in at La Coupole, even though I suspected that particular restaurant charged an arm and a leg because of its reputation. To my surprise it wasn't too busy. I was immediately shown to a table for one overlooking the pavement cafe.

I studied the menu, trying to get used to the noise echoing around the room. I had sat here alone or in

252

company each time I visited Paris — sometimes very late at night, occasionally during the peaceful hours of the afternoon. I had once initiated a conversation with an American lady on the next table; it transpired that she was a doctor at a hospital in Tulsa. For some reason which I still don't understand, I didn't tell her that I was a doctor; instead I turned myself into an architect with a small practice in a town in Denmark. I must have been very drunk, I think, and amused by the idea of putting on a mask and pretending to be someone else. I vaguely remembered the meaningless and totally fictitious descriptions of a manor house I was busy designing.

I dismissed my memories of the American lady. After some indecision I plumped for a pasta dish and a beer. The waiter had beads of sweat on his forehead. Even before he had finished taking my order, he was on his way to another table.

My sense of being the oldest person was reinforced when I glanced around the restaurant. The waiters were young, and most of the diners were nowhere near my age. There was the odd middle-aged man or woman, but they were few and far between.

I ate my meal and ordered a Calvados with my coffee afterwards. By the time I emerged my head was a little woolly. I decided to walk all the way to the Swedish embassy on Rue Barbet-de-Jouy, near Varenne. I didn't need a map to find my way from Montparnasse. All thoughts of my age had vanished; I was enjoying being out and about on the streets of Paris.

I went wrong more than once, and it took me a long time to reach the embassy. The gold-coloured sign below the Swedish state insignia informed me that the consular section was open. I went to a nearby cafe and had an espresso while I thought through the events that had been set in motion by Louise's desperate phone call. I needed the embassy's help to track her down and possibly to obtain legal representation and support.

I crossed the street and went inside. The woman on reception spoke Swedish with a French accent. I explained why I was there.

"How old is your daughter?" she asked.

"She's forty. She's also expecting her first child."

"And you're sure she's been arrested?"

"She wouldn't lie about something like that."

"But she didn't tell you where she was?"

"She didn't have time. That's why I'm here."

"And she's accused of being a pickpocket?"

"I'm afraid that might be how she makes her living, but I'm not sure."

She looked a little dubious. I nodded, hoping to make her understand that I wasn't exaggerating. She picked up the phone and spoke to someone on the other end.

"If you wait over there by the newspapers, Petra will come down and you can explain your business to her."

"My daughter is not 'business'. She's a person."

I sat down by the newspapers and contemplated a portrait of the king and queen. It was crooked. I got up and gave it a push so that it was even more askew.

254

Petra couldn't have been more than twenty-five years old and looked like an overgrown child in her jeans and a thin top straining over a generous bust. She was frowning as she held out her hand.

She sat down and asked, "How can I help?"

"Not here. This isn't something to be discussed in a corner where people come to read the newspapers. I'm assuming you have an office?"

She looked at me with something I interpreted as distaste. I realised we wouldn't be going anywhere.

I told her what had happened, giving dates and times, from Louise's initial phone call to my arrival in Paris, and the fact that I hadn't managed to contact her. I also explained that we hadn't known about one another until Louise was an adult, and that I had only recently realised that she probably made her living as a pickpocket. At least sometimes. Hopefully not all the time.

I could see from Petra's name badge that her surname was Munter, but it didn't give a title. She took notes while I was talking, occasionally raising her hand to stop me until she had caught up.

"This can't be the first time a parent has turned up at the embassy, worried because their child has disappeared or ended up in prison," I said. "You must know what I ought to do."

"First of all we need to find out where she is. We have official channels."

"So you're responsible for what the receptionist referred to as my 'business'?"

"I'm a trainee," Petra said. "I'm at the bottom of the heap. But I'm the one who kicks this upstairs or makes the decision not to pursue the matter."

"And you're going to kick it upstairs?"

"I think what you've told me is perfectly true."

"I'm worried about my daughter."

She made a note of my mobile number and the name of my hotel.

"We should know more tomorrow," she said, rising to her feet to indicate that the meeting was over.

"My daughter is pregnant," I said again. "She was scared when she called me."

Petra Munter gazed at me for a long time. She suddenly seemed to have grown up, no longer the teenager I had seen when she walked into reception.

"I'll make sure something is done, but the French don't like foreign thieves operating here. They don't exactly get a slapped wrist."

"So what do they get?"

She pulled a face but didn't answer. I pictured Louise sitting in the same cellar where I had once spent the night.

Petra walked me to the door and I shook her hand.

"Someone will contact you tomorrow," she said. "You have my word."

As she walked away, I remembered something else.

"I need a passport," I said. "A few weeks ago my house burned down. Everything was destroyed. I travelled here on a provisional passport, but I'd feel better if I had a proper one."

"We have an excellent machine here," she said. "It produces a Swedish passport within a very short time. But you could just as easily wait until you get back home."

I left the embassy, making a mental note of the opening hours, and set off back to Montparnasse.

My mobile rang. There was a lot of traffic, so I hurried into a side street before I answered. It was a Swedish number that I didn't immediately recognise.

It was Jansson.

"I noticed you weren't at home," he yelled.

Jansson always yells down the phone. He has never been able to accept that distance is irrelevant when he makes a call or when someone calls him. I remembered old fru Hultin, who lived on Vesselskär for a long time after she was widowed. I used to help her out with her bad feet now and again.

"Jansson screams like a jay," she would say whenever he came up in the conversation. She herself spoke so quietly on the phone that it was hard to make out what she was saying. She probably thought that everyone in the archipelago was sitting by their phone, listening to the latest gossip about her corns.

"How do you know I'm not at home?"

"I happened to be passing. The police have been looking for you."

"They haven't phoned me."

"They came by boat. Something to do with the fire."

"Have I been charged?"

"I don't know anything about that."

"So what did they say?"

"They just asked if I knew where you were."

"But you didn't?"

"No."

"I left a note for Alexandersson before I left. He knows I'm away."

"So I don't need to worry?"

"Why would you worry? Was it you who set fire to my house?"

"Why would you say such a thing?"

"I'm in Paris."

"What the hell are you doing there?"

Jansson rarely swears. Just as he rarely uses his beautiful singing voice.

"I'm the one who's looking for the police, rather than the other way round."

"I haven't a clue what you're talking about."

"It seems as if Louise has got into some difficulties, but I'd rather you didn't spread that throughout the archipelago."

"I would never do such a thing."

"Both you and I know that you would. During all those years when you were a postman you spread just as many rumours as letters." Jansson said nothing, but I knew he was offended. "The police must have said something else," I went on.

"They asked me to let them know when you came back."

"And of course you said you would?"

"What else was I supposed to say?"

"Has there been anything in the newspaper?"

"No."

I wondered what I should ask Jansson to do; I didn't want anyone thinking I had fled from my homeland.

"So you're really in Paris?"

"My battery's running out; you're breaking up."

It wasn't true, but Jansson would carry on trying to draw the story out of me unless I ended the call right now.

"Talk to you later," I said and hung up.

I was sweating. The fact that the police were looking for me could only mean they were convinced I was guilty. I hated sympathy, particularly when it was offered by people as stupid as Jansson. Only I have the right to feel sorry for myself.

I strolled along Boul'Mich and stopped at the bistro where Jean-Paul Sartre and Simone de Beauvoir used to spend their days. There were lots of people inside, so I sat down at one of the pavement tables. I had a coffee and two glasses of Calvados. My trip to Paris was beginning to resemble an alcohol-sodden escape from my isolated island, where the ruins of my burned-out house lay waiting for the winter snow.

I tried to think through what would happen when I found Louise. I didn't even know what she was accused of.

I couldn't focus. I headed back to the hotel, my pace getting slower and slower. When I glanced at the shop windows, I saw an old man's face looking back at me. A lady by the name of Madame Rosini was on duty instead of Monsieur Pierre, and gave me my key. They were very much alike, somehow: the same faint smile, the same warmth. There was no sign of Rachel.

I lay down on the bed and fell asleep. In my dream the house was burning down once more. I ran outside to escape the blinding light, only to be transported straight back to my bed. Over and over again the darkness metamorphosed into dazzling searchlights, searing my eyeballs. My dog, who died several years ago, came back to life. I also thought I saw my last cat, running away with her fur on fire.

It was dark when I woke up. I got undressed and had a shower. The water was just as cold as the sea; I couldn't work out how to adjust the taps.

I had just wound the biggest towel around my waist when my phone rang — a Swedish number again. I hesitated; should I answer? Was it Jansson or someone from the police?

It was Lisa Modin.

"What's the hotel like?" she asked.

"Is that why you're calling?"

"I'm going to come over."

"Today?"

"Tomorrow. Don't ask me why."

"I'm really pleased."

"Don't expect anything."

"Why do you always say that?"

"I just want to make sure you're not expecting anything."

"When are you arriving?"

"I don't know."

"I'll come and meet you."

"I don't want you to do that. Have you found your daughter?"

"I've been to the embassy; they're hoping to be able to help me tomorrow."

The connection was broken; perhaps Lisa had ended the call. I tried her number but couldn't get through. However, she was coming to Paris, and she knew which hotel I was staying in. That must mean she wanted to see me. Everything was changing. I got dressed and went down to reception. Monsieur Pierre was back, looking less than clean-shaven.

I asked whether a Madame Modin from Sweden had booked a room for the following day. He studied his computer screen, then shook his head.

"No Madame from Sweden, I'm afraid. Just a Canadian lady, Madame Andrews, who comes to stay with us once a year, in the autumn."

I went out into the mild November evening. I ambled down to Gare Montparnasse, bought a Swedish newspaper, then went into a little restaurant that seemed to serve only French customers. I couldn't see any tourists. I ordered sweetbreads; they weren't very nice, but I was hungry. I drank wine and thought about my daughter, Lisa Modin and bloody Jansson — I would never be able to work him out.

When I had finished eating I drank a cup of coffee while I flicked through the newspaper. I realised I had already read it while I was waiting at the airport.

I left the restaurant feeling unexpectedly cheerful. I set off towards the Latin Quarter, even though my legs were aching from all the walking I had done during the day.

On the way I was once again overwhelmed by the feeling that I was older than everyone else.

I thought about Louise. Had someone at the embassy managed to track her down in the labyrinth of Paris police stations?

It occurred to me with something that might have been sorrow that I had never allowed myself to be Louise's father. When she suddenly came into my life, I regarded her as more of a nuisance than a joy for a long time. Needless to say I had never admitted this to her. Nor had I confronted Harriet with my feelings, although I did blame her. She had robbed me of my daughter. Even though Louise was now part of my world, I would always be incapable of loving her the way I imagined one would love a child.

But perhaps that love would blossom when I met the child she was carrying? Or was that already a lost cause?

I wandered the streets, unable to reach any kind of clarity. Eventually I decided that the birth of a child meant the beginning of a new story in the great chronicle of mankind.

I had reached the lower part of the Jardin du Luxembourg when I remembered a jazz club I used to frequent whenever I came to Paris: Caveau de la Huchette. I knew exactly where it was. Perhaps it was still a jazz club? I needed a goal for my evening stroll.

I went into a bistro for a coffee. I noticed that a black woman who was sitting at a table with a man of about the same age kept glancing over at me. I looked around to see if she might be trying to attract the attention of someone else, but there was no one there — just the window panes glimmering in the light of the street lamps. She was perhaps ten years younger than me. I didn't recognise her. I concentrated on my coffee, but every time I raised my eyes she was staring at me.

She must recognise me. Or possibly she thought she knew who I was, which seemed more likely.

She stood up abruptly and came towards me, pushing her way between the tables. Her husband, or whoever her companion was, seemed totally uninterested.

She spoke to me in English; I naturally assumed she had mistaken me for someone else.

"I'm sure I recognise you," she said. I gestured to the chair opposite, and she sat down. "I remember your face," she went on. "From a long time ago. My mother was the same; she could recognise a person she had met only once, thirty or forty years earlier."

"And you can do that?"

"Yes."

"But I have no idea who you are. Your face doesn't ring any bells, your voice hasn't triggered anything in my memory."

She looked at me searchingly.

"Now I'm certain," she said. "When we were both young you came to the customs office here in Paris to pick up a typewriter someone had sent you — I don't remember which country it was from. You had to pay import duty because it was new, but you didn't have any money. In the end I let you take it without paying anything. You were almost in tears."

Now I remembered not just her but the whole situation. I had gone to Paris with a burning ambition to become a writer. I had sent a letter to my father, asking him to buy a typewriter and send it to me. I promised I would earn enough money through my writing to be able to pay him back. I didn't think for a moment that he would actually do it, but one day I was summoned to the French customs office. And it was indeed the woman sitting opposite me who had allowed me to take away the pale blue typewriter in its black case without paying the import duty.

"How can you possibly remember that?" I asked her.

"I don't know. I just saw you and I knew exactly who you were. You pleaded with me; you were young and poor. Was it Ireland you came from?"

"Sweden."

"How did things turn out for you? Did you become a writer?"

"I became a doctor."

"And what happened to the typewriter?"

"I sold it a few years later when I ran out of money." She nodded and got to her feet.

"Sometimes people do meet again," she said. "I'm glad I inherited my mother's ability to recognise faces."

She smiled and went back to her table. I was astounded. She didn't seem to be telling her husband what had transpired.

I left the bistro; my legs were no longer aching, my footsteps felt light. For a while I was an old man allowing myself to forget about my burned-out house.

The club was exactly where I thought it was. I paid and went in. It was still early. My memories from all those years ago involved going down the stairs to a cellar bar late at night; now it was only eleven o'clock. The staircase and the cellar bar were the same, but when I reached the bottom step I realised I should have taken a closer look at the poster outside to see what kind of music was on tonight. The instruments and amplifiers arranged on the stage in the far corner told me it wasn't going to be either modern or trad jazz. When I glanced around in the semi-darkness I could see that a reggae band was taking a break; there were dreadlocks and brightly coloured Rasta hats everywhere. However, there were plenty of older men and women with greying dreads sitting at the tables; I wasn't the only person of my age.

I went to the bar and ordered a glass of Calvados. When the music burst into life behind me, I felt a wave of warmth flood my body.

I stayed by the bar and carried on drinking. The compact dance floor was soon packed; everyone seemed to be dancing with everyone else. Small, almost imperceptible movements of the legs and hips. The gentle sway made me think of the smooth swell of the sea.

A woman wearing a colourful turban was standing next to me at the bar. I asked if she would like to dance; I was astonished at my own courage. She said yes. We shuffled onto the floor. I learned the basics of dancing when I was at school, but on the few occasions when I danced with Harriet I was embarrassed by my ineptitude. Now, even though the floor was so crowded, I felt at more of a loss than ever. My partner noticed at once; I was moving as if I had hooves. Her disappointment was obvious; she looked at me as if I had deceived her, then walked away and left me there. Total humiliation.

I went up the stairs, followed by the sound of reggae music, and out onto the street.

I had almost reached my hotel when I took out my phone for some reason. It hadn't rung, but I discovered that there was a text message from Louise: *Where are you?*

I tried to call her, but I still couldn't get through.

"I'm here," I said out loud to myself. "I'm actually here."

CHAPTER
SIXTEEN

I hated the woman who had left me on the dance floor. With every step I took towards my hotel, I subjected her to increasingly vicious attacks in my head.

On a dark street just before I reached the Gare Montparnasse a drunken man came up to me and asked for cigarettes. I told him I hadn't smoked for thirty years.

I was afraid he might attack me, but the tone of my voice clearly made him think again, and he staggered away.

I had difficulty sleeping that night. The incident in the club hurt; I was still embarrassed. I lay awake for a long time. I thought I could hear the guests in neighbouring rooms starting to make preparations to leave, and a cleaning trolley trundled past. I wondered if it was Rachel, starting work at this early hour.

It was five o'clock by the time I managed to doze off in my brown room. At eight my mobile rang; it was the embassy, a man who introduced himself as Olof Rutgersson. I wasn't sure I understood his title.

"We still haven't managed to locate your daughter," he said.

He had a nasal voice; I'm sure it wasn't his fault that it gave his tone an air of arrogance.

"What happens now?"

"We will definitely find her. After all, Paris is a city not a continent. She's probably under local arrest, but that does mean the search will take time. I'll be in touch as soon as I have something further to communicate on this matter."

I wanted to protest at the way he expressed himself: "something further to communicate on this matter"?! But I said nothing; I needed him.

There were hardly any guests in the breakfast room, where the gigantic head of a kudu with large curly horns hung on the wall next to etchings of bridges over the Seine. Monsieur Pierre had once again been replaced by Madame Rosini, while a short Vietnamese girl took my order for coffee.

There was a bottle of sparkling wine in an ice bucket, and I couldn't resist the temptation. My anger towards the woman who had abandoned me on the dance floor dissipated.

After breakfast I took a short walk to the railway station and bought a Swedish newspaper. When I got back to the hotel I sank down in a worn leather armchair in reception.

I liked the hotel. Lisa Modin had made a good choice. Before I started reading the paper, I asked Madame Rosini if they had received a booking for a Swedish lady. They hadn't. She must have decided to stay somewhere else.

I leafed through the paper; it was half past ten. Rachel came down the stairs carrying a basket of cloths and cleaning products. She smiled before making a start on the glass door.

My phone rang; it was the man from the embassy.

"Good news," he said. "We've found your daughter. She's at a police station in Belleville."

"What on earth is she doing in that part of the city?"

"I can't answer that, but I'll come and pick you up."

Exactly one hour later a chauffeur-driven car with diplomatic plates pulled up outside the hotel. I got in beside Olof Rutgersson. He was aged about fifty and rather thin. His face was grey, colourless.

As we drove off I asked him to tell me what he knew.

"I haven't got much to report," he said. "We found her through our usual channels and the extraordinarily poor computer system used by the French police. That's all I know. The important thing now is to assess her position so that we can work out how to proceed."

"You're talking about my daughter as if she were a ship," I said.

"It's just words," Olof Rutgersson replied. "By the way, I suggest you let me do the talking when we arrive. I have diplomatic status. You don't."

He made a few calls; I noticed he had a small tattoo just above his wrist. It said *MUM*.

We were in a traffic jam, and Rutgersson was talking on his phone when I recognised the street, one of Haussmann's wide boulevards.

I knew where I was. One day almost fifty years ago I had come up from the Metro exactly where our car was currently stuck in a queue of impatient drivers. It was during the period when I was working illegally, sitting in a little workshop in Jourdain repairing clarinets under the quiet guidance of Monsieur Simon. I don't remember how I got the job, but it didn't pay well. The workshop was in a backyard, and it was cramped and dirty. Apart from Monsieur Simon, who was a kind man, there was another young man working there who was fat, short-sighted and downright unpleasant. As soon as Monsieur Simon was out on some errand, he would start having a go at me, telling me that I was a burden because I had clumsy fingers and always arrived late in the mornings. I never argued with him, I simply despised his cowardice and wished he would drop dead among his saxophone valves.

Sometimes Monsieur Simon would send me out to various music shops to deliver instruments that had been repaired. It was as I emerged from the Metro with a parcel under my arm that I had found myself in the middle of a huge crowd. At first I thought there had been an accident, but then I realised people were waiting for someone to pass by. I peered down the road and saw President de Gaulle approaching; he was standing in an open-topped car. I had the instrument under my arm, and I made a movement with the other hand to get my cigarettes out of an inside pocket. I immediately felt two pairs of hands seize my wrist and shoulder. I dropped the clarinet. The two men, who I later realised were plain-clothes security guards, had thought I was reaching for a gun.

When they were satisfied that I had no evil intentions, and that my parcel contained a clarinet and not a bomb, they simply shrugged and let me go.

By that time the president was long gone, and the crowd had begun to disperse.

"I once saw President de Gaulle just here," I said to Olof Rutgersson.

He was busy sending a text and didn't hear what I said.

"I once saw de Gaulle," I repeated. "Just here. Almost fifty years ago."

"Of course you did," he replied. "Of course you saw de Gaulle just here. Fifty years ago."

I felt like punching him. After I'd taken his phone and chucked it out of the car window. I wished I were that kind of person. But I wasn't.

I didn't notice the name of the street on which the police station in Belleville was situated. Rutgersson leaped out of the car with an energy I found surprising. He had spent the journey yawning, hunched over his phone. Now he was transformed. He repeated his earlier exhortation to let him do the talking.

A young drug addict was throwing up in the shabby reception area while two uniformed officers observed him with distaste. A plain-clothes officer behind the tall desk nodded to Rutgersson when he waved his diplomatic pass. After a brief telephone call an older officer who walked with a stick emerged from another room. We accompanied him to an office where the air was thick with dust from a desk piled high with papers and shelves bellying under the weight of books and files. I had the sense of having been transported several hundred years back in time. The premises of law enforcers must have looked like this during Napoleon's day.

The man lowered himself laboriously into the chair behind the desk; I realised he was in considerable pain. His stiff hands told me that he probably suffered from severe rheumatism.

Olof Rutgersson took the visitor's chair on the other side of the desk and waved me to a seat by the door. He spoke fluent French. He also spoke very quickly, with the emphasis typical of those who tolerate no contradictions. I found it difficult to follow the conversation, but I did grasp that there was some doubt as to whether Louise was actually at this police station. The officer, whose name was Armand, sent for a younger colleague who couldn't help either. When the two Frenchmen had finished talking, Rutgersson stood up and came over to me.

"It's always the same with the French police," he said. "You can never get any sense out of anybody."

"So Louise isn't here?"

"The French police often lose people, but of course we're not giving up. I expect the Swedish police are the same."

After yet more confused conversations and various junior officers running in and out, it seemed that Louise had been at the station, but earlier that morning she had been transferred to a custody suite on the Île de la Cité. Armand was unable to tell us why. He drank cup after cup of strong black coffee; as he grimaced at

272

the temperature of the liquid, I saw that he had bad teeth, which made me feel slightly nauseous. Olof Rutgersson showed great tenacity, insisting that he wanted to know why Louise had been moved and what exactly she was accused of. He didn't get any answers. The van that had collected her and a number of other individuals who were under arrest had taken all the paperwork.

"Was she with anyone else?" I asked.

Rutgersson passed on the question, but no one could tell us whether Louise had known any of those who had been arrested at the same time.

It took half an hour, with Rutgersson getting increasingly annoyed, before he realised there was no point in staying in Belleville. When we left the police station, he wanted something to eat, so we went to a nearby cafe while the chauffeur waited in the car. I drank tea while Rutgersson had coffee and a sandwich.

My phone rang; it was Lisa Modin. Rutgersson listened discreetly to our brief conversation.

"The girl's mother?" he asked.

"She's dead. That was a friend."

"I'm sorry. I didn't know you'd lost your wife."

"We weren't married, we just had a daughter together."

As we left Belleville, the traffic heavier now, Rutgersson went back to making calls and sending texts. He wore a wedding ring on his left hand. I tried to picture his wife but without success.

I was waiting for Lisa to call back. I hadn't been able to work out whether she was already in Paris. The thought of sharing a room with her, lying right next to her, sometimes drove Louise out of my head completely. I was too old to have a guilty conscience. I didn't want to end up like my father. As he got older and was plagued with severe joint pain, he began to brood about the people he had treated badly or bullied during his lifetime. Even though he had been just as shabbily treated by unpleasant maître d's and toffee-nosed customers, it was as if he was determined to spend the time he had left atoning for his sins.

I remember one occasion just after my mother's death when I went to visit him in the small, dingy apartment in Vasastan. I had recently qualified as a doctor, and had taken my stethoscope and blood pressure monitor with me to show my father that I was now able to check those aspects of his health that he constantly worried about.

I stayed the night, going to bed early because I had to be at the hospital in the Söder district the following morning. My father had a tendency to wander late at night. He had spent so many years as a waiter that he rarely went to bed before three o'clock in the morning.

I suddenly woke up without knowing why. The door of my bedroom was ajar, and I could hear my father dialling a telephone number. I wondered who he was calling at this hour. I got out of bed and crept over to the door; I could see him sitting there with the receiver pressed to his ear. When he didn't get an answer, he gently replaced it and crossed off a name on the handwritten list in front of him.

274

He was asleep when I got up in the morning. I looked at the piece of paper by the telephone; it was a list of names, people I didn't know. Next to some of the names he had made a note that the person in question was dead. There were also various telephone numbers followed by a question mark.

The next time I visited him, I asked him about the nocturnal calls. Who was he ringing? Who were the people on his list? He told me without hesitation that they were people he thought he had mistreated during his life. Now, before it was too late, he wanted to call them and apologise. Unfortunately many of them had already passed away, which he found very difficult to deal with. I wondered whether that was why he had started neglecting his clothing; he no longer bothered to change if there were stains on his shirts or trousers.

He died six months after our conversation. I have no idea how many of those on the list he managed to speak to by then, but I kept it when I cleared his apartment. It had been in my desk drawer ever since, until my house burned down. Now it was gone for good.

We drove across the bridge to the Île de la Cité and found the address we had been given. Olof Rutgersson brandished his diplomatic pass like a crucifix, and within no time we had tracked down someone who would be able to tell us where Louise was. A female preliminary investigator called us into her spacious office, which I was surprised to see contained a grand piano, a Bechstein. She asked us to sit down and opened the file in front of her on the desk. She turned to me because I was Louise's father, but Rutgersson immediately took over; he was the one who wanted answers to our questions. The woman, who was wearing a wine-red skirt suit and had a small burn mark on one cheek, spoke just as quickly as Rutgersson. I had no chance of following the conversation. I had begun to change my opinion of Rutgersson; he seemed to be taking his task extremely seriously. He was not indifferent to what had befallen Louise after all. From time to time he interrupted the Frenchwoman, and gave me a brief summary of what was being said.

Eventually the picture became clear. Louise had been arrested after stealing a wallet from someone's inside pocket on a crowded Metro train near Saint-Sulpice. It appeared that she had been taken to Belleville, which was some considerable distance away, because the local custody facilities were already full. There was no doubt that she had stolen the wallet. The elderly victim hadn't noticed anything, but a fellow passenger had seen exactly what Louise had done and had grabbed her. It turned out he was a civilian employee of the French police.

There was no evidence that anyone else was involved, but she probably hadn't been working alone.

Louise had been arrested and would be formally charged. According to Rutgersson, over the past twelve months the French police had made a point of tackling the increase in muggings and the large number of pickpockets operating in Paris, which had almost become like Barcelona, the pickpockets' European paradise. When I asked him to find out if it would be possible to let Louise off with a caution because she didn't have a criminal record in France and was pregnant, the French officer merely spread her hands wide. It seemed unlikely that Louise would be released any time soon.

"Can't they just fine her?" I asked.

"It's too early to discuss any kind of penalty," Rutgersson replied. "The most important thing right now is to see her and hear her version of events."

"The most important thing is that she knows we're here," I said. "Everything else is secondary."

A uniformed officer led us through corridors, down stairs and passageways, moving deeper and deeper underground. I began to wonder if this really was the place where I had been held when I was picked up by the police in 1968. I thought I recognised the whitewashed vaulted cellar, the steel doors, the wooden benches, the distant sounds of people shouting to one another. The place was a maze; you could get lost at any moment and never find your way out.

Eventually Rutgersson and I were shown into a windowless room with a dark-stained wooden table and a few rickety chairs. We waited, Rutgersson with a kind of exaggerated calm, while I became more and more agitated. Then the door opened and Louise was brought in by a female officer. She was wearing her own clothes, a pair of trousers and a shirt I recognised. She was very pale. For the first time I could remember she looked pleased to see me. She usually regarded me with some degree of caution, but not this time.

She wasn't handcuffed, and the officer made no attempt to stop me from hugging her.

"You came," Louise said.

"Of course I came."

"In my life people don't usually come when I need them."

I introduced her to Olof Rutgersson. The police officer had stationed herself by the door and seemed to have no interest in our conversation. We sat down at the table, and Louise immediately began to tell us what had happened.

She admitted stealing the wallet on the crowded train. I no longer had any doubt that this was how she made her living, but she was prepared to admit only this one incident. I had some sympathy with her; why should she reveal to Rutgersson that her principal source of income was whatever she managed to steal? We had established a tacit mutual understanding. She had been arrested for the theft of this one wallet, nothing else.

"Are you so short of money?" Rutgersson asked when she fell silent.

Once again I changed my mind about him. I had thought he was an energetic and efficient embassy official; now I saw a remarkably insensitive individual sitting beside me.

"Why else would she have stolen a wallet?" I said. "Don't forget she's pregnant, and that her inheritance, my house in Sweden, burned to the ground just a few weeks ago."

Rutgersson looked at me in surprise, and I realised I hadn't mentioned my house. I told him the story, and he nodded to himself.

"We'll sort out legal representation for you," he said. "Unfortunately the embassy can't cover the cost, but we can advance you the money for the time being."

"Will it be expensive?" I asked.

"Not necessarily."

"Then I'll pay."

He nodded and took out his phone, but there was no signal deep in the bowels of the building. He exchanged a few words with the officer, who let him out. I heard his footsteps hurrying up the stairs as he sought daylight and a phone signal.

I took my daughter's hand. I wasn't used to doing such a thing. For the first time since that day almost ten years ago, when Harriet had told me that the woman standing in the doorway of her caravan in the forests of Hälsingland was my daughter, I actually felt as if she was.

I wished that Harriet was still alive, able to see that at long last Louise and I had found one another.

I asked her how she was feeling. I asked about the baby. She answered quietly that everything was fine. Eventually I couldn't avoid asking why she hadn't turned up for lunch that day, why she had simply left a note under my windscreen wiper.

"I just needed to get away."

I left it there. Her response made it clear that she didn't want to tell me why she had suddenly taken off.

We got quite close while Rutgersson was upstairs chasing a phone signal. I felt I understood my daughter better than I had in the past; she was running away, but nothing more.

I had one more question.

"You called me. Did you call anyone else?"

"No."

"Why me? Of course it was absolutely the right thing to do, but just a few days earlier you'd gone off and left me without a word."

"There's no one else I can ask for help."

"You've always said you have a lot of friends."

"That might not be true."

"Why would a person lie about something like that?"

"I have no idea what other people do, but I don't always tell the truth. Just like you."

I could tell from her voice that she didn't want to continue the conversation. We'd gone this far but no further. She had called me. No one else.

Rutgersson returned; there was something weasel-like about the way he moved. He brandished the phone as if it were a gun. He always seemed to be in a hurry.

"Madame Riveri will take on your case," he said before the police officer had time to close the door behind him. "She's helped us out in the past; on three separate occasions she's managed to get Swedish citizens out of tricky situations. We can safely leave matters with her."

He shook hands with Louise and wished her luck.

"Unfortunately I can't stay," he said. "I have a meeting at the embassy. But Madame Riveri will keep me informed."

He left the room, and I could hear his footsteps dashing up the stairs.

"He's been a great help," I said.

"I'm glad he's not the father of my child," was Louise's response.

I didn't understand what she meant. Or perhaps I did.

Madame Riveri was about fifty years old and elegantly dressed. She moved and talked in a relaxed manner which left no one in any doubt about her opinion of her own ability in legal affairs. With a firm gesture she dismissed the female officer and took a notebook out of her bag. When she realised that Louise's French wasn't good enough to sustain a meaningful discussion, she switched to English. I now heard in detail how Louise had travelled around on the Metro looking for a suitable victim. Madame Riveri wanted to know exactly where and when she had boarded the first train, where she had changed and why she had chosen that particular man as her target. The way Louise answered convinced me that she trusted Madame Riveri.

They spoke about the baby, but the identity of the father wasn't mentioned. Finally Madame Riveri asked if this was the first time Louise had committed a crime. She said it was, but I could see that the other woman didn't believe her. Louise's dexterity spoke of a great deal of practice over a long period.

"What you have just told me is not true, of course. However, it will help our case if you are a first-time offender who just happened to get caught."

Madame Riveri snapped her leather-bound notebook shut and slipped it into her bag.

"I would ask you not to speak to anyone unless I am present," she said. "We'll have you out of here in a couple of days, three at the most. I doubt if it will be sooner, but it is possible."

She got to her feet, shook Louise's hand then nodded to indicate that she wanted me to accompany her. The police officer escorted Louise away and I trotted up the stairs after Madame Riveri; she was moving so fast that I found it difficult to keep up. When we were out on the street and the heavy door had closed behind us, she gave me her card.

"I'll pay whatever it costs, of course," I said.

She gave me an ironic smile. "Indeed," she said. "But we don't need to discuss that at the moment."

I wanted to find out what was going to happen next, but she hailed a cab and disappeared without even saying goodbye.

I set off for my hotel. There was rain in the air. I stopped on the bridge over the Seine and watched a barge as it passed beneath me. A woman was hanging out washing, and there was a pram anchored to the deck. I jumped when someone tapped me on the shoulder. I turned and looked straight, into a dirty, unshaven face. When the man asked me for money, there was no avoiding his bad breath. I gave him a euro and walked away.

I remembered my father confiding his great fear: he was terrified that one day he would be unable to pay his bills and would end up living on the street. I never understood why he told me that. Perhaps he wanted to warn me? But I was careful and always made sure I had money put aside in case of something unexpected.

When I reached the hotel, Monsieur Pierre was back with his warm smile. I went into the bar and had a cup of tea as a change from all that coffee before taking the lift up to my room.

I had just lain down on the bed when my telephone rang. It was Madame Riveri; she had arranged an appointment with the magistrate's court for the following day to request that Louise be released and deported from France. She wanted to know if I would be able to pay for my daughter's flight to Sweden; I told her that wasn't a problem.

I fell asleep, and in my dream my father was running around a deserted pavement cafe. It was very windy, and the napkin over his arm was flapping like a partially torn-off wing. I tried to call out to him, but I couldn't force a single sound from my throat.

As my father fell over, I woke up with my heart racing. I sat on the edge of the bed and tried to slow my breathing. After a few minutes I checked my pulse: ninety-seven. Much too fast. I lay down again and thought about my heart. Had I lived a life that put me at risk of an unexpected heart attack? I tried to dismiss the idea but without success. I took a tranquilliser from the pack I always carried with me and waited for it to take effect.

My phone rang again; this time it was Lisa Modin.

"I'm in Paris. Where are you?"

"At the hotel you booked for me."

"Is it OK?"

"Yes. Where are you?"

"At the station — Gare du Nord."

"Not Gare Montparnasse?"

"I'm on my way there."

"Are you staying in this hotel?"

"No, but not far away."

"I'll come and meet you. Just tell me where you are in the station, and I'll come over."

"There's no need. I know where my hotel is."

"I've always dreamed of meeting a woman arriving in Paris."

She laughed, briefly and with a hint of embarrassment.

"I've found my daughter," I said. "I'll tell you more later."

"Pick me up in an hour. I've only just got here; I need to sit down and get used to the idea."

I promised to meet her, then I went down to the bar and ordered a mineral water. Monsieur Pierre was just getting ready to hand over to the night porter.

Thirty minutes later Lisa rang to tell me she was in a small cafe next to a big Dubonnet sign.

There were still plenty of people in the station, but the rush hour was over. I immediately spotted the Dubonnet sign; Lisa was sitting alone, drinking tea next to the barrier separating the cafe from the waiting room. She was wearing a dark blue coat, and her suitcase was by her feet.

I thought how pretty she was, and that she had come to visit me.

I was just about to go over to her when my phone rang. I thought it might be Louise, so I answered.

Needless to say, it was Jansson.

"Am I disturbing you?" he asked. "Where are you?"

"It doesn't matter where I am. What do you want? If you've developed some new imaginary illness, I don't have time for that right now."

"I just wanted to call and tell you there's a fire."

At first I didn't understand what he meant, and then I went cold all over.

"What's on fire? My boathouse?"

"The house on Källö. The widow Westerfeldt's house."

"Has it burned down?"

"It's still burning. I just wanted you to know."

The call ended abruptly; I guessed that Jansson had failed to charge his phone, as usual.

I thought about what he had said; I hoped the widow Westerfeldt had managed to get out. Her house was very similar to mine. It had been built along the same lines by skilled carpenters at the end of the nineteenth century.

I stood there clutching my phone. I was finding it very difficult to process what Jansson had said, but surely it must mean that I couldn't possibly be a suspect? Unless of course there were natural causes behind this latest blaze.

I couldn't know, and yet I was sure. There was a pyromaniac or an arsonist loose on our islands.

I slipped my phone into my pocket, and when I looked over at Lisa again she had seen me. She waved hesitantly, as if she really wanted to hide the gesture.

I waved back and went over to her table.

CHAPTER
SEVENTEEN

We started off talking like strangers who just happened to be sitting next to one another. I ordered wine from the waitress, and we raised our glasses. I brushed against her hand and said I was pleased to see her. I asked pointless questions about her journey; her responses were equally meaningless.

She suggested we should settle the bill; I wanted to pay, but she refused. When I offered to carry her case, she shook her head.

We went to her hotel together. I still hadn't said anything about Louise, and she hadn't asked. I was preoccupied with that horrible phone call from Jansson, and the fact that the widow Westerfeldt's house was in flames right now.

We walked along in silence. Eventually I said, "Paris is always Paris."

"Always," Lisa replied.

Her hotel, the Mignon, appeared to be more modest than mine. A dark-skinned young man was on duty at the small reception desk; apparently guests were issued with some kind of plastic card instead of a heavy key. I waited while Lisa registered and handed over her credit card.

286

"I'm tired," she said. "I need to sleep."

"312," I said. "I'm sure that's a good room. If you're up on the third floor, you won't be disturbed by the traffic."

"I'll see you tomorrow."

The bar next to reception was just about to close.

"Just a few minutes," I said. "Stay for a drink. I've got news."

She hesitated. "I need to wash my hands. I won't be long."

I watched her disappear into the lift; a couple speaking Danish rather too loudly collected their key card and I went into the bar. The woman behind the counter didn't exactly look pleased to see me.

"I won't stay long," I said apologetically. "A glass of red wine, please. A guest who's staying at the hotel will be down shortly. We won't stay long."

She nodded without speaking, poured me a glass of wine then went into the kitchen at the back. I wondered how many bars I had visited in my life. Thought about the endless hours I had spent hunched over wine glasses and coffee cups.

When Lisa came in I could see that she had combed her hair and changed her blouse. The barmaid emerged from the kitchen and asked her what she wanted; Lisa simply pointed to my glass.

"The bar is closing," I said. "She seems a bit annoyed with us."

"My room is small," Lisa said. "I was kind of disappointed, but then I noticed how quiet it was. You were right: I couldn't hear the traffic at all."

"I've found Louise, and she has a lawyer who's helping her. We're hoping she'll be released either tomorrow or the following day, if the judge is sympathetic."

"You must be so pleased. I should have asked about her as soon as we met."

"I'm relieved. A man from the Swedish embassy helped me; without him I would never have found her."

The barmaid brought the bill over, and this time Lisa let me pay. We emptied our glasses and stood up; before we had even got through the door, the lights had been switched off.

"I've got something else to tell you as well," I said when we were waiting for the lift. "Jansson, the man who brought you to the island, called to tell me that a house on a neighbouring island is on fire. Right now, tonight."

"What? And was that deliberate too?"

"I don't know, but fires are rare out on the islands. There's something strange going on. It's frightening."

For the first time since she saw me at the railway station, Lisa actually seemed interested in talking to me. I was disappointed; a burning house was clearly more important than the man who wanted nothing more than to get close to her.

"We can talk about it tomorrow," I said, preparing to leave. "When shall I call round?"

"Let me come to your hotel, then I can see what I booked for you."

We arranged for her to be there at ten. When I got outside I was overcome by the urge to set off into the night, to see where life might take me. Without further thought I went over to a taxi waiting by a lamp post, and asked the driver to take me to the Place Pigalle. He was North African, and he was playing loud music. I asked him to turn it down as we drove off, but he pretended not to hear me.

I had had enough. I yelled at him, told him to pull over. I threw him a handful of euros and got out of the car.

"Fucking music!" I shouted at him through the open side window.

He shouted something in response, but I didn't understand. I had already turned and was walking away. I was afraid he might come after me; if he attacked me, I wouldn't stand a chance. I heard the car screech past; the driver didn't even look at me.

I was so scared I was shaking. I knew I ought to go back to my hotel, but instead I got into another taxi. This one was driven by a grey-haired man; I guessed he was part of the distinguished tradition of Russian taxi drivers in Paris. His radio was switched off. The interior of the car smelled of sausages and strong tea. When I asked him to take me to the Place Pigalle, his only response was a brief nod. He dropped me off near the Moulin Rouge, and I went straight to the nearest bistro.

I drank. A lot. Partly due to relief, because I thought Louise would be released within a day or two, and partly because of Jansson's phone call. I couldn't believe he would have contacted me if this new fire hadn't also been started deliberately.

But I drank mainly because I had realised that whatever reasons Lisa Modin might have had for coming to Paris, they were nothing to do with my hopes and dreams. She might be interested in me as a person, but not as a man.

I kept ordering, kept drinking. Eventually I called Jansson. It was a long time before he answered; he sounded out of breath as he shouted in my ear.

"It's me," I said. "Where are you?"

"We're trying to stop the fire from reaching the barn, but the lovely old house is beyond saving."

"Hold the phone away from your ear."

"What?"

"I want to hear the fire."

He did as I said, and I really thought I could hear the roar of the flames.

"Did you get the widow out?" I asked when he came back on the line.

"They've taken her to the Sundells' place on Ormö so that she doesn't have to see this."

"Take a picture."

"A picture?"

Jansson didn't seem to understand.

"Have you got a camera phone? Take a picture and send it to me."

"Why?"

"Because I want to see that what you're saying is true. I want you to send a picture to my phone, here in this bar where I'm drinking myself into a stupor."

"Why?"

"Why am I drinking or why do I want a picture? I'll tell you when I get home. I'll say it one more time: I'm in Paris. I'm waiting for that picture."

Jansson did as I asked. I had another drink, then my phone pinged. I looked at the image; it was terrible. You couldn't see anything of the house, just a formless glow.

I held the phone up to the barman.

"My house is burning down," I said.

He looked at me but didn't say anything. I could understand why.

I went out into the night. I had neither the courage nor the desire to speak to the women hanging around on the street, but I suddenly recalled a New Year's Eve, the year before I met Harriet, when I had a relationship with a girl who worked in an ironmonger's shop.

At Christmas I realised I didn't want to carry on seeing her, but I didn't know how to tell her because she would be devastated. I needed time to think. A few days before New Year's Eve I was in the apartment where she lived with her parents, who happened to be away. The original plan had been that we would celebrate the New Year quietly together, which was something I wanted to avoid at any price.

I told her I had to go out to buy some new shoes. I had already left a note under her nightdress so that she would find it at bedtime.

I didn't go to a shoe shop; I went straight to Arlanda and flew to Paris. In my dishonest message I had written that of course I loved her but that I needed to be alone for a few days. My love was just too overwhelming.

In Paris I found a cheap hotel not far from Clichy, slept until twelve every day and spent my nights in various bars in the Pigalle or Les Halles, which at that time were in the city centre. The whole time I was trying to pluck up the courage to approach a prostitute. The women on the street scared me. I fancied one of the women who hung out in a bar I frequented, but I didn't have the nerve to speak to her either. Every night I slunk around like a randy tomcat, sticking close to the walls to avoid a stray kick. It wasn't until New Year's Eve, the day before I was due to fly home, that I ventured into one of the many bars where I thought I might find prostitutes.

Heavy curtains covered the window, a single lamp burned outside. As I seized the door handle, I had no idea what to expect. Would there be a lot of people, a lot of women? I stepped into the dimly lit room and discovered that it was virtually empty. An elderly man who resembled little more than a shadow was moving around behind the bar, the bottles sparkling in the mirrored wall. He glanced at me, assessing whether I was a punter who should be allowed in or someone who was likely to cause trouble, and gave me a nod. I had a choice: the empty tables and red chairs, or one of the leather-covered stools. The only woman in the place was sitting at the far end of the bar smoking a cigarette. I avoided looking at her, ordered a glass of wine and tried to appear as relaxed as possible. Music poured out of invisible speakers. I ordered another glass of wine, and the bartender wondered if I would like to buy the woman a drink. Naturally I said yes, and he gave her something that might have been a weak Martini. She raised her glass, I did the same. Despite the poor lighting I could see that she was in her thirties. She had brown hair cut in a pageboy bob, she wasn't heavily made up, and was as far from my idea of a prostitute as it was possible to be. However, I was aroused by the thought that she was for sale. I had three hundred francs in my inside pocket; was that enough? I hadn't a clue about the price of women in Paris, neither then nor now.

I stayed there until the bells had rung in the New Year on the radio behind the bar. Only one other male customer turned up all evening, and he and the woman knew one another. Perhaps he was her pimp. Just before he left they had a row about her lighter, which she insisted he had taken. It got quite nasty, and I wondered if I ought to leave. But the lighter turned up, everything calmed down, and the man disappeared. When the door closed and the curtain keeping out the cold fell back into place, the woman suddenly moved to the stool next to mine. She told me her name was Anne. I don't remember what I said, possibly that my name was Erik or Anders. She asked where I came from; I said Denmark. What was I doing in Paris? Taking a break from my post as the manager of a bank in Copenhagen. I removed all traces of who I actually was. As if that made any difference. She asked for another drink; I nodded to the bartender, although I was starting to worry in case the drinks were sold at inflated prices. Surely the business couldn't be profitable if they only had one customer on New Year's Eve?

I wondered what my girlfriend in Stockholm was doing. Was she sitting in her parents' apartment thinking about me? I didn't know, but I was glad I had flown to Paris. When I got back I must find the courage to tell her that our relationship had no future.

Anne gently nudged me with her leg.

"You know we can get together in the room at the back," she said.

"Yes," I said. "Yes, I know."

I didn't say any more; I was grateful that she didn't push it.

It was half past twelve. From the street came the sound of the odd firework and the shouts of people celebrating. I offered her another drink; I was terrified that she would suggest we withdrew to the other room. The initial temptation was gone; all I wanted now was an escape route. We sat there in silence. Every fifteen minutes, almost as if she were obeying an inaudible signal, she lit a cigarette with her Ronson lighter. As the flame sprang into life, I saw that her nails were bitten to the quick.

I asked for the bill. I paid and gave her a hundred francs. She took the money and smiled; I stood up and left. People were still partying. In the distance I could see the flare of rockets soaring into the air in Montmartre. I lingered for a little while; after ten minutes, just as I had decided to move on, Anne came out. She was wearing a suede coat trimmed with fur and a beret. I said hello as she walked past; she looked at me as if she had been molested. I was definitely someone she no longer knew.

I walked through Paris on that long, cold winter's night, and the following day I flew home. I hadn't bought any shoes. Nor could I bring myself to end our relationship. It wasn't until the beginning of February that I managed to say the words, to harden my heart against her despairing sobs, and finally to walk out never to return. Thirty years later I happened to bump into her; by then she was married and had three children. One of the first things she said was that now, with hindsight, she was very glad I had left her. If I hadn't, our life together would have been a disaster.

I walked around Place Pigalle trying to remember where that bar had been. All the buildings looked just as they had back then, but I still couldn't work out where it was. Eventually I thought I'd found it; I was sure I recognised the door, the closed curtains. It was still a bar. I hesitated before I went in. I was afraid I would be opening a door to the past. I even feared the same woman would be sitting there smoking her Gitanes. In order to bring myself back to the present day, I took out my phone and looked at the picture of the fire again. Should I call Jansson? I decided against it, put away my phone and went into the bar.

Everything was different. A new counter, brighter lights, a television with the sound off. A few men were sitting at the bar; there was a young barmaid with a ring through her nose and a gemstone in her left ear.

There were no other women; this came as a relief rather than a disappointment. However, the relief worried me; did I no longer know what I wanted? Was I incapable of drinking without keeping my thoughts under control?

I left the bar, hailed a taxi and went back to my hotel. I dropped my clothes in a heap on the floor and got into bed. From the room next door I could hear the sound of a television. I looked at my watch; it was quarter past two. I banged my fist on the wall behind the bed a few times, and the noise stopped.

This is the point I have reached, I thought. I'm just an old man, lying alone in his bed in a hotel in Paris, feeling unwell. My daughter is under arrest in the bowels of a French police station, and a woman who doesn't love me is staying in a hotel nearby.

I was woken by my phone ringing: Jansson. It was six o'clock. The curtains were moving in the draught from the window; during the early hours of the morning the wind had got up over Paris.

"The fire is out," Jansson said. "Did I wake you?"

"No. Do they know how the fire started?"

"Alexandersson seems to think it's exactly the same as your house."

"What?"

"The fire started simultaneously in several different places."

"So we have a lunatic on the loose in the archipelago. I was fast asleep when my house went up in flames, and now someone has set fire to an eighty-five-year-old lady's home."

"The dog must have woken her," Jansson said thoughtfully. "If she hadn't had the dog, the smoke could have killed her before we got there."

"Thanks for letting me know. Have the police been looking for me? Do people still think I set fire to my own house?"

"I've no idea what people think."

"I'll be back in a few days."

"I've never been to Paris. Sometimes I feel as if I've never been any further than Söderköping."

"Didn't you go to the Canaries, years and years ago?"

"I don't remember."

"Send me another picture," I said finally. "If you're still there."

The picture arrived a couple of minutes later; the house was a ruin. The fire had died down, although I could still see smoke and glowing embers. The coastguard had rigged up bright floodlights, illuminating the remains of the house with a ghostly brilliance. It was just possible to make out the shadowy figures of those who had helped to put out the blaze.

I got out of bed and looked down at the courtyard. Leaves and rubbish were swirling around in the strong wind. There was no sign of the rat I had spotted the previous day.

Lisa was waiting in reception when I went downstairs at ten o'clock. She rose to her feet as soon as she saw me.

"Let's go out," she said. "I need some fresh air."

She turned into Rue de Vaugirard without knowing what she was doing. I hadn't told her that this had once been my street, the longest in Paris. We walked towards Porte de Versailles; after about half an hour, when the gusts of wind were making it hard to walk, she led me to a bistro that I recognised from the time when I used to live nearby.

I remembered an occasion when I had had some money and decided to treat myself to breakfast before I embarked on the long trek to the clarinet workshop in Jourdain. I had ordered a hot chocolate and a sandwich. The elderly man who served me, who was probably the owner of the bistro, had stopped dead and bent double, banging his head on the metal counter. Everyone could see that he had been stricken with severe pain of some kind. It was early in the morning, and the bistro was full of people eating and drinking before they went to work. A man in blue overalls was standing next to me with a glass of red wine; he knocked it back just as the man behind the counter collapsed.

I don't know what happened next. I couldn't cope with the groaning, so I emptied my cup, picked up my food, put the money in a little plastic dish and walked out.

I went back the next day — in fact I went there almost every day for a month — but I never saw the elderly man again.

One day, over a month after the incident, the waiters were wearing black armbands on their white shirtsleeves.

I had never been back since then. Until now. I recognised the colour of the walls, although the tables and chairs had been replaced. Of course I didn't recognise any of the staff or customers. What was familiar, I realised, was the sound of glasses being dipped into the washing-up bowls.

Lisa led me to a corner table next to the window overlooking the pavement section, which was closed. The tables and chairs were piled up and chained together. I felt as if I were looking at animals in a stall, waiting for the winter.

"I used to live near here," I said. "But you couldn't possibly have known that."

"You must be wondering why I've come to Paris," Lisa said. "We don't know one another. You're here to look for your daughter. But why have I come? I've even lied to my editor about the reason for my trip."

"What did you say to him?"

"That's my business. It's nothing to do with you."

Her tone was sharp, and we didn't say anything else for a while.

After we'd finished our drinks, we continued on our way. Rue de Vaugirard seemed endless, just as I remembered from when I had lived there. I recalled a Saturday afternoon when hordes of young people came pouring down the street. Later I found out they were on their way to a concert at Porte de Versailles where an English pop group that everyone was talking about was playing. They were called the Beatles. I knew nothing about their music; I lived in the world of jazz, although

I did occasionally attend the organ recitals in the church at Saint-Germain.

This whole excursion seemed utterly pointless. I stopped.

"Where are we going?"

"Nowhere. Or to another cafe."

"Why have you come to Paris?"

"Let's keep walking," she replied.

We went into a bistro near Rue de Cadix; it wasn't lunchtime yet, and there were very few customers. We sat right at the back. The waiter was old and walked with a limp. Lisa ordered a bottle of red wine; she chose the most expensive item on the grubby wine list. Her selection made me feel even more anxious. The waiter — who stank of sweaty armpits — brought the bottle and two glasses. Lisa noticed the smell too. She smiled at me.

"I came because I was wondering what you really think."

"Think about what?"

"I've noticed how you look at me, from that very first time when I wanted to hear about the fire. I wasn't really surprised when you turned up asking to stay the night. You're not the first man who's stood there howling on my doorstep."

"I wasn't howling. And what I told you was absolutely true."

She frowned, as if my answer had annoyed her. When she spoke I realised she was angry.

"You don't have to lie to me."

"I haven't lied to you."

She pushed away her glass and leaned across the table.

"You've lied to me," she insisted.

"I haven't."

"You have!"

This came out as a yell; she sounded like my daughter. In my peripheral vision I could see that the waiter had noticed what was going on, but he simply turned away and carried on wiping down tables.

That's what the world is like, I thought vaguely to myself. People turning away everywhere you look.

I tried to remain calm, to pick up my glass without shaking. I swallowed the contents and got to my feet. I put some money on the table without saying a word, then walked out. I headed down the street as fast as I could; when I reached the Metro station at Porte de Versailles, I hurried underground and caught the train to Montparnasse.

I immediately regretted my actions. What had Lisa been trying to tell me? I sat in that rattling train carriage feeling totally exposed. She had seen inside my grubby old-man's thoughts and decided to find out what I really wanted. Did I actually imagine that there could be any kind of romance between us? Didn't I realise that she was offended now she had discovered what my motives were?

I carried on past Montparnasse and didn't get off the train until we reached the Right Bank. I was in Châtelet once more. When I emerged into the daylight, it had started raining. I went into a newsagent's and bought an umbrella.

I had just put it up when my phone rang. I stood outside a shoe shop under the projecting roof.

It was Olof Rutgersson. He immediately asked where I was.

"Out in the rain," I replied. "With a newly purchased umbrella."

"I just wanted to let you know that Madame Riveri will be picking up your daughter at three o'clock this afternoon. I knew she was good, but even so I have to say this is sensationally fast. She must have had a very positive personal relationship with the judge in charge of the case. Your daughter will be released. Madame Riveri is going to call you to arrange a meeting place. For the exchange."

"The exchange?"

"She hands over your daughter, you pay her for her work."

"Is Louise being deported?"

"I don't know, but if our esteemed Madame Riveri says she's going to be released, then she's going to be released. And that's the most important thing."

"Thank you for all your efforts too."

"The Swedish Foreign Office and our embassies are always happy when we manage to achieve a positive outcome in any situation. Please let us know when you and Louise are safely back in Sweden. It might be as well if she avoids any further pickpocketing activities in France; she now has a criminal record, and French justice has a long memory."

We ended the call with a few polite phrases. I put my phone away, thinking that Lisa Modin would never upset me again. Nor would I bother her with my dreams of some kind of relationship.

I ambled along in the rain, choosing my route at random. I wondered if I had ever visited as many cafes as I had during these few days in Paris.

Jansson called again. I asked if there was any new information about the fire, but there wasn't. However, there were rumours of a connection between this latest blaze and the one that had destroyed my house.

"Perhaps I'm no longer regarded as an arsonist?"

"That was never the case."

"Don't lie to me. There's no point."

"People are afraid it will happen again."

I could understand that. Fear spreads quickly, especially among the elderly. I sat there at my table thinking how ironic it was that out in the archipelago I was one of the younger residents. At least during the autumn, winter and early spring.

I was still thinking about Lisa. I tried to make myself feel contempt for her, but I couldn't do it. I shouldn't have walked out; I should have let her finish what she had to say. I'm sure I would have been able to convince her that she was wrong. I wasn't the man she thought I was.

I stayed in the cafe until lunch was over and there were only a handful of customers left. A blind woman patted her guide dog, who was lying at her feet. Seeing her wrinkled hand stroking the dog's fur was like witnessing a movement that had gone on for all eternity.

My grandfather had dominated my childhood out on the island, but my grandmother had been there too, providing the security I didn't recognise or value until I was an adult. In the final years of her life she lived in a home, suffering with severe dementia. She used to go outside at night because she believed that my grandfather was at sea in a heavy storm. Even when there wasn't a breath of wind, the storm raged within her; she was constantly worried about her husband.

They died only a few hours apart. First her, then him. There was no life for the one left behind when the other had gone. According to what I had heard, from Jansson needless to say, my grandfather had found out in the morning that she had passed away. He had folded up the newspaper he was reading, put his glasses in their case and lain down on his bed. Two hours later he was gone too.

My reminiscences were interrupted by the sound of my phone. This time it was Madame Riveri, suggesting that we should meet. She had made a note of my hotel; could I be there in an hour? She would bring Louise.

I thanked her, paid for my coffee and went back to the hotel. A brief power cut on the Metro was alarming; what if I wasn't there to receive Louise and Madame Riveri's bill? Fortunately the problem was short-lived and I was there in time. While I was waiting I asked Monsieur Pierre if there was a room available for tonight. There was, but I didn't make a booking because I had no idea what Louise's plans might be.

304

It had stopped raining. I went out into the street as the appointed time approached. I thought I caught a glimpse of Lisa; I never wanted to see her again. No, that wasn't true. I didn't want to give up my dream, however hopeless it had turned out to be.

Madame Riveri and Louise arrived by taxi. Louise was very pale. We went into the hotel; Madame Riveri went off to the ladies' powder room and left us alone in the deserted bar.

"I know nothing about the life you live here," I said, "but if you like you can stay in the hotel tonight. They have a room."

She nodded without saying a word. I went back to reception and booked a single room.

"It's for my daughter," I said.

"I assume she's the lady sitting in the bar?" Monsieur Pierre said. "May I ask if the lady who arrived with her is your wife?"

"No. Louise's mother is dead. I'm on my own."

"I'm sorry to hear that," Monsieur Pierre said sadly. "It's not good for any human being to live alone."

Madame Riveri returned; she was in a hurry. I thanked her for everything she had done and asked if it had been difficult to secure Louise's release.

"I explained that she was pregnant and pointed out that she didn't have a criminal record. Then it was fairly straightforward, particularly as the judge and I get on very well. I also told him that Louise's father had come to Paris to take her home."

"She's staying here tonight, then we'll see what happens."

Madame Riveri took an envelope out of her bag.

"There's no rush as far as the payment is concerned, but don't forget about it. If you do, you'll be sorry."

She said goodbye to Louise, then swept out of the hotel.

I went up to Louise's room with her, which was on the same floor as mine. She didn't have a bag with her; I asked if she had any money. She didn't.

"I need clothes," she said.

I gave her some money. I wanted to ask her where she had been living in Paris, where her belongings were, but I knew this wasn't the right time. No doubt she was grateful for my help, but she didn't want to be under an obligation to me.

Before I left her room I asked if she'd like to have dinner with me later.

"I'm too tired," she said. "I want to wash off the dirt from prison, then I need to sleep."

"I'm in room 213," I said. "We'll have breakfast together tomorrow when you're feeling better."

That evening I ate in a Chinese restaurant nearby, then watched a black and white Fernandel film on the television in my room. Louise wasn't the only one who was tired.

I woke just after midnight; someone was knocking on my door. I stumbled across the room to find Louise standing there. She seemed to be shivering.

"Can I sleep here?" she said.

I didn't ask why. I had a big double bed; she lay down on the unused side and turned away from me.

306

I switched off the light. After a little while she reached out with one hand. I took it and held it, then we both fell asleep.

CHAPTER
EIGHTEEN

My house was on fire. The staircase leading to the ground floor seemed endless, not the twenty-three steps I had counted out loud as a child. I kept on running, but the staircase just kept on growing longer as the fire came closer and closer. I stumbled and fell, and then I woke up.

Louise was fast asleep. She hadn't moved at all; her hand was still in mine.

I listened to her breathing. I could hear the breathing of many of the people I had listened to during my life. My father's heavy, often irregular snores that came and went, silence giving way to something like a growl, then silence once more. My mother's virtually inaudible breathing. My grandfather: sometimes he didn't seem to be breathing at all, then he would loudly draw air into his lungs. My grandmother's snores, often accompanied by whistling noises, as if the wind was blowing through the gaping cracks in the boathouse.

Strangely enough, I had no recollection of Harriet's breathing from when she had slept beside me. She would often complain that I woke her up with my snoring. She had left no traces of her sleep; I searched my memory, but I couldn't find her sound.

308

Thinking about all those sleeping people made me drop off again. When I woke a few hours later, Louise had got up. She was standing by the window peeping through a gap in the curtains, the grey light falling on her. Her belly was clearly visible now. A baby was growing in there, and I didn't even know the name of its father. The sight evoked an intense feeling of joy. I had never experienced anything like it.

Louise noticed that I was awake. She turned to me, still holding onto the curtain.

"Thanks for not snoring," she said. "I've slept away those terrible days in prison."

"You were certainly in a deep sleep," I said. "I woke up and thought you were far, far away."

"I dreamed about a dog. It was wet, and its fur almost looked like a coat of rags. Every time I tried to get near it, it started howling as if it was frightened of me."

She crawled back into bed, while I got up, shaved and had a wash. I dressed and went down to the breakfast room. Louise joined me after half an hour. Now I recognised her. That washed-out pallor had gone, and she ate with a good appetite.

"Why haven't you asked me where I live?" she said.

"You usually complain when I ask you questions."

"That's just your perception. What are you going to do today?"

"That's entirely up to you, but maybe we should go back to Sweden?"

She looked at me searchingly, as if my words had taken her by surprise.

"Not yet," she said. "I want to show you where I live. If you're interested?"

"Of course I am."

I thought I ought to tell her that Lisa Modin was in Paris, but I decided to leave it for the time being. If there was one thing I didn't want right now, it was my daughter storming out of the hotel in a temper.

I told her about Jansson's calls and showed her the pictures he had sent.

"Weird," she said. "Creepy. Where's this island?"

I tried to explain but without success. She said she understood, but I was pretty sure she hadn't a clue which island I was talking about. However, she was relieved that I could no longer be suspected of arson.

"Did you believe it?" I asked. "Did you believe I set fire to my grandparents' house?"

"Not really, but you have to remember that I don't know you particularly well."

"The torch," I said. "Why did you deny that it was you flashing the torch?"

At first she didn't seem to know what I was talking about, then she shook her head with a smile.

"It amused me, messing with your head."

"But why?"

"Perhaps because you treated Harriet so badly."

"But I looked after her when she was sick!"

"Maybe, but not before. Not when you were together. She told me."

"You made me row across from the skerry in the middle of the night — wasn't that enough?"

"No. I thought about you and Harriet a lot that night."

I didn't want to hear what Harriet had said about me, so I changed the subject.

"Did you steal my watch when you brushed against me?"

"If I have a speciality, it's taking people's watches."

"You must be very skilful; I didn't notice a thing. But you could have told me it was you."

"I knew you'd realise eventually — that's why I left it behind."

She got to her feet, even though she didn't appear to have finished her breakfast.

"Let's go," she said. "I want to go home."

We went upstairs and put on our outdoor clothes. I allowed myself to be led by my daughter, just as I had followed Lisa Modin the previous day.

We took the Metro and changed trains at Châtelet, using the same line on which I had travelled to Jourdain all those years ago. I wondered if it really was such a small world — would we end up getting off there? However, Louise didn't move until Télégraphe, two stations further on. Many of those who disembarked were North Africans. Around me I could hear just as much Arabic as French. The station was terribly run-down, with the alcoholics who had always been there sitting or lying on several of the benches. They looked like statues that had fallen over.

When we emerged from underground, I thought of Morocco or Algeria.

Louise glanced at me with an unexpected smile.

311

"Some people feel scared when they arrive here," she said.

"Not me. I might not know for sure, but I have a good idea of what the world really looks like."

We followed a winding street lined with old buildings, with crumbling plaster facades and layer upon layer of graffiti, which somehow managed to intensify the greyness rather than brightening the place up. A woman in a full hijab came towards us carrying a screaming child. A group of men sat smoking in a doorway. When I peered into the darkness I saw an elderly man feeding another man with a soup spoon, his movements slow and measured.

Louise was walking quickly. She seemed to be in a hurry to get home, but I thought she was also running away from the time she had spent in that subterranean cell.

She turned into a cul-de-sac and stopped at the last building, which was next to a high wall. It was a four-storey apartment block, just as dilapidated as everything else I had seen on our way from the Metro.

"This is my island," she said, pushing open the door.

The stairwell was filled with the aroma of exotic spices. From one apartment I could hear music that mostly consisted of the sounds of a monotone flute, beautiful and melancholy. We went all the way up to the top floor; it annoyed me that I was out of breath. Louise waited for me on the landing.

"This is where I live," she said. "But I don't live alone."

She had a bunch of keys in her hand and turned towards the door.

"Hang on a minute," I said. "I need to know what to expect."

"My apartment."

"You just said you don't live alone?"

"I live with my partner."

"Your partner?"

She placed a hand on her belly. "My baby has a father."

"I've asked you about him, and you wouldn't tell me anything. And now all of a sudden I'm going to meet him?"

"Yes."

"Does he have a name?"

"Yes."

"Any chance you could tell me what it is? What he does? How long you've been together?"

"Do we have to have this discussion on the landing? His name is Ahmed."

I waited for her to go on, but instead she unlocked the door. I followed her into a dark hallway; it reminded me of the apartment in which I had lived on Rue de Cadix.

"Ahmed will be asleep," she said, pointing at a closed door. "He works nights as a security guard. He's from Algiers." She led me into the kitchen, which was small and cramped. I tried to picture Ahmed, to whom I would be related when the child was born, but nothing came into my head.

The kitchen was freshly painted and smelled of turpentine. The cooker and the fridge were old; the table and chairs could easily have been retrieved from a skip. I realised that Louise and this man called Ahmed were poor. Obviously life as a security guard and a pickpocket wasn't very lucrative.

Louise made coffee; I sat down on the chair nearest the window. The adjacent block was just a few metres away, and a radio or some kind of stereo was playing loud music in the distance.

"I have to know," I said. "Do you really make your living as a pickpocket? You're clearly not very good at it — you got caught."

"You know what I used to be like," she said. "When we first met."

I remembered only too well. Louise had turned up in a picture in the newspaper, which Jansson, needless to say, had got hold of. Louise had stripped naked in front of a group of international politicians to protest about something or other — I no longer recall what it was. I had realised then that my daughter was a rebel, as unlike me as it was possible to be. Where I had always been frightened and insecure and put on a front, pretending to be brave, she had burned with a passion for her beliefs and had thought it possible to bring about change through a lone protest.

I wondered what had happened to all the anger that had been directed at politicians and a world she couldn't bear?

"I have to make a living somehow."

"That's why you became a pickpocket?"

314

"I've never stolen from anyone who couldn't afford to lose what I took."

"How can you possibly know that?"

She shrugged.

"Does Ahmed know about this?"

"Yes."

"And is he a pickpocket too?"

She hesitated before she answered.

"There's a part of my life you don't know about," she said eventually. "I'll tell you. The year after Harriet died, I hitched all the way to Barcelona. On a few occasions I had to fight off men who thought I'd got into their cars to do them a service; I always had a steel tail-comb at the ready. In the Pyrenees I once had to stab a guy in the cheek. I was afraid he might die; the blood was spurting all over the place.

"Anyway, I managed to get out of the car before anything happened. I was going to Barcelona to join a demonstration against Spain's abortion laws. I had a friend, Carmen Rius, who lived in a part of the city called Poble Sec; the people there are not exactly rolling in money. We took part in the demo, but then Carmen asked me to go with her to Las Ramblas, an area frequented by tourists. She didn't tell me what we were going to do, she just said I should stick close to her and take anything she passed to me. Her English wasn't very good, and my Spanish was even worse, but I went along with her all the same. I watched as she approached a Japanese tourist, a *guiri* as she put it. The woman had a rucksack on her back, and one of the pockets was open. Carmen removed a wallet so fast that I hardly saw her do it. She gave it to me and hissed at me to hide it. I slipped it into my handbag and Carmen disappeared. The Japanese tourist hadn't noticed a thing. I realised then that Carmen was a *carterista,* a pickpocket. I was astonished at how easy it had been.

"When I asked her how it felt to be a thief, she insisted that no one who lost their wallet or phone would go under. She never went for the poor, only tourists who could afford to travel, and therefore could also afford to lose a few possessions. I allowed myself to be persuaded, and she taught me how to do it. After a few weeks Carmen let me have a go. An Asian tourist with her money in her back pocket was my first victim. It went well, and Carmen said I was now a fully-fledged *carterista.* Strangely enough I wasn't nervous at all. I stayed for six months and became part of a group of four women working together."

She paused and waited for my reaction.

"Now you know how it started."

I was sure that she was telling the truth. She really did want me to know.

"Ahmed," I said. "You said he's from Algiers, but you're telling me about Barcelona?"

"I didn't meet him there. Carmen was arrested, and I moved to Paris. I met him through friends of friends, and we were a couple."

"Did you tell him you were a pickpocket?"

"Not right away. Not until I was sure we were really together."

"And what did he say?"

"Not much. Nothing. But he's not a pickpocket, even though he does have fantastic fingers."

"But he lets you do it? What kind of a man is he?"

Louise leaned across the table and grabbed my hand.

"A man I love. The only man I've ever loved before, although in a different way, was Giaconelli the shoemaker. When I met Ahmed, I understood what love could be."

I gave a start; there was a man standing in the doorway. I had no idea how long he'd been there. He was unshaven with cropped dark hair and was wearing a white vest and striped pyjama trousers. His bare feet were extremely hairy.

"This is Fredrik, my father," Louise said in English. "And this is Ahmed, my partner."

I stood up and shook his hand. He was considerably younger than my daughter, probably no more than thirty years old. He smiled at me, but his expression was watchful.

He pulled out a stool and sat down at the table. He looked as if he was expecting me to say something. Everything to do with my daughter was completely incomprehensible as far as I was concerned. I would never be able to work out how she had become what she had become.

"I believe you're a security guard," I said tentatively. "I hope we didn't wake you."

"I don't sleep much," Ahmed replied. "Perhaps deep down I'm already an old man. I believe you sleep less as you get older."

I nodded. "Before that final slumber we sleep less and less over a number of years. As a doctor I ought to know why, but I can't give you a reason."

Louise poured coffee; Ahmed didn't want any. I could see the love in her eyes when she looked at him. As she walked past him with the coffee pot, she quickly stroked his hair.

I asked Ahmed about his parents.

"My father is dead. He worked on the docks in Algiers, and he was struck by a steel hawser from a ship. The tension was too tight, and it broke. He lost both legs and bled to death."

"I'm very sorry to hear that."

"Thank you."

"And your mother?"

"Dead."

He didn't explain how she had died, and I didn't ask.

"Do you have any brothers or sisters?"

"Two who are unfortunately no longer with us, one still alive."

I thought that Ahmed was surrounded by many dead people. I tried to change the subject and asked about his job.

"I look after stores where I could never afford to shop. Every night I enter a world which is otherwise closed to me."

He looked at Louise.

"To us," he corrected himself. "And to our child."

"Congratulations, by the way," I said. "I know these days people often find out in advance whether it's a boy or a girl?"

Ahmed frowned. "We would never do that."

"We're just having the scans to make sure everything is OK, given my age," Louise said.

I was finding the situation difficult to deal with. I suspected that Ahmed regarded me with a kind of controlled contempt. The fact that Louise was so besotted with him also bothered me. There was something submissive about the way she looked at him, the way she caressed his head. This was a Louise I had never seen before.

I couldn't think of anything else to say. I almost felt insulted. Louise's life choices were beyond my comprehension. She was a pregnant pickpocket living with an Algerian immigrant who had a hopeless job working nights as a security guard.

Ahmed got to his feet and left the kitchen; I wondered if he had read my mind.

"He seems very nice," I said to Louise.

"Do you really think I would have chosen to have a child with a man who wasn't nice?"

Before I had time to answer, Ahmed was back. He had put on a pale blue shirt and a pair of shorts with Arabic lettering down the sides. He was carrying a glass bottle on a wooden stand, like a classic ship in a bottle.

"A present for you," he said. "I might have to earn my living as a security guard at the moment, but this is the kind of thing I really want to do."

He carefully put down the bottle and adjusted the table lamp so that I could see the contents.

This wasn't a sailing ship that had been pushed through the narrow neck of a bottle to rest on stiff blue waves and then erected with the particular magic that characterises that patient art. This bottle contained a desert, its dunes billowing very differently from the waves formed by the sea. There was an ornate Bedouin tent, the opening allowing a glimpse of the interior, where men in white sat on soft cushions and veiled women served coffee or brought hookahs. Outside the tent a Bedouin dressed all in black was sitting on a horse, handing the reins to a servant. His turban was skilfully wound around his head.

I had some knowledge of the art of creating ships in bottles. My great-grandfather, who had worked on cargo ships on the North Sea before returning home to become a fisherman, had made a model of the *Daphne*; she went down off the treacherous Skagen reefs one Christmas Day in the 1870s. A Danish fishing boat went out into the storm and managed to save the crew, but eight of the rescuers died. When I was a child my grandfather explained that the ship, with its tall masts and its tattered sails, had been pushed through the neck of the bottle while lying flat. Using a clever system of the finest threads, it was then possible to raise the masts and fix the sails, and to secure the ship on the waves, which were made of coloured modelling clay.

However, the Bedouin camp Ahmed had created was far more impressive than any ship in a bottle that I had ever seen. His technique and skill were outstanding. I realised that with those fingers he would probably be an excellent teacher for anyone who wanted to become a pickpocket.

"It's beautiful," I said. "Is this setting, with the tent and the man on the horse, something you've experienced yourself?"

"I grew up in the kasbah in Algiers. The desert was far away, outside the city, but I saw pictures and films. And my father was a Bedouin; he spent his entire childhood as a nomad, with tents erected in a different place each evening."

"I should have brought you something," I said. "But I didn't have much warning about this trip."

"I'm grateful that you helped Louise get out of prison."

"Thieving in Paris isn't a very good idea," I said, immediately regretting my choice of words.

"It's over now," Louise said crossly. "Going on about it is no help at all."

Ahmed reached out and placed his hand on her arm.

"Your father is right. I don't think Fredrik will mention it unnecessarily."

He pronounced my name with a French accent, presumably to be polite. I was sorry about my earlier suspicions.

He stood up.

"I think I need to sleep for a couple of hours more," he said.

He gave a slight bow and left the kitchen. Louise went with him, and I got ready to leave. After a few seconds she came back; I was standing there with the Bedouin bottle in my hand.

"There's something else you need to know," she said. "Put down the bottle."

I did as she said and followed her into the room beyond the kitchen.

"This is also my life," she said as she opened the door.

The room was small, painted white, simply furnished. A bed, a fitted carpet, a ceiling light. And a wheelchair. The chair was facing the window; I could just see hair and the back of someone's neck.

"This is Muhammed. We don't need to whisper; he's deaf."

Louise went over to the wheelchair, and the person sitting there immediately produced a stream of incomprehensible noises. Louise turned the chair around. Muhammed was a seven- or eight-year-old boy. His face was distorted by a grimace that seemed to have stiffened into a rigid scar. He stared up at me. I had the feeling that the twisted mouth could let out a scream of angst at any moment.

"This is my father Fredrik," Louise said in French, while simultaneously writing something on a screen linked to a computer attached to the chair.

She jerked her head to indicate that I should come closer.

"He can't move his hands, but you can say hello by touching his cheek."

I did as she said, almost recoiling when I felt the boy's skin. It was ice cold.

I knew there were a number of chronic illnesses where people are completely lacking in subcutaneous fat. They are very cold and can often suffer from a range of different mental or physical problems. Perhaps he had hydrocephalus, or water on the brain as it is sometimes called. However, his head didn't seem unnaturally swollen, so I had doubts about my diagnosis.

"Who's his mother?" I asked.

"Muhammed is Ahmed's brother," Louise explained. "Their mother had a breakdown when he was born and it became clear that he would never live a normal life. She sought refuge in mental illness, but Ahmed was determined to take care of him. That's why he moved to France. For the first few years he looked after Muhammed alone, then I turned up. He will be like a brother to the child I'm expecting."

"What's the diagnosis?"

"He has many problems. Apart from the deafness, his brain isn't fully developed. He can't talk, and he'll go blind within the next few years."

We went back to the kitchen.

"Leave the bottle," she said. "I'll wrap it up safely, make sure it doesn't break."

"I realise you won't be coming back to Sweden with me."

"Not right now. Not before the child is born. After that we might move to Sweden — out to the island, once the house has been rebuilt."

I didn't know what to do. Part of me wanted to put my arms around her, hug her as tightly as I could. Another part simply wanted to run away from the whole thing, go back to the caravan.

She asked how long I was thinking of staying.

"I'm leaving tomorrow," I said. "You're out of prison; you haven't been deported. I know what your life is like. There's nothing to keep me here, and staying in a hotel is expensive."

"You could stay here."

"Cities don't suit me any more. I need to go home. I'm longing to get back to my island and my burned-down house."

Louise thought for a moment, then said, "I'll come to your hotel this evening. I'll bring the bottle with me."

We said our quiet goodbyes in the dark hallway. I felt unsure of myself, like a young child. I don't like it when I can't understand things.

Out on the street I paused for a moment. It would be many hours before we saw one another. Without really making a conscious decision I headed for the Metro and travelled south. I changed trains and eventually got off at the Bastille. Slowly I walked towards the Hotel de Ville. I ought to book my ticket home. Something was irrevocably over. Meeting Louise's family had made it clear to me that we lived in different worlds, yet I still hoped it would be possible to change things, that our worlds could come together in the future.

Once again I started to observe the people passing by on the street. When I occasionally saw an older person, it served merely as a confirmation that we were the exceptions.

I made a phone call; after a long wait I was eventually able to book a seat on a flight leaving at 11.30 the following day.

I continued my long walk to Montparnasse. A female busker made me stop. She was singing old jazz songs in a powerful vibrato. The hat in front of her was well filled; I added a euro, and she smiled her thanks. Many of her teeth were missing.

My legs were aching by the time I arrived at the hotel. Monsieur Pierre was on reception, counting the contents of a cash box.

"I'm going home tomorrow," I said.

"Monsieur has finished with Paris for now?"

"Possibly for ever. You can never tell, at my age."

"Quite right. Growing older is like walking on thinner and thinner ice."

The bar was open but empty. I ordered coffee.

As I was passing reception on the way up to my room, I heard Monsieur Pierre in an inner room, which was hidden by a dark red curtain. He was humming along to some music I recognised. I listened for a moment and realised it was Offenbach.

There was a message on my bed to say that Rachel had been my cleaner today. I lay down and dozed off immediately. When I woke up after what I thought had been a long sleep, I saw that only twenty minutes had passed. I tucked the duvet around my legs and leaned back against the bedhead. In my mind I returned to the apartment and the moment when Ahmed had suddenly appeared in the kitchen. I saw his disabled brother; I thought about the gentle way Louise had stroked Ahmed's head, her tenderness towards his brother. She had allowed me access to her life, but to me it had felt like walking into a room where nothing was familiar.

It seemed to me that I had a daughter who had great empathy for others; sharing responsibility for such a severely disabled child was impressive. How she could combine activities such as helping terminally ill patients to see Rembrandt's paintings one last time with her "work" as a pickpocket was beyond me. But I was a part of her and she was a part of me. This was a story that had only just begun. I wondered whether Louise understood me better than I understood her.

This is how far I have come. From a waiter's house in Stockholm to a hotel room in Paris. Once I was a successful surgeon who made a mistake. Now I'm an old man whose house has burned down. Not much more than that.

I do not fear death. Death must be freedom from fear. The ultimate freedom.

I got out of bed, fetched some sheets of paper from the brown folder on the desk and tried to formulate my thoughts. But no words came, no sentences. Only childish maps of imaginary archipelagos, with narrow sounds, hidden inlets and strange, bottomless depths filled both sides of the paper. It was the only map of my life I was capable of creating.

I thought about Ahmed and the remarkable Bedouin in the bottle he had given me. Perhaps I ought to give him one of my imaginary archipelagos, from a part of the world that was completely unknown to him?

I went out and wandered around Montparnasse for a while before heading for the Metro station exit where I assumed Louise would eventually arrive. It was cold and dark, and the people hurrying up and down the stairs were all absorbed in their own lives.

No one saw me, no one was missing me.

Louise turned up just before seven. She was carrying the bottle, wrapped in newspaper and brown paper. She was surprised to see me waiting and asked if something had happened. I had the feeling that she was worried about me.

"I'm going home tomorrow," I said. "I don't like dramatic farewells. Neither do you."

She laughed. Just like Harriet, I thought in surprise. I'd never noticed that before.

"Well, at least we're alike in one way," she said. "Dramatic meetings or goodbyes can often be unpleasant."

She handed over the package and told me to be careful, particularly when I put it in the overhead locker on the plane.

"32B," I said. "I'll be squashed between two other people."

Then there was no more to say.

"I'll come," she said. "We'll come. But you need to go home and build a new house. You can't die until you've done that."

"I have no intention of dying," I said. "And of course I'll make sure the house is built. I'm not going to leave you a ruin."

We hugged, then she turned and went back down the stairs. I watched until she disappeared. Perhaps I was hoping that she would turn around, change her mind?

I went to a nearby bistro and drew my old house on the white tablecloth. From memory, in full detail, I couldn't imagine building anything different.

It was nine thirty by the time I went back to the hotel. A light drizzle was falling on Montparnasse. I hoped all the walking I had done during the course of the day would help me sleep.

Monsieur Pierre had gone home; I had never seen the night porter before. He was very young and had a ponytail and an earring. I wondered briefly what Monsieur Pierre thought about sharing a workspace with him.

Then I noticed Lisa Modin sitting in one of the armchairs in reception. She stood up and asked if she was disturbing me.

"Not at all. I've just said goodbye to my daughter. She's been released from prison, but she's staying in Paris."

I didn't mention Ahmed or his brother.

"I've been given a bottle with a Bedouin encampment inside it," I continued. "One day I hope I'll be living in a house with a shelf I can put it on."

Lisa didn't say anything, she just carried on looking at me.

We went up in the lift. I placed the brown package on the desk in my room, then I sat down on the bed. Lisa sat down beside me. Neither of us said anything. When the silence had gone on for too long, I told her I was going home the next day.

"Me too," she said.

"Maybe we're on the same flight?"

"I'm going by train. Didn't I tell you? I'm scared of flying. My train leaves at 16.20."

"Hamburg, Copenhagen, Stockholm?"

"That's right. I came here because I wanted to see you; I don't know why. I'm not sorry I yelled at you; what happened, happened. But I don't want my trip to have been completely pointless."

"Perhaps we share a feeling of loneliness," I said.

"Sentimentality doesn't suit you. Our expectations are different. I have none, but that's not the case with you. Expecting nothing is an expectation in itself."

"We could lie down on the bed," I suggested. "Nothing more."

She took off her jacket and her shoes. They were red and had higher heels than any of the shoes I had seen her wearing before. I took off my jumper.

Lisa was the second woman with whom I had shared a bed during my stay in Paris. Last night Louise had lain here, her breathing deep and steady. Now I had Lisa Modin by my side.

I thought about the desert and the Bedouin tent and the horse.

It was a moment of great calm, the beginning of freedom. Suddenly the fire and my flight from the blinding light were far, far away.

CHAPTER
NINETEEN

We didn't touch each other that night.

We talked for a long time about the city in which we found ourselves.

Lisa started to tell me about herself. The whole of her childhood had been almost unbelievably harmonious. She could remember moments when she had been so bored that she had wondered if life really was an endless, tedious road. She also talked about her fear of flying, which she had never managed to conquer. It had started on a long-haul flight home from Sri Lanka. At some point during the night, as she curled up in her seat on the darkened plane, she had suddenly understood that she was ten kilometres up in the air.

"I was being carried on the shoulders of emptiness," she said. "Sooner or later the weight would become too great. I've never set foot on a plane since."

Our nocturnal conversation came and went in waves. She told me she had spoken to the priest on the phone.

"I asked him about the bear's tooth that was supposed to have been found on Vrångskär, but he didn't know what I was talking about. There was no bear's tooth in his house, in the church or in the parish hall."

"That's what I said," I replied. "I told you it was just something I'd heard. Even a non-existent bear's tooth can become a legend."

We talked about all the poor people we had seen on the streets of Paris.

"Poverty is getting closer and closer to us," she said. "No one can escape."

"Sometimes I think that the period and the country in which I have lived is a great big, wonderful anomaly," I said. "I have never been without money, unless I have deliberately made that choice. We know very little about the world our children will inherit."

"Perhaps that's why I've never wanted children," Lisa said. "Because I could never guarantee that they would have a good life."

"You can't think that way. In the biological world children are the sole purpose. Nothing else matters."

It was after three when we fell asleep. First Lisa. Her breathing was rapid, then slow, rapid again, silent, then it settled into a gentle snore. She slept as if she was awake. Cautiously I rested my head on her shoulder; she didn't stir.

We woke up at almost the same moment. When I opened my eyes and turned my head, Lisa was lying there looking at me.

"I just woke up," she said.

It was seven o'clock. She sat up.

"I'm glad you didn't throw me out yesterday."

"Why would I do that?"

"I shouted at you."

"I expect you felt you had good reason."

She lay back down after gently moving aside my outstretched arm.

"Thank you for not trying it on," she said. "You might have thought I came here offering myself on a plate."

"Why would I have thought that?"

"Because it would have been a perfectly natural reaction."

"Not for me."

She leaped out of bed and pulled back the curtain.

"What is it that makes you different from other men?" she asked.

"I am the way I am."

She looked irritated, and the conversation stalled. I got up and she disappeared into the bathroom. I stood by the window looking down into the courtyard while I waited. She had come to the hotel, and she had stayed the night. That must mean something, even if I still didn't know what it was.

She emerged from the bathroom with the same energy about her that I recalled from the first time we met. I suggested that we should have breakfast together, but she shook her head with a smile.

"We could have had dinner on the train if you weren't flying home," she said.

She gently stroked my face before she left the room. For some reason I hoped Rachel wouldn't see her.

After Lisa's abrupt departure, I went down to the breakfast room even though I wasn't hungry. Monsieur Pierre was on reception, gazing at his computer screen.

The breakfast room was very quiet, with just the odd guest concentrating on their boiled eggs and coffee.

When I couldn't bear to sit there any longer, I went to Monsieur Pierre and asked for my bill. I paid with my card, but I was suddenly worried in case there wasn't enough money in my account.

There was no reason to be concerned. If I didn't start spending significantly more money, there would always be enough. In spite of everything I had a good pension from my career as a doctor.

I left a tip of ten euros and asked Monsieur Pierre to pass some of it on to Rachel.

"She's an excellent person," he said. "We're very glad to have her."

I headed towards the lift, then turned.

"Who owns the hotel?" I asked.

"Madame Perrain, whose father started the business in 1922. She's ninety-seven years old, and unfortunately she's very ill. The last time she came here was twelve years ago."

I thanked him and got into the lift. When I stepped out on the second floor, my key in my hand, I made a decision without really thinking things over. I would catch the same train as Lisa Modin. I wouldn't fly. Seat 32B might be occupied, but not by me.

I slept for a few hours more then left the hotel. Even though it was still quite a long time before the train was due to depart, I took a taxi to the Gare du Nord. I was done with the city; I would return only if it was to see Louise and her family. I was ready to leave Paris for good.

The taxi driver had dreadlocks and was playing Bob Marley. I hummed along, and as we were waiting at a red light he turned and smiled. His teeth were white, but sparse on the top row. I thought about my visit to the former jazz club where they now played reggae; I asked him if he knew the place.

"Of course," he replied as the lights changed to green.

I left Paris to the sound of "Buffalo Soldier". I gave the driver a generous tip when he dropped me off at the station. I had arrived here the first time I came to Paris, as a very young man with terrible toothache and hardly any money. Now I was leaving. I had got into a taxi in this spot back then; now I was getting out of one. In spite of the distance between those two journeys, they were somehow linked.

I bought a ticket, assuming that Lisa would be travelling second class. I wandered around the station, trying to remember what it had looked like fifty years ago. I was sure my train had been pulled by a steam engine, and that I had sat in the very last carriage.

I called Jansson. I didn't tell him I was on my way home. He had nothing new to report about the fire, but everyone on the islands was getting worried; they were afraid a seriously malevolent individual was on the loose.

That was the word he used — malevolent. It didn't sound quite right on Jansson's lips. If he had sung it in his fine tenor voice, it might have sounded more convincing, like something in an opera. I asked whether the police had found any similarities with the fire that had destroyed my house, but Jansson had no answers for me. He kept going back to the fear of something yet to happen.

I went into a newsagent's and bought an English medical journal, which I slipped into my bag.

Half an hour before the departure time I made my way to the right platform. I stood next to one of the iron pillars supporting the roof; I wanted to see Lisa before she saw me.

She arrived fifteen minutes later; the train had just pulled in. I followed her at a distance, like a scruffy private eye. As she climbed aboard I saw that I was right: second class.

Just as the conductor was about to close the doors, I followed her on board. I stayed by the toilet until the train set off. After all these years my final journey home had begun.

I could see Lisa in the sparsely occupied carriage. Her eyes were closed, her head resting on the wall by the window. Fortunately she had chosen a spot with an empty seat opposite. I sat down as quietly as I could. After a minute or so she opened her eyes and smiled.

"I ought to be surprised," she said. "But somehow I'm not."

"The first time I came to Paris I travelled by train," I said. "As I told you last night. But I've never left Paris on a train. I've stood by the roadside with my rucksack many times, hoping for a lift, but now I have the opportunity to make that missing journey home by rail."

"It's good to see you," she said. "I haven't been looking forward to this trip, but now maybe it will be different."

"Why did you come? I can't make this long trek without knowing the answer."

Before she had time to respond, the brakes squealed, triggering a memory of the very first time I arrived in the city. The same squealing brakes, people losing their balance, someone swearing. It was as if I had cracked through a shell and stuck my head out into a world that no longer existed.

We travelled through the suburbs, the train picking up speed. There was no one else in this part of the carriage. Lisa had her back to the engine; I asked if she wanted to swap places.

"Those who were going to be executed were always transported facing away from the direction in which they were going," I explained. "It was so that they wouldn't see the gallows or the executioner's block as they approached."

"I'm fine here, thank you."

Once again an incident from my youth came into my mind. I was standing out in the winter cold with a frightened girl; I think her name was Ada, and she had a great big Farah Diba hairstyle. I was drunk on arrak, somehow obtained from Hasse the baker's son, the boy everyone wanted to be friends with. Before Ada had time to take evasive action I threw up all over her white shoes. The occasion was a school dance; I had been evicted because of my intoxicated state. Ada regarded herself as my girlfriend and had therefore felt obliged to share my humiliation. But now she ran straight back into the warmth, where well-behaved couples were dancing together to a jazz band with a blind double-bass player.

What was I thinking now, as we sped through the outskirts of Paris and a little man dragged a big heavy suitcase along the aisle of our carriage? Was I hoping not to be abandoned, as I had been all those years ago?

I rested my head against the wall and folded my arms.

We crossed the Belgian border. Our tickets were on the table in front of us; I pretended to be asleep when the conductor came along to check them.

Lisa stood up.

"I'm hungry. I'm going to the restaurant car."

I went with her. A man sitting across the aisle was watching a film on his tablet; I asked him to keep an eye on our bags, and he nodded. Lisa led the way; the restaurant car was packed, and we had to wait for a table. The waiter spoke French with an Eastern European accent. Outside the window darkness had fallen. We both ordered chicken; we ate, we drank.

"You were crying in your sleep," Lisa suddenly said.

"Was I?"

"People rarely cry for no reason."

"I have no recollection of that at all. Nor of any dreams."

The waiter topped up our glasses. He had developed the skill of pouring drinks on a moving train without spilling a drop, even when the carriage jolted and lurched.

"I once took the overnight train through Switzerland," I said. "I was on my way to Italy. In the restaurant car I was seated at a table with a woman of about my age who was on her own. I was very young at the time. For some unknown reason we were drinking some kind of sugary punch. I was knocking back three glasses to her one. I had the crazy idea that I might be able to tempt her to my sleeping compartment; I had booked first class in an excess of arrogance and because I had plenty of money. I don't know why I was so well off; I had just started training to be a doctor. If I remember rightly, it was the Easter holidays, and I had decided to go to Rome on a whim. Nothing happened, of course. When the restaurant car closed, she thanked me and disappeared. I staggered back to my compartment, opened the window and passed out, drunk. When I woke up in the morning, the bed was covered in snow. The inside of my mouth felt as if it were coated in a layer of syrup that had set. I have never had such a terrible hangover, neither before nor since. I was ill for days. My only memory of Rome is the suffocating traffic; I was furious because I had wasted my money on such a dreadful trip. I had thrown away a wonderful experience for God knows how many glasses of punch."

"I also have a memory of Rome," Lisa said, "although my trip was a bit more successful. I went there with two friends, one whom was about to start working there as an au pair for a Swedish diplomat. We went along to provide moral support during her first week. One day I went for a walk on my own; the other two had caught a cold and stayed in bed. I met a man called Marius, and a few evenings later I lost my virginity behind a tree in the gardens of the Villa

Borghese. The whole thing consisted of inept fumbling on both sides. We were supposed to meet the following day, but I didn't turn up. I still wonder what became of him; I wonder if he ever thinks of me."

The restaurant car was beginning to empty. We were drinking coffee; Lisa had ordered a pudding, but it was far too sweet, and she hardly touched it.

She suddenly asked why I had turned up at her apartment that evening.

"You already know the answer."

"I know nothing. But I have a suspicion."

"Which is?"

"That you were hoping I would let you into my bed. How could you think such a thing?"

"I didn't think anything. I hoped."

"You snooped among my papers. You found a secret in my wardrobe."

She angrily tossed aside her napkin, then she waved to the waiter, who appeared to be half-asleep on a stool by the kitchen door. He immediately brought over the bill, which he had already prepared. I wanted to pay, but Lisa took it. She said I had already spent more than enough. She gave the waiter a ridiculously large tip, and he beamed at her. It was the first time we had seen him smile all evening.

We went back to our carriage; this time I led the way, opening the stiff doors as we moved through the train.

The man who was supposed to be keeping an eye on our luggage was fast asleep, with the film still playing on his tablet. The bags were still there.

"Where are we?" Lisa asked when we had settled down. She had snuggled up under her coat, legs tucked up on the seat.

"Maybe Germany?" I said. I looked at my watch. "We'll be in Hamburg in five or six hours; there's always a break there."

"Wake me up when we get there. I love the fact that nobody knows where I am. A train racing through the night. If I could write novels, I would write about this journey."

"Would I be in your story?"

She didn't answer. She had already closed her eyes and pulled her coat over her head.

I must have dozed off too. I woke up when the train stopped, and in the pale light on the platform I could see that we were in Hamburg. The man opposite got up and left. Lisa was still sleeping, one leg dangling off the seat.

We were exactly on time; it was quarter to three in the morning. In contrast to my trip all those years ago, there was no need to change trains, although we would be waiting here for thirty-five minutes. I touched Lisa's shoulder through her coat. She threw it off as if she had been attacked, blinking at me in bewilderment.

"We're in Hamburg," I said. "We'll be here for half an hour."

"I was asleep," she said, still only half-awake. "Such a deep sleep. I dreamed about a hole that suddenly opened up."

"I'm going to get some fresh air," I said.

340

Lisa pulled on her shoes, stood up and ran her fingers through her hair.

"Can we leave our bags?" she asked.

"Someone usually walks up and down keeping an eye on the train. Anyway, we'll be able to see what's going on from upstairs."

We were quite close to an escalator leading to the upper floor, where shops, cafes and the ticket office were located. It was cold when we got off. A man in uniform was already patrolling the platform, monitoring the train.

I asked if Lisa was hungry.

"Are you?" she said, sounding surprised. "At three o'clock in the morning?"

We bought two cups of tea to take away from a cafe. A long-haired man with a grubby rucksack was fast asleep at one of the tables. It seemed to me that he had been there for ever, the timeless vagabond, constantly reborn, always looking exactly the same. A small group of apathetic, possibly homeless youngsters was sitting at another table. They formed a sharp contrast to a couple in their thirties who were tenderly stroking each other's cheeks and hair.

Lisa walked over to the barrier; from up here it was possible to see every platform in the almost deserted station, with its domed roof made of iron and glass, the panes grubby with the accumulated dirt of so many years. She placed her cup on the barrier.

I took a risk and put my arm around her. She didn't resist, but she gently pulled away.

"Don't do that," she said. "Just stay where you are. If things happen too fast, they always go wrong."

A scruffy, emaciated junkie came up to us, begging for money. I gave him one euro; when he asked for more, I shouted at him to clear off. He moved away; Lisa watched him go.

"I don't understand how people find the courage to have children," she said. "When the result could be a beggar in a railway station."

"That's rather cynical. Life guarantees nothing but constant risk. That also applies to having children."

"Did you never think that way? When you were waiting for your daughter to be born?"

"I knew nothing about her. I've already told you that."

We threw our empty paper cups in the bin and went back to the train. Some new passengers had joined our carriage. I wondered whether to suggest that Lisa and I should move so that we could sit next to one another, but I realised she wouldn't want to. There was no need to ask her. As soon as she sat down she had established the boundaries and closed her eyes, as if I had no access to her world.

We continued our journey northwards. I don't know if Lisa slept, but she snuggled under her coat once more. I sat gazing out into the night, with fragments of memory swirling around in my mind like truncated film clips. When the conductor passed by, I asked if there was a buffet car open. He shook his head, explaining that there was a drinks machine at the back of the train. I knew it was unlikely to contain anything alcoholic.

342

We arrived in Stockholm on time, having eaten both breakfast and lunch on board. Lisa had accepted my offer of a lift home. Neither of us mentioned the brief embrace in Hamburg. I couldn't decide whether it all seemed like a dream to her, something that hadn't really happened. For me the reverse was true. I had sat opposite her for hours as the train took us to Copenhagen and on through the Swedish autumn landscape. I wondered if it was possible to yearn for a person who was less than a metre away.

She spent much of the journey absorbed in a book about the history of Swedish journalism. I had nothing to read but my pocket diary. I went through all the different names listed for each day of the year, tried to imagine myself as something other than Fredrik. Only Filip seemed even remotely possible. When I had run out of names to consider, I picked up my pen and made anagrams out of Fredrik Welin and Lisa Modin. Hers was easier to have fun with than mine.

Refkrid Nilew wasn't as interesting as Masdi Olin.

We caught the train from the central station in Stockholm to the airport. A cold rain was falling. I collected my car and spent ages circling and trying various exits before I eventually found the right one and picked Lisa up outside Terminal 3.

Southwards through the rain. The heat inside the car was unpleasant. The traffic was heavy, everyone was in a hurry. It didn't thin out until we were past Södertälje. I asked Lisa if she was hungry.

"I'm just enjoying the trip; I don't want it to end," she replied. "I'm like a child who can never get enough."

"Enough of what?"

She shook her head and didn't say any more. I could see the wet surface of the road shimmering in the headlights, and I thought I probably felt the same. This trip could go on forever as far as I was concerned.

We had reached the dark depths of the Kolmården forest when she asked me to stop in a parking area. She got out of the car and disappeared into the gloom. I switched on the radio and listened to the news; it seemed to me that I had heard it all before. I turned it off as Lisa got back in the car. It was pouring with rain now and her hair was soaking wet.

"So what's going on in the world?" she asked.

"Everything. All over again. Or afresh. Always the same, always different."

Outside Norrköping we stopped at a service station for something to eat. Lisa tasted her food, then pushed away the plate.

"We ought to complain," she said. "That's inedible."

"I'll go and say something."

"No — if I can't do it myself, nobody is going to do it for me."

She pulled the plate towards her and ate small forkfuls of the fish gratin. A quarrel flared at a nearby table: a couple of young men started fighting before their companions managed to calm them down.

We drove on through the darkness. I had to slam the brakes on just past Söderköping when a hare ran across the road. We didn't say much during the journey, we just shared the silence, which I found difficult. I wanted to talk to her, but I didn't know what I wanted to talk about.

We arrived at Lisa's apartment block shortly after ten. The cold rain was still falling. I put my jacket over my head and lifted her suitcase out of the boot.

"How are you going to get home tonight?" she asked.

"I don't know yet."

"Stay here."

I could hear from her voice that this wasn't an offer made on the spur of the moment; she had been thinking about it for a while. I grabbed my bag, locked the car, and we hurried over to the door.

As we reached the bicycle stands I stumbled and cut my leg. By the time we reached Lisa's apartment, I was bleeding heavily. In the bathroom she washed and bandaged the wound.

The trip to Paris was over.

As I sat on the toilet watching her tend to my leg, I knew that we were getting close to a critical moment.

I just didn't know what it was.

PART FOUR

The Emperor's Drum

CHAPTER
TWENTY

The first thing Lisa did after bandaging my leg was to open the balcony door wide. The chilly night air came pouring in.

I watched as she gathered up her post. She was obviously a woman who read a lot of journals and magazines and disliked junk mail.

She asked me what I wanted to eat. Tea. Sandwiches — liver pâté, sardines. She told me to make myself comfortable on the sofa. I offered to help her get it ready, but she just shook her head.

I realised she was having doubts about whether she should have invited me to stay.

I sat down and thought about all the times I had been in a similar situation: alone with a woman with no idea what might happen.

I recalled the first time I had made love, well over fifty years ago. Some friends had told me this girl had "loose morals" and was always up for it. I think her name was Inger and she used to turn up at the school dance. I was fourteen years old. I danced badly and regarded these occasions as a necessary evil in order to lure girls into adventures. At least that's what I told myself. I spotted her over by the wall. The girls were waiting for the charge from the opposite side of the room, where the boys were poised on invisible starting blocks. I had fortified myself with arrak supplied by Hasse the baker's son, who pinched it from his father's bakery, then sold it at a premium in small glass bottles that he bought from the pharmacy. I wasn't drunk, just far enough gone to have the nerve to dash across the floor. Inger hadn't a clue who I was. We moved around the floor like small, sweaty icebreakers, forcing our way through the crowd. This wasn't a dance, more an evening of pushing and shoving. I don't think we said a single word to one another.

After two "dances", I suggested that we should go. She asked where. I didn't know. Just away from this dance floor that stank of sweat, booze and cheap perfume. Then she made it very clear that there was no one at home.

She lived in a suburb — I can't remember the name of it. Bagarmossen, perhaps? We travelled on the underground, still not talking. She was wearing a brown skirt, boots that indicated she had big feet, a white blouse and a dark red coat. She didn't look in the least like a girl with loose morals who was prepared to go to bed with just about anybody. Then again, what did that kind of girl look like?

She lived in a three-room apartment in a 1950s block. On a shelf I saw a photograph of her father in a conductor's uniform. I sat down on the sofa, which was covered in cushions, embroidered with various quotations that I have long since forgotten.

Inger disappeared into the bathroom. I heard the toilet flush and wondered what to do. What awaited me was both terrifying and irresistible.

She emerged from the bathroom, stood in front of me and offered me an unexpected helping hand. "Do you want to fuck now, or shall we wait a bit?" she said.

She didn't explain what we would be waiting for.

"Now," I said, feeling my face go red.

She nodded, walked towards the door of her little bedroom, then turned and raised her eyebrows. I immediately got to my feet and followed her. She pointed to the bathroom.

"You can use the blue towel."

I have almost no memory of what happened after that. She had turned off the light, undressed and got into bed; there were soft toys everywhere. I took off my clothes and got in beside her. During a fumbling embrace when I sometimes wasn't sure whether I was groping teddy bears or her breasts, I pushed inside her and immediately came. She giggled, I cursed my incompetence and angrily tossed several furry creatures on the floor.

"It's impossible to fuck among a pile of bears," I snapped.

Inger giggled again but said nothing.

I stayed for an hour. We still didn't talk. Then I got dressed and left.

"See you," I said.

"No," she said. "You won't."

I sat on Lisa Modin's sofa all these years later, wondering what Inger had meant. Didn't she want to see me again, or did she realise that I had got what I came for and was no longer interested in her?

I wondered briefly what had happened to Inger, with her brown skirt and her alleged loose morals. Was she still alive? Had she had a good life? I never saw her again.

My reminiscences of that first inept and humiliating experience were pushed aside as Lisa asked me to join her in the kitchen.

Lisa and I ate and chatted about nothing in particular, then she asked me to clear away and wash up while she used the bathroom. I wiped the table, closed the balcony door then sat on the sofa until she came out in her bathrobe and went into the bedroom.

"There's a towel on the side of the bath," she called out.

I thought about Inger. So different, and yet so similar.

"Is it blue?"

"It's white — why?"

By the time I had showered and dried my hair, she had turned off the bedroom light, leaving only a floor lamp burning in the living room. I walked over to the bed, let the towel fall and crept between the sheets.

We lay in silence in the darkness. I reached for her hand, but it was clenched into a fist. I didn't try to open it.

She was asleep when I got up at six and left.

It was cold as I walked to the car. The place was deserted. Driving along the road was like passing through a skilfully constructed set on which no film would ever be made. I imagined that everyone who lived there carried a clapperboard around with them all the time, hoping that they would be able to use it one day.

I drove to the water and got out of the car. In spite of the chill I walked up and down the wooden quay trying to make sense of what had happened last night. My only conclusion was that I really didn't understand Lisa Modin. Why had she travelled to Paris?

There were no answers. I carried on down to the harbour; I met a car en route and had to slam on my brakes. I thought I recognised a marine engineer, who was clearly drunk. Jansson had once hinted that this guy was an alcoholic, but then you could never be sure when it came to Jansson. People he disliked were always alcoholics.

I pulled into my parking space at Oslovski's house. A light drizzle had begun to fall. I got out my bag and was about to call Jansson to ask him to pick me up when I decided to check whether Oslovski was at home and had already started working on her car in the garage. I knew she was an early riser. The gravel drive was freshly raked, the curtains closed. I listened for any sounds from the garage, but all I could hear was the wind blowing off the sea. I thought I might as well go up to the garage anyway. As I rounded the corner of the house, I saw that the door was ajar. Oslovski must be there; she was always very careful about locking up.

Nordin had told me that Oslovski had once been in his shop, searching for money in her trouser pocket.

She had taken out the biggest bunch of keys Nordin had ever seen. He had often wondered how a person who lived in such a small house could possibly need as many keys as a prison guard.

I knocked on the door, simultaneously pushing it open. The light was on.

Oslovski was lying on the cement floor behind the car, which was jacked up. As usual she was wearing her blue overalls, with the company name ALGOTS just visible in faded letters.

I didn't need to touch her to know that she was dead. She was lying on her back with one leg bent underneath her, as if she had tried to stop herself from falling. She was holding a spanner in one hand, and blood had trickled from her head onto the hard floor. Her eyes were closed. I went over, knelt down and checked her pulse; she was dead but not yet cold. Nor had her skin begun to take on the yellow, waxy pallor that comes after death. She had been dead for an hour at the most. There was nothing to indicate an assault; she had suffered either a stroke or a heart attack. Or perhaps a haemorrhage had sent her to her death with no warning.

I sat down on a grubby stool next to the wall where the tools hung in their designated places. I mourned her. Perhaps not as a friend, but as a person who had brought a certain security with her presence in my life.

First Nordin, now Oslovski. I was increasingly surrounded by dead people. The child growing in my daughter's belly only partly redressed the balance between the living and the dead.

Afterwards I couldn't explain why I did what I did, but I got up from the stool, took the bunch of keys out of Oslovski's pocket and went over to the house. From the harbour I could hear the morning bus into town struggling up the steep hill. I waited until the sound of the engine had died away, then I unlocked the door.

I had never been in there before. The closest I had come was on the odd occasion when Oslovski had appeared and we had chatted on her tiny veranda. I had always felt that she wasn't just standing there to talk to me; she was acting as a kind of sentry, making sure no unauthorised person crossed the threshold.

I stood there in the dark hallway; I was aware of the bitter smell that always seems to accompany loneliness. Had my own house smelled like that before it burned down?

I switched on the lights and walked slowly through the three rooms. On the steep staircase leading up to the attic were piles of newspapers and countless carrier bags from various grocery shops. I realised that Oslovski, in her isolation, had become a manic hoarder. The whole place was in chaos. Clothes, bundles of fabric, shoes, galoshes, hats, skis, a damaged kick sled, furniture, broken lamps, fishing nets. It was indescribable. Only the room containing her bed was remotely tidy. I paused in the doorway, struck by something I couldn't quite put my finger on. Then I realised that in spite of the mess everything in the house was spotless. The piles of newspapers were dust-free, the sheets on the bed were clean. The cluttered kitchen contained a washing machine and a tumble dryer. In a bin bag on the floor next to the sink I could see the packaging from a French fish gratin, which might well have been Oslovski's last meal. A single red chair with a plastic seat pad stood next to the small dark green Formica table.

It was clear that Oslovski had never expected or wanted dinner guests.

I went through the house one more time. Chaos and pedantic neatness, side by side.

I stopped. I had the feeling I had seen something to which I should have reacted. At first I couldn't work out what it was, then I realised it was to do with her bedroom.

I went back up the stairs; as soon as I walked in I knew what it was.

The sheets had a sky-blue border adorned with stars. I had seen those same sheets very recently — in the deserted house in Hörum. There was no doubt. The bed in that house was made up with exactly the same sheets as those on Oslovski's bed.

Oslovski must have been a lone vixen, I thought. She wasn't running towards Golgotha, but perhaps she had a den with two exits. One where I was now, the other in the dilapidated house in Hörum. Perhaps she hid there when her fear of whatever it might be became too much for her?

Oslovski had lived close to us for many years, yet she had remained a stranger. Had she ever wanted to develop a closer relationship with us? Perhaps her fear, wherever it came from, was so great that she preferred to live alone in her den, with more than one exit and entrance?

She really had taken almost everything with her, I thought. She had left only a made-up bed in a house that was falling down, and a partially restored DeSoto in a garage. And a mystery no one will ever be able to solve: the mystery of loneliness.

I was sure it was Oslovski who had used that bed in Hörum, although I would never know why.

She had disappeared without a sound, leaving a cold, inaccessible trail.

The stale, musty smell was making me feel sick. I went out onto the veranda and called Jansson.

"It's me."

I knew he always recognised my voice.

"Where are you?"

"I'm fine, thank you for asking. I'm down by the harbour. Oslovski is dead."

There was a pause before Jansson responded; he sounded completely taken aback. "Oslovski is dead too?"

"What do you mean, too?"

"I was thinking about Nordin."

"Yes, Oslovski is dead. I found her in the garage. Either a massive stroke or a haemorrhage, I suspect."

When Jansson spoke again, after another pause, he was on the verge of tears.

"She was so lonely."

"We all are. We die alone. At least when we're born we have company."

Jansson's lachrymose mood suddenly switched to anger. "What the hell is that supposed to mean?"

"It means exactly what I said: at least we have our mother with us when we're born. Even if she's half-crazy with pain."

Silence once more. This time I didn't bother waiting.

"I want you to pick me up," I said. "In two hours. I need to sort out this business with Oslovski first."

"What were you doing in her garage?"

"I usually stop by to say hello. She never let anyone into the house, but I used to pop into the garage when she was working on her old car."

"A Cadillac, wasn't it?"

"A DeSoto."

"And she died, just like that?"

"We can talk about it when you pick me up. In two hours. I need to call the police now."

Jansson reluctantly let me go. I went back into the garage and replaced the keys in Oslovski's pocket. To be on the safe side, I checked her pulse one more time.

Oslovski was and remained dead.

I called the emergency number, gave my name and location, explained that I was a doctor and that I had found a dead woman in a garage. When I was asked if a crime could have been committed, I said no.

The unnatural life Oslovski had lived had ended with her death from natural causes.

I went out onto the road and waited. When it got too cold I went and sat in the car. In my mind my fingertips were caressing Lisa Modin's shoulders.

It was forty-five minutes before a police car and an ambulance arrived. When I saw them coming down the hill towards the harbour, I went out into the road to meet them. I didn't recognise the two police officers. One of them reminded me of my daughter: the same determined look, which could be interpreted as stand-offishness by those who didn't know her.

We went up to the garage with the paramedics, two older, stronger men. I told them about Oslovski and the fact that I had her permission to park my car on her property. We stopped outside the door.

"She's in there," I said. "I'm a doctor, and I'm sure she's dead."

I waited outside. I was finding the thought that Oslovski was gone more and more depressing. I had never really known her, but we had lived at the same time. She was one of the people with whom I had shared my life, and now she was gone. A part of my world had disappeared.

The paramedics came out.

"We're not allowed to transport dead bodies in the ambulance," one of them said.

"We've sent for the body wagon," the other one said. "Looks like a stroke to me."

I went in to join the two police officers, who were gazing down at Oslovski.

"There's a wound on her head," the female officer said.

"She would have sustained that when she fell," I said. "If you have a massive stroke you go down like a bird that's been shot."

"We'd better take a look in the house," the other officer said.

"She usually carries her keys in her pocket," I said.

I waited on the veranda. They rummaged around in the house for a while and came out when they had found her ID card.

"The way some people live," the woman said.

I didn't reply. I gave them my details, locked my car and walked down to the quayside. Another doctor would come to certify the death. While I was waiting for Jansson I did some food shopping and bought a newspaper. The cafe was open, so I decided to have breakfast.

As soon as I saw Veronika, I realised she didn't know about Oslovski. She hadn't seen or heard the ambulance or the police car.

"You're early," she said with a smile. "Coffee? I can't honestly recommend the Mazarins!"

"Come and sit down," I said, pointing to a table by the window.

She looked puzzled.

"Rut is dead," I explained. "Rut Oslovski. I found her in the garage, where she'd been working on her old car. They'll be taking her body away shortly."

Veronika recoiled, as people do when something unexpected has occurred. Her eyes filled with tears. I knew she was one of the few people Oslovski used to talk to. They might only have chatted about the weather, but at least they had a conversation.

"But what on earth has happened?"

"She was lying on the floor with a spanner in her hand. I'm guessing she had a stroke or a haemorrhage. She hadn't been attacked, anyway."

We sat there talking quietly, neither of us really able to process the morning's events. Veronika brought coffee, along with sandwiches defrosted from the previous day.

"She was lonely," Veronika said.

"Lately I had a feeling she was frightened," I said.

Veronika frowned. "What do you mean?"

"I thought she'd changed."

"She was always frightened, all the years I knew her."

"Do you know why? Did she ever say anything?"

"No."

"But what do you think?"

"I don't know. I suppose you can be scared without knowing why."

"Where did she come from?"

"I've no idea. There was always something . . . inaccessible about her."

"She repaired jetties and worked on her car. Who was she really?"

"I don't know."

Jansson would be here soon. I wanted to distract Veronika before I left.

"How's the woman who won twenty-five thousand kronor a month for twenty-five years getting on?"

"Just because you have an arsehole it doesn't mean you have to be one," Veronika said pensively. "But that's exactly what she is. She's boasting about the fact that she's going to spend the winters in Thailand."

I'd never heard Veronika talk that way before. As far as I was concerned, she had always been the quiet owner of the cafe, but now she was suddenly something different. Something more. I was embarrassed.

I saw Jansson's boat approaching and got up to leave. Veronika was lost in thought.

"We'll miss her," I said.

She nodded but didn't say anything.

Jansson was waiting on the quayside.

"Is it really true? Is Oslovski dead?"

"You don't know me very well if you think I'd lie about something like that."

He pulled a face. "There are too many people dying. It's like an epidemic."

"It's just coincidence," I said. "Death is breathing down the back of our necks, but no one knows when the blow will fall."

I stowed my bag and my groceries in the boat. I didn't want to make this conversation any longer than necessary; I wanted to get home to my caravan. Jansson understood; he cast off and clambered aboard with some difficulty. That particular activity exposes the ageing process. About five years ago I had discovered that I could no longer leap easily into my boat without losing my balance. My joints had grown stiffer. Old age has arrived when you can no longer jump aboard. I watched as Jansson shuffled along, almost hating those stiff joints of his, and reversed away from the quayside. I sat in the prow, hunched against the wind and the autumn chill.

We travelled to my island in silence. Once again I was surprised not to see the house among the bare trees. I still hadn't managed to get used to the blackened ruin.

Jansson skilfully hove to. The ability to come alongside a jetty with a barely noticeable bump hadn't left the former postman. I lifted my, bags ashore and was about to give Jansson his hundred-kronor note when he took off his cap. I knew this meant that he wanted to say something.

"What do you want? Can't it wait? I've had a long journey — I'm tired."

"My heart feels funny. I'm frightened."

Under normal circumstances, when Jansson turns up with his aches and pains and asks me to examine him, I know from the start that it's all in his mind. But this morning it was different. I nodded in the direction of the bench and climbed out of the boat. Jansson followed suit. I went into the boathouse and fetched my stethoscope. When I came out he was already taking off his thick jacket.

"Take off your shirt and jumper too," I said.

Jansson did as I asked. He sat there, naked to the waist, his skin covered in goose bumps in the cold wind. I listened to his lungs and his heart, asked him to take deep breaths. His lungs sounded fine, but as soon as I picked up his heartbeat, I knew there was something wrong. I must have checked Jansson's heart a hundred times over the years; I had never had any cause for concern. But now it was different: I could definitely hear an arrhythmia.

As I stepped back I could see the fear in his eyes. Jansson had become an old man.

"It might be a good idea if you pop into the clinic, ask them to do an ECG," I said.

"Is it serious?"

"Not necessarily. It might be nothing, but at our age it's a good idea to have an ECG now and again."

"Is it fatal?"

"If you don't go to the clinic, it could be. Put on your clothes and go home; tomorrow you can take the bus into town. The clinic will look after you."

Jansson got dressed in silence as I put the stethoscope away. I came out of the boathouse to find him bent forward on the bench, hands clasped as if he had suddenly felt the need to say a prayer. He looked up at me as the door creaked shut.

"Why don't you tell me the truth?"

"I am telling you the truth. You need to go to the clinic. Don't worry unnecessarily. I just picked up a little murmur; I'm sure there's an explanation, and medication can work wonders these days."

"I've been reading about the heart," he said. "It starts beating long before we're born. I think a lot of people believe that doesn't happen until the umbilical cord is cut."

"It happens on the twenty-eighth day," I said. "That amazing muscle starts working on the twenty-eighth day, and after that it usually stops only once. Death is the end of a race, after all, but we don't charge through and break a tape. If the heart were a bird with wings, you could well have flown to the moon and back several

364

times before it decides that it's time for those wings to rest."

Jansson nodded. I realised he knew all about the wonderful heart muscle's life and death.

We sat in silence on the bench, two old men in a spot meant for major and minor truths. Jansson was sixty-nine years old, I was seventy. So together we were one hundred and thirty-nine. If I counted back in time, that took us to 1875, when surgeons operated wearing a starched collar, sometimes evening dress.

"We're not allowed to learn to die," Jansson said.

"What do you mean?"

"In the past death was a part of life. Now it's completely separate. I remember I was six years old when my grandmother died. Her body lay on a door in the parlour at home. There was nothing odd about that. Death was a natural part of our lives. Not any more. We no longer learn to die in this country."

I understood what Jansson meant. His fear was totally genuine, and yet there was something about his reaction that puzzled me. It was as if the Jansson I had known was casting off his skin, like a snake.

"How do you learn to die?" he whined.

I had no answer. Of all the dead people I have known while they were alive, none has given me a rational explanation of the ability to handle death, which sooner or later will catch up with me too.

We don't just die alone. We never know how we are going to die, even if a medical diagnosis can be made.

As I sat there next to a worried Jansson I thought about a black and white photograph I had seen many

365

years earlier — an image that had frightened me more than any photograph I have ever come across.

It must have been taken during the early 1950s. A chimney sweep on a roof in Stockholm decides that it is time to end his life. He is about sixty years old. He attaches a steel cable to one of his brushes, loops the cable around his neck, and fixes the other end to the square chimney. Then he balances on the ridge. He must have been standing there for quite a long time, because he has been spotted. Some men up a ladder are trying to persuade him not to go through with it; there must be a photographer up another ladder, but of course I can't see him. Their efforts are in vain; the sweep throws himself off the roof. The camera clicks a fraction of a second before the cable is pulled tight, and the man dies as it breaks his neck and slices into the skin and sinews of his throat. The chimney sweep dangles there for ever in that final void. On his face is etched either determination or despair; I have never been able to decide which, in spite of the fact that I have spent many hours staring at that photograph.

Did the chimney sweep teach me to die? Does the picture reveal anything of the mystery hidden in that final moment? What is it about the chimney sweep's leap out into the unknown that has both repelled and fascinated me over all these years?

This is what I have left, I thought. Sitting on a bench with another old man who also finds it difficult to clamber into his boat without hurting his knees or losing his balance. Here we sit, hunched in silence, complaining that we don't know how to behave when death comes for us.

I didn't like this. I didn't want to sit here with Jansson, moaning and groaning about the misery of getting older. I nudged him with my elbow.

"Do you want a cup of coffee?"

"I was thinking about Oslovski. And now you're shoving me as if you hate me."

"I don't hate you," I said in astonishment. "Why would you think such a thing?"

"You thumped me."

"I did no such thing, for God's sake! I just gave you a nudge!"

"I know you've always thought about killing me," Jansson went on. "Just as I learned to read a letter through the envelope, I can see what's going on inside your head."

He got up, unhooked the mooring rope and did what he could no longer do: he jumped down into the boat. Needless to say he fell over as the boat rocked. He banged his head on the gunwale, opening up a small cut. I thought about Oslovski lying dead on the floor of her garage next to her DeSoto.

Jansson reversed away from the jetty with blood dripping from his eyebrow. Perhaps he was in the first stages of dementia?

I didn't even wait until he had rounded the headland before going up to the caravan. A little mouse scuttled out when I opened the door. It's one of life's great mysteries, how mice can get into a sealed room.

The phone rang just as I sat down with a cup of coffee. It was Lisa Modin; she asked about Oslovski straight away. I pictured her at her desk with her notepad in front of her.

"How do you know about it?" I asked.

"I have people who keep me informed."

"Police officers?"

"Sometimes."

"Paramedics?"

"Not so much."

"Undertakers?"

"Occasionally."

"Is this where you say you are not at liberty to reveal your sources?"

"That's right."

"I was the one who found her."

"I didn't know that."

I explained how I had pushed open the garage door and found Oslovski lying on the concrete floor with a spanner in her hand. As I told Lisa my story it was as if I was only just beginning to grasp what had happened. The death that comes to others is every bit as incomprehensible as that which will one day come to me.

"Was there anything suspicious about her death, as far as you could see?"

"Like what?"

"I'm asking you."

"The post-mortem will show natural causes — a stroke or a haemorrhage. It could be something else of course."

"Such as?"

"I don't know. You'll have to wait for the post-mortem."

"Did she still have her glass eye?"

The question took me by surprise. Who had told Lisa about Oslovski's eye? Had I mentioned it?

"You told me about her when we were out on that island," she said, answering the question I hadn't asked.

I vaguely remembered.

"Yes, it was still there."

Silence; perhaps she was making notes.

"What are you doing?" she asked.

"Drinking coffee."

The conversation came to an end even though I would have liked it to continue.

After a few minutes the phone rang again; I hoped it was Lisa, but it was the churchwarden. He introduced himself as Lars Tyrén and he asked if I was happy to be one of the bearers for Nordin's coffin. The funeral would take place at eleven o'clock on Friday morning; I promised to be there early in order to go over the ceremony in advance.

"Isn't he being cremated?"

"He will be laid to rest in the family grave." I drank my coffee, thinking that I needed to go and buy a dark suit.

Lisa didn't contact me again, and I didn't call her either. I did, however, speak to Louise every day. There was a different tone between us now. We talked about Harriet each time we spoke; I also noticed that she was pushing me to get things sorted out with the insurance company so that I could make a start on the construction of the new house.

I went into town and bought a suit. I went into the most exclusive gentlemen's outfitters I could find and chose black Armani. Because I didn't know whether ties at the funeral were to be black or white, I bought one of each. Before I picked out a white shirt, I was assured that it wasn't made in China, but in a factory in Turin.

The suit cost six thousand kronor. In spite of myself, I was pleased that I had allowed myself to splash out.

A strong north-easterly was blowing as the day of the funeral dawned. It had been an unusually windy autumn. Jansson's boat bobbed and rocked in the squall. He was wearing a black tie with his suit.

Oslovski's house was locked up when we picked up the car. Jansson gazed around curiously. He insisted on seeing where I had found Oslovski's body, but the garage was locked too.

We drove to the church. I managed to put on my black tie, with the help of the rear-view mirror.

Nordin's coffin was pale brown, with a bouquet of roses resting on the lid. The priest talked about Nordin as the eternal servant. His words made me feel sick; they sounded so false. Nordin had been a good person, but none of the residents of the archipelago had forgotten that he sometimes refused credit to those who were less well off. No doubt many people regarded him as a complete bastard.

We carried the coffin through the gusts of wind to the family grave in the western corner of the churchyard. The oldest inscription informed us that landowner Hjalmar Nordin had passed away on 12 March 1872.

As we lowered the coffin, I exchanged a glance with Jansson. I had the impression that he felt as if he were lowering his own coffin.

The ceremony was over. We walked over to the parish hall for coffee and sandwiches, but all I really wanted to do was run away. Suddenly the proximity of death frightened me.

It took me completely by surprise.

I hurried into the hall.

I took shelter inside the den.

CHAPTER
TWENTY-ONE

The first snow fell on the archipelago on 1 December. When I stepped out of the caravan, stark naked, to take my dip in the cold water, the ground was white. There wasn't a puff of wind. Nature was holding her breath as autumn turned into winter. My bare feet left prints in the thin covering of snow. I climbed down the ladder, inhaled and counted to ten with my head under the water. The cold burned my skin. Back on the jetty, I was shivering so much my teeth were chattering. But I had no intention of giving up my dip, however cold it became or whatever thickness of ice I had to chop my way through.

I hurried back to the caravan and made my breakfast. On this particular morning I put on one of the blue Chinese shirts; the collar had already started to fray. I looked at my face in the shaving mirror: it was pale, my eyes increasingly sunken. My hair was thinner, the hairline receding. I had a sore that refused to heal at the left-hand corner of my mouth. It could be an ingrowing wart. As I stared into my eyes, I saw a person I only partly recognised.

A duel was going on between the man in the mirror and the man standing on the floor of the caravan.

Time had passed, and time continued to pass. It was already several weeks since the trip to Paris, Oslovski's death and Nordin's funeral. Veronika, who keeps herself well informed about what is going on in the archipelago, told me that Oslovski's post-mortem had confirmed my suspicions: she had suffered a massive stroke and died in seconds. The PM had also revealed that her body was riddled with cancer, with the primary tumour in one of her adrenal glands.

No one had been able to track down any relatives. I went to her funeral. She had left instructions stating that she wanted to be cremated. The church was sparsely populated. I couldn't understand why Jansson wasn't there; his absence upset me. His curiosity at least should have brought him there.

I occasionally spoke to Lisa Modin on the phone. Every time our conversation ended I wanted it to continue. She would often call back the following day, and I began to realise that in spite of everything she had the same need to talk to someone as I did.

Jansson had followed my advice and taken himself off to the clinic, where an ECG had revealed exactly what I had suspected: signs of a disturbance in the cardiac conduction system. He was now on medication and no longer had any symptoms. However, I noticed that he was constantly expecting the problem to recur. Every time he turned up I listened to his heart. When I assured him that it sounded perfectly normal, he didn't believe me.

He told me that the residents of the islands were afraid that there would be another fire. Apparently the police were getting nowhere. Jansson thought the arsonist was an outsider. That was the term he used: an outsider. Someone who travelled around starting fires, only to disappear.

Louise and I continued to grow closer through our phone calls. I was visited by representatives from the insurance company. Kolbjörn Eriksson and a relative who was a carpenter were contracted to build the new house; in the best-case scenario, it would go up during spring and summer the following year.

The day the first snow fell, I went into town to shop for groceries. As usual I parked outside Oslovski's house; no one knew what was going to happen to the place because there was no will, no family.

When I had locked the car I suddenly decided to walk up to the garage.

The door had been forced. Whoever had broken in had done so with such violence that the lock had been ripped out of the wood.

The DeSoto was gone. Someone must have driven up in a truck or recovery vehicle and towed it away. All the tools were exactly where they should be on the walls; only the car was gone.

I immediately called the police and reported the break-in. As the situation wasn't regarded as an emergency, the operator informed me that it would probably be more than two hours before a car was dispatched.

I gave them my details because I had no intention of waiting around for that long.

The break-in and the theft had upset me. This was an attack on Oslovski. A dead person is dead, but to steal the car that she had worked on for so many years, determined to restore it to its former glory, that was still an attack.

I bought long johns, gloves, a woolly hat, a scarf and a thick winter coat. I made sure none of them had been made in China. Oddly enough, the hat was from Indonesia. Afterwards I went to the restaurant in the bowling alley for something to eat. I hadn't touched a drop of alcohol since I got back from Paris; I didn't miss it at all.

Before I went back to the harbour, I called in at the small electrical shop. It was owned by Johannes Rudin, a man with a hunchback. He had been there all those years ago when I had visited the shop with my grandfather to buy a new radio. According to Jansson, Johannes had recently turned eighty-five and had no intention of retiring.

I had decided to get a TV for the caravan. Listening to the old transistor radio wasn't enough; I wanted something to look at.

Johannes listened with one hand cupped behind his ear as I explained about my caravan, then he pointed to the smallest flat-screen TV in the shop.

"You'll need an aerial," he said. "You can put it up yourself if you're a bit of a handyman."

I paid and carried the TV and aerial to my car. When I had stowed everything away and straightened up, I saw a poster informing me that it was time to book a table at the bowling alley restaurant for Christmas and New Year.

I decided to organise my own New Year party. In my caravan. I would invite Jansson and Lisa Modin. It would be cramped and hot and sweaty with the three of us, but a New Year celebration in a caravan was something different. About as far from an event in a restaurant as it was possible to get. I would ask Veronika to prepare the food, while I would provide the drinks.

I drove back to the harbour. My decision was challenging, but I had good reason to say goodbye to a difficult year. At the same time I wanted to celebrate the fact that my daughter and I had deepened our relationship, and that hopefully a child would soon come into the world. Of course Louise, Ahmed and Muhammed would also be welcome if they wanted to make the journey from France to the archipelago. Then the caravan really would be crowded, but we could manage.

To my surprise, Lisa said yes when I rang and invited her for New Year's Eve. She said she was looking forward to the party. I asked what she was doing for Christmas, and she told me she was going to Crete. That made me feel jealous, but of course I didn't say anything.

Jansson offered to arrange a small fireworks display.

Veronika came up with some suggestions for a simple menu, and we reached an agreement on the cost and all the practical details.

Snow fell from time to time, but it soon melted away. Fear still drifted across the islands and their sparse population like a sea fret, but there were no more fires. Jansson kept me informed; the police didn't seem to have any leads, and it looked as if their investigation had ground to a halt. I kept wondering who had burned down my house and why. Sometimes I thought there was something I had missed, something I ought to have realised, but I didn't know what it was.

No one seemed to have any idea what was going to happen to Oslovski's house, but one day Jansson paid me an unexpected visit. He clambered up onto the jetty and we sat down on the bench. He had brought a magazine about vintage cars containing both articles and small ads. He turned to the advertising section, with pictures and prices.

He pointed, and I immediately saw what he meant. Oslovski's car was for sale, and the image had been taken inside her garage. The thieves had photographed the car before they moved it.

Oslovski's DeSoto Fireflite, manufactured in 1958.

I could still remember her telling me that this particular model had had a short production run — only 4,192. One of the most unusual details was that the exhaust pipe actually came through the bumper. The advert stated that the bodywork was a mixture of Wedgwood Blue and Haze Blue. No price was given; there was a phone number for interested parties to call.

"How did you find this?" I asked. "I didn't know you were into old American cars."

"My nephew called," Jansson said. "I'd told him about the break-in and the fact that the car had been stolen. He knows everything about vintage American cars, and he guessed this might be the one. He was right."

"You've got a nephew?"

Jansson took out his phone and handed it to me instead of replying.

"It's best if you call. My voice starts trembling if I get nervous."

A woman answered.

"It's about the car," I said. "The DeSoto. I was wondering how much it was?"

"A hundred and eighty-five thousand."

Her voice sounded muffled, as if she were speaking through a handkerchief.

"Can you tell me something about the car? Background, previous owners, that kind of thing?"

"You'll have to talk to my brother about all that, but he's not home at the moment."

"When will he be back?"

"I've no idea."

"Can I come and see the car? Where is it?"

"You need to talk to my brother."

"Surely you can tell me where the car is?"

She saw through me.

"Try again in a few hours," she said dismissively and ended the call.

Jansson had leaned closer to listen in to the conversation; it felt as if we were an old married couple, sitting there on the bench in winter chill.

Two swans flew past. We watched them until they were out of sight.

"Bastards," Jansson said. "Stealing a dead woman's car."

We went up to the caravan for a cup of coffee, then we played cards. Jansson won every game.

After an hour and a half, by which time we were both tired of playing, I rang the number again. No one answered. In a sudden burst of energy I called the magazine's advertising desk and informed them that one of the cars on their "For Sale" pages was stolen. The man I spoke to was very concerned and asked me to report it to the police.

I did as he said. When the officer suggested that I report the matter via the police service website, I flared up, telling him I was sitting in a caravan on a remote island, with no internet access.

I don't think he really grasped my situation. He noted down the details with an air of indifference, as if he wanted to let me know from the start that this was going nowhere and that a prosecutor would immediately dismiss the possibility of an investigation.

Oslovski was like a piece of human flotsam that had drifted onto our shores. Jansson had started a collection for a headstone, but it was difficult to get people to contribute. I think he ended up paying most of the eventual cost himself, but at least I was there when the stone was erected in the churchyard. Oslovski was placed between one of the archipelago's last pilots, who happened to be a relative of Veronika from the cafe, and a landowner from Röda Furholmen who was notorious for his unpleasant behaviour when he'd been drinking. Occasionally some unknown person would lay flowers on her grave.

In the middle of December a storm swept in across the archipelago. It came from the Baltic to the south-west, and struck with full force in the middle of the night. The gusts of wind were so strong that the caravan shook. I went out into the sleety darkness with my torch, shoring up my home with tree stumps and plastic barrels filled with water. I had just finished and gone back inside when there was a power cut. I undressed and dried myself with a recently purchased towel made in Cambodia. I still had the LPG stove, and I made some coffee in spite of the fact that it was four o'clock in the morning. I had a candle on the table, its flame flickering in the draught.

My telephone rang. I immediately assumed it was Jansson, wanting to know if my electricity had gone too, but instead it was a man speaking English with an accent. I couldn't work out who it was and thought it must be a wrong number. Then I realised it was Ahmed.

"I am at the hospital. Louise is having the baby."

The child was coming, much too soon. I could hear the anxiety in Ahmed's voice, but he told me there was no need to worry. Louise had asked him to call me; he promised to let me know as soon as the child was born.

I didn't get any more sleep that night. The child was so premature that it would have to be placed in an incubator. The storm and the hurricane-force gusts outside the caravan felt like an ominous backdrop as I awaited the birth of my first and perhaps only grandchild.

I thought about Harriet. Once again I pictured her making her way across the ice with her wheeled walker. I found it difficult to remember what she had looked like on that occasion, but in my mind's eye I could picture her as a young woman, back in the days of our messy relationship. I experienced an intense sense of loss. Or perhaps it was longing. Which isn't quite the same thing.

One night she and I and Louise had slept together in the caravan before it was moved to this spot. Now Harriet was gone, and Louise was lying in a hospital bed in Paris, giving birth to her child.

The candle flickered again, and memories passed through my mind like uneasy shadows. My father was there, my mother, my grandparents — and various women with whom I had had relationships or whom I had never managed to conquer. I was there too, among the shadows. Perhaps I was the one slinking along close to the walls of the caravan, making sure the light never fell on my face?

At ten to six the phone rang again. It was Ahmed: Louise had had a girl. The baby didn't weigh much, but everything had gone well. She was in an incubator, as I had expected.

Ahmed said the baby looked like me.

That wasn't true, of course. Newborn babies, especially if they are premature, don't look like anybody except themselves. They are unfinished sketches that will develop in an unknown direction.

I went out into the darkness and the wind. Still no power. I used the torch to light my way, dizzy with joy. I hadn't expected to have such strong feelings. I went into the boathouse, with the wind howling and whistling through the gaps. I sat down on one of my grandfather's old eel traps, which he had used right up until the last year of his life. By now the net was so fragile with age that it tore if I pushed two fingers into one of the holes and spread them apart.

I felt a tremendous urge to tell someone what had happened, but who could I call? Jansson or Lisa Modin. Perhaps Veronika or Oslovski? But Oslovski was dead, and I had never had her phone number anyway.

I tried Lisa, hoping I would wake her. Which I did.

"You," she said. "At this hour — what time is it?"

"Half past six. I've just become a grandfather."

"Congratulations. Is it a boy or a girl?"

"A girl."

"Did everything go well?"

"I believe so, but the baby is premature. That always carries risks."

"Will they put her in an incubator?"

"They already have. I must confess I'm lost for words."

"And you chose to call me? That's nice."

"I don't have anyone else to call."

"I'm sure you do."

"Perhaps we could have a drink, wet the baby's head?"

"Not at half past six in the morning."

"At the weekend?"

"Maybe. Ring me in a couple of days."

"You ring me."

She promised to get in touch, and I immediately began to look forward to seeing her again. It was a long time since the trip to Paris.

I called Jansson.

"I've got no power," he said. "If that's what you wanted to know."

"Louise has had her baby. A little girl."

There was a pause, then he said, "Isn't that a bit early?"

"Yes, but everything's fine. I hope."

"In that case allow me to congratulate you on behalf of the entire archipelago."

Sometimes Jansson expresses himself in the most peculiar way. His words can border on pomposity, but right now it felt as if he really meant it: he was representing the collective joy of the islanders. He had made me a part of the ever-dwindling population of the archipelago. I was no longer an outsider.

"Thank you," I said.

Then we talked about the storm. Jansson had contacted the electricity company, and they hoped to have the power back on by nine. Apparently a substation where the cable left the mainland had been damaged. In addition, the wind had brought down a large number of trees.

When the conversation was over, I went back to the caravan, lay down and waited for the dawn. As the grey light filtered in, I went outside again. Up on the hill, not far from my grandfather's bench, an oak tree had come down, the roots sticking up like a giant mushroom that had been kicked to pieces. I walked all the way around the island and was able to ascertain that the fallen oak was the only casualty. All the other trees had survived. The topsoil might not be very deep out here, but the trees are tough, clinging on with their claw-like roots.

I fetched my handsaw and cut a slice from the trunk of the oak. It seemed to take forever; I was dripping with sweat by the time I finished. I went down to the jetty for a dip, then dried myself off in the caravan. I took my magnifying glass to the boathouse, sat down and counted the rings. To my surprise, the tree was older than I could have imagined. After checking again to make sure, I concluded that the first ring dated from 1847. The following year, when the oak was no more than a sapling, the European revolutions took place. I worked my way outwards, as if I were on the edge of eternity. I placed my finger on the line separating 1899 and 1900. A war begins in 1914, another in 1939. I was born in 1944, the year before the war ended. And now the tree had fallen in a December storm, all those years after it began to grow.

I left the slice of wood in the boathouse, went outside and sat down on the bench, which was sheltered from the wind. The waves were still choppy, and there was the odd squally shower from time to time.

The power had been restored, just as the company had promised Jansson. All the lights came on at five past nine in the morning, and late in the afternoon I noticed that the wind had started to die down, although far out at sea the waves were pounding the reefs on the surface. Once again I walked around the island.

I couldn't stop thinking about Louise and my granddaughter. Ahmed rang again in the evening and told me that all was well with Louise and the baby. Of course he didn't mention what both he and I knew: that there were many hurdles to overcome for a child born so prematurely.

"Have you chosen a name?" I asked for the want of anything else to say.

"Not yet."

I heard him laugh. I still couldn't understand what Louise saw in him, but his laugh gave me a clue.

That evening I sat down to plan my New Year's Eve party. I noted down the food I had discussed with Veronika and made a list of the beer, wine and spirits I would buy. All the time I could picture that tiny baby in her incubator.

When the storm had passed, I went over to the mainland and talked through the whole thing with Veronika. She didn't think I needed to buy crockery; she could lend me whatever was necessary from the cafe. She would also bring chairs because there was only one chair and a stool in the caravan.

"Tablecloths?"

"Yes, please."

She jotted everything down on the back of a receipt book.

Then we talked about Oslovski. The story of the stolen car, Jansson and the magazine, and my peculiar conversation with the woman on the phone, whose brother was apparently selling the car, was the talk of the town. Veronika knew all about it.

"They must be local," she said. "Someone who knew what she had in the garage."

"Do people suspect anyone in particular?"

"No."

I wasn't sure if I believed her. The answer had come much too quickly. Perhaps she had someone in mind, but I let it drop. I was convinced that the DeSoto would never be recovered.

We spoke about the precarious financial situation of the cafe, and Veronika confided in me that she had started to think about moving.

"To a different cafe?"

"To a different country. I might open a cafe, I might not."

"You'd be missed."

"Maybe, maybe not."

The bell over the door pinged and a dozen or so people came in.

"The local council," Veronika whispered. "They're going out into the archipelago to plan where to put the new toilets. Can you believe it takes that many civil servants to make a decision?"

Before I picked up the car, I went to the chandlery. Needless to say, my wellingtons hadn't arrived.

I drove into town and did my shopping for the party. I loaded the five bags I filled into the car before going to the bank and the pharmacy to stock up on cash and medication. I stopped outside the shoe shop. It was closed, the window empty.

Every now and again I have a little flutter on the horses. I know nothing about harness racing and I'm too idle to study the form before I place a bet, but on one occasion, twenty years ago, I was almost horrified to find that I had won no less than ninety-six thousand kronor — 96,322 kronor, to be exact. I will never forget that moment.

When I received the money I went to South Africa, even though apartheid was still in force. I hired a car at Nelspruit airport and drove to the Kruger National Park. I spent a week there, driving from one overnight post to another. I experienced the ever-present arrogance of the whites towards the blacks. There was a strange silence everywhere. The whites spoke to the blacks or coloureds only when issuing an order. I never heard a relaxed conversation between the races. I was terribly upset and tried to show kindness towards the blacks who served me at mealtimes or topped up my car with petrol, but my friendliness made them wary, suspicious.

I travelled around the vast park and encountered all the wild animals I had hoped to see. I had the constant feeling that the animals saw me twice as often as I saw them. A boa constrictor had half-swallowed a wild-boar cub. A pride of lions was tearing at a zebra. I was a visitor, a polite guest cautiously knocking on the door of untamed nature.

I spent the rest of the money on some expensive suits and dining at exclusive restaurants. I even bid fifteen thousand kronor for a statue of the Buddha at an antiques auction. I lost it when my house burned down.

I went into the betting shop in the town centre and worked out an improvised system of a couple of hundred lines on harness races in Solänget. God knows where that was. Needless to say I didn't recognise the names of any of the horses or the drivers, but I decided I preferred a horse called Bumblebee's Brother to another in the same race with the name Wolfskin. The owner of the shop was a man whose bald head had an indentation to the left of his temple. According to Jansson, who knew all about everyone's medical problems, the man had had an accident with his tractor when he was trying to get his old motorboat into the water one spring many years ago. Jansson thought it was remarkable that he had survived without suffering brain damage, but during my years as a doctor I often saw people whose heads were a very odd shape as a result of accidents without any loss of their mental capacities. In particular I remembered a young academic researcher who was regarded as a mathematical genius both before and after a car accident. His head looked like a cone.

I handed over my betting slip, put the receipt in my inside pocket, then went to the restaurant at the bowling alley for something to eat.

I had just left the restaurant when Louise called. The odd snowflake was drifting through the air. I went back inside and stood by the lane; there were no noisy games in progress at the moment.

She was fine, but naturally she was worried about her baby.

I asked as many questions as I could think of about the unit where the child was being cared for. Louise felt that all the staff were very experienced and knew what they were doing.

"What can I do for you?" I asked.

"Pray."

"Pray? But I'm not a believer!"

"You can pray anyway."

"OK. I can say a prayer and send it off in all directions, backwards and forwards in time, straight out into the universe and down into the depths of the sea."

"Thank you."

"Is there anything else you want me to do?"

"Not right now."

Louise assured me she was getting all the support she needed from Ahmed. Then she started talking about Muhammed in his wheelchair.

"His eyes are like light," she said. "They move at the speed of light, looking into worlds I know nothing about. One day he will receive answers to all the messages he sends out."

"I don't really understand what you mean," I said. I asked if they had chosen a name for the baby yet.

"She's going to have three names, and later on she can choose which one she prefers. Rachel, Anna and Harriet."

I thought about Rachel who had cleaned my room at the hotel in Paris. I thought about Harriet. No one in our family was called Anna; perhaps the name was linked to Ahmed and Islam?

"Pretty names," I said. "So what are you calling her at the moment?"

"We vary it from day to day."

"I want to see her," I said.

"That's really why I called. I'm sending a picture to your phone."

"Are you coming home for Christmas?"

"This is home. Besides, she's still in an incubator."

"If you're short of money, I can help."

"This isn't about money. Build the new house."

Because I couldn't bear the thought of losing the closeness we had achieved, I quickly dropped the subject. She asked if it was raining or snowing. Talking about the weather is always the last resort, but it calmed us both down. No angry ripostes, no hostile silences.

The photograph of Rachel Anna Harriet arrived immediately after the call ended.

My grandchild, barely visible in the incubator, looked like no one but herself. I couldn't see anyone else in her little face, not even Ahmed. I stood there by the bowling lane and realised I was moved. There on my phone was a new person who had just begun to participate in the dance of life. A little girl with three names who would live, if she achieved a ripe old age, until the end of the twenty-first century.

I didn't stop looking at my phone until a group of young men arrived for a game. They spoke a language I didn't understand; presumably they belonged to the group of refugees who had just been billeted in the town.

I drove down to the harbour, keeping an eye out for foxes all the way, but nothing happened this time. All I saw were some crows flapping away from the remains of a dead badger on the road.

Oslovski's house was deserted; no one appeared to have crossed the neatly raked gravel drive. I carried my bags down to the boat, which was moored by the petrol pumps, and went to show Veronika the picture of my grandchild.

"She's very pretty," she said.

"I don't know about that. It'll be a while before we can say one way or the other."

"I've been thinking," Veronika said. "Maybe Paris is a city I could move to? I know you've been there."

"Paris is a very big city. It's easy to disappear if you don't know why you're there."

I headed back down to the quayside, then changed my mind and called in at the chandlery, where fru Nordin was drinking coffee with a plate of Danish pastries in front of her. As a doctor I ought to say something about her obesity, but then I noticed that her eyes were suspiciously shiny, as if she had just been crying. No doubt she was still grieving for her husband.

I didn't show her the photograph on my phone; I just asked for new batteries for my torch.

The sun broke through the clouds as I travelled home. I decided I would ask Jansson to sing at the New Year party, just as he had sung at Harriet's midsummer party a few weeks before she died.

I couldn't think of a better ending to the old year or a better start to the new one.

Perhaps I could even ask him to sing "Ave Maria"?

The same as last time. Now as then.

CHAPTER
TWENTY-TWO

One day Louise and Ahmed decided that their baby would be called Agnes. All thoughts of Rachel and Harriet disappeared.

Agnes. A beautiful name that no one in our family had ever had. A beautiful name for a very small person.

A few years before they died my parents had been seized by a sudden urge to find out more about their background. They both knew their maternal and paternal grandparents, but that was it; anything further back lay hidden in a thick fog. They dug through church records and regional archives; they sought information from the few relatives who were still alive. I remember sensing a silent competition between the two of them: who would succeed in tracing their family back the furthest? The only way each of them felt they could achieve some kind of nobility was to find out more than the other.

When they died, they left behind a decent family tree, but there was no Agnes. On my mother's side they had discovered, to their boundless shame, that a brother of her great-grandfather had been executed — beheaded, in fact — on a hill just outside Västerås. He had been a guardsman; he had got into a drunken quarrel with a comrade and had killed him, stabbing him twenty-one times, as the court record meticulously noted. King Karl XV had refused to show him any mercy, and Karl Evert Olaus Tell had lost his head early one morning in 1867.

This knowledge sent an icy wind whistling through their research. When I came home for a visit from medical school, I noticed that all the papers relating to the family tree had disappeared from their place of honour on the bureau with the secret compartment where I had once found a pair of old spectacles when I was a child, but no hidden treasures. One evening when my mother had dozed off and my father had drunk a fair amount, he had revealed the humiliating truth about the executed guardsman. The discovery somehow lurked beneath the surface like a silent, grotesque, corrosive accusation against my mother.

Gradually they started looking into their past once more, but the joy and excitement had gone, replaced with a sense of anxiety about what they might find in the yellowing documents.

It is difficult to imagine two more reluctant researchers than my parents. They had taken on a task of which they were now ashamed. The archives sent a poison coursing through their veins.

Needless to say, they didn't come across any more murderers. To their surprise they learned that they both came from the sparsely populated inland area of Västerbotten and the equally desolate forests of Härjedalen. There was Finnish blood on my father's side, and on my mother's an unexpected diversion to Russia.

But no Agnes. The little girl in Paris was Agnes the First.

From time to time the police contacted me, occasionally with a question but usually to tell me that they still had no answers. The fire seemed to have come out of nowhere.

Louise and I spoke on the phone every day. Occasionally Ahmed would start the call, and we would exchange a few words before he handed over to Louise. I thought I detected a new tone in her voice, although I couldn't quite pin it down. Hadn't the child's arrival brought unadulterated joy? Was Louise tired? Was she experiencing the fear that so often accompanied new motherhood, particularly when it involved a premature baby? I always ended our conversation with an assurance that I was there if she needed my help.

We also spoke about the burned-out house. She told me she often dreamed about it, saw it rising from the ashes. Another recurring dream she dismissed as embarrassingly childish. Every morning the Carpenter Elves had raised the wooden walls by one metre, using their old-fashioned skills. Nobody knew where they came from, nobody heard the sound of their hammers during the night. The house kept on growing, but the ruins were still there, black and cold, just as they had been after some unknown person came along and set the fire.

I promised Louise that our house would be rebuilt; I stressed that promise again on the day she told me the baby's name was Agnes.

"In the old days people used to give their children several names," I said. "Even if they were poor, they could shower their children with a wealth of names. I had a classmate with seven Christian names, even though he was the poorest of the poor in my school."

"Do you remember the names?"

"Karl Anton Axel Efraim Hagbert Erik Olof. His surname was Johansson."

"My daughter will only be called Agnes," Louise said. "She'll never be in any doubt about what her name is."

One morning I noted the fact that Agnes was one month old as I took my morning dip in the ice-cold water. The weather was changeable, as temperamental as an irascible human being. It snowed, the snow melted, the wind blew from all directions, then there was the kind of windless calm that really belongs to high summer. It could rain for four days non-stop, with constant cloudbursts hammering down on the fragile roof of the caravan.

No one knew what was going to happen to Oslovski's house. There were rumours about the lights being on from time to time, so people started to believe the place was haunted. Someone mentioned her glass eye, claiming that at night it was transformed into a sparkling prism which seemed to find light in the darkness. At least these rumours meant the property was safe from break-ins or vandalism.

The gravel drive was always pristine; no one went near the house. It was as if people doubted whether Oslovski had actually died. Perhaps she had just gone off on one of her mysterious journeys; no one knew where she went or why. Except to track down parts for her car, which remained missing.

"It's always been desolate around here in the winter," Jansson said one day. "But now it's worse than ever. As if empty can become emptier."

I knew what he meant. The silence in the archipelago intensified during the winter. It wasn't just the quayside crumbling away and the iron bollards rusting; it was as if the sea itself didn't really have the heart to fill the harbour basin with water any more.

At Oslovski's wake I took the opportunity to ask Jansson if he would sing at our New Year party. He recoiled as if I had suggested something inappropriate.

"It would make the party just perfect," I said with a smile.

Jansson chewed his lower lip like an awkward schoolboy who hadn't done his homework.

"I can't sing any more."

"Of course you can!"

"And besides, 'Ave Maria' isn't the only song I know," he said stubbornly.

"Fine," I said. "That's fine."

We didn't discuss it any further, but I knew I had his word. He would sing when we were gathered in the caravan, as midnight approached.

I went through the catering one more time with Veronika. We had settled on hot-smoked salmon for the main course, with soup to start and apple cake to follow.

"I would have invited you," I said. "But there isn't enough room in the caravan."

"I'm going to Iceland on New Year's Day," she said.

I looked at her in astonishment.

"Iceland? Isn't it even colder there than it is here?"

"I don't care about the weather. I'm going because of the Icelandic horses."

"Is that where you might move to?"

"Perhaps."

Her phone rang; I gathered from the conversation that it was someone enquiring about a birthday party. I picked up my jacket, pulled my hat down over my ears and waved to her. She smiled at me as she began to make notes on a turquoise pad.

There was an old newspaper lying on one of the tables, so I checked my betting slip. I hadn't won anything, of course.

I headed home, the boat buffeted by choppy waves. I felt as if the sea might solidify at any moment, petrifying the waves, the spume, the boat and me.

A grey sea like this one was like a clockface without hands. Or a room where the walls have fallen down. Sometimes I had a vague premonition that the sea was the force that would one day take my life.

In order to avoid the even rougher waters as I reached the part of the bay leading to the open sea, I followed the inner shipping lane. It was a longer route, but it was sheltered from the north wind almost all the way, except for the very last part of my trip. I passed an island where the bare branches of the oak trees reached up into the sky. I thought I caught a glimpse of a wild boar slipping away into the undergrowth. I let the engine idle and allowed the waves to carry me, hoping the animal would reappear. The next island was called Hästholmen; a geology professor called Sandmark had once built a summer cottage there. I had seen him when I had accompanied my grandfather to the harbour as a child. Sandmark always wore a black beret and a baggy British khaki uniform, and he lived until he was a hundred and seven years old. Back then it was Jansson's father who delivered the post; according to Jansson, Professor Sandmark had died on his jetty, having just received a pension payment. Jansson's father had been standing there with the notes in his hand when Sandmark sank silently to the ground and died on the spot.

Jansson's father had been particularly upset by the fact that the professor had collapsed without so much as a groan of pain, fear or protest.

The summer cottage was in a terrible state. I didn't know for sure, but I thought it was owned by two granddaughters, two sisters who hated each other because one had become rich while the other had failed in life.

My phone rang; it was Jansson.

"I'm sure," he said.

"Sure about what?"

"That the arsonist isn't local."

"Did anyone ever really believe that? Apart from when I was the prime suspect."

"I've gone through every single person who lives out here on the islands. It can't be any of them."

"What do we really know about people?" I said. "What do you know about me? What do I know about you?"

"Enough to be confident in what I'm saying."

I had the feeling that our conversation was going round in circles.

"What do the police think?" I asked, purely for the sake of something to say.

"I imagine they probably think the same as me, but where do they start looking?"

Jansson chuckled, as if he had said something funny, then he became serious again.

"I'd really like to hear your view," he said. "On who's behind all this. These house fires."

"I'll give it some thought, but right now I'm out in the boat. It's cold."

"We need to talk about this."

"You're right, we need to talk about this. At some point."

I ended the call and put my phone back in my pocket. Something about our conversation was bothering me. Even though Jansson had spoken as he always did, something wasn't right. I just couldn't work out what it was.

What did I really know about Jansson, apart from the fact that he had delivered the post for years in all weathers? He had an extensive knowledge of everyone who lived out on the islands. Everyone knew Jansson, the helpful postman in the archipelago. But who really knew him?

I went over the conversation in my mind. I didn't feel any better, and I still couldn't decide where the anxiety was coming from.

400

I accelerated and headed home. A few Canada geese were flying around beneath the grey clouds, unable to find their route south.

Back home I solved a chess problem in the local paper; it was much too easy. The most stupid amateur could work out that a combination of moves involving a castle and a bishop would quickly lead to checkmate for the black pieces. I felt like contacting the paper to complain about the way they regarded their readers as idiots, but of course I didn't do it. Those occasions when I have felt like protesting and have actually done so are few and far between.

It was hot inside the caravan. In spite of the fact that darkness had fallen, I undressed, picked up my torch and went to the boathouse. I climbed down into the water and forced myself to swim a few strokes before the cold got too much for me. I was on my way up the ladder when I heard my phone ringing; I had left the door of the caravan ajar. I set off at a run, but slipped and fell over one of the wet stones in the grass.

I put my clothes back on before I checked to see who had called. I could only think of two people: Louise or Jansson.

It was Lisa Modin. I called her back, but it was ages before she picked up. I was about to give up when she answered, sounding surprised to hear my voice.

"You called me but I couldn't get to the phone in time," I explained. "I'd just been for a dip and I was down by the jetty."

"I didn't call you."

"But my phone is showing your number."

"I don't understand that — I didn't call you."

"And I'm not mistaken."

She was breathing heavily, as if she had just run a long way uphill.

"I'll call you back," she said. "I need to check this out."

I sat down to wait; she rang me after ten minutes.

"I didn't call you," she said yet again. "I must have accidentally pressed a button when the phone was in my pocket."

"So you didn't intend to speak to me?"

"Not right this moment, no."

"In that case it's probably best if we end this conversation now."

I rang off before she had the chance to say any more and threw my phone down on the bed. It was still lying there when it started ringing again. I ignored it. I couldn't work out what I was doing.

I did, however, send a text an hour later. *You're still welcome to come to the New Year party. Unless you've changed your mind.*

She didn't reply until after midnight, by which time I had given up hope that she would still come. The display showed just one word: *Yes.*

I lay there for a long time, thinking about that one word. *Yes.*

I was woken at dawn by cramp in one leg. I wondered if I had developed diabetes; cramp in the calves is a common symptom. However, I wasn't drinking large amounts of water or getting up to pee during the night.

I dug out a blood glucose meter from one of the plastic bags where I keep my medical supplies; the reading was 6.9. I didn't have diabetes.

In a burst of impatient energy I tidied the caravan. I hadn't really touched the place since I moved in. I lit a fire in an old oil drum where my grandfather used to burn his rubbish and chucked in all the crap I had accumulated over the past few weeks. I got rid of one of the blue Chinese shirts; the colour had already faded, the cuffs were frayed and the stitching around the buttonholes was coming undone. I fed the shirt slowly into the flames.

When I was a child, if I had toothache I would sometimes take revenge by pulling the wings off insects. A painful bruise could be eased by drowning a pretty butterfly or by laying a perch on the shore and letting it suffocate.

Now I took my revenge by torturing things that were already dead. This time the Chinese shirt would pay the price.

Later in the day I rowed out to the skerry. The tent was still there, although the recent storm had ripped out some of the pegs. The stones and twigs I had positioned to reveal the presence of an intruder were exactly where I had left them. Nor had anyone lit a fire among the soot-covered rocks.

The sea was calm now. On my way back to the island I looked for the drift net I had seen earlier in the autumn, the net that carried on fishing even though no one would ever empty it.

That night there was a heavy snowfall in the archipelago. At dawn I undressed and went down to the
water completely naked, using my torch to pick a path
through the snow.

Winter had arrived. Soon it would be Christmas,
then New Year.

The snow stayed until Christmas but melted away on
the third day, when warmer winds blew in from the
south. I hung coloured lanterns between the boathouse
and the caravan. Veronika brought extra chairs and
crockery, along with some of the food. We did a trial
run, setting everything out in the caravan; it was a tight
squeeze, but it would be OK.

New Year's Eve was cold and clear, and there wasn't
a breath of wind. At three o'clock in the afternoon
Veronika got everything ready and gave me my final
instructions concerning the food. In order to make
things easier for me, the soup was in Thermos flasks;
she had also lent me an extra LPG hob, which we set
up in a sheltered spot behind the caravan.

We drank a toast to wish each other a Happy New
Year, then said our goodbyes on the jetty as I waved her
off on her trip to Iceland.

Jansson arrived at seven, having picked up Lisa Modin.
Burning torches lit the way to the caravan. Jansson spent
half an hour sorting out his firework display.

The three of us sat down at the little table and we ate
and drank from half past seven until just after eleven.
By then we were all tipsy, the food was gone, and it was
so hot inside the caravan that Jansson had taken off his
shirt and was sitting there bare-chested. When Lisa

went out for a pee, I asked Jansson if it wasn't time for a song. He brightened up as if he had been afraid that I wouldn't mention it. However, he didn't want to sing just yet; he would prefer to wait until midnight.

"'Ave Maria'," I said. "You have to sing 'Ave Maria'."

"I promise, but I have another song too."

I couldn't help wondering what it might be.

"'Buona Sera'," he said. "Made famous by Little Gerhard in Sweden in the 1950s."

I thought I remembered the song he was talking about, but I would have preferred the combination of "Ave Maria" with something other than Little Gerhard.

"Excellent," I said. "Very good."

Lisa came back, her gaze slightly unfocused. She tripped and laughed at her own clumsiness.

I had a bottle of champagne on ice: Veuve Clicquot. I remembered the name from a wedding anniversary that my father hadn't forgotten, much to my mother's surprise. He had come home with this very label. When Louise arrived with Agnes, Ahmed and Muhammed one day, we would also celebrate with Veuve Clicquot.

We finished off a bottle of red first, then I went outside and called Louise, who was at the hospital.

"You're drunk," she said. "I'm glad to hear it!"

Midnight was approaching. Jansson insisted that his watch was accurate to the second; none of us wanted the TV or radio on. The thermometer by the caravan door was showing plus two. The coloured lanterns were reflected in the calm, shining water, and ragged clouds drifted slowly above our heads. Jansson led the way up to my grandfather's bench; I could hear him quietly warming up his voice. I took Lisa's arm when she stumbled, and she didn't pull away.

We were surrounded by silence. Jansson fixed the beam of the torch on his magic watch. I tried to picture Louise, Agnes and her family, Muhammed in his wheelchair, all of them perhaps gathered by a window.

We stood there on the hill as if we were the last people in the world. Jansson began to count down the remaining seconds of the old year. I gripped Lisa's cold hand, and still she didn't pull away. With the other hand I felt in my pocket to make sure I had my cigarette lighter to give to Jansson so that he could start his firework display.

"Now," Jansson said, his voice trembling with excitement and emotion.

The year was over. Jansson launched into "Buona Sera". Lisa clearly recognised the song but was as taken aback as I had been at Harriet's last midsummer party, when Jansson astounded us all with his powerful voice. He held the torch so that it illuminated his face from below, giving him a ghostly pallor, but neither Lisa nor I were bothered about his appearance. It was his voice that exhorted us to look to the future. And then came "Ave Maria". The cold winter's night disappeared, and summer bloomed all around us. I could see Harriet sitting there with a glass of white wine in her hand and Jansson standing at the end of the table singing in a way that simply knocked all the air out of our lungs.

Afterwards, when he had fallen silent, I saw that Lisa had tears in her eyes. So did I, and perhaps even Jansson himself. We passed the schnapps around, drinking straight from the bottle as you do when you are with friends. We wished each other a Happy New Year and praised Jansson's wonderful voice. I asked him to start the firework display; the bangs and the not particularly impressive rockets echoed among the rocks and flared against the night sky, only to disappear in seconds. However, Lisa and I applauded Jansson's brave attempt to frighten away the evil spirits with fire and smoke.

When it was over we went back to the caravan. Jansson seemed tired and refused another drink.

"I'm going to head home," he said. "It's late for an old postman who isn't used to performing."

"I had no idea you could sing like that," Lisa said. "A Jussi Björling out here among the rocks and skerries!"

"I'm happier keeping quiet," Jansson said, getting ready to leave. He seemed anxious, restless.

We walked down to the jetty with him. To my surprise he appeared to be stone cold sober as he made his way over the slippery rocks to his boat.

He moved quickly, as if he were suddenly in a hurry. The feeling I had had before, that I didn't understand him at all, came back to me. However, right now I just wanted to make sure he actually left and didn't change his mind.

"You sang beautifully," I said.

"Mozart and Little Gerhard," Lisa said. "Extraordinary."

"Schubert," Jansson said. "Not Mozart."

"Who wrote the Italian song?"

Jansson shook his head. He didn't know.

"Off you go," I said. "It doesn't matter who wrote 'Buona Sera'."

Jansson fired up the engine while Lisa and I stood shivering on the jetty. He had put on his leather cap, which was looking rather scruffy after all the winters he had worn it while delivering the post.

We could hear the sound of bangs and whooshes in the distance.

"Vattenholmen," Jansson said.

"What's the name of the people who live there? Erlandsson?"

"They own a mail order company selling health products," Jansson said. "They've been reported to the police several times for making false promises, claiming that their creams and herbal preparations can cure everything from eczema to cancer."

"That house they built can't have been cheap."

"No, but the smell of scandal lingers around most people who make a ridiculous amount of money."

With that he bobbed down through the hatch and started the engine with a good spin of the flywheel. He reappeared, waved a hand in farewell and reversed away from the island. We stayed there until the red and green navigation lights had vanished around the headland.

I went into the boathouse and switched off the coloured lanterns, then we went up to the caravan.

"He sang so beautifully," Lisa said.

"I wanted it to be a surprise," I said. "He hides his voice as if he were carrying around a huge, possibly dangerous secret."

"Why was he in such a hurry to leave?"

We had stopped outside the caravan. I didn't have an answer; Jansson often resembled an indolent cat, reluctant to stir unnecessarily, but then he would suddenly turn into a completely different feline, moving across the rocks like lightning.

We went inside. Veronika had supplied me with several black bin bags and some paper carriers. I asked Lisa to put the empty bottles in the paper bags, separating plain and coloured glass, while I dumped the remains of the food in a bin bag. I had asked Veronika why she had given me more than one black sack.

"They come in useful if you want to throw up," she said. "Saves you doing it just outside the caravan."

I didn't think anyone had suffered from the amount we had drunk, although I couldn't swear to it of course.

I tied up the bag and pushed it under the caravan, then put an untouched crate of beer in front of it.

When I had finished I couldn't resist glancing in through the window. Lisa was sitting on the bed with an unlit cigarette in one hand. In the other she held the lighter I had given Jansson to start his firework display.

She looked up, straight at the window; I didn't have time to move away. She called to me to come in, then she reached out and switched off the light.

She had unrolled the mattress on the floor for me, and she got into the bed. I wanted to reach out and touch her, but I didn't dare. Right now I was grateful that I didn't have to be alone. I wondered if she felt the same.

She began to talk, perhaps because she had been drinking, perhaps for other reasons. She told me about a man who had once been part of her life, a man she still hadn't forgotten.

"It was before I started trying my hand at journalism," she said. "I couldn't decide what I wanted to achieve — or if I actually wanted to achieve anything at all. I worked in a paint shop to earn a living; ask me whatever you like about different kinds of paint and brushes, and I'll have an answer for you. One day a man came in and bought a small tin of blue paint. As soon as I saw him, I knew he was the one I wanted to live with. A few days later he came back and bought another tin. We started chatting; he was doing up an old cupboard. And so we became a couple. He had an incredibly boring job as an office clerk working for the local council, and every time he came home it was as if there was a great darkness surrounding him. He wasn't much to look at either, but I loved him to distraction. And he loved me. We were together for four years, but one day he got home from work, surrounded by that black cloud, and told me he didn't want to live with me any more. That was almost fifteen years ago, but to be honest I still haven't forgotten him."

She fell silent.

"Why are you telling me this?"

"So that you'll know."

"I don't want to know."

"What do you want?"

"Right now I'm just happy that you're here. Tomorrow I might feel differently."

We both lay awake, and the conversation edged along. She had cautiously opened one or two of her doors, just a fraction, and allowed me to peep inside.

410

It was very hot inside the caravan. The heater was on the highest setting, but neither of us could be bothered to get up and turn it off. I started to believe that there was a closeness between us after all, beyond all my expectations.

My phone rang; it was too late for Louise. It must have been at least three o'clock in the morning. I swore and wiped the sweat off my face. Lisa told me to pick up; the caller was probably drunk, so it would be a short conversation.

The person on the other end wasn't drunk at all. It was Jansson, and he was scared. I could tell that his body was shaking just as much as his voice was trembling.

"There's a fire," he yelled in my ear. "Karl-Evert Valfridsson's house is in flames! If you go outside you'll see the glow in the north-west."

I did as he said; the flames were shooting up into the air from Karstensön, where the Valfridssons' large house was located.

"I'd only just fallen asleep. I don't know what woke me up, but now I'm here," Jansson shouted. "Anyone who can help needs to get over to the island!"

"Are the Valfridssons out of the house?"

"They're away, the house is empty. It's going to burn to the ground."

"What's happened?"

Jansson didn't reply, which was answer enough for me. The arsonist had struck again.

"I'm on my way," I said. "We're both on our way."

When I went back inside, Lisa had switched on the light and got dressed.

"Another fire," she said. "Is it what I'm thinking?"

"It's arson," I said. "We need to go over there and do whatever we can to help."

"Has anyone died?"

"No."

I got dressed as quickly as I could, then we hurried down to the boathouse.

I asked Lisa to sit in the prow with the beam of the torch pointing out across the water as I didn't have any navigation lights. I sat in the stern with a chart on my knee, illuminating it with my phone from time to time. It was no more than two nautical miles to Karstensön, but there were several reefs along the way that I wasn't entirely sure of.

As we swung out into the bay, the Valfridssons' house blazed like an enormous midwinter sacrificial feast.

We were heading straight into the fire.

Boats were coming from all directions.

The New Year had started with yet another burning house.

CHAPTER
TWENTY-THREE

Once again I saw a house transformed into a blackened ruin.

The Valfridssons' house burned with the same fury that had obliterated my home. The old house stubbornly resisted, but the blaze was stronger. It reminded me of a lion, its jaws embedded in the throat of a dying gazelle.

There were about thirty of us running around with buckets of water and hosepipes, yelling at one another. Then the coastguard arrived and started up the pumps, and we stopped running around. Alexandersson, who was a little tipsy, took charge. I knew everyone there. We all wished each other a Happy New Year in the middle of the chaos, as we tried to do something useful.

I noticed that Lisa Modin was extremely capable. She took the initiative, and people listened when she made suggestions.

But of course there was nothing we could do. The whole place was already in flames by the time we arrived. At about five o'clock in the morning the roof began to collapse, the hot tiles shattering as they hit the ground. The windows burst, oxygen poured in and gave new strength to the conflagration. The heat was so intense that everyone had to move back.

I stood beside Alexandersson, sooty sweat pouring down his face.

"Another one," he said. "Who's burning down our property out here on the islands? What have we done to deserve this?"

"Is it the same as my place?" I asked. "A fire that starts everywhere and nowhere?"

"We don't know yet, but I'm sure the answer is yes. Same method, same lunatic."

He shook his head then spat out something black and unpleasant, possibly a plug of snuff, and went back to his pumps and hoses.

Lisa was sitting on a rusty old kick sled next to a barbecue covered with a torn boat tarpaulin. The glow of the flames lit up her sweaty face. From Paris to a blaze in the middle of the night on one of our islands, I thought. We had almost spent an entire peaceful night together, until Jansson's phone call shattered the intimacy.

Where was Jansson? At first I couldn't see him, then I spotted him lurking in the shadows, where the glow didn't reach his face. There was something strange about his body language. I moved closer; his eyes were fixed on the house and he still hadn't noticed me. Now I realised what was odd about his posture. His hands were clasped in front of him, as if he were saying a silent prayer, but was it directed to himself or to some fire god whose name I didn't know? His body was as rigid as if he were a wooden sculpture or a scarecrow.

414

He saw me just as I thought about the scarecrow. He immediately pulled his hands apart, as if I had caught him doing something embarrassing. I knew that embarrassment was the thing Jansson feared most of all; dropping a letter in the sea, letting the wind rip a pension payment slip out of his hand and watching it dance away across the water. Perhaps that was why he rarely sang, because he was afraid that one day a false note would come out of his mouth?

I went and stood beside him. He stank of sweat and booze, his best party shirt blackened with soot.

"At least no one was at home," I said. "No one died."

"It's still a terrible thing."

"You mean the fact that it's another arson attack?"

Jansson gave a start, as if I had said something unexpected.

"What else would it be?"

"But who the hell is creeping around out here in the early hours of New Year's Day?"

We didn't say any more. I watched the people slowly moving around the fire and wondered if Jansson was thinking the same as me: that it could well be one of them who had started it.

I glanced at Jansson, but his expression gave nothing away.

It was seven o'clock by the time Lisa and I left. The house would carry on burning for several hours, but there was nothing anyone could do. Alexandersson had managed to contact the owners, who were staying in a hotel in Marseilles. Before we left he told me that fru

Valfridsson had screamed so loudly that he thought his eardrum might burst.

I knew the lady in question; she was about my age and very thin. She had once come over to my island in a little motorboat to ask if I would look down her throat; she thought she had developed a tumour. I sat her down on the bench outside the boathouse, pushed down her tongue and checked her throat. There was no tumour. When I told her I couldn't find anything, she burst into tears. I was completely taken aback. With some patients it's obvious that they are going to have a strong reaction, whether the news is good or bad, but I was unprepared for Hanna Valfridsson's tears.

And now she was screaming in despair in a luxury hotel in Marseilles.

Before I started the engine I had asked Lisa where she wanted to go, and now we were heading for the harbour in the darkness. It occurred to me that I had far too much alcohol in my blood to drive my car, but then again I couldn't imagine there would be too many police officers hanging around this early on New Year's Day, hoping to catch someone in the middle of nowhere driving under the influence.

Oslovski's house was still locked up and deserted, but I stood for a moment looking at the window to the left of the front door. I wasn't sure, but I thought the curtain, which was closed, looked slightly different. I couldn't work out exactly what had attracted my attention; perhaps it was my imagination, or perhaps I was hoping that someone had been inside, that the place hadn't been abandoned.

416

Lisa asked what I was staring at.

"The curtain," I said. "But to be honest, I'm not sure. I thought maybe there was someone standing there watching us."

"The fire was quite enough," Lisa replied. "No more ghostly goings-on, thank you."

We drove into town in silence, through the morning mist that sometimes concealed the forest by the roadside. Lisa switched on the radio to listen to the news.

There had been riots in the Paris suburbs. A firefighter had been badly injured when he was struck on the head by a rock.

A major jewel heist had been discovered this morning in Moscow, involving one of the biggest jewellers in Russia.

Someone had died because of a drug called Spice.

A snowstorm was slowly moving in from the east, but they weren't sure how far south the snow would reach.

Lisa turned off the radio and asked me to stop. I pulled over on a logging track and she got out. When I realised she wasn't going for a pee, I undid my seatbelt and followed her. There wasn't a breath of wind. She had walked a few metres and was almost out of sight. A little further and she would disappear completely. That frightened me; I didn't want her to cease to exist, to vanish without a trace among the tall pine trees.

"It feels as if I'm part of a different story," she said.

She spoke quietly, as if she didn't want to disturb the silence all around her. As I stood watching her I thought she was like an animal, a deer perhaps, alert to the possibility of attack at any moment.

"Different from what?" I asked.

She didn't turn around.

"The one I'm usually in. Sometimes I detest all those meaningless articles I write for the paper, words that are dead the moment someone reads them. People delouse a newspaper, picking off the words in the same way they pick lice off their bodies."

I didn't really understand what she was saying, but there was no doubt that she meant it.

"I want to write something else," she went on. "Not books, I'm not good enough for that. I would be consumed with envy whenever I thought about those authors who really know how to choose their words, to create an unforgettable piece of work. Maybe I want to draw maps of places where no one has ever set foot? In the old days they used to let the cows wander free so that they would find the shortest and best route home. Let me go and I will find the forgotten pathways."

We stood in silence in the forest for a little while. This was my seventieth New Year's Day. The thought of how few I had left was a frightening one. I shuddered, and Lisa turned to face me. She was smiling.

"Coffee," she said. "I'm going to write a detailed account of last night's fire."

Everything was quiet in her apartment block. As if to protest at the unwelcoming silence, she stomped noisily up the concrete stairs. A dog started barking, but stopped when a man yelled at it. I followed one step

418

behind and reached out my hand, but I didn't touch her.

She made coffee while I sat on the sofa where I had once tried to sleep.

We drank our coffee at the kitchen table, ate a couple of sandwiches, didn't say much.

"I ought to get some sleep," she said as she cleared the table. "Otherwise I'll think it was all a dream."

"I can assure you that house really did burn down."

Lisa leaned against the draining board and looked at me.

"What's going on out there on your islands? Houses going up in flames in the small hours. I'd never experienced the roar of a fire until last night."

"It was arson," I said. "There's no proof yet, but everyone knows. Someone who helped to put out the fire probably started it."

"It shouldn't be impossible to find out who's responsible," she said almost crossly. "There aren't very many of you. There are comparatively few inhabited islands."

"No one profited from burning down my house. Who has anything to gain from destroying the Valfridssons' property? Or from seeing the widow Westerfeldt's pretty home collapse in ruins? It seems like total insanity to me."

"Could it be revenge?"

"We all have our differences; envy can eat away at someone over the years. But surely no one would go so far as to risk people being burned alive!"

"The desire for revenge can send you crazy."

419

"We're too simple for that kind of thing out here on the islands."

"You don't come from the islands."

I looked at Lisa in surprise.

"I don't, but my family does. I also have a profession which the local residents approve of; I'm a doctor, I'm regarded as useful. I have a kind of honorary status as an islander. I probably don't really 'belong' in the archipelago; I don't have a stamp on my soul. But I'm accepted."

We didn't say any more. I could tell from her expression that she didn't agree with me, but it wasn't worth pursuing the matter.

As if it were the most self-evident thing in the world, we went and lay down on her big bed. I listened to her steady breathing as it grew deeper. At first I saw the flames dancing, then I fell asleep.

It was ten thirty when I woke up. My head felt heavy, my mouth was dry. I could hear the muted sound of the radio from the kitchen, the clink of coffee cups. I coughed, and a chair scraped. Lisa appeared in the doorway in her dark blue dressing gown with a glass of water in her hand.

"If you feel the way I do you'll want a glass of water," she said.

I drained the glass as she watched.

"Painkillers?" I said.

She came back with the same glass, this time full of a sparkling analgesic solution.

I drank it down and leaned back against the pillows.

"How's it going with your article?" I asked.

420

"I haven't started it yet. But soon."

"Are you going to write about the voluntary firefighter who's sleeping in your bed?"

"I don't think anyone would be interested in that."

My phone rang; it was Kolbjörn, the electrician. He didn't ask where I was, he simply wished me a Happy New Year then got to the point. He's not a man who converses unnecessarily.

Apparently a small group of those who had helped out last night had come to a decision and were ringing round other residents of the archipelago. Kolbjörn had been asked to contact me.

I could tell from his gravelly voice that he was hungover. Or perhaps he was still drunk. There were rumours that he was something of a binge drinker, but no actual proof. He had never given the impression that he had been drinking when he worked for me, nor in my grandparents' day when he was a young electrician serving his apprenticeship with a man called Ruben. That was before he joined the merchant navy.

"We're going to have a meeting in the local history association centre," he explained. "We've decided to wait until Twelfth Night. Two o'clock in the afternoon. We want as many people as possible to be there; we're going to talk about these arson attacks and what we can do."

"To stop them?"

"To catch whoever's responsible. Then they'll stop."

"Any suspects?"

"No."

"I'll be there," I said. "Two o'clock."

Lisa had left the bedroom while I was on the phone; the door of her study was ajar.

She was sitting at her desk, writing. Her dressing gown had ridden up her thighs. I realised that my need for sex was not a spring that had dried up for the rest of my life. That definitely wasn't true.

However, I didn't want her to see me peeping through the door. I moved away, made a noise with my glass and sat down at the table.

She emerged with the notepad in her hand.

"I'm writing about the fire, but I'm saying that I ended up there because I was at a New Year's party on one of the islands. I'm not mentioning any names."

"Shouldn't you at least mention Jansson's name? The former postman who was at the party? If nothing else, it would please him greatly if he appeared in the local paper. His first name is Ture."

Suddenly I realised she wasn't listening. She looked anxious, but her voice was firm when she spoke.

"I'm used to being alone. Right now I need to be alone. And I need to write."

"You won't even notice I'm here. I've perfected the art of being quiet."

"That's not what I mean. I need to close everything down around me."

I sat down on the chair in the hallway to tie my shoes. Lisa stood in the kitchen doorway, still holding the notepad. When I got up and attempted to give her a hug, she moved away.

"Not now," she said. "I'm not being unkind, that's just the way it is."

422

I drove to the harbour. In a field next to the long inlet I saw a skier making his way over the thin covering of snow. A dog was racing along in front of him, as if tracking some unknown quarry.

I parked the car in its usual place. A biting wind was blowing in off the sea. I couldn't resist the temptation to go and take a look at Oslovski's garage, but it was all locked up. Through the dirty window I could see the emptiness left behind after the theft of her DeSoto Fireflite. I had a lump in my throat; I missed the person called Oslovski, the person I had hardly known but who had been close to me. Her glass eye had seen me more clearly than others' eyes. Perhaps I was actually experiencing grief at her loss?

I walked down to the harbour, which was deserted on this New Year's morning. As I set off for home, the black sea seemed to be feeling the cold just as much as I was.

It snowed during the night of 5 January. When I reached the local history association centre, which was situated in an inlet below the church, I could see footprints leading up from the jetty. I squeezed my boat in between an old wooden craft from Krutholmen and Holmén the pilot's Pettersson boat from 1942. It looked as if a lot of people had turned up. The tracks in the snow made me think of a flock of crows that had wandered around for a long time before flying away.

The aroma of coffee and a welcoming fire greeted me as I walked into the spacious room. Kolbjörn

Eriksson nodded, then came over and shook hands. His own hand was as big as a bear's paw.

"Thanks for coming," he said.

"It's good to see so many people here."

"Do you want to say something?"

"Why would I do that?"

"Well, your house was the first to burn down."

I shook my head; I had nothing to say. In the coffee queue I exchanged a few words with people I rarely saw. My ability to remember names has declined dramatically over the years; sometimes I think that much-feared gateway is slowly opening for me. One day I will walk through into the land where memory has been swallowed up by forgetfulness.

I had just got my cup of coffee when Louise called. She knew about the fire, but I hadn't mentioned the meeting. I quickly explained where I was and promised to call her back later. She said that Agnes would soon be out of her incubator, which made me feel both happy and relieved.

I had counted fifty-six people when Wiman, a retired priest who lived on Almö, clapped his hands and asked for silence. Personally I had never heard him preach, but many people had told me that he divided his parishioners. For some incomprehensible reason, a number of those living out on the islands were annoyed because he never stressed the constant presence of hell and the devil during his sermons. Those who lived on the mainland, however, thought he was an excellent priest who never brought up the darkness of evil unnecessarily when he was standing in the pulpit.

424

Wiman welcomed everyone, blew his nose, wished us a Happy New Year and blew his nose again. Then he raised his voice with practised ease and bellowed that there must be no more of this insanity, no more setting fire to houses out on the islands. We must all learn to keep a closer eye on our neighbours' property and take note of any unfamiliar vessels in our waters. We must take responsibility for our brothers and sisters. There was no need for any formal organisation; however, Kolbjörn Eriksson, Ture Jansson and Wiman himself were joining together as a committee. One of them would always be available if anything happened, if anyone had suspicions or was worried.

He opened the discussion to the floor to be met by silence — no one was used to a priest letting others speak. Again he encouraged everyone to ask questions or to comment. Eventually an old fisherman called Alabaster Wernlund from Torpholmen, one of the smallest fishing communities in the archipelago, got to his feet, making an enormous amount of noise with his chair. Everyone knew that he was hard of hearing, that he had a volatile temper and that he not infrequently called the coastguard when he got it into his head that large-scale smuggling was going on around his island. He might be eccentric, but everyone also knew that he had a sharp mind and couldn't be bamboozled by fancy talk.

He was wearing a red woolly hat and the kind of orange hi-vis jacket you usually see on construction workers.

"What are we going to do if it turns out that this pyromaniac is here in this room? Surely that's just as likely as the idea that he's coming over from Denmark?"

Pontus Urmark immediately stood up. He was a skinny carpenter from the far end of the small islands in Kattskärsvarpen. He might have less sense than Wernlund, but he had just as much of a temper.

"Why the hell would an arsonist come from Denmark?" he said. "Haven't they got their own islands?"

"Belgium, then, if you prefer that!" Wernlund yelled.

Wiman tried to intervene, but it was already too late. The two men were standing at opposite ends of the hot room, sweat pouring down their faces like two actors fighting over the right to a riposte on stage. Urmark, whose profile resembled that of Karl XII, had the loudest voice, but Wernlund was a worthy opponent; he knew exactly when to make his poisonous remarks.

The quarrel ended just as suddenly as it had flared up. They both sat down in sullen silence, but they were watching one another and might easily launch a fresh attack.

Wiman used the lull in hostilities to return to how important it was for those of us living out on the islands to look out for strangers who appeared in the harbour or on boats around the archipelago. At that point his audience seemed to come to life. Many people wanted to speak or at least waved their hands to show that they were engaged in the debate. A young fisherman from the southern part of the archipelago stood up and said

426

in a trembling voice (I'm not sure if he was nervous about addressing the gathering or flustered because of what he was going to say) that it was these strangers — foreigners, in fact — who were responsible for dragging Sweden further and further down. Perhaps one couldn't blame these mysterious foreigners for eradicating the fish in the waters of the archipelago; that was down to "the bloody Polacks" as he insisted more than once. Not people from the Baltic countries or Russia. No, the lack of perch these days was definitely down to the bloody Polacks. But the foreigners were clearly responsible for everything else: any form of crime, particularly the theft of outboard motors, break-ins and these arson attacks. Sweden had abandoned its borders. The Sweden that had once been ours had been handed over to the hordes who were now allowed to pour across its borders and help themselves.

I sat in my corner listening to this agitated young man, his freckled face glowing in the heat. He was obviously convinced that he was speaking the truth. At that moment his faith was greater than Wiman's had ever been. He carried on ranting about foreigners and the politicians who allowed them to ravage our country. He cursed uncontrolled immigration; he applied his verbal branding iron to the forehead of everyone with evil intentions, be they beggars or pickpockets, who were running amok mainly in our cities, but whose presence was increasingly being felt in rural areas and now around our islands.

Then he burst into tears. It was such a shock that the whole room stopped breathing. He covered his face with his hands, his whole body shaking as he slumped back down on his chair. He had come alone; there was no wife or relative to comfort him.

I realised later that his tears were a call to arms. Islander after islander stood up in support of the young man, saying how right he was. Xenophobia, based on nothing more than myths, hearsay and what a friend of a friend had allegedly experienced, settled over the room like a fetid cloud. Few people took a different view. Wiman did his best, but he lacked the strength — and perhaps the conviction. The only one who really protested against the tone was Annika Wallmark, who had a small ceramics workshop just outside the town, but as she was a well-known radical, no one took any notice of her. Murmurs broke out as soon as she opened her mouth.

Veronika had sprained her foot falling off her horse during a trek in Iceland, and had come back limping. She said what we all knew: that we could only guess at the identity of the perpetrator. There was a significant risk that we would start looking for a scapegoat and spreading even more toxic rumours.

What did I say — the doctor with a daughter who was a pickpocket in Paris? I didn't agree with the young fisherman, nor did my views match those of Annika Wallmark.

I said nothing. The meeting and all those voices turned into a labyrinth, simultaneously threatening and reassuring. We would keep an eye on each other's houses, we would watch any unfamiliar vessels with eyes more used to looking out for seabirds during the hunting season. We had shifted every last scrap of suspicion from ourselves to those nameless individuals who had invaded our country.

I said nothing, but as Wiman began to draw the meeting to a close I experienced an unfamiliar, nasty taste in my mouth. I thought about Louise and her Ahmed; if he had turned up here and heard how he was regarded, as a representative of all those foreigners, I'm sure he would have fled. Would I have been able to defend him?

Something unfamiliar was hiding beneath the surface I knew so well, and it frightened me.

I walked back to the boat with Jansson. It was dark by now. We could hear muttered conversations here and there between those who had been at the meeting; the breath coming out of their mouths was like a series of smoke signals.

Down on the jetty there was a little shed where the association stored its flags and flagpoles. I stood in the doorway as Jansson changed out of his suit and into warm maritime clothing. A bell rang in my head as I watched him, but I couldn't understand why.

Jansson carefully folded up his suit and put it in a plastic bag. I still couldn't work out what the situation reminded me of.

Something was bothering me, but what?

We went out onto the jetty; some of the boats were already on their way, their navigation lights showing. Someone was locking the doors up at the centre.

Jansson and I nodded to one another, and he disappeared down the hatch to fire up his engine. I switched on my torch, pulled the cord to start my engine and set off for home.

The late afternoon was very cold. The ice had started to form in the inlets and along the coast. If the temperature continued to fall, most of the archipelago would soon be surrounded by ice.

Back in the warmth of the caravan, I was finally able to shake off the unpleasant feeling from the meeting. I had seen and heard people I thought I knew, but who had turned out to hold opinions I would never have expected.

What had I expected? What had I thought about these people's view of the world beyond the islands?

I was sitting there with a cup of coffee, still unable to answer my questions, when Lisa Modin called. We had spoken a few times since the morning of New Year's Day, but when I had wanted to go and see her or suggested that she should come to me, she had said no. I had been careful not to try and persuade her; I was afraid she might withdraw completely.

"How was the meeting?" she asked.

"Who wants to know?"

"I want to know."

"Lisa Modin or the journalist?"

"We're the same person."

I had told her I was going to the meeting; after all, Kolbjörn Eriksson had called me when I was lying on her bed. But how could she know it was over and that I'd got home just a little while ago?

"Who've you been talking to?"

"I'm talking to you."

"How do you know the meeting is over?"

"I guessed."

I didn't believe her. She must have spoken to someone; the only person I could think of was the woman no one listened to.

"You've been talking to someone, and I know who it is. Annika Wallmark."

"I never reveal my sources."

"She pops up from behind her potter's wheel, gossiping and talking about all kinds of stuff, and no one gives a damn."

"Why don't you just tell me how the meeting went, instead of trying to get answers to impossible questions?"

"It was well attended and we were all in agreement. We're going to keep an eye on what's happening to our neighbours' houses. We islanders have added an eleventh commandment. We're going to transform ourselves into vigilantes, so to speak. It sounds pathetic and it is pathetic, but it's also true. It was Wiman, the priest, who said those words."

"Can you tell me any more?"

"No."

"What was the atmosphere like?"

I had the feeling that she knew considerably more than she was letting on. Did she have other contacts? Jansson? Hardly. Nor the young fisherman who had started crying. Wiman, perhaps?

I realised I didn't trust anyone who had been at the meeting. I tried to change the subject: when would she like to come and visit my caravan again?

"Not yet."

"Maybe I'm too old and boring. It would be better if you just came straight out with it. Old doctors can usually cope with the truth."

That was a lie. If anything distinguished us from other people, it was probably the fact that we were less well equipped to deal with the truth.

"No," Lisa said. "You're not too old. But both of us are solitary by nature."

When the conversation was over, I went back to my cup of coffee. I still thought there was a chance that I might manage to break out of my loneliness through meeting Lisa Modin, in spite of everything.

I was aware of a growing sense of happiness. There was Lisa, there was Louise and there was the baby. I felt nothing yet for Ahmed and Muhammed, but perhaps it would come one day.

I lay down on the bed, with the radio quietly playing music that was supposed to be calming.

I had just dozed off when I woke with a start. At first I didn't know why, but then I realised.

When Jansson called me after the New Year's Eve party to tell me that the Valfridssons' house was burning, he had said that he had been at home and had been woken up. And yet he had been wearing at least some of the same clothes from the party when I met him later, at the fire. I had reacted, but without giving the matter any further thought.

I lay in bed with the radio still playing. I recognised an old song: "Sail Along Silvery Moon".

Thinking about Jansson's clothes made me anxious, but I still didn't know what it was that I had discovered.

It was like an unexpected reef in what I thought was a well-charted shipping lane.

CHAPTER
TWENTY-FOUR

The cold never loosened its grip during the week following Twelfth Night. Ice began to form in the bays and inlets. I still didn't need an axe to cut a hole when I went down for my morning dip, but a thick mist lay just above the surface of the water, which was growing blacker by the day. Soon the ripples would turn to ice.

Two days after the archipelago meeting I was sitting in the caravan playing patience when I felt unwell. It was like a nausea in my head rather than my stomach. I left the cards, put on my jacket and went outside. I didn't know what was wrong. I had spoken to Louise the previous evening, and everything was fine. She promised to send me some new pictures of Agnes. When I asked if she and Ahmed needed any financial assistance, she just laughed and said she would let me know when poverty really moved into their apartment.

I had also spoken to Lisa Modin; she was in her car on the way to Stockholm, so it had been a short conversation. She was going to a school reunion, having accepted the invitation after much hesitation. She promised to call me when she got back.

I walked around the island. The frost sparkled like glass on the site of the fire and the blackened remains of my house. I went up to my grandfather's bench, pulling on the gloves that were in my pocket.

We were approaching the depths of winter. Almost every year there is a point when the islands and bays close their doors. No one is allowed in or out. The shops are shut, the curtains drawn. Sometimes it happened as early as the end of November or the beginning of December, sometimes not until February.

In some years the archipelago didn't close down at all. My grandfather used to say that if the sea didn't ice over and the snow didn't cover the skerries, then come summer the fishing would be poor. I had once asked Jansson if that was true, and he had firmly answered no. However, when I told him that was what my grandfather had said, he immediately changed his mind.

The nauseous feeling in my head had now turned into a vague, nagging pain. I decided to row across to my tent. Perhaps I had spent too long sitting at the table in the caravan and needed some exercise. I went down to the boathouse and pushed out the skiff. There wasn't a breath of wind. I rowed with powerful strokes and immediately started sweating. After every fifteenth stroke I rested on the oars for a moment before carrying on.

When I was five years old, my grandfather built a little boat for me to play with. He used Masonite board, with a prow and stern made of pine and oars of alder. That boat had been my most cherished possession throughout my childhood.

Could I make something similar for Agnes? Probably not; it was far too big a job for an inexperienced carpenter. However, perhaps I could ask Kolbjörn Eriksson? I had heard that he was exceptionally talented in the skilled art of boatbuilding.

I reached the skerry and pulled the skiff ashore. The tent was securely anchored in the little hollow; I had come over to check on it every time we had had high winds, but it had stood firm.

I immediately saw that I had had visitors. The bank of stones forming a wall around the cooking area had grown, and someone had made a hook on which to hang a pot to boil water. I opened the tent flap and was struck by a smell I recognised: acetone. Could my mysterious visitor be a woman? Acetone made me think of nail polish, which Harriet had used. And hadn't Louise been wearing nail polish when I saw her in Paris?

Of course I also realised that there was a more disturbing possibility: acetone is an important ingredient in the production of synthetic drugs, above all the narcotic known as Spice. Was a junkie seeking refuge in my tent from time to time?

I found this idea upsetting. All my life I have felt antipathy towards those who sully their lives with drugs. As a surgeon I often had to operate on someone who had taken something and been involved in an accident, or been stabbed in a dispute over those expensive commodities. As they lay there on the table, helpless under the knife, I frequently thought that I was

436

doing what I was supposed to do, but that I really didn't care what happened to them afterwards.

When I attempted to discuss this with my colleagues, none of them seemed to agree with me. I soon gave up, deciding that I was probably ill-suited to my profession when it came to my views on the value of certain individuals.

No doubt that was partly why the smell in the tent bothered me so much. I crawled outside, closed the flap, wondered whether I ought to take down the tent, then went on a tour of inspection around the skerry. In a crevice, neatly covered by torn-up moss, I found a small rubbish heap. I rooted through the empty milk cartons and bread wrappings and came across a scrap of black rubber. At first I thought it was a piece of a tyre from a bicycle, then I realised it was actually neoprene and therefore more likely to have come from a diving suit. However, this was an unsatisfactory conclusion; no one dived in the waters off these islands in the winter. Nor could it have drifted ashore on the southern side of the skerry where I found it; the wind out here is almost always offshore.

So it couldn't be part of a diving suit. All of a sudden I knew: it came from a wetsuit worn by surfers to keep out the chill from the wind and water. My visitor was the black-clad windsurfer who had turned up in the autumn and on several occasions had headed out towards the open sea with his board and his sail.

I stood scanning the horizon, but there was nothing to see except the banks of cloud slowly drifting in from the Gulf of Finland.

I walked around the skerry again, but I couldn't find any more clues.

I didn't have time to worry about the identity of my visitor. As I set off for home I decided it was the moment to tackle the insurance company so that the construction of the new house could get under way. I didn't have time to wait, either for my own sake or for the sake of my daughter and granddaughter.

From time to time I rested on the oars and gazed down into the dark water, hoping to spot another drift net floating silently along in the depths like a predator seeking its prey. But the sea was empty and black, with no hint of light.

Back on the island I pictured the new house slowly rising from the ruins. Even though all my photographs had been destroyed in the fire, I knew that the local history association had commissioned a photographer to document all the houses and boathouses in the archipelago during my grandparents' day. The pictures were kept in the association's archive collection. I should have thought of that when I was at the meeting; Wiman was the archivist and would have been able to help me.

I had been asked to join the association's board more than once, but I had always refused, feeling slightly more guilty each time. Jansson, who had served on the board several times, had told me there were no more than four meetings a year; the work was not arduous. It was an important organisation that did a great deal to fight for those who lived in the archipelago.

However, I knew that Jansson wasn't telling the whole truth. I had heard rumours, even without Jansson's assistance; there were deep divisions between various members and groups. At times it seemed as if open warfare raged between different factions. I had never really understood the reasons behind this seething tension, but something told me it was essentially down to the fact that there was only one dung heap and far too many aspiring cockerels.

I called Wiman; I began by saying how well I thought he had handled the meeting, then I asked about photographs of my house. He promised to look through the archive to see what he could find.

"Things weren't kept in particularly good order in the past," he said. "The archive is in a state somewhere between chaos and a complete mess, created by the archivists with the apparent aim of making it impossible to find what you're looking for."

He was in danger of tipping over into his preacher's voice, so I quickly ended the call.

I spent the next few hours playing poker with myself. It's the saddest expression of loneliness I know. I never feel more overwhelmed by weariness and unhappiness than when I'm trying to win money off myself. There is no deeper form of isolation.

I sat there for a long time that evening making notes about the new house; I hoped to start building in the early spring. There was no need to lay new foundations, so it was just a matter of removing the burned-out ruins. I intended to ask both Jansson and Kolbjörn Eriksson for advice; I would ignore whatever Jansson said, but I didn't want to incur the sullenness and ill will that would follow if I didn't consult him. Kolbjörn was the one I trusted.

That night I dreamed of caves. I was wandering around in a darkness that became so heavy I could hardly breathe. At that point I woke up. There were mice scampering around on the roof of the caravan. I listened for the wind, but all was calm.

For a brief moment I thought I might never wake up if I went back to sleep. Death was suddenly very close.

But I did fall asleep, right in the middle of that thought, surrounded by mice seeking shelter from the cold.

The following day I called the insurance company. I had expected a long-drawn-out infuriating duel between myself and uncooperative bureaucrats, but once I got through to Jonas Andersson, everything was very straightforward. A little too straightforward, perhaps. Were there invisible pitfalls ahead, to be revealed only gradually? However, I chose to believe what Andersson said. The new house would be built, starting in the spring. If necessary he could send me a list of suitable building firms in the area, recommended by the insurance company.

After lunch I had just decided to call Kolbjörn when I heard Jansson's boat approaching. I went down to the jetty to meet him. Sometimes I thought I could tell from the sound of the engine what mood Jansson was in and what he wanted from me. It was all in my mind, of course, but the idea amused me.

440

He moored by the jetty but didn't switch off the engine, which meant he was intending to stay for only a short time. There was therefore no danger that he would ask me to examine him because of some new imaginary ailment.

He climbed onto the jetty; we shook hands and then he reached inside his thick jacket and handed me a letter.

"You've retired," I said. "You don't deliver the post any more."

"Wiman asked me to bring you this."

I took the envelope, which wasn't sealed. It contained old black and white photographs of my grandparents' house. I merely glanced inside; I didn't want to reveal the contents to Jansson. However, as I slipped the envelope into my pocket I realised he knew exactly what was in there; he had already opened it, of course. I felt an almost irresistible urge to push him into the cold water. Perhaps he noticed something because he took a step back. I smiled.

"Could you tell your successor that from now on I would like my post delivered again, please?"

"You've changed your mind?"

"Yes, just now. Thank you for bringing the photographs."

"What photographs?"

I thought I ought to come straight out with it, put into words what everyone in the archipelago knew: that during his long years as a postman Jansson had read final demands, letters of condolence, threatening letters, friendly letters, letters that didn't say much at all. He had read the lot. And now he stood here pretending he didn't know what was in the envelope from Wiman.

"I'd like you to leave now," I said in a pleasant tone of voice. "I have a lot to do today. Can I pay you for the delivery?"

He shook his head and clambered down into the boat, but remained standing with one hand on the bollard.

"Could it have been Oslovski?" he asked.

I didn't understand the question.

"Who burned down the houses."

"Why the hell would she have done that?"

"Nobody knew anything about her. She was a foreigner. God knows what a person with one eye is capable of."

I was astounded by his grotesque logic. What could the fact that Oslovski had one eye possibly have to do with the arson attacks? I usually let Jansson's stupid comments go, like water off a duck's back, but not this time.

"Of all the possible pyromaniacs, Oslovski is the least likely. Besides which she's dead."

Jansson was offended. He let go of the bollard and cast off the mooring rope. For once we didn't wave to one another as he reversed away from the jetty.

I went back to the site of the fire. A couple of crows pecking among the sooty ruins rose into the air and flapped away. I would bury Giaconelli's buckle when the foundations were tidied up, ready for the new house; it would be a token, a memorial to the house

442

that had once stood there — but also a memorial to the man who had been a master shoemaker.

I happened to be listening to the radio once when a world-famous soprano who had appeared on stage in the biggest theatres all over the world was being interviewed. She was asked what the most important thing was for an opera singer.

"Good shoes," she had replied without hesitation.

I understood what she meant. Good shoes in which to walk, stand and work are every bit as important for a fisherman as for a surgeon.

Right now I longed for the wellington boots I had ordered months ago, which still hadn't arrived.

I took out my phone and called the chandlery. Eventually fru Nordin answered; I wondered if I had woken her. Perhaps she had made herself a bed in the storeroom for the time of year when customers were few and the bell over the door rarely pinged? I suspected she was one of those people in the archipelago who went into hibernation when winter began to press down on the earth.

My wellington boots still hadn't arrived.

I sat down at the table in the caravan with Wiman's photographs spread out in front of me. The oldest was from around 1900. The porch hadn't yet been built. My grandfather was standing by the front door with my grandmother on a stool next to him. They were still young. My grandfather had a moustache; the bushy beard was still far in the future. On the back of the picture was a note stating that it was probably taken by

Robert Sjögren, who travelled around the islands at the turn of the century.

I went through the pictures one by one. Most were taken from the front; the back of the house didn't appear anywhere.

In one of the photographs, dated "Summer 1946" by an unknown hand, the white garden furniture had appeared. The porch had been added over twenty years earlier. My grandparents were sitting on the ribbed wooden chairs with cups of coffee and a plate of biscuits. In the half-shadows, as if he were slightly shy of the unknown photographer, sat a man named on the back as Adolf Sundberg.

I suddenly remembered him; he came walking towards me as a distant memory, growing clearer as he got closer. Adolf Sundberg lived to the age of a hundred and four. He was born in 1899, and even as a young man he had said that he intended to live during three centuries. Which he did — he passed away in 2003.

He often visited my grandparents. He was a good raconteur, so I would often hang around as he sat on one of those white chairs drinking coffee.

He once told a story about his family that my grandparents discussed for ages afterwards. Was it true or not? I can't have been more than ten years old at the time, but that was when I really understood the huge, almost immeasurable distance between a lie and the truth, between a tall tale and an account of something that had actually happened, something no one need ever doubt.

Adolf Sundberg had arrived in the archipelago as a stranger. His family originated inland, in the town of Alingsås far away in Västergötland, on the plains stretching down towards the sea. He had served on board two-masted wooden ships carrying cargo around the inner archipelago, but after a quarrel with a captain about a broken compass, he had signed on with *Blåsut*, which was lying idle in Västervik, before it set sail again, travelling between Gävle and Copenhagen. After a few years he came ashore, married a girl from Kalmar and took over the farm her uncle had owned. That was how Adolf Sundberg from Västergötland came to the islands. At a haymaking party where a great deal of schnapps had been consumed he told the story that was a discussion topic for ever afterwards, when people met and wondered how reliable Adolf Sundberg actually was.

In Alingsås, he said, his grandparents had owned a pharmacy. One of the most popular products back in the 1840s was leeches. His grandfather had come up with the brilliant idea of breeding leeches in an old fish pond in the municipal park, instead of the ornamental carp that had once occupied the muddy, evil-smelling water. Every time the supply of leeches dropped and the glass jars in which they were kept began to look empty, Adolf's grandmother knew what was coming. There was no point in protesting, even though she found the whole process utterly humiliating. They would set off from home at first light, Grandfather carrying a long pole and Grandmother dressed in a simple shift, which she concealed beneath a capacious coat. She probably put up a bit of a fight when they reached the pond, but to no avail. She stripped naked; her body was fat and shapeless. She waded out into the pond until the water covered her breasts. Grandfather held out the pole so that she would have something to grab; if she fell over she would drown, because she couldn't swim and Grandfather would never be able to drag her out. Then she stood there as the eager leeches sank their teeth into her ample body. When she had had enough, she made her way back to dry land with the black leeches firmly attached, mainly to her backside. When Grandfather sprinkled salt on them they let go and dropped into the glass jars.

This exercise was repeated at regular intervals. After a while everyone in Alingsås knew about the strange pantomime played out early in the mornings during the warmer months. Curious onlookers hid behind bushes and in the undergrowth, gleefully watching as the naked matron ploughed through the water before complaining as the leeches fastened themselves to her flesh.

This was Adolf Sundberg's story. Everyone believed it deep down but felt obliged to express their doubts with regard to its veracity. You couldn't just send a naked old woman into a fish pond, using her body as bait to catch leeches. It wasn't possible. Admittedly some men mistreated their wives, but this was beyond the bounds of decency.

I spent a long time gazing at the picture of Adolf Sundberg with his cup of coffee. From far away I heard the voices coming back to me: my grandfather's slow,

446

almost hesitant way of formulating a sentence, my grandmother, who didn't say much but spoke with the utmost precision, using beautiful similes taken from a seemingly inexhaustible store. And then Adolf Sundberg, with his domed hat, his bushy beard and his shiny waistcoat; over the years the stains and grease marks had combined to form a patina that was never washed away.

They would always sit there on those white chairs, even though they were all dead and the chairs had been lost in the devastation of the fire.

The last black and white photograph had been taken on my grandfather's seventy-fifth birthday, 19 June 1957. The photographer, Tage Palmblad, had gathered a large group of people around the porch and the garden furniture, with my grandfather right at the front, my grandmother by his side. When I studied the picture more closely I discovered to my surprise that I was there too, squeezed in between two of my grandmother's cousins, who were considerably more interested in how they appeared than in giving me enough room.

I was thirteen years old when that picture was taken: my hair bleached chalk-white by the sun, short trousers, a striped top, sandals, skinny body, unsure of myself in front of all those people.

I thought I would invite everyone I had got to know in the archipelago to a house-warming party when my new home had risen from the ruins. I would sit right at the front, with Louise and her family beside me.

I called Wiman to thank him for his speedy response to my request.

"There might be more pictures," he said. "But as I explained, the archive is in a real mess, and I haven't had time to sort it out yet."

"These are fine — more than enough for those who are going to build my new house."

"Did you know that the Österströms' place on Skarsholmen was built at the same time?" Wiman said. "If I've understood correctly, they used the same builder."

So whoever I chose could use the Österströms' house as a detailed model.

"It hadn't occurred to me, but of course that's very important because there are no drawings. In the old days the master builders and their clients were their own architects."

After the conversation with Wiman I went up to my grandfather's bench with my binoculars so that I could check on my tent, but there wasn't a soul in sight.

Twilight was beginning to fall. I shivered. I had almost reached the caravan when I heard my phone ringing on the table. I stumbled on a root and banged my chin on the edge of the caravan. When I reached up to check the damage, my hand came away covered in blood. I staggered inside and grabbed my phone as it stopped ringing. I wiped my bloody face with a tea towel; I could feel with the tip of my tongue that I had lost a tooth from my lower jaw. I picked up the torch and went back outside to see if I could find it in the grass.

448

I couldn't find the tooth. Had I swallowed it without noticing? I went back inside, put some ice cubes in a plastic bag and held it against my lips. It took a long time for the bleeding to stop. I looked at my mouth in the shaving mirror; the tooth had broken off cleanly, and the root was lost in congealed blood. When I pressed the gum with my finger, I felt a sharp, stabbing pain. I would have to go and see the dentist tomorrow; it was too late now. I could probably find an emergency dentist in town, but I didn't want to set off at this hour.

I took some strong painkillers then checked to see who had called. It was Louise. I rang her back, but the number was busy. I tried again; still busy. I lay down on the bed clutching my mobile. The thought of having to spend time going to the dentist annoyed me. Or perhaps I was just tired. Growing older meant losing a little bit of energy every single day. And one day it would be completely gone.

I dropped off to sleep, only to be woken by Louise on the phone. I didn't ask how she was, or Agnes, or the family; I simply launched into an account of my bleeding mouth and my broken tooth. However, she interrupted me.

"Agnes is sick."

Her voice was almost breaking. I sat up straight and clamped my jaws together, which was a painful mistake.

"What's wrong with her?"

"They don't know."

"What are her symptoms?"

"She screams all the time. She's in pain."

"In her tummy?"

"Her head."

"Her head?"

"Oh God, I don't know. No one knows."

Her fear became mine. I had no doubt that whatever was wrong, Louise's reaction was definitely not unwarranted. I racked my brains for an answer. I had never specialised in paediatrics, nor had I been involved in anything other than routine surgical procedures on children. The fact that it was something to do with the head was worrying. A baby's heart and brain are fragile.

I tried to calm both Louise and myself. I asked her to tell me what had happened; could she tell me any more about Agnes's symptoms? What exactly had the doctors said?

Apparently the whole thing had been very fast. That morning Agnes had suddenly started screaming. Nothing had helped, not even an attempt at breastfeeding. Louise had taken her to the hospital while Ahmed stayed at home with Muhammed. In the children's emergency unit they had immediately admitted her for observation and tests. Louise was calling from the hospital; I wrote down the name on the back of a packet of crispbread.

Her explanation didn't enable me to reach any conclusion about what might be wrong with the child. It was very unusual, but not unknown, for babies to suffer a brain haemorrhage. On the other hand encephalitis, or inflammation of the brain, sometimes affected small children and could be life-threatening. Nor could a tumour be ruled out. The French doctors were trying to establish a definite diagnosis at this very moment.

I asked if Agnes had a temperature. She didn't, but the pain in her head was still there. Louise was waiting for her to undergo a brain scan.

I asked if she wanted me to come. She said no, but I could tell from her voice that she could easily change her mind.

She didn't want to stay on the phone because she was waiting for Ahmed to call. She promised to let me know as soon as she had any news.

"If nothing happens, call me anyway," I said. "I'll keep the phone with me all the time, and it's fully charged."

Clutching the phone as tightly as if it were a rosary, it seemed to me that death was suddenly present in the caravan. I didn't want him here. I called Lisa. I didn't ask where she was or if I was disturbing her, I simply told her what had happened.

"That sounds terrible," she said. "Do you want to come over?"

"No, but thank you for asking."

"Are you really going to sit there in the caravan all by yourself?"

I didn't reply. More than anything I wanted to stagger down to the boat, hope the engine started and head for the mainland.

"Perhaps you could come here?"

"There isn't room for the two of us and so much worry in your caravan."

I asked if I could reach her during the evening, and she said yes.

"What are you doing right now?" I asked.

"I'm praying that there isn't anything seriously wrong with your grandchild."

"That's what you're thinking. What are you doing?"

"I'm standing here holding my gloves and a bag of groceries. I'm on my way home."

Silence drifted by. A gust of wind shook the caravan.

"Thank you," I said and ended the call.

I went out into the cold air and took a deep breath. It was already dark. I went down to the bench on the jetty. My phone rang again; it was Louise. Agnes was about to undergo an MRI scan; the doctors still hadn't reached a firm diagnosis, but I could tell from her voice that she was more scared than the first time she called. I don't think I was able to hide my own panic at the thought of what must not happen.

It was a brief conversation; Agnes was being taken away on a trolley, and someone told Louise to switch off her phone.

I shivered and went back to the caravan. Proximity to death turns time into an overstretched elastic band, making us constantly afraid that it will break. The information about Agnes was too vague; I thought I ought to speak to one of her doctors, but my French wasn't good enough. I knew that fear was drilling deep holes in Louise, and there was nothing I could do to help her.

I had a sleepless night; Louise called at first light to tell me that Agnes had a mild form of meningitis. She would have to stay in the hospital for a week or so, then hopefully everything would be fine.

We both started crying; we were exhausted. At least now we could rest.

I was woken by the sound of an engine at some point during the morning. My jaw was aching where my tooth had broken off. I drank a scoop of water out of the container on the draining board. I knew Jansson was on his way; no other engine sounds like his.

I was sitting on the bench by the time he rounded the headland. He hove to, leaving the engine running. I relaxed; he wasn't intending to stay long this time either. He looped the mooring rope around the bollard and clambered ashore. We shook hands and discussed the essentials: the weather, wind direction, the banks of cloud over to the east, the temperature, the ice and the fact that the Enberg family, who farmed sheep and fish, had a ten-year-old daughter who played the double bass; she had just been given a grant of three thousand kronor by the Lions.

I waited impatiently for Jansson to tell me why he had come. I didn't want to run the risk of him staying any longer than necessary, so I didn't mention Louise's calls or my lack of sleep.

"I'm going to visit my brother," he said at last, when there was nothing more to say about the weather.

"You've got a brother? I've never heard you mention him."

"We don't have much contact with each other. He's a few years younger than me, and he left long before you moved here."

"But you've never even told me that you've got a brother!"

"Of course I have."

"Where does he live?"

"In Huddinge."

"Stockholm . . . and that's where you're going?"

"I'm setting off first thing tomorrow morning, and I'll be away until Sunday."

I did a quick calculation: he would be away for three days.

Jansson got to his feet. "It's many years since I was in Stockholm," he said as he unhooked the mooring rope. "Perhaps it's time to see how the capital city is getting on."

"Have a good trip, and say hello to your brother from me. What's his name?"

"Albin."

We waved to each other as he reversed away from the jetty. I found it very strange that Jansson had never mentioned his brother in all the years I had known him. Or had I forgotten?

I managed to get hold of a dentist who was willing to see me. The trip and the treatment took three hours; by the time I got back the pain had gone.

The following day I woke early; I had slept for many hours. Louise rang at eleven o'clock that night and told me that the doctors now had Agnes's illness under control. She promised to call me the next day. That night I went to bed with a feeling of relief that I didn't recognise from any other time in my life.

454

It was cold and still when I woke up. As I sat at the table with a cup of coffee, I was struck by a thought that I immediately pushed aside. But it came back.

I would go over to Stångskär and visit Jansson's house. He had once told me that he kept a spare key under a stone in the garden.

I couldn't explain why I needed to go there; perhaps it was something to do with the unease I had felt when the Valfridssons' house burned down?

At ten o'clock in the morning I left the island and set my course for Stångskär. From time to time the boat sliced through thin shards of floating ice. Another week of this cold, and the ice would be here to stay.

Jansson's boathouse and his old slipway lay in a south-facing inlet, where he and his boats were sheltered from the worst of the storms coming in from the north and west. I switched off the engine and drifted towards the jetty. His boat wasn't there; he really had gone to see his brother. I climbed out and called his name a few times just to make sure he really wasn't around. I walked up to his two-storey house, which was one of the oldest in the archipelago. I knocked on the door but no one answered. The key was well hidden, and it took me a while to find it. As I inserted it in the lock I wondered once again why I was making this secret visit. I thought about Oslovski's house and about the deserted house deep in the forest. And now here I was at Jansson's red-painted cottage with its sparkling windows and freshly painted decorative carving above the porch.

I went inside. Jansson kept the place very clean. The floors were spotless; everything in the kitchen shone. In that way he reminded me of Oslovski. I went upstairs and into what must be his room. The bed was neatly made, slippers side by side, no clothes lying around. The other rooms were empty because he never had visitors. The beds were made up, but for what reason? Could they be an expression of his loneliness, his longing?

I went back downstairs. In the living room he had draped a sheet over the television. The house didn't suit Jansson at all. He should live in completely different conditions.

Finally I went into the laundry room beyond the kitchen. Again, everything was in perfect order. The pale January sun shone in through the window. Clean clothes were arranged on hangers, underwear folded in baskets. I suddenly remembered Jansson bringing me underpants after my house had burned down.

I was just about to leave when I noticed the laundry basket, which contained items that had not yet been washed. I saw the shirt and trousers Jansson had been wearing at my New Year's Eve party and when I saw him later at the fire.

I couldn't help picking them up. They told me nothing that I didn't already know. I was just about to put them back when I noticed another shirt underneath. This one had black sooty marks on the lower part of the sleeves. I lifted it to my nose; it stank of petrol.

My head was spinning. I felt as if I could see everything with perfect clarity.

The night when my house burned down, a dazzling light had flared up.

That's how it must have happened.

When I went back to the boat a little while later, I was afraid.

I hoped I hadn't left any traces behind.

CHAPTER
TWENTY-FIVE

I thought about the Japanese garden my daughter had described to me.

The Ocean of Emptiness.

That's what it felt like as I headed home from Jansson's island. It was as if Stångskär had metamorphosed into a fortress where Jansson had hidden himself with all his secrets. I now knew what I had understood, but I didn't understand what it was that I knew. Jansson had become transparent, yet at the same time he was far, far away. If I stretched out my hand, I would never be able to reach him.

I switched off the engine and tried to think, but my head was all over the place.

I continued my journey home; as I reached the bay I saw someone moving around outside my tent on the skerry. I turned into a narrow inlet that is navigable only in a small boat like mine. This enabled me to approach the skerry from the side where a high rock face made it impossible for anyone to see me from the tent. Like a hunter I was also careful to stay downwind of my prey. I killed the engine and used the oars instead. Rowing this boat was hard work, even when I flipped up the engine.

My head was full of Jansson, but there was still a little bit of room left to find out who was using my tent and my skerry.

I hove to next to the steep cliff, where a number of depressions in the rock made it possible to scramble ashore. I remembered carving my name at the water's edge in this very spot when I was a teenager, but there was no trace left now. I crawled across the rock like a clumsy lizard to see who was outside my tent, but there was no one in sight. Whoever it was had gone inside and zipped up the flap. Two separate strands of distaste and anxiety were fighting for space inside my mind: Jansson's insanity and a concern that the person in the tent would turn out to be violent.

The surfboard and sail lay where I usually left my boat, looking like an insect that had been washed ashore.

I took a step away from the tent and accidentally kicked a pile of stones. Before I had time to scurry back to the boat, the tent flap opened.

The boy was fair-haired and couldn't have been more than seventeen years old. He was wearing a black neoprene suit and I immediately noticed a tear on one shoulder, which he had made a reasonable job of repairing with masking tape. His eyes were dark; I couldn't tell whether he was afraid or simply watchful. There was something about his hair that bothered me: it was too blond, too white. It looked as if it had been dyed by someone who didn't really know what they were doing. But why had he changed the colour of his hair? In order to become someone else or because of an impatient desire to make himself different?

I signalled to him to come out; for some reason I didn't think he spoke Swedish. He crawled out and sat down; I sat down too. My anxiety was gradually giving way to a growing curiosity.

"I haven't taken anything," he said suddenly. "I have only rested."

He spoke Swedish with a slight accent; perhaps he came from the north?

I was about to ask him his name when he leaped to his feet and ran towards his surfboard. It happened so fast that I only just had time to get up. He pushed the board out into the water and jumped onto it. He was extremely agile, moving like a sure-footed animal with a gleaming black coat. There was enough wind to fill his sail.

I was overcome with a strange mixture of fury and impotence. I yelled after him, "Hey! Hey you!"

With hindsight I can't think of a more pointless thing to shout. He didn't turn around, of course. I watched him disappear around the southern headland.

Soon the ice would form, and he would no longer be able to windsurf.

The tent flap was fluttering in the breeze. I crouched down and drew it back. There wasn't much inside, just an empty plastic bottle, several screwed-up pieces of paper and the remains of a packet of biscuits. I crawled in and smoothed out the sheets of paper. They looked as if they had been torn off a squared pad. On some of them he had played noughts and crosses with himself. Several of the games were unfinished, with no winner.

There was some writing on one of the pages. His handwriting was ornate, almost old-fashioned. It took me a little while to work out what it said.

The same text was repeated twice, like a refrain:

> Some poems fade away in days
> Then daybreaks and dreams
> Have agreed on a victor

I could read the words but found it difficult to understand what he meant. Was it a poem or a message he had decided not to send to an unknown recipient? Was it for me, the man who had put up the tent and provided him with a refuge?

I tucked the piece of paper in my pocket and left the tent. With some difficulty I managed to scramble up the steep cliff to the top, where I could look out across the bay.

There was no sign of him. He could be hiding among the islets in the small archipelago known as Hällarna, which is unnamed on maritime charts.

A little further out lay Satansgrundet, or the Devil's Reef, which was shaped like a chopped-off pillar sticking straight up out of the sea. He could hide there if that was what he wanted.

I stayed at the top of the cliff until I started shivering. Back at the tent I took a pen out of my pocket and wrote a note on the reverse of one of the unfinished games of noughts and crosses.

Nice poem. You're welcome to use the tent, but naturally I'm curious about who you are.

I thought for a moment, then signed it: *Fredrik.* I added my phone number, then I placed the piece of paper in the middle of the groundsheet, zipped up the flap and set off for home.

I wondered what the boy's name might be. He was no Erik or Anders — then again perhaps that's exactly what he was?

It occurred to me that the only person I knew who would have done the same thing was my daughter. In a way he was her brother. He was a visitor from a new age that I would only have time to brush up against.

I hoped he would get in touch.

I didn't start the engine, I simply allowed the boat to drift towards my island. Dusk was beginning to fall. The ice would come late this year.

A few weeks of intense cold followed. The ice reached further and further out to sea. I lay in the caravan listening to the movement of the sea and the ice. If I placed my hand on the wall, it soon felt chilled to the bone. However much I turned up the heating, there was a constant battle between the bitter cold outside and the heat inside.

Needless to say I spent a great deal of time thinking about Jansson and the discovery I had made at his house on Stångskär. I have never experienced so many confused and contradictory emotions, not even when I botched the operation that destroyed my life as a doctor. I brooded about him during the day and dreamed about him at night. On several occasions I sat there clutching my phone, ready to call the police, but I just couldn't do it. The idea that Jansson could have let me burn to death in my house was too improbable, too appalling.

I think I was most afraid of the day Jansson would return from his mysterious trip. How would I confront him? He had said he would be away for three days, but several weeks had passed.

There were days when I walked around in the cold stillness of feeling as if I were confined in a cage. I forced myself to carry on taking a dip each morning, but not even the icy water could make me think more clearly. In my head Jansson had been transformed from a friendly seafaring postman into something that could only be described as a monster.

I spoke to Louise every day; Agnes was now fully recovered. I didn't ask any questions about how they lived their life or where they got their money from. I found it difficult to imagine Louise going out and earning her money as a pickpocket with a baby at home, but I had no way of knowing, and perhaps I didn't want to know.

It was after one of these conversations with Louise that I remembered an occasion when my father had come staggering home much too early. He was drunk, his hair a mess, and he was furious. The rage was etched on his face, every muscle seemingly set in the throes of an agonising cramp. I could also see the despair in his eyes. I must have been about ten years old at the time. My mother pushed the door to, leaving it open just a fraction. Looking back, I realise she did this so that I would be able to follow what was said, and perhaps so that I would learn how a person could be utterly crushed yet still be open to solace and have the ability to overcome his humiliation.

I couldn't see much, but I heard every word.

It was the same old story: my father had fallen out with the maître d' and been fired on the spot. He had thrown his cloth on the floor and simply walked out. The maître d' had followed him into the street, and they had stood there yelling at one another until there were no words left. It had been raining. They had stood there like two dripping-wet dogs.

My father was often fired under dramatic circumstances. It was by no means unusual to find him sitting at the kitchen table moaning while my mother slowly persuaded him to regain his faith in humanity, and above all in himself. But on this particular evening he said something quite different from the standard litany of complaints about the indignities to which he was constantly subjected.

Earlier in the day, while the restaurant was quiet, he had apparently flicked through a magazine left behind by a customer. He had read about a Chinese emperor who, long long ago, had ordered that a large drum be placed by the main entrance to his palace. Anyone who came along could stop, strike several powerful blows, then pass on their complaint to a servant, who would immediately convey it to the emperor. Everyone had the opportunity to put forward a grievance without the risk of incurring imperial rage.

"These drums don't exist anywhere," my father fumed. "There isn't a single place where we can wield our drumsticks to make sure that someone listens to all the injustices we have to suffer."

Why did I think of my father and the emperor's drum after I had spoken to Louise? There was no connection. A waiter and a pickpocket had nothing in common. The only thing I could come up with was that both of them wanted to live in a different, fairer world where justice applied to everyone.

I jotted down a few words on a scrap of paper.

The emperor's drum. My father's tears at the kitchen table. What's the connection?

The following day when I was in the caravan I heard Jansson's boat approaching. My heart started racing. I opened the door and listened. There was no doubt: it was definitely Jansson.

He seemed exactly the same as usual. The way he raised his right arm slowly, a little stiffly, before he waved with fingers outspread. He didn't stop waving until I had returned the gesture. I couldn't believe he had discovered my secret visit to Stångskär; if he had, he was hiding it very well.

He had run the mooring rope from the prow to the roof of the wheelhouse, and when he reached the jetty he flung it to me. I caught it and looped it around the nearest bollard.

Jansson clambered ashore.

"My brother was fine," he said, perching at the end of the bench. "But the trip was a bit longer than I'd planned."

465

He took off his left boot and shook out a fragment of a pine cone, then put it on again.

I stood looking at this man, whom I had known for so many years. I realised now that I had known only a small part of a complex, splintered individual. I had never had any suspicion that a terrifying figure was hidden behind the ordinary person who had delivered the post to the island for so long.

Did he himself know who he was? Do any of us really know who we are?

I had no answer. The only thing I was clinging to at the moment was the incomprehensible.

A grey-haired postman who was also a ruthless arsonist.

If the bright light hadn't woken me, I would have burned to death. The widow Westerfeldt could also have been the victim of the terrifying power of fire. And Jansson had had no way of knowing whether the Valfridssons were out on their island or not.

Standing there in front of the man on the bench, I felt utterly helpless.

"You don't usually come over for no reason," I said.

"I just wanted to tell you that my brother is fine, but living in a big city seems like an insecure kind of existence to me."

"What do you mean?"

"How can you keep tabs on yourself when other people are pushing and shoving and bumping into you all the time?"

I was struck by the thought that Jansson might not even have a brother. Could that be as much of a lie as everything else? The man sitting there on the bench had set fire to my house, then invited me to stay with him when my house no longer existed. He had even brought a wellington boot to replace the one I had lost in the fire. He had celebrated New Year's Eve with me; he had said he was going home to bed, but instead he had set fire to another house. And in between these two incidents he had also burned down the widow Westerfeldt's home.

I couldn't put it off any longer. I had to face up to him.

"Why?" I said.

Jansson looked at me.

"Sorry, did you say something to me?"

"There's no one else here."

"I didn't quite hear what you said."

"Yes, you did."

Jansson didn't seem to have any idea that I knew. How could he be so sure that no one had found any evidence? Wasn't he even on his guard?

"Coffee would be nice," he said abruptly.

During all the years he had been coming to the island, he had never asked for coffee. I wondered if it meant anything. Should I be afraid? If he could burn down a house in which someone lay sleeping, he could whip out a hammer and smash my skull.

We went up to the caravan side by side, Jansson with his usual slightly rolling gait. He sat on the bed while I made coffee. He asked after Louise and Agnes, he talked about Lisa Modin, but when he started enquiring about the plans for the new house, I felt like throwing the boiling water over his face and hands.

I didn't do it, but I did stop making the coffee.

"I want you to leave," I said. "I want you to leave and never show your face here again."

Jansson looked startled.

"What do you mean? I don't understand what you mean."

I had opened the door, but he was still sitting on the bed as if he really didn't understand.

Of course he did. He might not have noticed that I had been in his house while he was away visiting someone who might possibly be his brother, but he certainly realised that I knew he was responsible for the arson attacks.

"You've opened the door," he said. "But I still don't understand what you want. Are you throwing me out?"

I closed the door. Now I wanted to prevent him from leaving.

Why had he burned down my house when I was lying there fast asleep? Was it me or the house he wanted to destroy? Or was it something else?

"I know it was you," I said. "I know, and I can give the police enough information to warrant an investigation, which will see you charged and convicted. I have proof — clothes in your laundry basket, stinking of petrol.

"I wonder if, deep down, you wanted me to find out the truth. Wasn't that why you came here to tell me you were going to visit your brother? Who may or may not exist. You hoped I would go over to your island. If you'd really wanted to hide the evidence, you would have washed everything to do with the fires. You're like one of those criminals who writes letters to the police to give them clues. But who are you?

"Have you always been waiting for the moment when you can start setting fire to houses, and perhaps killing people at the same time? Has it always been your dream? Is that what you thought about as you travelled around with your letters and magazines and pension payment slips? Did you think that one day you would turn into a completely different person — the good, kind postman who becomes evil?"

Jansson didn't say a word.

"That shirt in your laundry basket might not be enough to convict you," I went on. "But I'm sure the police will find further proof. Unless of course you decide to confess. They'll lock you up for years. Given your age, you'll probably die in prison. Or maybe they'll decide you're insane, in which case they'll put you away indefinitely in a mental institution, along with other crazy people. Mind you, going to prison isn't the worst thing; you could probably cope with that. But can you live with the fact that people out here in the archipelago will hate you? That the only memory you will leave behind is the image of a wicked man who stopped delivering the post and started burning down the beautiful houses on these islands?"

Jansson was no longer pretending that he didn't understand. He was slumped on the bed, his hands resting heavily on his knees, his head drooping. "Why?"

469

I yelled. "Why did you call me with a handkerchief over your mouth and warn me about the police?"

He didn't respond. He was motionless, as if he had turned to stone, fixed in a denial that couldn't be smashed to pieces with a hammer.

I stood by the door feeling every bit as helpless as I presumed Jansson himself was feeling.

"Why?" I said again. "Why did you want to kill me?"

He straightened up and looked at me with nothing but surprise.

"I didn't want to kill you. Why would you say such a thing?"

"I was asleep. I could have burned to death."

"I would have helped you out. If you hadn't woken up."

"So you stood there watching the fire take hold?"

"I was waiting for you to wake up."

I tried to imagine the scene: I had come rushing out of the raging inferno wearing mismatched wellington boots, and Jansson had been standing there in the shadows. Only then did he leave, returning before long to help put out the fire.

He was still looking at me, but he was gazing beyond me, far into the distance, at horizons known only to him. I would never find out why he had done what he had done. There were no answers, least of all in his own head. A light had gone out within him; a darkness had come creeping in, a darkness that he wanted to illuminate from the outside, with torches in the form of burning houses.

470

Jansson got to his feet; I stepped aside. I watched him walk slowly down to the jetty. For the first time ever I saw him move without purpose.

The boat reversed away from the jetty. I went up to my grandfather's bench. It was too cold to sit down; I simply stood there looking out to sea as the ice floes drifted by. Nothing was in a hurry any more.

I wondered what to do. I ought to call Alexandersson and inform the coastguard, of course, but I couldn't do it. I had to understand this myself before I could expect anyone else to do so. I couldn't just ring up and announce that Jansson was the guilty party; no one would believe me.

I imagined myself sitting in the caravan with Alexandersson, telling my story. He would simply stare at me, then he would ask if I could really prove what I was alleging. A shirt that smelled of petrol was not enough.

The story in my head just wouldn't make sense to anyone else. The fact that to me it all seemed to fit together wouldn't help at all.

I knew that Alexandersson would ask why Jansson had set fire to our homes.

Why?

My response had to be that I didn't know. Only Jansson himself could answer that question.

What would happen if he was arrested? There would be an initial sense of relief throughout the community, but this would soon be followed by a feeling of angst because one of the archipelago's most trusted inhabitants had turned out to be the perpetrator.

If Jansson was the arsonist, who could we trust in future? Something would come to an end out here on the islands, perhaps the last thing that was holding us together. Trust, a willingness to provide support for anyone who needed it — and not just by carrying each other's coffins when the time came.

In my mind I could see everyone huddled together on their jetties or in the harbour. Our impotent attempts to understand. No doubt more than one person would angrily say that we should go and burn down Jansson's house on Stångskär, but of course no one would be prepared to do it.

I thought about Jansson with a mixture of rage and astonishment. His loneliness had been so much greater than mine after all.

Time passed. I still didn't say anything. No one seemed to suspect Jansson. According to what I heard, the police had no leads; the investigation into the arson attacks was going nowhere.

I considered sending an anonymous letter to the police, accusing Jansson. I didn't do it, though; I didn't quite trust my own judgement, mainly because deep down I still couldn't believe that Jansson was a completely different person from the man we had all thought he was.

I wondered if he was ill. Could he have developed a tumour that had damaged part of his brain and distorted his thought processes? I dreamed more than once that he had set fire to the caravan, and that I ran screaming out into the night.

472

On 30 April, Walpurgis Night, Kolbjörn arrived on his cattle ferry with his son Anton and one of Anton's friends. Together we managed to get the caravan on board. Kolbjörn had brought along an electric cable, which he ran from the island to the skerry. He chuckled at the thought that this was completely illegal but assured me there was no risk of dangerous short circuits.

We towed the ferry across with my launch; Kolbjörn took several photographs on his phone.

"It's forty-five years since we last transported cows on this ferry," he said. "But my father always insisted we should keep it; you never know when it might come in useful. And here we are, using it to move a caravan."

He stood in silence for a moment, contemplating his ferry.

"It's weird," he said. "The police haven't got a single lead or a single suspect for the arson attacks."

"I suppose it's not that easy," I replied. "No one seems to have gained anything from the fires."

Kolbjörn pulled a face and shook his head.

"I'm trying to understand, but it's impossible. I'm sure they're doing their best. Maybe we should all take a practical approach, like Jansson."

I gave a start when he mentioned Jansson's name, but he didn't seem to notice.

"Why, what has Jansson said?"

"He's written a letter to the council, suggesting that they provide everyone who lives out here during the autumn and winter with a fire extinguisher, free of charge."

"Really?"

"I think it's a very sensible idea."

It crossed my mind that I was going crazy. Where was Jansson heading with this? Why was he mocking the residents of the archipelago?

"I think the council will give us our fire extinguishers," Kolbjörn went on. "But I don't suppose Jansson will get any thanks for it."

"No," I said. "I don't suppose he will."

My voice was unsteady. Kolbjörn glanced at me. I smiled. The smile said: I'm absolutely fine.

Kolbjörn had carefully prepared the ground on the skerry. He had laid out a track made of thick planks of wood and had set up a complex block and tackle system. Everything worked perfectly, and the caravan was soon settled in its new home. Kolbjörn connected the electricity while I opened a bottle of champagne. We drank a toast as if it had been schnapps.

That night I slept on the skerry for the first time without needing to use my tent. I dreamed that I was on board a boat; the skerry had broken away from the bedrock and was carrying me to the distant Öresund Sound.

I woke up early the next morning. It was the first of May, and the air was warm. I had told Kolbjörn and Anton to wait until after the holiday before they made a start on the house, but Kolbjörn had said there was no point in hanging around.

After breakfast I went over to the island. They arrived at nine, the ferry laden with a small digger, a shed and an unconscionable number of tools. I sat on the bench by the boathouse and watched as things got under way. Anton was a real grafter. I could see that he took the same intense pleasure in his work as his father. It wouldn't take long before his digger had cleared the ruins and made room for my new house.

They packed up for the day at about six. A blackbird landed on the roof of their shed, the first one I had heard this year.

I walked down to the jetty with them.

"I want to bury a token, a memorial under the new house," I said to Kolbjörn as Anton started up the engine.

"How big is it?"

"It's just a small tin containing a shoe buckle." He looked intrigued.

"It's a very fine buckle," I went on. "It holds a special meaning for me."

"I'll ask Anton to dig a hole right in the middle of the foundations. If there's a rock in the way we can take it out with a non-explosive demolition agent."

I waved to them as they left; I wondered what on earth a non-explosive demolition agent might be.

The ferry had only just vanished around the headland when the prow of another vessel appeared; it was a fast aluminium boat that I didn't recognise at first. However, as it drew nearer I could see the advert for the cafe adorning the port side and realised it was Veronika's boat.

She had never visited me on the island, apart from when we were making preparations for my party. I was worried; something must have happened.

She climbed onto the jetty with the mooring rope in her hand. I could tell from her expression that my premonition was well founded.

"Has the coastguard been in touch?" she asked.

"No?"

"So you don't know anything?"

I sat down on the bench; I didn't want to collapse if she told me something terrible. She was still holding onto the boat like a dog on a leash.

"Jansson has gone. He headed straight out to sea in his boat. The coastguard was on the way in from Landsort and saw him far beyond the archipelago. They went over to check if everything was all right; Jansson seemed perfectly normal. He told them he was going to turn back very soon. Alexandersson decided to let him be; after all, Jansson is Jansson. When he got back to the office, there was a message on the answering machine: Jansson yelling that he didn't want anyone to come looking for him, and no one would find him anyway. The coastguard went straight back out and they're going to carry on searching until dark. Of course everyone is wondering if Jansson has gone mad."

I listened to Veronika with no sense of surprise whatsoever.

Jansson was leaving us. He would fill his body with sleeping tablets, weigh himself down with a grappling iron, chains and the anchor, and make a small hole in the boat so that it would sink slowly. No one would ever be sure what had happened. No one would find him.

"He's always been a little strange," I said tentatively.

476

"I often think he's one of the most normal people out here on the islands. What do you mean, strange?"

"Perhaps I mean he's . . . very individual. He's not married, he doesn't have any children."

"I'm not married. I don't have any children."

"You're not seventy years old."

"Jansson is shy, but there's nothing else wrong with him. What if he's planning on killing himself? Something must have happened."

It was as if Veronika had given me the solution. We were sitting on the bench where I had examined Jansson so many times without being able to find anything wrong with him. Perhaps I had found something at last.

"As a doctor I have a duty of confidentiality to my patients," I said. "I haven't told anyone else what I'm about to tell you. If it gets out, I'll know that you have betrayed my confidence."

"I would never do such a thing!"

I knew she wouldn't say a word.

I quickly ran through possible diagnoses where there was only one conclusion unless a miracle occurred.

"Jansson has cancer," I said. "An aggressive, incurable cancer. It started in the pancreas and has spread to the liver. He's unlikely to last until the summer."

Veronika understood. A doctor always tells the truth. Perhaps she had chosen to come and talk to me because she suspected that Jansson was ill? There could be no other explanation for his departure.

"Is he in pain?"

"It's been possible to alleviate it so far, but I don't know about the future."

"Is there nothing that can be done?"

"Nothing."

There wasn't much more to say. Veronika was still clutching the mooring rope.

"I can't do this any more," she said after a while. "I'm going to sell the cafe, do some travelling."

"Where will you go?"

"Not straight out to sea, at any rate."

She got to her feet.

"I wanted you to know," she said. "And now I know."

Her boat zoomed away from the jetty.

No one would ever find Jansson. If he had decided to take the truth about the house fires with him to the grave, then that's what he would do. The last letter would never reach its destination.

Nor would he set off and fall over the edge of the horizon. If I knew Jansson as well as I thought I did in this respect, he had fooled Alexandersson. When he was alone he would change course and return to the inner archipelago. There were many areas with a depth of almost a hundred metres where he could scuttle his boat. No one would find him because everyone would believe he had disappeared far out at sea.

I got up from the bench. It was a simple, crystal-clear moment in my life. My clinic on the jetty was closed and would never reopen.

Kolbjörn and Anton started building my house. I helped out as a labourer, although I was probably more of a hindrance than a help. However, I could provide information when there was any uncertainty about what a particular detail might have looked like; the house in my memory had never burned down.

By the end of June Kolbjörn said I would be able to move in during August.

Veronika had sold the cafe to an Iranian couple; I decided to arrange my own house-warming party.

Lisa Modin often came to visit, watching as the new house emerged. I still longed for the love she couldn't give me, but I became increasingly grateful for her companionship. I was an old man who had gained a female friend. I could bear to contemplate my face in the mirror. I shaved meticulously, I didn't neglect myself. Thanks to Lisa, I had something to look forward to. She helped me resist my tendency to depression.

However, I was under no illusions. One day she would go away, to another newspaper, a TV company, another town. I didn't know how I would react when that day came, but I still had Louise and her family, who were also my family.

Louise promised to come to my house-warming; she would bring Ahmed and Muhammed too, not just Agnes.

But during all those weeks as the house progressed I kept thinking about Jansson, Oslovski, Nordin. I couldn't for the life of me understand why I should stop communicating with old friends just because they were dead. I carried on talking to them, listening to them, remembering them. I carried on trying to picture Jansson's death, Nordin's final moment, and I wondered whether Oslovski had had time to realise that death had come to call on her in the garage with her 1958 DeSoto Fireflite.

In these people I saw myself, and during that spring and summer when my house was being built I also came to understand that other people must see themselves in me.

July was unusually warm, followed by a great deal of rain in the first weeks of August.

I moved in on 27 August, even though several of the rooms were still unfurnished. Lisa Modin arrived in the evening and stayed overnight. In her own room, of course. The following day Kolbjörn would pick up Louise, Agnes and the rest of my family from the harbour and bring them over.

Early in the morning I went for my dip, then checked my blood pressure on the bench that was now part of a defunct clinic.

I was an old man, but as a doctor I was able to tell myself that I was fine.

I walked right to the end of the jetty and threw my stethoscope in the water. It drifted towards the seabed like a dead snake.

At that moment I saw something; I couldn't believe my eyes, but then I realised it actually was a perch. It wasn't very big, but there was absolutely no doubt in my mind.

A fish had returned and presented itself to me like a gift.

The stethoscope had settled on the bottom. In a few days it would be buried in the mud, which ultimately consumed everything.

As I stood there on the jetty, my telephone rang. It was Margareta Nordin.

She told me that my wellington boots had finally arrived. There was no mistaking the joy in her voice.

I went up to the house that had risen from the ruins. I thought about the day almost ten years ago when I had removed the enormous anthill from under the dining table in the living room. That too had been a day of great joy.

In the new dining room I placed a table I had found among the dead swallows in the loft at the boathouse. On the table was the glass jar containing birdlime and the remnants of the old birdcage. I would often leaf through the *Guide to the Capture and Care of Songbirds* at night before I fell asleep.

One day I would understand why my grandparents had spent their time catching birds with lime spread on twigs. I had no intention of giving up. It was a task that suited an old man like me.

I contemplated the apple tree, which I had washed with soap and water. It had regained its original colour, but I didn't know whether it would bear fruit.

Beneath the floor of the house, buried in the ground, lay the tin containing Giaconelli's shoe buckle. It gave me a sense of security to think that the buckle had survived the fierce flames.

It was already late August.

Soon the autumn would come.

But the darkness no longer frightened me.

Afterword

There may be some readers who think they recognise the islands, bays, skerries and people in this novel, in spite of the fact that no archipelago in the world can be laid on top of my geographical and human map to produce a perfect match.

I often think about the invisible postglacial rebound when I write. It is a constant, even though we are unable to perceive it with our eyes or our other senses. A shoreline is always something unfinished, slipping away, drifting. A piece of fiction relates to reality in the same way. There may be similarities between the two, but above all it is the difference that determines what has happened and what could have happened.

That is the way it must be because the truth is always provisional, always changeable.

Henning Mankell
Antibes, March 2015

AN EVENT IN AUTUMN

Henning Mankell

Kurt Wallander's life looks like it has taken a turn for the better when his offer on a new house is accepted, only for him to uncover something unexpected in the garden — the skeleton of a middle-aged woman. As police officers comb the property, Wallander attempts to get his new life back on course by finding the woman's killer with the aid of his daughter, Linda. But when another discovery is made in the garden, Wallander is forced to delve further back into the area's past.

A TREACHEROUS PARADISE

Henning Mankell

Cold and poverty define Hanna Renström's childhood in remote northern Sweden, and in 1905, at nineteen, she boards a ship for Australia in hope of a better life. But nothing prepares her for the life she will lead. After two brief marriages, she finds herself the owner of a bordello in Portuguese East Africa. As Hanna's story unfurls over the next several years, we watch her in this "treacherous paradise," as she wrestles with a wrenching loneliness and with the racism she's meant to unthinkingly adopt. And as her life becomes increasingly intertwined with the prostitutes, she moves inexorably toward the moment when she will make a decision that defies every expectation society has of her, and, more important, those she has of herself.

THE SHADOW GIRLS

Henning Mankell

Tea-Bag, a young African girl, has fled a refugee camp in Spain for the promise of a new life in Sweden. Tania has made a long and dangerous journey to escape the horrors of human trafficking. Leyla has come with her family from Iran. All of them are facing challenges in their new home. Meanwhile, celebrated poet Jesper Humlin is looking for inspiration. Harried by his mother and girlfriend, misunderstood by his publisher and tormented by his stockbroker, Jesper needs a new perspective on life. A chance encounter with Tea-Bag leads him into the shadow world of the immigrant experience in Sweden. Initially he sees the girls purely as material for his next work, but soon discovers they have very different ideas.

THE PYRAMID

Henning Mankell

When Kurt Wallander first appeared, he was a senior police officer, his life in a mess. His wife had left him, his father barely acknowledged him; he ate badly and drank alone at night. *The Pyramid* chronicles the events that led him to such a place. We see him in the early years, doing hours on the beat; witness the beginnings of his fragile relationship with Mona; and learn the reason behind his difficulties with his father. These thrilling tales provide a fascinating insight into Wallander's character. From the stabbing of a neighbour in 1969 to a light aircraft accident in 1989, every story is a vital piece of the Wallander series, showing Mankell at the top of his game.